TRADING SECRETS

RACHAEL ECKLES

APHRODITE
BOOKS
—
NEW YORK

APHRODITE
BOOKS
—
NEW YORK

Copyright © 2020 by Rachael Eckles

Published in the United States by Aphrodite Books LLC, New York.

www.aphroditepublishinghouse.com.

APHRODITE and the Aphrodite logo are trademarks of Aphrodite Books LLC.

eBook ISBN: 978-1-7349018-0-1

Print ISBN: 978-1-7349018-1-8

Cover design by Meghan Spiro

Cover image: DepositPhotos.com Stock Photo

Aphrodite Logo by Jana Feldberg

10 9 8 7 6 5 4 3 2 1

First Edition

To Everyone Who Has Believed in Me Along the Way. Thank You. (A reminder for Mom, Daddy, and Jessie: Don't worry! This is fiction, not an autobiography.)

Turns out it was mostly a lie.

But, at least for a short while,

It was a beautiful one.

—Russell Brand

CONTENTS

PROLOGUE

The moment the blues walked into her office, Celeste knew something was wrong, terribly wrong. Her heart pounded, and her throat tightened. The two nondescript men in NYPD uniforms exchanged somber glances. The shorter one cleared his throat and began talking, but Celeste's hearing was muffled. She replayed the words in her head, struggling to make sense of the situation.

"Ms. Donovan ... listed as his emergency contact ... accident while flying in the Berkshires ... rough patch ... plane down ... body badly burned ... next of kin identified him ... truly sorry for your loss, ma'am."

Then they were gone, and she was alone on her sofa with no recollection of how she had gotten there. Was it the same day or a week later? Her face was streaked with dried tears, her tongue heavy and coated from her vices. A near-empty Macallan and overturned Xanax container taunted her from the coffee table. She reached for the prescription bottle and emptied the last two pills into her hand, washing them down with a gulp of scotch. Fred Warren's warnings all those weeks ago were legitimate—she was in danger, grave danger. But she had failed to realize the love of her life was in danger as well.

Theodore's gone. And I could've stopped it.

PART I

BEFORE

1

HEAVY SCOTCH AND LOOSE WOMEN

Forty-one-year-old Celeste Donovan rushed through the lobby of the Savoy Hotel to embrace each of her three best friends—Savin, Mark, and Jack. Well, not rushed, exactly—rushing was nearly impossible while wearing 120-millimeter Louboutin knee-high boots and a Tom Ford leather mini.

"Hey, fellas! I'm surprised you made it after last night! What do you have in mind for this evening? Heavy scotch and loose women, I presume?"

Jack grinned devilishly as he pulled a flask out of his interior sport coat pocket and swallowed a long pull. Blond with chocolate eyes, long lashes, and strong dimples, he could have passed for Celeste's twin at just an inch taller than her lithe five-foot-ten stature. He was closer to her than her biological brother in more than just looks, the only one who knew her explosive secret from all those years ago and protected her when it mattered most.

Mark launched into his predictable tirade of complaints. "You know how I hate London. Too rainy, and the women are dreadful. Sav, you'd better have something fantastic in mind. I didn't take a red eye from Shanghai to hear Celly discuss whatever the fuck men pay to hear her say." Mark complained about any place that did not have an abundance of Asian or Brazilian women. He smoothed an imaginary wrinkle on the front of his slim-cut cerulean Prada shirt and straightened his bespoke navy blazer, the colors set off dramatically against the backdrop of his smooth dark skin.

Savin's eyes twinkled. "Still the same old insufferable fuddy duddy we know and love, aren't you? Never fear! I have an evening of adventure and intrigue planned for us, with the first stop at—"

"Don't tell us—I want to be surprised." Celeste never got tired of Savin pulling strings to get them into strictly A-list locales around the globe, places plebeians never knew existed. Money could buy your way into a lot of places, but not everywhere, and that is where Sav came in. He was Lebanese, with the proverbial tall, dark, and handsome vibe, and he used his looks and charm to his advantage whenever possible.

Jack helped Celeste into her signature Max Mara cashmere coat. London weather was dreadful year-round, but in the dead of winter, the frigidity was intolerable. She wrapped a turquoise silk scarf around her neck, repositioned her sleek blonde ponytail, and stuffed her hands into her gray fox-fur-lined Italian leather gloves.

"Quit dawdling, the car is waiting!" Savin urged with a grin. "It was bad enough we had to listen to your soapbox speech for the eleventh time." Celeste shot him a weary glance. She was fully aware the three guys had gotten sloshed at the hotel bar instead of attending her panel discussion at the Managed Funds annual conference, where she had upstaged her nemesis, Fred Warren. After the session, Fred had eyed her up and down with a look of disgust and refused her extended hand. *Why does everyone take everything so personally these days?* she mused. She had puckered her lips to reveal her dimples. "It's all fun and games, Fred!"

"Fuck off, Celeste," Fred said, as he turned on the heels of his $900 loafers and stormed off. Her grin broadened, and she sighed in satisfaction. *His paunch is even bigger than last time I saw him. He really should lay off the porterhouse-and-scotch diet.*

"Fred was red-faced and fuming by the end. You missed a good show, boys!"

The mammoth doors were opened simultaneously in front of them by unseen bellhops, and they walked out into the twilight, descending into the Maybach waiting for them.

"Olly, please take us to Dante," Savin barked to their driver, Oliver, in the tone only Brits could pull off—not truly polite, but not quite rude either. He pretended to operate with an air of intrigue, though Brits were hardly notorious in New York, where he and Celeste ran one of the most successful hedge funds in the world, Donovan & Clarke Capital, or D&C for short. He was sitting in the rear-facing bucket seat next to Mark, and Celeste and Jack were sitting across from them. Mark ceremoniously pulled out a flask, likely Macallan 25 (nothing less than 25 for Mark).

"Really taking us back to the old days, aren't you, Mark? I expect you'll be chasing your scotch with a few lines of blow," Celeste joked.

"I deserve it. Shanghai was terrible this week. I worked around the clock but finally closed a deal. Investors calling me twenty-four seven, screaming. Then a shitty flight delay. I tell you—flying first class is not what it used to be. I can't believe I endured such pedestrian disaster."

"Yet you're going back at the end of the week?" Celeste inquired.

"Yeah, I have some, uh, business to get back to in Shanghai. Moving into a new place."

"You flew commercial?" Savin asked in disbelief.

It was the first time they were all together in at least a year, and they excitedly spoke over one another, interrupting as only true friends can. Celeste laughed as they poked fun at her (many) conquests. She had only ever had one serious relationship, with Omar Santos, and that had imploded a decade earlier. She managed to escape, but not without serious harm. Rather than cower in fear and allow him to destroy her, Celeste had vowed revenge and channeled her pain. Unbeknownst to Omar, Celeste and Savin were behind one of the most noteworthy insider trading schemes in history that nearly bankrupted Omar, to the tune of over $1 billion. He had disappeared from New York shortly after and had not resurfaced in the past ten years. Celeste rested easy, knowing he was out of her life for good, though she had subsequently sworn off love as a useless extracurricular activity more suitable for other women. Like jogging or philanthropy. She now preferred relationships based on more ... carnal interests.

"Celly circa 1999 at the Shore Club pool—remember the Euro she was straddling in the pool? And the hickey on the back of her thigh?"

"That was a bruise from my workout!" she protested. They erupted into laughter.

"Remember that asshole from Bear Stearns? Facundo? That was classic. How many minutes did you know him, Celly, before you disappeared with him and took off all your clothes?"

Celeste kept her love life private to the outside world with an air of haughtiness—after all, she would fuck whomever she damn well pleased—but these three men had witnessed dozens of Celeste's disappearing acts when a hot or powerful (the two were typically mutually exclusive) man was present. The fact that she rarely saw a man more than once or twice was not helpful for her defense, either.

"You're a bunch of weirdos. What forty-year-old men discuss such things?"

"Oh, come on, Celly. We're just taking the piss out of you!" Savin exclaimed.

"Celly, you're up." Jack held out a small mirror with two decent-sized rails of coke split out from several grams and a silver vintage Tiffany straw for her.

"Oh, Jesus." She rolled her eyes. The coke was fluffy and yellow, uncut Colombian from the looks of it. Celeste licked her pinkie finger, dipped it in, and brought a tiny bit of the powder to her tongue. She was pleased with its purity. "I hate to pass it up, darling, but none for me tonight."

After learning how a regular meditation practice improved cognitive function considerably, Celeste had begun working more intensely with her longtime guru, Swami Shivarajananda. Her practice had led her to realize she no longer had the desire to stay up until 8 in the morning doing illicit drugs, though admittedly, it had been fun while it lasted.

Savin and Mark also rebuffed Jack's offer. "More for me!" Jack said with a Cheshire grin and proceeded to clean the mirror.

The car came to a stop in front of the restaurant, and Oliver rushed to open the door for Celeste. She took his hand and climbed out of the car, moving with the grace and regality of royalty while hanging onto her in-your-face sexiness.

Dante was one of London's newest hot spots and the city's latest addition to the Michelin list, receiving two stars. In addition to its exquisite cuisine, Dante's ambiance was perfection, with low lighting and contemporary art from living artists on nearly every wall. Celeste used the same dealer when she needed a new piece for her collection. The dining room consisted of large, round booths covered in the softest ivory calf leather, with no stuffy tablecloths. Savin never disappointed—he always placed them among the socialites. Not that they were interested in socializing with anyone.

The maître d' recognized Savin immediately and straightened his tie when they made eye contact. "Mr. Clarke, your table is ready as you requested."

"Thank you, George," Savin said.

A uniformed man assisted Celeste out of her coat, and George personally escorted the foursome to the most visible table. The server, a tall, athletic twenty-something man with nearly shoulder-length dark hair and pleasant dark eyes, approached the booth once they shuffled in. *No wedding ring and hot as fuck,* Celeste noted.

"Hello, Mr. Savin, nice to see you again." The waiter looked to the others. "Good evening. I am Antoine. I will be taking care of you tonight. Any friend of Savin's is a friend of mine. May I get you a drink while you look at the menu?" Antoine's French accent was heavy, a huge turn-on and one of the reasons Celeste loved having a pied-à-terre in Paris. She could sit for hours with gelato and a book in Jardin des Tuileries listening to the French converse.

Antoine cleared his throat, flustered as Celeste openly ogled him. She knew the moment they made eye contact that he would be making an appearance in her hotel room tonight. She smiled coyly.

"Yes, darling. I'll have a Ketel martini, extra dirty, extra olives. I apologize in advance for my degenerate friends. I promise to try to keep them in line." Celeste winked.

Antoine chuckled. "Of course, Mademoiselle."

"Oh, please call me Celeste, Antoine." She liked the way his name rolled off her tongue. After nine years of French in school and a year abroad in college, her pronunciation was impeccable. Antoine's cheeks warmed to a deep blush, and he turned to Jack.

Jack was nearly cross-eyed from his nose candy and the flask of scotch he had polished off in the car, but of course he was prepared with a drink order. "A double Hibiki 21, neat."

Mark shuffled through the wine and cocktail menus with indecision. "How about a bottle of Dom White Gold? 1995? Four glasses, please. We have some celebrating to do." *An eight-thousand-dollar bottle of champagne. I wonder what he's up to,* Celeste thought.

Savin ordered his usual "Whatever Jack is having" and quickly dove back into the story he was telling about a recent trip to St. Lucia with his flavor of the month. Apparently, Tara (was that her name? Celeste stopped keeping track) gave mind-blowing head but was a snooze otherwise.

Sav was a serial monogamist; he had a new lady friend move in every couple of months. The turnover was almost as impressive as the tab he must have running with New York moving companies. Celeste found it all to be so dull. Why go to all that work for a little sex? The way she understood it, the longer a relationship went on, the more conflict and the less sex to be had. Sounded like all work and no play.

An unremarkable server dropped off cocktails for Celeste, Jack, and Savin. Pissed when his attempt to intrigue everyone with his mystery celebration had gone unnoticed for the second time that evening, Mark whined, "Doesn't anyone want to know what we're celebrating?"

"You can't hold a secret to save your life, so you'll tell us before the bottle arrives at the table," Celeste retorted.

"Fine, since you dragged it out of me!" Mark looked around at their barely interested faces, apparently savoring an unappreciated dramatic pause. "I'm ... expecting!" Three sets of eyes stared blankly back at him.

"Another indictment? What else is new?" Jack joked. He wasn't too far off base, though. No one could survive these days in the mysterious world of global finance without an investigation or an audit. Mark's firm had paid a $4.3 billion fine the previous year when the SEC attempted to make an example of them. Billion-dollar fines were the only recourse for the SEC to hold rogue finance types accountable, though the price tag did not sting for billionaires; it was an annoyance rather than a deterrence. While the DOJ could pursue criminal charges, a guilty verdict was unlikely after an appeals court limited the scope of insider trading, and these guys knew it. Still, the government was trying to exercise its muscle; subpoenas had become a semiannual affair, even for those on the straight and narrow like Celeste and Savin. *Though we don't always play by the rules.* Celeste grinned to herself. With their $400 million proceeds from the Omar takedown, they had launched D&C unencumbered, unheard of for two inexperienced kids in their twenties.

"No, dumbass, a kid!"

Three jaws dropped as Mark sat back, satisfied to have finally gotten their attention.

"Wait, I don't understand. I didn't even know you were seeing anyone seriously," Celeste protested, ignoring the twinge in her chest.

"Her name is Jin, and we started seeing each other a few months ago. She got knocked up right away. I know it seems fast, but I dig her. We even had an ultrasound last week ... and I'm going to ask her to marry me when I get back to Asia. Celly, that's why I came this week, so you would help me pick out a ring. I wouldn't even know where to start."

Celeste had been pregnant once, but it had ended as unexpectedly as it came when Omar decided to use her as a punching bag after a night of drinking. She pasted a smile on her face, determined not to let old memories ruin the moment.

"Jewelry is my department, darling," she said. *Marriage, not so much.* "And Harry Winston. You always start at Harry Winston. We'll find the perfect ring." She was surprised at the tears that welled in her eyes, bursting with happiness for Mark and touched he had chosen her for the job.

"All you pricks are in the wedding. Assuming she says yes, and I hope she does, I'd like to have the wedding in the fall after the baby is born. Celly, we'll figure out what to do with you. I already told Jin about you and your, eh, troubles getting along with other women." Every girlfriend the men had ever had despised Celeste.

"You tell ONE woman she looks fat WHEN SHE ASKS YOU if she looks fat and suddenly you're the bitch. I'm so misunderstood." She feigned a frown.

"Celly, it was her wedding day, and she is your sister-in-law," Savin reminded everyone. They all laughed, mostly because Celeste was not bothered in the least.

"I will say one thing—fat or not, she's in line for sainthood for staying married to my idiot brother that long." Celeste and her brother had been estranged since their parents' death while Celeste was still in college, save for a call from him every few months asking for money.

As news that Mark was going to have a child began to sink in, Savin and Jack barraged Mark with questions.

"Boy or girl? I could never have a girl. Imagine when she started dating. What if she dated a dickhead like you?"

"What month is she in? Does she throw up every day?"

"Have her tits gotten hard? Huge?"

"When you're fucking, are you worried about denting its head?"

Though she laughed at their ridiculousness (for they were totally serious), Celeste was still proud of them. For selfish pricks, they were all in their own way thrilled for Mark, and no one had even tried to talk him out of settling down. Probably because she, Savin, and Jack had a long way to go and no understanding of how disruptive marriage and a child would be. A glance over at Jack escaping to the restroom for a bump was all she needed or know that—without question—she would not be the last one settling down.

Antoine approached them and placed the cocktails on the table.

An assistant lingered behind with the precious bottle of Dom. After the show of putting the champagne on ice was completed, Antoine locked eyes with Celeste at the exact moment when she was sucking an olive off a cocktail toothpick. She paused and swallowed, keeping her eyes locked with Antoine's, and then broke into a seductive smile.

Savin watched the entire exchange and rolled his eyes. "The poor guy." He turned to Celeste, scolding under his breath, "Seriously, Celly, get a room."

She winked and asked a few questions of her own.

"When is she due? How tall is she? Does she have long, slender hands or short stubbies? Do you know if she rounds or squares her nails?"

I'm not picking out a gorgeous ring for a fatty or an ugly, she thought. *God, I'm as terrible as they say. But I've been working so hard lately. I deserve a few things for myself ... and I'll be there anyway.*

Savin insisted they all order the club steak entrée. "When in London, as they say." "No, Savin, no one says that, and no one eats club steak. No one actually likes London cuisine except you," Jack corrected. After several cocktails and a delicious meal (ignoring Savin's recommendations was always the best idea), she looked around to see most of the other tables still occupied with hip urbanites. Although their party days were behind them, they often closed down the town when they were together. Tonight would be no different.

Celeste excused herself to freshen up and slide a hotel room key to Antoine. She tried to be discreet in front of the boys, though discretion was not always her strong suit.

Antoine was easy to find, heads taller than the other servers. She cornered him and said with a smile, "Antoine, I'm staying close by at the Savoy. I'd like you to stop by later."

He looked surprised and pleased. She took it as a compliment and of course as a yes that he would indeed join her.

"Room 1509." The penthouse suite to enjoy the view. She tucked the keycard in his pants pocket and walked away before he could say a word.

She was not interested in giving men her last name or phone number. It was too easy to search for her, and the last thing she needed was a man (or boy in this case) complicating her life. These less familiar encounters gave her the sex with no strings she needed minus the drama Savin was always managing.

She turned back and asked in flawless French, "Oh, and Antoine, would you point me to the ladies' room?"

The shock had vanished from his face, and in its place, was a beaming smile. Antoine was a fox, and she was already wet thinking about him inside her. In her tipsy state, she figured it was wise to escape now before she pulled him into the restroom with her.

"*Oui, ma chérie.* It's down this hallway and to the right."

Celeste used the restroom, and then she went straight to the mirror. She had to admit, even with the long day and jet lag, she still managed to look fantastic. There was little to do by way of improvement, though she went through the motions for the benefit of the other women in the restroom, adding a dab of her favorite highlighter, Touche Éclat, around her eyes and smearing her Dior lip gloss across her artificially plump, but natural-looking, lips. She tore herself away from the mirror and walked back to the table.

Savin was telling a lively story with wild hand gestures flying as he stood up to let Celeste slide into the booth, a story she had no doubt heard at least a thousand times. She noticed with displeasure two scantily clad ladies had joined the table, upset only because they were cheap looking and much too eager. *Really, who wears Herve Leger bandage dresses anymore anyway?*

"So we were at the craps table, and then the bastard bumped into me, nearly knocking me over. In my stumbling, I managed to roll two snake eyes ... paying out thousands!" Everyone erupted into laughter.

Celeste did not disguise her contempt for these childish women and let her mind wander back to Antoine. She fantasized about what she was sure was a large Frenchman's cock and shifted in her seat.

"Earth to Celly! Would you like another round?" Mark asked. She looked up, again directly into Antoine's eyes.

She cleared her throat, embarrassed because Mark had obviously said her name more than once.

"Yes, please. And I'm dying for a delicious treat …"

Antoine blushed again. "My pleasure, *ma chérie*." He disappeared to fetch the tiered dessert cart.

She ignored Savin's repeated jab ("get a room" in the form of a cough) and dove into what she had come to discuss—money.

"OK, Savin, we do need to take advantage of Mark being here and talk a little business." She stared pointedly at the two women whose names she didn't care to ask, willing them to leave her presence.

They squirmed and the bolder of the two said, "Um, well, we should be going. Are you guys going to the after-party we told you about?"

"I can speak for all of us when I say probably not. Nice to meet you." Celeste's tone was enough to make the two women stand up and scurry away. *Silly girls. You never appear desperate in front of a man.*

D&C was on the cusp of next-level profits in a market furiously scrambling to grasp the fortunes promised by artificial intelligence, or AI, investing. Celeste subscribed to the philosophy "If you're not first, you're last," and she despised nothing more than losing in the market. Being the most organized and driven of the four friends, she often had to steer them back to the task at hand.

"All work, and no play, this one!" Savin said. "Mark, we need you to lead our efforts in Brazil. We're changing investing as we know it by developing teams locally instead of sending New York assholes in, and we have people on the ground in every one of the financial markets except São Paulo. We can talk numbers tomorrow. Two months or so, and then you're back to wherever it is you live these days." Savin sat back, looking proud of himself.

Celeste jumped in. "Mark, this is our make-or-break moment. We need this team established yesterday, two weeks ago, five years ago. You're the only one with the contacts to build the team. We need you." It wasn't a heavy lift (ever) to get Mark to spend a few months in South America, especially in Brazil. He spoke flawless Portuguese, loved the culture, and particularly loved the women. Celeste often wondered why he did not move there permanently.

They had decided to focus their infrastructure investments in key emerging markets, such as the BRIC countries, Brazil-Russia-India-China, and a few countries in Africa. With the volatile American market on the verge of collapse due to the instability created by populist politics ("The US has quickly become the largest clusterfuck of all," Celeste liked to point out), she viewed emerging markets as the more stable investments in the mid to longer term. They also served as laboratories for innovation in finance because their governments were willing to look the other way if enough money was thrown at them.

"Did you all not hear me when I said Jin is pregnant? And the getting engaged part? I can't steal away for two months."

Oh, shit. So this is what happens when one of your friends starts growing up. Your business plans get wrecked. Yet they needed someone on the ground, and Mark was the obvious choice, the only choice. Celeste switched to another tactic.

"Of course, darling, Savin didn't mean to be insensitive. What if we rent you a spectacular beach house on Ipanema in addition to an apartment in the city and you bring your lady friend with you? You can't tell me a pregnant woman wouldn't enjoy a few months by the beach!"

Mark relented a bit. "We'll talk tomorrow at brunch. I need to run this by Jin."

Jack perked up again as if on cue and just as suddenly seemed bored. "No more business talk. Or kid talk. Snooze."

Jack had made several millions that he invested in an unstable market when they were in their mid-twenties. He gambled it all on an IPO for an organic supermarket chain (before organic was ubiquitous) and got lucky—he was now worth hundreds of millions of dollars. He retired, private jet and all, by the time they were twenty-eight. Now he spent most of his time traipsing around the world, though Celeste wished he would find someone to settle down with. Of the four of them, he needed it most; however, she supposed they were all lonely in some regard. She hoped Mark was happy, she truly did, but she had witnessed too many terrible endings to put much stock in this relationship thing he was trying, baby or no baby. None of them were the marrying kind.

It's lonely at the top.

They decided against dessert because it was time for a change of scenery. Savin tipped Antoine 400 euros over his usual 45 percent of their bill. She was pleased with his etiquette. She winked at Antoine as they tumbled out of the booth, collectively much drunker than any of them had realized.

"See you soon, Antoine," Celeste cooed under her breath.

Antoine seemed to have lost the blush. She was certain he was propositioned often. Although probably not by women like her.

"Room, uh, 1509, right?" he mumbled so only Celeste could hear.

His heavy French accent only drew her in further, staring now at his full lips, imagining them all over her body. As if his broad shoulders and long, lean body weren't enough.

She would have one more drink with the boys at their favorite after-hours spot and then slip away for an evening of getting fucked by Antoine. Soon he would be all over her body, and she was pleased to spy a rather large bulge almost hidden in his baggy black waiter pants.

———

CELESTE WAS THE LAST TO SLIDE INTO THE CAR THROUGH THE DOOR Oliver held open. She looked around to see that everyone had lost steam, despite their grandiose plans to stay out all night. Oliver dropped them off at the hotel, and she hugged each of the guys good night as they got off the elevator. Brunch was the following day at 1 p.m., and she knew the guys would want to get up and work out, read the papers, check the markets. *Leaving plenty of time to jerk off in the shower, knowing these three,* Celeste mused.

The elevator door opened to her penthouse suite. She was a bit obsessive when it came to her surroundings, and her assistant regularly coordinated with the hotel butler staff to make sure everything was to her liking. The wet bar was stocked with Evian and her organic snacks. The bathroom sink was home to all her makeup, lined up in perfect rows by order of application. She opened the boudoir to find her silk negligees hanging alongside her dresses and suits.

No sooner had she slipped into her deep-navy Agent Provocateur bra and garter belt than she heard a knock at the door.

The entire suite was illuminated with a warm candlelit glow, thanks to the turndown service. Celeste swung the door open in excitement, though outwardly calm and confident. Antoine looked even more gorgeous by candlelight, and his eyes were dark with desire. Brooding (he was, after all, French), he bent down to kiss her cheek, then walked past her and tossed his coat on the sofa. Gone was the boyish, shy façade; in its place, a man's desire. He turned to her, grabbed her waist, and pulled her against him, their foreheads nearly smacking.

Antoine picked her up and carried her to the bedroom, throwing her down on the California king bed. *Nothing like an excited admirer in bed*, she thought as he ripped off his shirt and several buttons flew to the floor. She grabbed one of the condoms she had placed on the nightstand and handed it to Antoine. She was reckless with men and perhaps shared her body too freely ... but she made sure she was safe when she did so. He ripped open the condom and put it on, and she arched her back as he slid inside her. He was well endowed as she had guessed (men did not have Antoine's swagger without a big dick or a lot of money).

Celeste took all of him in. Tiny beads of sweat glistened on his defined shoulders, and his hair moved in rhythm with him pounding her—deep, intense, and methodical. She put her arms above her head on the bed, and he obliged by coming closer to her and holding her wrists with one hand, rubbing her clit with the other, his dick sliding in and out with the right amount of friction.

"*Mon Dieu*, Celeste," Antoine muttered. "My God, *tu me rends si dur.*"

"Yes, believe me, I can feel how hard your dick is, and I'm not complaining," she responded breathlessly.

Antoine maneuvered her so that she was on top of him. His thumbs held her hip bones as he moved her back and forth on his cock, which hardened even more when she rubbed her clit, feeling him pulsating inside her as a low growl of desire escaped his lips. She leaned her head back in pleasure and felt tingles take over her body once more as he exploded inside her. They climaxed together, Antoine shouting, "*Mon Dieu, mon Dieu!*" over and over, and then collapsed into a heap.

The two lay together silently for what seemed like an eternity, Antoine lightly snoring, Celeste counting down the seconds until it was appropriate to kick him out. She walked into the bathroom, closed the door, and turned on the shower. Steam filled the room while she washed a tiny smudge of eyeliner from her face. Once satisfied, she stepped into the shower, noting her products lined up precisely as she liked. Celeste demanded excellence from her team, and it did not go unnoticed.

Refreshed, she put on a silk robe and returned to the bedroom, where Antoine was still in the spot where Celeste had left him.

"Would you like a towel before you go, Antoine?" Celeste had never liked sleepovers. He stood up and rolled off the condom, then went to the bathroom and flushed it. She retrieved a silk negligee from the closet and slid it over her head while he dressed.

Relieved, she thought, *Finally.*

As she ushered him to the door, Antoine turned to her with a hopeful expression. "Please let me know the next time you are in London. You know where to find me."

"Of course. Good night!" Celeste patted his chest and closed the door.

She waited until the elevator doors closed, and then she climbed into bed and snuggled into the silky sheets, falling to sleep with a "just had a great fuck" grin on her face.

2

SPRING FLING

Two weeks later, Celeste exited the elevator and walked down the hall to Savin's apartment. Angelo, the firm's longtime security guard, stood outside the behemoth front door. Celeste noted a nightclub bouncer look-alike in a black suit lurking in the corner with a list. Angelo beamed when he saw Celeste, a reprieve from his typical stoic demeanor meant to intimidate. Angelo fit the stereotype —a tall, well-muscled former pro football player who had suffered a career-ending knee injury. He stood six foot eight, formidable with his bulging muscles protruding out of his white T-shirt. He was a teddy bear on the inside, but he would go to any lengths to protect her. He had proven his loyalty and resourcefulness years earlier when Omar had hurt Celeste. While she did not have specifics, Jack had intimated that Omar had paid dearly for his mistakes in a campaign led by Angelo and the man who had since become the firm's attorney, Johnny Carolo.

"Angelo. Long time, no see! You're always sending one of your guys to watch over me—are you tiring of me?" Angelo laughed and wrapped her in a bear hug.

"It's better when you don't see me—that means you're safe these days, Celeste!" Angelo opened Savin's door and stepped inside.

"Savin has outdone himself tonight. The party is in full swing, and of course, you're the most beautiful woman to arrive." His expression turned somber. "Try to stay out of trouble."

"Never, darling!" Celeste said with a laugh as she entered the party. The door closed behind her, and she scanned the foyer and ballroom. Savin's usual invite list was here. Heavy hitters like her from the hedge fund world (except all male, of course) and their model girlfriends, as well as bankers, entrepreneurs, and everyone in between. A few select celebrities who weren't too unbearable. She knew most everyone here and was interested in speaking with only a few of them tonight.

This evening was Savin's inaugural Spring Fling. Celeste had been in São Paulo the previous week closing a major deal with Roberto Barbosa, one of their primary investors and the man who had given them seed money to start their firm long ago, when she received an urgent text from Savin demanding her attendance. She reminded herself to fire whoever had taught him how to send high-importance text messages. His constant hysteria was unbearable.

"Celly. Get your ass back to NYC. My Spring Fling is this weekend!"

"Sav, it's early March and 30 degrees. Hardly spring. Stopping over at Roberto's new Rio resort."

"No!!!!! Need you here!"

"It's fucking cold! Beach days needed. Roberto's already arranged the jet, etc."

"Have a little faith, Celly! It will be a lovely spring evening. Roberto's flying in anyway. Please tell me you'll be there?"

"Fine. But you owe me."

Celeste scanned the foyer and ballroom. Savin's event planners had outdone themselves. The party was complete with out-of-season bouquets and an excellent playlist. Uniformed cater waiters milled around with champagne and hors d'oeuvres. Upon seeing her, Cat, one of the bartenders Celeste recognized from the renowned Cipriani's downtown, beckoned to her from behind the bar.

"Compliments of Savin. He said I'm allowed to share this with only you," Cat said, handing Celeste the flute. Celeste recognized it as a prestige vintage from the Moët cellar in Epernay, France, a bottle from Savin's permanent collection. She downed the champagne (she knew she should savor it, but she needed to be a little tipsy to tolerate the crowd) and, after Cat poured her a refill, walked toward her friends mingling in the center of the crowd.

Then she saw him. Rather, she felt him, felt his stare from across the grand room. He stood alone at the back bar, gazing at her intently, unabashedly, before breaking into a grin. Celeste knew she had never seen him before; with dark, almost-black hair and ice-blue eyes, he was the type of handsome a woman remembered. His smile was unnerving. Celeste broke away from this strange man's gaze, scanning the room to find Savin. She turned to walk to the other end of the columned ballroom, where Savin was speaking with two men she vaguely recalled meeting in the past.

Savin and company widened their circle to include her. "The lady of the hour and the brains behind our little operation. Celeste Donovan, of Donovan & Clarke Capital, these are a couple of my mates from boarding school, Edward and Triston."

Celeste smiled radiantly to hide her discomfort about the mystery man. "Yes, we've met once before, no?"

The man she remembered as Edward took her hand and brushed it with his lips. "I would never forget such a remarkable woman. I believe we met at Bungalow 8 for one of Savin's birthday soirées many years ago."

"Yes, now I remember," she fibbed as she pulled her hand away from him. She hated being touched by strangers unless she had chosen to take them to bed and they were in the process of giving her an orgasm.

Savin dove back into a tale of his outlandish behaviors. "Mum was none too happy to hear from the headmaster that I was once again caught drinking during class—twenty-five-year-old scotch stolen from her liquor stash, no less. I argued she couldn't be too upset since Father had ingrained in me a taste for only the best, but she wasn't buying it." Celeste looked around the room, nodding and smiling to greet her business colleagues and the women they had brought—all of whom predictably despised Celeste. According to her stylist at Bergdorf's, she was one of their favorite topics. *God forbid a woman makes her own money and ages gracefully.*

"Roberto! Good to see you! And so soon after our last visit!" Celeste said as she widened the circle for him and his guest. Roberto Barbosa was six feet tall, Brazilian with dark features, and larger than life with his booming voice, heavy Portuguese accent, and infectious baritone laugh. He was mildly overweight (or short for his height he liked to say), and his belly shook when he laughed. His hair was thinning and graying, but despite his weight and age, Celeste had to admit he was an attractive man. His money and charisma didn't hurt. He was always accompanied by a beautiful woman and was currently working on divorce number three because of his wandering eye.

Celeste hugged her client and then turned to the beautiful, petite brunette at his side. She extended her hand to the woman, expecting jealousy and petulance. The woman had long, dark Hollywood waves, glowing olive skin, a perfectly applied smoky eye, and tasteful Cartier studs. She was wearing a flattering fuchsia shift dress and had a gold Jimmy Choo clutch under her arm. The woman met Celeste's gaze and offered a firm handshake. Celeste liked her confidence and style immediately.

"I'm Samantha, but everyone calls me Sam. Roberto tells me you make him a lot of money."

Celeste laughed at Sam's candor. "This is true, I suppose. Roberto is one of our most valuable investors," she said with a smile.

She was thrilled that Roberto's lady friend was sharp, witty, and successful. Sam kept a place uptown to be close to her New York office when work brought her here from São Paulo (was it a litigation firm? Celeste forgot upon hearing) and trained with Celeste's former Pilates teacher when in town.

"New York truly is the largest small town in the world!" Celeste said. Their shared love for Geoff, the Pilates reformer master, bound them in conversation in a way normally foreign to Celeste.

"Well, duty calls. I must say hello to a few people before I can sneak out. Sam, it was lovely to meet you, and Roberto, so glad you were able to pop in. Let's have dinner the next time you two are in town," Celeste said with uncharacteristic sincerity. *Wife number three and Roberto's last mistress were both so terrible. Who would've guessed he could snatch up such a wonderful woman?*

AFTER MAKING ROUNDS AT THE PARTY, CELESTE WAS BACK AT SAVIN'S side, listening to more stories about the Edward/Triston/Savin show.

Celeste chimed in. "So did Savin tell you his little party theme? This is his Spring Fling in thirty-degree New York style." The group laughed as Savin dove into a story about how wishing winter away actually worked; he had watched it on the Discovery Channel one night when the Ambien was not working after Tara moved out a few weeks prior. Edward and Triston rolled their eyes and chuckled along with Celeste, accustomed to Savin's antics.

In her peripheral vision, she saw a man appear right next to her and was startled when he placed a hand on her lower back. Celeste looked over and saw that it was *him*, the handsome man with the searing gaze from earlier. After a few glasses of champagne, Celeste had forgotten about him, but now the skittishness returned.

Savin greeted the man with a firm hug and a pat on the back. "Mate, so good to see you! Where have you been hiding?" Savin inquired, oblivious to Celeste's discomfort.

"If you'll excuse me, fellas, I need to get some air," Celeste interrupted. She escaped the mystery man's ice-blue stare and perfect face without a backward glance. Under normal circumstances, she would have fucked him two hours ago, but she was feeling anything but normal. On Savin's massive terrace, Celeste inhaled the crisp cool air. His Tribeca loft was one of her favorite vantage points, and its airiness gave the illusion of endless space in an overcrowded city where one never felt alone. Celeste sighed and took in the Manhattan skyline, happy to be back home after her travels. Even late in the evening and ninety stories high, one could feel the vibration unmatched anywhere else in the world. She, like all New Yorkers, thrived on the intensity.

Celeste glanced over her shoulder to see the mystery man walking toward the door.

Fuck.

There was no one with whom she could feign conversation before he stepped out onto the terrace. She appeared outwardly calm and uninterested, though inside she was disconcerted. She felt her cheeks flush, unaccustomed to men having such an effect on her.

It's the wine.

"Hello," mystery man said as he stood directly behind her and murmured in her ear. "I came over to talk to you, and you fled." He was much too close. *Nibble my ear, why don't you.*

His scent was a mix of raw masculinity and pheromones. She turned around and stepped away from him, realizing she had not made eye contact with him since a few hours before.

"Hello," she replied curtly. She did not trust herself to respond to his comment.

"Spectacular view, huh?"

"You know Savin, always has the best of everything." She bristled at the fact that he had a British accent. She would never let Savin know—he was too self-absorbed as it was—but she secretly loved Anglo accents.

"He does indeed. And your name is?"

"Celeste, but you already knew that, no?"

He nodded.

"How do you know Savin?" she asked. "He's been my business partner for many years, and I've never seen you before."

Confident and relaxed, mystery man dove in.

"Savin and I went to boarding school together in Buckingham. Then, true to form, he got in trouble for smoking pot one too many times in the quad—not to mention the fact that we treated class attendance as optional. Our parents kept us separated after that."

To her chagrin, she giggled at this. "Sounds like the Savin we all know and love!"

"Would you like a smoke? I rarely do but picked some up on a whim." He withdrew a box of Nat Shermans from his jacket pocket.

"Oh, no, I quit years a— ... No, you know what? I would love one." It would give her something to do with her hands while his eyes pierced through her. *If you stare into my soul, you deserve to see whatever darkness you find, mystery man.* Celeste smiled at that and relaxed a bit.

Their eyes met over the flame as he lit her cigarette. She inhaled deeply, waiting for the nicotine to calm her the way it used to. The serenity never came, and instead, she fell into a body-wrenching coughing fit after her first drag. Mortified, she looked up at mystery man, whose concerned look was quickly replaced with hysterical laughter.

"I don't mean to laugh, Celeste, but you have a certain *je ne sais quoi.* I didn't expect to send you into an emphysema spell. Are you OK, dear?"

Celeste burst into laughter despite herself. "I haven't smoked in ages; perhaps I should've said no." She realized how foolish she was acting toward this man who had been neither forward nor strange. The laughter led to tears threatening to roll down her face, a reality check that now was not the time to mess up her makeup. She straightened up and handed the cigarette to mystery man. He extinguished it on the ledge and threw it over the side.

"Tsk, tsk," she said. "That could have fallen on someone's head."

"Perhaps that was the intent," he said as he winked at her. "What do you say we get out of here? I'd love to take you out for a drink. Johnny's Place is right around the corner."

She was impressed. Celeste frequented the trendiest hot spots, but few knew of this swanky place. Intimate. Sexy. A well-kept secret.

"Well. I *suppose* I could use a change of scenery."

He moved closer and put his hand on the small of her back, beginning to lead her inside.

"I'll grab my coat, and then we can head out," she turned to tell ... *I never asked him his name.*

No sooner had she walked back into the ballroom than Savin was in front of her, and mystery man excused himself.

"So you've set your sights on Theodore, huh? Don't break his heart. He's the real deal, an old friend," lectured Savin.

"Theo—" *Oh, that's his name.* "I didn't set *my* sights on *him*. To the contrary, I was minding my own business ... Besides, somehow I think he can take care of himself." She smiled.

"He's a good guy, Celeste. I wanted the two of you to meet tonight."

"You arranged this? What the hell, Sav?" she scolded as he laughed at her reaction. Her heart fluttered as she struggled to keep her mind off the man's perfect lips.

"Why else do you think I demanded your presence? You need something more than a series of Antoines. I can tell you're starting to find it all so dull. And if I didn't know better, I would think that maybe you have a little crush, Celly." Celeste narrowed her eyes with a frown and prepared to turn and stalk off. She stumbled backward and ran smack into Theodore's chest. He was holding up her camel cashmere coat. Savin laughed at the uncharacteristic display of clumsiness.

Celeste looked up at Theodore with a question in her eyes. Theodore leaned to her ear, whispering, "I knew it was yours because your scent lingered on it."

"Ah. Yes, of course. And thank you."

Savin did not miss any of this exchange ... Or her blushing. She wished for the thousandth time that he were less observant. She was going to hear about this over Sunday brunch. He winked at the two of them and shook Theodore's hand.

"Great to see you, mate. Celly, I'll see you at brunch Sunday."

Celeste did not make a habit of leaving events with men, preferring to meet them after. As they made their way to the door, she told a couple of the wives who hated her how wooooooooonderful it was to see them, while Theodore (with his hand again at the small of her back) said goodbye to no one. In fact, he appeared to know no one besides Savin. A ghost.

Theodore pulled Savin's massive door closed as she strode to the elevator. Angelo raised his eyebrows and stepped aside to let them pass.

"Good night, Celeste. Be safe."

"Good night, Angelo."

Theodore stepped into the elevator after her, and yet again she caught her breath at his handsomeness. Thinking of nothing intelligent to say but needing to cut the sexually charged silence, she cleared her throat.

He said, "This is a strange thing I'm about to say ... but I'm not sure I've ever been more attracted to a woman than I am to you. I was immediately drawn to you when I saw you walk in, and I haven't been able to think of anything besides your eyes since. You are a vision."

Oh, come on! "We met like an hour ago." She hesitated to call him by his name. "Theodore, is it?" Celeste chuckled and looked away, at once disappointed that the four elevator walls were mirrored. It was impossible to avoid his gaze.

Her La Perlas were drenched. *I wish he would give me some space ... or fuck me right here in the elevator.*

As they stepped out onto the cold street, Celeste was relieved to feel the heat leave her cheeks. They walked in silence the two blocks to Johnny's and retreated down the steps into the warmth of the tiny sublevel jazz club, a fire crackling in the middle of the room. A quartet was playing in the corner. They strode to the bar, and he put his arms out to remove her coat. He doubled it over his arm.

"You are quite the gentleman."

"Any excuse to be close enough to touch you." She jerked her head around to look into his clear blue eyes, crinkled in mischief. *Two can play at this game.*

"What can I get for you, Miss Celeste? The usual?"

Celeste casually reached over the bar to stab three olives with a pick. She sucked the olives off slowly and deliberately, one by one.

She felt Theodore's eyebrows raise but ignored him and said, "Let's switch it up. Vodka martini tonight, Ketel. Extra dirty." She turned to Theodore and winked.

He appeared unruffled as he ordered, "What the lady is having."

Celeste struggled to gain the upper hand in the conversation. "So, Theodore, how is it that you know Savin so well, but you don't know any of our friends?"

"I like to keep a low profile. Better for business."

"Sounds mysterious. What brings you to town this weekend, mystery man?" He laughed, a masculine hearty laugh, his eyes crinkling at the sides again. Not the kind that made her cringe and wish for a vial of Botox to erase his crow's feet—Theodore had the manly crinkles representing a rich life of laughter and smiles. *God, he is delicious.*

"A secret mission, and only you can help me. I must save a fair maiden from a dragon!"

Celeste laughed. She straightened up when a more serious look came across Theodore's face.

"Honestly, you're part of the reason I decided to visit. Savin and I caught up a few months ago, and I complained that I haven't dated in a while. He said I 'simply must' meet you." His imitation of Savin's theatrics was spot on, complete with hand gestures.

Laughing in spite of herself, she inwardly cursed Savin. *So he was telling the truth; he arranged this, actually threw a party to set me up with his long-lost friend.* If she weren't so furious, she might have thanked Savin. She might yet; the jury was still out.

"Hmm, sounds like a very elaborate matchmaking scheme."

"Well, you know Savin. I must say, you exceed his description of you. His photos do you no justice, though I am happy to find you have as much substance as you have beauty."

"He sent you photos?" Her expression was stoic, but inside she was seething. *How pedestrian to send photos like a fucking Tinder profile.*

"Yes. But I must confess, I saw you a few weeks ago at an event. I tried to say hello, but you were hell-bent on flirting with a young waiter. In fact, I believe you told me to get the fuck out of your way and stormed off."

Celeste had the grace to blush as she recalled a man at the mayor's New York Fashion Week party stepping in front of her, then smiled. "Oh. Well, I suppose you were in my way, then." *No reason to deny having sex with that hot waiter—Brad or Brandon? Ben?—at this point.*

"Yes, I was going to say hello to you and Savin that night, but you were ... otherwise occupied, and Savin was tied up entertaining a crowd of twenty. I asked him not to tell you I was coming tonight, which was intended to avoid pressuring you, but as I say it aloud, I realize it sounds a bit ... creepy."

"I see. Well, now, here we are. Tell me a little about you." It surprised Celeste that she was not bored and wanted to hear what he had to say. She had two therapists, a Sherpa, a guru, a shaman, an acupuncturist, a yoga teacher, a personal trainer, an executive coach, and a priest. She figured she had covered the bases for emotional companionship and did not usually engage in much conversation with men.

"Happy to oblige. What would you like to know?"

"Where do you live?"

"Everywhere. Nowhere. Work can take me to two countries in one day and not home for a month or six. My lifestyle hasn't exactly lent itself to a relationship. Soon, though, I'd like to be able to stay in one place a little longer."

"What is your work, exactly? It sounds like Savin told you everything about me, so you must know he and I are business partners."

"Yes, I know a lot about your work. Savin says you're the most brilliant mind he's ever worked with."

"Is that so?" Celeste said with a laugh. "This is the first I'm hearing of my brilliance. We've always worked well together, Savin and I, but mostly because I let him complain about what a pain in the ass I am all the time. I'm sure I don't have to tell you that he is the real pain. Now, as for you, what do you do besides fly country to country in a G-4?"

Ugh, his sexy laugh again.

"My work is a bit complicated these days. Let's just say for now that I'm a modern-day Robin Hood." He paused and clinked her glass in cheers. "In all seriousness, I just shuffle money around."

Part of her wanted to move away from the work conversation and have his hands slide up her leg and ... She almost arched her back at the runaway train of thought.

Theodore entertained her with tales of him and Savin sneaking cigarettes and booze in grammar school. She had, of course, heard nearly every story from Savin, but she wondered why Savin had never mentioned a friend named Theodore. Savin's stories were elaborate, so the omission was odd.

"Some things never change," she said. "Savin's never met a rule he didn't want to break. Let me guess. He plotted out the entire scheme, down to the escape plan. When you succeeded and all went well, he had a total meltdown."

Theodore nodded. "They wouldn't expel us because we both excelled in our studies. To be fair, it wasn't entirely our fault. Trap dozens of young men in the countryside with no girls and leave them to run amok? I'm surprised we didn't end up in prison by age fifteen."

"Were your parents as absent as Savin's? Seems his parents dropped him off at age six and never returned." *Grabbing a drink with a man is a precursor to get drunk and fuck, Celeste, not explore each other's familial pasts.* This was the strangest date of her life, not that she had many for comparison.

"Yes, they were. My father was a successful banker with lots of women on the side, and my mother had an affinity for gossip and her favorite cocktail of wine and Xanax, preferably ingested together before noon. When both parents were home, their English passive aggression was deafening. It was all so cliché, and frankly, I wasn't sad to miss their day-to-day dramas. I'm happy to see age has brought them a bit more peace, as they seem to actually enjoy each other's company these days. My dad spends his time on the golf course, and my mother has kept up quite well with daily Pilates and her gardening. I have no living siblings and no extended family to speak of. Some cousins who come and go every few years when they need money."

"Wow."

"It's OK. I feel fortunate to have had a great childhood despite, or perhaps because of, my parents' absence. My nanny and my grandparents doted on me, and genuine love is really all a child needs to excel in life. What about you?"

"Whew, this is a heavy convo tonight, isn't it?" *The last thing I want to get into is my parents' death.* Theodore pivoted the conversation.

"I'd like to take you out to dinner before I leave Monday." He brushed her cheek with his hand. "Well, what I'd actually like to do is hole up with you in my hotel room until I leave Monday, but I should probably take you to dinner first."

On any ordinary date, his forwardness would be welcome, and she would have insisted they do just that—fuck in his hotel room that night with her graceful exit before morning. Now, though, she was uneasy. She had the sneaking suspicion this mystery man, with his flirting ease and the intensity with which he looked at her, was going to try a new approach with her.

"Um, sure, sounds nice." She yawned. Four hours of discomfort was exhausting. He noticed and placed two $100 bills on the bar, turning back to her so that they were face-to-face.

"May I walk you home?"

Celeste laughed. "I live in the West Village, I'm wearing five-inch heels, and it's thirty degrees out. It's safe to say I'm not walking home."

"You didn't seem to mind the cold when you fled to the terrace to avoid me earlier tonight." His eyes were enchanting, and she faltered, forgiving him at once for poking fun at her awkward behavior earlier.

"Allow me to drop you off," he said.

He helped her with her coat once more, his ever-steady hand returning to her back. As they stepped out to meet the harsh street lighting and city noise, she noticed a black Maybach waiting. The driver opened the back door for her, and she slid in after providing him with her address. He nodded and closed her door. Theodore walked around to the other door and slipped in next to her.

He was much too close. She was more than a little tipsy and knew she would have exercise supreme self-control to make it to her place rather than his hotel room tonight.

"So dinner tomorrow it is. Shall I ask my sources where to take you, or do you have something trendy and of the moment in mind?"

No restaurant opened in Manhattan without her knowing and dining there before it was on everyone's radar. She was a hedonist in every sense of the word, and food was no exception. On a whim, she decided to leave it up to him.

"I'm at your mercy."

"Perfect. I'll have a table for us at eight thirty."

Theodore reached for her hand and raised it to his lips, which were as soft and plump as she'd imagined earlier. His lips lingered as their eyes met, then he lowered his hand and ran his first two fingers along the length of her thigh—dangerously close to the still-wet triangle between her legs, his eyes dancing again at his effect on her.

The car arrived in front of her building, a glossy high-rise tucked in the middle of historic brownstones in the quaint West Village, much faster than she would have liked. Celeste loved her building, but most important to her was the round-the-clock security. Her twenty-four-hour doormen kept her protected. She appreciated them all but favored Jonah, who was working tonight.

Theodore got out of the car and came around to open her door.

"I can't wait for dinner," he said. He looked down in her eyes and wrapped her in a warm hug. The hard bulge she had been wanting to feel all night pressed against her through Theodore's pants. Not one for intimate contact that did not involve fucking, she struggled to return the hug in the least awkward way possible, standing on the tips of her toes to wrap her arms around his neck.

"Me, neither," she breathed in his ear and gave him a kiss on the cheek. She walked toward the door before her willpower crumbled, resisting the urge to turn back and look at him. Well, almost. She peeked over her shoulder and smiled to see he was as aroused as she was, still hard, staring intently exactly when she left him. Pleased, she turned to Jonah, who held the door open.

"Good evening, Miss Celeste."

"Hello, Jonah," she said in a singsong voice. She heard Theodore's car roll away once she was inside the building.

Jonah looked at her questioningly, and then lowered his eyes. She realized this was perhaps the first time she had left a man with a kiss at the door in the six years she had lived there.

Inside the elevator, Celeste exhaled. Theodore's presence was intense. He was intelligent, witty, and sexy as hell. It was rare that a man caught her attention for longer than it took to get undressed, but she felt ... electric when he was close to her. The last time she had felt like this was a lifetime ago.

Omar. The carnage from her relationship with Omar permeated every facet of her life, though she would hardly admit it to anyone. Her drive and her compulsiveness to keep men at arm's length were the result of what had happened during her relationship with Omar. When Omar revealed his violent tendencies, coke addiction, and affinity for prostitutes to Celeste, she and Savin, motivated by the boldness and naïveté of youth, plotted her escape route, the legendary insider-trading scheme leaving them $400 million richer, fuck-you money allowing them to start their own shop several years before. Omar knew nothing of their deceit, thought Savin had persuaded his father's colleague, Roberto, to sponsor the launch of D&C. This secret, if discovered, could have cost Celeste, Savin, and Roberto everything, including their lives. Fortunately for them, the statute of limitations had run out, and they no longer faced the threat of prosecution. Most importantly, Omar had been banned from the island of Manhattan, thanks to some of Jack's roughneck connections. *Fuck you, Omar. I won like I always do.*

Once inside her apartment, Celeste looked out her floor-to-ceiling windows covering three walls—the perks of having the entire floor—and took in her picturesque view: to the south, the odd-looking One World Trade building, which had been constructed a few years earlier on top of the World Trade Center ruins; to the north, the Empire State Building, peeking over the other high-rises.

This view never gets old.

Too wired for sleep, Celeste poured herself a glass of red wine, a complex Barbaresco, compliments of Jack, and settled on her chaise lounge. Jack owned vineyards on several continents, so she never wanted for exotic wines. Jack's holiday gift to her was predictable— an annual supply of only the finest. Other than the minor discomfort caused by Theodore this evening, all was well in her life. She and Savin had just finished a capital raise for their latest AI proposal, the analytics projecting returns head and neck above their usual profits. Theodore was just a pleasant man, albeit a steaming hot sexpot. Drinks, dinner, and great sex tomorrow night, and then on to the next one.

3

YOUR FIRST FIRST DATE

Meredith, Celeste's stylist, had chosen one of Celeste's most flattering body-hugging dresses—a sleeveless black number with a plunging neckline—along with open-toe burgundy suede booties and a gray YSL smoking clutch, for her date with Theodore. Simple, chic ... perfection. Celeste retrieved her latest purchase from the Agent Provocateur bag on the island in the middle of her walk-in closet—a black silk demi bra, suspenders, and thong. She removed the tissue and laid the pieces out, fingering the luxurious fabric. *Gorgeous, but maybe commando is more appropriate.* She heard the elevator arrive and wrapped herself in her silk kimono.

You will be eating out your heart, and hopefully my pussy, tonight, Theodore. She was wet at the thought of his head between her legs as she walked out to the foyer to meet her glam squad—Ty, her hairstylist, and Patrick, her makeup artist.

"OK, so Patrick and I realized on the way over, we've never actually gotten you ready for a date before!" Ty gushed. "Have you ever been on a date? We got a bottle of bubbles to celebrate the occasion."

"Your *first* first date, Celly! Oh my God!" shrieked Patrick.

She shot them a dirty look, took the bottle from Ty's outstretched hand, and walked over to the bar to pop the cork. After filling the champagne flutes and distributing the glasses, she responded.

"Of course this isn't my *first* first date. I fail to see what the big deal is."

"Fuck that. You're a terrible liar. Even Meredith agreed in our group tex—"

"What does it take to get good help these days? Help that isn't so —insolent ... and invasive." Celeste sought to lighten the mood and switched gears to Ty's favorite topic—himself. "What happened to your sex friend from the other night?"

"Oh em gee! You'll never believe it. He called me—like picked up his iPhone and dialed my number—CALLED me...and asked me out again. I didn't know whether to swoon ... or file a restraining order!"

Patrick looked unimpressed. "You said he had a big dick, right? Just let him buy you dinner and stop overthinking."

"Yeah. For once, you're probably right."

Celeste reached for her iPhone to turn on some music and set the mood while two of her favorite men poked, prodded, and coifed her into perfection. She refused to admit it to anyone, even herself, but the stakes were high for this date. She felt out of sorts around Theodore, could not maneuver the situation to exercise the supreme control she exhibited in every other aspect of her life. She hit play on her playlist, and her Sonos wireless speaker system came alive with the latest pop song. A text from Monty, the firm's driver, confirmed he would retrieve her at 8:15 p.m.

"Mon, it's the wknd," she texted back. "Send someone else. Enjoy the fam!"

"Miss Celeste, happy to pick you up. See you at 8:15."

"Unnecessary, but thank you!"

CELESTE BLOCKED OUT THE LIVELY BANTER BETWEEN PATRICK AND TY, lost in thought. What was it about this man? She had not slept at all, thinking of Theodore's lips, his smile, how his body felt against hers when he hugged her. For once, she was even going to arrive on time (not that she would let Ty and Patrick know this; they would collapse in fits of laughter at her crush). She took a swig of the last of her bubbles and stared at her reflection in the mirror. "Nice work, guys! Now get out of here, so I can get dressed!"

"Fine, but we're taking the champs with us!"

Celeste laughed. "There's a bottle of vintage bubbles in the fridge if you'd like to take it also."

"Oooo, she's offering us the good stuff. Celly, you know I'll never turn down Dom, so you'd better mean it if you're offering."

"Yes, I'm fully aware. Be young, and have fun tonight, while I die of boredom on a date with this forty-something man." She rolled her eyes for effect, hoping that Ty and Patrick bought it. Luckily, they were both lost in texts when they got in the elevator, no doubt planning how to score their next eight ball and where to go for a night of dancing and debauchery. Oh, how she missed those days. In contrast, she was going on a dinner date at 8:30 with an age-appropriate man and was planning to arrive on time. She was losing her edge.

How times had changed. She used to feel so ... alive pissing Omar off. She recalled the fits Omar used to throw when she would arrive twenty, thirty, forty-five minutes late after he had given her "very explicit instructions" to arrive on time. "Fuck you," she would respond loudly, making a mental commitment to be an hour late the following evening. That volatility was pervasive throughout her relationship with Omar, with constant ups and downs. Tonight, she would arrive on time. *Only because it's Saturday night and because they could give the table away*, she reasoned.

Celeste took her time dressing with great care to ensure every piece was in place. When the reflection staring back at her on her dressing platform was perfection, she gathered her bag and coat and rode the elevator down. Her phone read 8:14 p.m.

"Have a wonderful evening, Celeste," Jonah called from his perch with a wink. That man knew more of Celeste's secrets than she cared to admit.

"Thanks, Jonah! Don't wait up," she teased.

Monty stood by the car holding a massive display of pink peonies —her favorite and also nearly impossible to get because they were out of season.

"What's all this, Monty? These are exquisite!" It wasn't her birthday, so she was unsure why the team would buy her a gift.

"They are from a Mr. Theodore? He arranged for me to pick them up?" he said with a question in his voice, though he was never one to pry.

"Is that so? Well, let's give them to Jonah. He'll put them upstairs." Jonah materialized outside at that moment and took the oversized vase out of Monty's hands.

Celeste climbed into the car wordlessly, wondering the meaning of the flowers. Once Monty was settled into the car, she tried to draw him out.

"I assume Savin coordinated all this with the flowers? I don't appreciate him making you gofer around running errands. On a weekend, no less!"

"I'm happy to share in bringing a little romance to your life, Miss Celeste." Monty smiled. "There's one more thing." He turned to the back seat and handed her a card. *Celeste* was scrolled across the front in calligraphy.

"Romance? I don't under—Ohh." She cut herself off when she saw a man's scrawl at the bottom.

Looking forward to a lovely evening with you, Celeste.
   —Theodore

Celeste rolled her eyes and flopped the card down on the seat. "I knew this was a bad idea," she muttered to herself.

She felt Monty watching her reaction in the mirror, beaming from ear to ear. This was probably the kind of cheese-dick thing he did for his wife on a monthly basis in exchange for a blow job.

"This Theodore seems like a class act, doesn't he?" Celeste frowned at Monty's question and replied with a noncommittal "Perhaps," then busied herself with her phone, making clear she was finished speaking for the duration of the ride. She softened her frown as they pulled up to the restaurant, refusing to let Theodore see any sort of reaction. This was turning into a definite "fuck him, leave before dawn, and forget it happened" type of evening. *Flowers on a first date? I mean, really.*

When she entered the restaurant from the bustling Soho street, she was greeted by the man of the hour himself and the maître d', Hiroto, at the door. The restaurant, Rakuen, had just earned its debut in the Michelin Guide for New York City, and scoring a table there was almost as hard as getting a ticket for the opening night of *Hamilton* with the original cast had been (which could be done with enough money, she learned, when she paid a small fortune for tickets in the seventh row—rumored to be the best view in any Manhattan theater). Judging from their easygoing postures and facial expressions, Theodore and Hiroto were old friends.

A ghost who no one on Wall Street knows but is friendly with the maître d' of the hottest restaurant in Manhattan.

"Here she is." His clear blue eyes were twinkling, his dark hair was perfectly placed, and his bespoke sport coat and tailored jeans were impeccable. Her attraction to him was visceral, instinctive, animalistic. Butterflies fluttered in her stomach, and she was once again wet at the sight of him. She drew in a sharp breath, tried again to regain composure, and turned to thank the doorman—reminding herself that Theodore was just a man, like any other man she had conquered and discarded.

"You look incredible, darling." Theodore embraced her lightly, leaving her salivating. He removed her gray cashmere coat and fox fur shawl, and a tiny man appeared out of thin air to retrieve it. The hostess, a tall, voluptuous brunette whom Theodore gave no more than a glance, led them to their table—in a small back room close to the kitchen. A private room and clearly the chef's table. *How does he...?*

"Thanks, Tessa," he said as she scurried away.

Theodore pulled out Celeste's seat, then leaned in and murmured in her ear, "You look fucking fantastic." A chill ran down her spine at his proximity, and she realized it was the first time they were alone. She smiled and pulled away from him as she sat down. Theodore slid her chair in and settled into his own.

"So, I've never tried this restaurant. You're my first!" Theodore exclaimed.

"The chef's table, huh?" Celeste asked plainly. She considered herself in the know, and she was friendly with most of the restaurateurs in Manhattan; in fact, she had invested in a few places herself. How he had managed to score a last-minute table, the chef's no less, and yet was unknown in New York was a mystery. She was not sure whether she was impressed or jealous.

Celeste's instinct was to act aloof, but he was much too close ... the walls closing in on her, the candles, his masculine scent. She was dizzy with desire. There would be no feigning a lack of interest tonight.

"It's amazing what level of anonymity money can buy," said Theodore. "More on that later. Now you. How was your day, beautiful?"

At that moment, their server, Mitch, whom she remembered from previous dinners here, slipped in the room without a sound.

"Miss Celeste, what would you like to start off with?" Mitch asked.

Feeling it wise to avoid dirties tonight, she ordered a glass of champagne.

"What are we celebrating?" Theodore asked with raised eyebrows.

"Your going-away party!"

He chuckled. "In that case, we'll have a bottle, Mitch."

They ordered the Omakase, the chef's menu, and every course was more delightful than the last. Theodore was as sensual a foodie as she was, savoring the tastes and textures of their decadent meal like only a true hedonist can. He revealed he was a sophisticated cook, and they laughed as she shared what had happened the last time she attempted to use her oven (full building evacuation and no fewer than four fire trucks full of New York's finest determined to save her from her cooking). By the end of the meal, almost two bottles later, they were canoodling like old lovers. Two bottles because "you cannot possibly celebrate properly with only one bottle of champagne," Theodore had explained.

This is why I don't do dinner dates. She at once hated herself for getting involved and reveled in his gaze. There was only one place to go—Theodore's room at the St. Regis. Once they climbed into the Maybach waiting for them, the driver put up the privacy window. Celeste kidded, "Presumptuous to assume I'm joining you this evening, isn't it?" She normally despised this coy cat-and-mouse game that women played with men, for there was no shame in sexuality. She was intolerant of the slut shaming that went on in the media, and she bankrolled Planned Parenthood, National Women's Law Center, and other women's empowerment organizations—but here she was acting like a virginal schoolgirl in Theodore's presence. *Oh, fuck it.* One look at his hard dick in his pants, and she dropped the act.

They began tearing at each other's clothes when Theodore sensed her acquiescence. He cupped Celeste's naked breast under her dress with one hand, the other hand in her hair pressing her lips to his. When Theodore's driver dropped them off, they hurried through the lobby, taking little notice of the scene at the King Cole, the bustling hotel bar. Theodore led her to the back elevator, and they struggled out keep their composure as it inched to the top floor. He opened the door to the Dior Suite, renowned for its inspiration from the fashion house's atelier and exceptional butler service. The sitting room looked magical with Fifth Avenue lights sparkling through the windows. Celeste whistled. Theodore bent to kiss her, then stepped away to the bar, where a red aerating in a carafe and two Bordeaux glasses sat. He poured the wine and brought the glasses over, and they settled on the couch. The soft lighting and jazz humming in the background enhanced the palpable sexual tension. Yet Celeste felt an unfamiliar force holding her back from making the first move.

Please touch me again. Touch me anywhere.

As if he read her mind, Theodore reached over to brush away a hair caught in her lip gloss. She inadvertently let out a purr as his hand moved to her shoulder, and a shiver ran down her spine as his hand trailed down her arm. He kissed her wrist, then suckled her index finger. Her nipples hardened.

Theodore stood up and pulled Celeste into his arms. She thought he would lead her into the bedroom, but instead he held her in a slow embrace. He rocked his hips in rhythm with hers, swaying to the music playing over the speakers. After two songs, her body was throbbing with desire. While she had to admit the foreplay was a little sexy, she was growing frustrated with this prolonged pre-fuck dance.

"Please take me into the bedroom and fuck me."

"Since the first time I saw you, Celeste, I've wanted to feel you. I've never wanted a woman more than I want you right now. But you must know—I'm going to take my time with you. I want to know every inch of your body. I want to make you come over and over again. I don't just want a quick fuck."

"I'm not a patient person, Theodore."

He let her lead him into the enormous bedroom. Theodore lit candles on the bedside table, and the flames danced in his sparkling eyes. He unzipped her dress at a glacial pace, placing his lips on each body part he exposed. When the dress fell to the floor, he stood back and admired her naked body. She felt shy. Dozens (upon dozens, if she were honest) of men had seen her nude, and she never felt the least bit self-conscious. Until now.

"You are magnificent," he said with conviction.

She went to him and pressed her lips to his while removing his shirt and then his pants. His cock bulged in his boxer briefs. They walked to the bed, and Celeste lay back on the fluffed pillows, yearning to feel him inside her.

Theodore had other plans. He knelt on the floor with the nimbleness of a twenty-year-old, pulled her legs apart, and began suckling her inner thighs. He entered one finger inside her, moving it in and out, and his other hand caressed her breast. Try as she might, she could not look away from him, entranced by the intimacy of the moment. He slid in a second finger and made figure eights with his tongue on her clit. Theodore owned her pleasure, leisurely building her climax while inside she felt like clawing her way up the walls. Though his face was serious, his eyes held a playful twinkle. It was clear he enjoyed watching Celeste squirm with impatience.

His fingers gently, then more forcefully, stimulated her G-spot. Within moments, her body began to tingle all over, and then she threw her head back as the orgasm washed over her. Theodore continued his licking and teasing, satisfied only when Celeste's body tensed again in orgasm. She ejaculated this time, wetting the comforter beneath her. Celeste had long since viewed men as prey, something to be conquered and discarded. This time, though, she was his prey. She had never felt more turned on—or more vulnerable. He looked into her eyes without blinking, a deep, intimate stare intensifying her unease. *Has anyone ever died from anticipation of wanting someone to fuck them?*

Celeste took in the view as he removed his boxer briefs and grabbed a condom out of his jeans pocket. He was strong, manly, rugged. His broad chest was sprinkled with dark hair. His cock, which was thick and erect, reached up to his navel. He was in all aspects physically perfect. But that wasn't all. She had seen many beautiful men; they were a dime a dozen. Theodore was something more. He was smart, witty, and, dare she say, interesting.

"I hope you don't think I'm finished with you," he growled as he held the condom in his hand, clearly intending to make her wait longer. Oh, his teasing was delicious ... but she was accustomed to being in complete control in the bedroom. Men never fought her when she took charge. In fact, she controlled her entire interactions with men. She carefully chose them, fucked them, forgot about them. Things were much simpler without having the "feels," as Ty would say. She stood up and pressed her naked body against his. He finally succumbed and put the condom on, and they were in bed in an instant. *Now this is what I was looking for.*

Their bodies fit well together, and he slid his protected cock inside her while caressing her cheek and looking her in the eye. She let out a small cry of pleasure. He filled every ounce of her with his hardness, and his breathing in her ear was more than she could take.

Once satisfied that Celeste had climaxed again, Theodore let out a loud "Oh fuck, you feel amazing, Celeste." She felt his cock pulsating, and just the thought of his orgasm, the intimacy of it all, led her to come once more.

Celeste was no stranger to orgasms—she had several a week either by her own hand or from someone's dick—but five or six in one session was unusual with a virtual stranger. She was gutted, empty, but only in the most satiated way. She closed her eyes in satisfaction.

"Oh, Celeste," Theodore murmured huskily. "I've wanted you for so long. Longer than you know." He leaned some of his body weight against hers.

She opened her eyes to see something foreign in his. Openness. Honesty. Vulnerability.

"Since you saw Savin's photos or saw me in person *yesterday*?" she asked coyly to lighten the mood. Theodore did not take the bait but continued the slow, deep rhythm of in-and-out, until she was wet once again and ready to be fucked.

"Actually, we've crossed paths a few times over the years," Theodore said nonchalantly, savoring her wanting.

"There is zero possibility of that. I would have without a doubt remembered you," Celeste said. She grimaced, regretting her candor. "Er, where did we meet before Savin's? Or the mayor's party, though I don't really count that as meeting."

She reached up to kiss him, moving her hips against him.

"Gorgeous, you don't get to skip the good parts. I want to know everything about you, and I want you to know me."

Celeste continued to buck her hips but stayed on his slow rhythm, in part because she sensed he would not give up this pillow talk time. *At least he's fucking me while being emotional.*

"Many years ago, you and I had dinner together."

Oh, Jesus, not another Brad/Brandon situation. This island is so fucking small. As Theodore had noted last night, at the mayor's party, Celeste had pursued a twenty-something waiter only to find she had bedded him a year prior. To top off the situation, she had forgotten his name was Brad, calling him Brandon. *Well, he was still a good fuck, even if he was easily forgotten.*

"Oh?"

"You don't recall, that's OK. You were fairly fucked up."

"And when was this magical encounter?" Celeste said haughtily.

"At one of Omar's dinners." At the mention of his name, Celeste lost her lady arousal.

"You know ... Omar?" She attempted to hide her stammer but failed. He pulled himself out of her and lay next to her. *I am one story away from getting the fuck out of here.*

"I do. I also know what he's capable of, so I was surprised to see such an intelligent, alluring woman by his side. It was some sort of work dinner. You and I sat next to each other, but you didn't look away from Omar once during the entire meal."

So this was post-Omar-fucking-every-woman-in-sight, then. Celeste's relationship with Omar a decade earlier was a nightmare after he went off the deep end. She was not surprised she was closely monitoring Omar in such an overt, humiliating way, but it shocked her that she had been oblivious to this delectable man.

"I'm sorry, I don't remember this at all. Omar and I had a somewhat ... tumultuous relationship, so I was distracted much of the time."

"Yes, I recall a blowup at some point during dinner. There were a few other dinners, too, but as you may have noticed, I try to keep a low profile. Enough about that. I only wanted to be honest that we've met, so you'll know how long I've wanted to make love to you. More later. Now it's time for me to make your legs shake again."

After what seemed like hours more of Theodore's delicious teasing, they came together and then collapsed in exhaustion, synced blissful sighs escaping their raw, overkissed lips. Celeste laid her head on his chest and gently twisted his chest hair between her fingers, caressing his skin. Goose pumps popped up on his chest, and she felt his cock hardening against her leg. She was still tingling between her legs, wanting his touch once more. She straddled him for one more quick lovemaking session. Then she lay in his arms once more, their limbs intertwined.

"What are you thinking about?" he asked.

"Mmm ... not much of anything, really. Just enjoying the moment. You?" Celeste couldn't remember the last time someone had fucked her sleepy. And with that, she dozed off, content in his arms, thoughts of Omar, work, and scrambling out the door far from her mind.

———

Celeste awoke to Theodore nuzzling her neck. "Good morning, gorgeous," he said into her ear.

"Mmm, good morning." She stretched her limbs, instantly aroused as his hand trailed from her breast to between her legs, caressing her clit. His hard dick pressed into her back, and they both began breathing faster. She was soon mounting him, and they fucked for another hour, a repeat of the previous night's multiple orgasms. When they awoke from a nap later in the morning, Theodore rolled over and reached the phone. He rang the front desk.

"Yes, good morning. Breakfast would be wonderful. Yes, two will be dining." Theodore nodded in agreement. "The Fifth Avenue sounds delicious. Thanks."

Theodore rose from the bed and disappeared into the bathroom. He returned in a bathrobe, holding another one out for Celeste. She stood up and stepped into the robe in his outstretched arms.

They had sex once more after breakfast before Celeste felt the need to escape. She hated goodbyes (and walks of shame after 12 p.m., and in fact, everything about sleepovers), and it was nearly time for Celeste's 2 p.m. brunch with the guys. She pulled herself out of his arms and gathered her clothes from the oversized ottoman.

"This was just ... lovely, Theodore. Thank you for a wonderful evening." *Hopefully, this is what one is supposed to say in such situations.*

"I had an incredible time, Celeste. I have some upcoming travel, but I'll be in touch."

"OK, sounds great," Celeste said breezily. She kissed Theodore on the cheek and turned to leave.

"Wait, Celeste." Theodore walked in front of the door to face her.

"You are the most mesmerizing woman, inside and out, with whom I've ever had the pleasure of spending an evening. I had a magnificent time, and I can't wait to see you again."

"Oh, that's sweet, darling." She patted Theodore on the chest and walked out of his room, this time without a backward glance.

SHE TOOK A CAB TO AVOID MONTY'S KNOWING EYES. WHEN CELESTE walked into her building twenty minutes later, Jonah was standing behind the concierge desk and smiled cheerfully when he saw her.

"Miss Celeste, I have another special delivery for you. Shall I carry it up?" He was holding another enormous bouquet, this time the most delicate cascade of orchids she had ever seen.

"That would be wonderful, Jonah," she said casually.

Seated on the sofa in her living room a few moments later, Celeste opened the card Jonah had left with her.

Thank you again for a lovely evening, Celeste. I will be in touch soon.

xx T

Celeste rolled her eyes. *"I'll be in touch?" Am I an interviewee he's decided not to hire?*

4

SKIRTING THE EDGE OF DECENCY

Twelve years earlier, as twenty-nine-year-old Celeste sprawled across the palatial bed in Omar's lush Plaza suite, she had not yet grown accustomed to the luxe life the next decade would bring when she had her own wealth. Last night had been another late one with Omar and his friends. She had slept over again, despite the nagging voice inside that this was too much, too soon, too fast. The past few months with Omar had flown by in a blur. He was visiting New York at least two weeks a month, stating it was for business, though Celeste suspected his true motivation was to see her. He said he was in love with her. Maybe she was even in love with him, too, but how could one ever be sure? There was a red flag or two, so did that negate her feelings? She had questions upon questions but no girlfriends to confide in. She did not relate to fairy tales and preferred hearing news of stock market performance and volatile geopolitics over watching *Sex and the City* episodes and browsing online dating sites in search of "The One." Omar provided her with companionship, luxurious getaways, and adequate sex (at least in the beginning), so she played the part of the smitten younger girlfriend. Perhaps she even was.

The night she met Omar, she had been out at a club with the boys "entertaining clients," which is what they called their cocaine-infused Wednesday night ragers that rolled into Thursday morning. This was when Wall Street had been a disaster with excess—not that it had cleaned up much, but at least they had all aged out of some of their bad behavior. They had been tucked in a corner booth, far removed from the chaos below in the enormous two-story nightclub. Celeste came out those evenings to get high and take a random man home, not to socialize. She watched with disdain as her friends flirted with the flies, as she not so affectionately nicknamed the sad little women who swarmed around bankers whenever they smelled money.

She was bored with the tragedy at her table that night, so she walked to the restroom to freshen her Dior gloss. She did not notice Omar hovering by the bar at first. After a quick makeup touch-up (and a pick-me-up in the form of two key bumps) in the lush ladies' room, she exited the bathroom and nearly bumped into a tall, dark man. His gleaming smile did little to dispel Celeste's annoyance that he was blocking her path. Celeste needed nothing but sex from men, so she resented a man who invaded her space under the guise of a free drink or two she could buy for herself.

"Excuse me," she said forcefully as the man simultaneously pivoted and began shepherding her toward the bar, hand on her lower back guiding her like chattel.

"You must let me buy you a drink," he stated with a heavy Brazilian accent. Up close, Celeste could see that the man was older than she had originally pegged—perhaps in his late thirties or early forties—but had to admit he was extremely good-looking. However, she preferred the younger crowd with hard abs and unrelenting sex drives over Viagra and hip replacements. With his dark, flawless features, he could have passed for any number of nationalities, Persian or possibly even Italian, but his accent was a dead giveaway. Celeste glanced over at her friends, assessing her options. Another bottle of bubbles had arrived at the table, and the flies gathered round and cheered at the sparklers the servers had brought out with the bottle. It was all so dull, really. She glowered and turned back to the handsome but otherwise unremarkable man and accepted the calculus that he was the least boring option at this point in the evening. She zoned out while he droned on about his jet, properties, and investment firm. *Duh, every douchebag in New York has all of the above.* When he turned his back to order another round, she sneaked out without providing him with so much as a name.

It wasn't until a few weeks later that she noticed him again, this time at the Mandarin Oriental in Time Warner for a five-figure-a-plate fundraiser for some disease or poor-children-in-Africa cause. She no longer kept track of these do-gooder events she was required to attend because her firm threw around millions for philanthropy.

She was standing with Savin and Mark at a high-top cocktail table, half listening to Savin's girlfriend woes and half resorting to her internal boredom with life dialogue. Celeste perused the room for an interesting prospect and locked eyes with none other than Omar, though she had not caught his name yet.

"Celly, want another drink?" Savin had asked.

"Sure. Belvedere martini ..."

"Yes, yes, extra dirty, I know," Savin said with annoyance and walked away.

She had not given the man a thought since the night they met and did not intend to spend the evening listening to him carry on again. Rather than looking away, though, he started walking toward her. She gave Mark a "save me from the man fast approaching" look, but he misinterpreted it as a "beat it" look. When Omar arrived at the table, he thrust his hand out to Mark while looking at her.

"Omar. And who is this man hogging your attention when you should be sitting with me, Celeste?"

Mark cleared his throat. "Mark." He looked back and forth between Celeste and Omar and mumbled, "I just realized I needed a refill. Celly, what are you drinking?"

"Savin is supposed to be getting me a drink, but he's apparently disappeared. I'm fine for now," Celeste said. Mark turned and walked away. *Guess I'm going to have to get rid of this man myself.*

"Now that he's out of the way, where were we when you so rudely skulked off the other night?"

"Never mind that, *Omar.* How do you know my name?"

"I have my ways," Omar said. "I had to find out who you were so I could see you again. And you should know that once I set my mind on something, I get it."

"Oh, is that so? Well, I hope you're not inferring that I'm a *thing* and that by showing up uninvited to this ...," she gestured behind her, trying to remember the name of the gala, "... event, you've somehow gotten *me.*" Celeste picked up her Chanel clutch. "If you'll excuse me, my friends are waiting."

Omar did not miss a beat. "You're as sassy as you are beautiful. How about I apologize for being a presumptuous jerk and you give me the good fortune of allowing me to start over with you?" His ability to turn the conversation around so swiftly without an apology was admirable, and even though Celeste recognized he was manipulating her, she relented because his wide smile was admittedly more than a little sexy.

And just like that, he had negotiated his way into her life and was becoming a permanent fixture. What was more concerning for her, though, was that he had also found a way into her heart, making it harder to ignore her feelings for him these days despite his bad behavior.

Celeste shook off the memory and walked into the bathroom where Omar was showering. She opened the glass door and stepped into the steamy water. Omar leaned to kiss her on the cheek and then forcefully pulled her toward him, his flaccid penis against her stomach. Celeste pushed him away lightly, knowing how this shower would end—with an argument where he blamed her for not making him hard—and she would end up late for work. "You know I have an important pitch meeting today. I only have time for a quick shower!" she scolded Omar.

"What meeting?"

It was all she had talked about for weeks. She shot him a dirty look.

Omar smiled, oblivious, and looked down at her with a thoughtful expression. "You know, you no longer have to work.

Frankly, I can give you anything you want, and in exchange, you can give me what I want—you all to myself." *Sure, two or three months into a relationship, just pack up your fledgling career you're building into a little box and throw it off the Empire State.*

Celeste laughed at Omar's proposition while she lathered shampoo in her hair. "Yes, but darling, we've been through this before. I'm not interested in being a kept woman. I *like* working. I like the kill as much as you do."

Omar laughed. "You're cute. Don't dismiss it without thinking it through, Celeste. You're much too beautiful to work." *As if the two are mutually exclusive.* She refrained from rolling her eyes because that had resulted before in a lecture on how she had to respect him, for which she did not have time this morning.

"Of course I'll think about it," she said, with no intention of considering it more than she already had. She was relieved when Omar switched to a different topic, as was his frenetic nature.

"Dinner tonight? At Per Se, eight thirty."

"Sure. We'll talk later; I have to dash home before work." She rushed through her shower routine, kissed him as she hopped out, and toweled off quickly. She had scored this meeting with a potential client, Stan Hobbs, a storied investor looking for young talent with fresh ideas. Everyone knew Stan invested in the next big thing, so a yes from him would pack a punch. The stakes were high, and she wanted everything to run smoothly for their meeting. Even though she had been with the bank for only nine months, she was hungry for a bigger challenge, something to make her mark. She and Savin were pitching Stan today on ideas they had sketched out around what they were calling "robotics investing." The field of high-frequency trading was new and ever-evolving, but based on their research, they had come up with an innovative strategy to automate investing and use computer technology to mimic investor behavior. The only thing missing was the capital to execute. They would sell to the highest bidder and make him or her wealthy (or wealthier) quickly. With the market in the dumps after the 2008 crash, they figured someone would be hungry enough. They hoped Stan was their guy.

"STAN'S GOING TO SAY NO," SAVIN SAID WITH DEFEAT.

The two had skipped out on a few hours of work that afternoon following the meeting to rehash and figure out their next steps. "Well, of course he's going to say no," Celeste retorted. "If they don't wire the money then and there, the answer is always no."

She stared into her glass of scotch, disappointed but determined to remain optimistic. She refused to let one bad meeting derail their plans. "Sav, let's look at this differently. Stan just wasn't the right fit. His risk tolerance is lower than ours. But we'll find the right investor. It's only the first day of the first week of our four-week push."

Like Celeste, Savin could not stay down for long. It was one of the reasons they made a good team. "You're right. The positive was that he didn't throw us out of his office the moment we arrived."

"Right. He was interested. He at least had confidence we weren't full of shit, and it was clear no one had pitched him the idea before we did," Celeste said brightly. "Not bad for two kids at the bottom of the food chain."

They paid for their drinks and sneaked back in to work to finish up another boring day of trading for Celeste and analyzing potential mergers for Savin. Celeste was one of the best on her team, but this gave her little solace. She found most of her colleagues to be legacy buffoons, hired because their dads were in finance and had pulled some strings. It was like being the tallest midget.

Celeste left the office around 8 p.m. and found Omar's driver, James, waiting outside her office in a Suburban. She rolled her eyes. She had told Omar a hundred times not to send Suburbans for her. "Have you ever tried climbing in and out of those climate-suffocating monstrosities in five-inch heels, Omar? Well? Have you?" she asked in frustration as he laughed it off each time. "Celeste, for someone who does not want to be a kept woman, you certainly have a lot of demands. Don't worry, though; I find it adorable." He would kiss her forehead condescendingly and return to whatever conversation was more important than anything she said.

"Miss Donovan, Omar sent me to fetch you for dinner. He gave me strict orders to bring you directly to the restaurant and said that in the event you insisted on making your way to your apartment, I was to give you this to override your protests." Omar knew well enough to know that she would have otherwise changed at home and been thirty minutes late to dinner. Celeste took the envelope from James's outstretched hand and stuck it in her stately maroon Fendi bag. She adjusted her miniskirt and black boots, ascending into the back seat with James's assistance. At least sitting in the cross-town traffic would give her time to freshen her makeup. But first, the envelope.

Celeste slid her immaculate French-manicured nail under the crisp navy seal to open the envelope. She recognized the stationery—Omar left her notes on mornings when he had an early flight, the mornings she slept in and then took advantage of the luxurious whirlpool tub. The Plaza permitted late checkout only for its most valuable patrons, of which Omar had become one. *OLS* was written in gold-foiled letters at the top of the ivory notecard. Omar Luiz Santos. In his now-familiar scrawl, he delivered his ask:

Dear, come straightaway to dinner tonight. I have a surprise for you and can't wait to share. Love, Omar

---

Love? What the fuck is he up to?

Celeste shrugged to James with a pout. "Fine, you can take me straight to the restaurant, though now I'm going to be early. I *loathe* arriving early."

James winked at her in the rear view. "I promise to take the long way, Miss Donovan."

Celeste pulled out her Gucci makeup clutch and set to work on a dramatic smoky eye, intended to draw attention away from the fact that she remained in work attire, while James skillfully wove in and out of Manhattan rush hour traffic but, true to his word, taking as long as possible.

Omar was on his best behavior when Celeste arrived. His jet-black hair was slicked back, and he was wearing his banker date uniform—Prada dress shirt (for the slim men; the chubbies could not pull that off), blazer, and Gucci loafers with no socks. She despised the no-sock look. He kissed her grandly in what Celeste had come to realize was a desire to invoke jealousy among the other patrons, hugging her close to him as they walked to what was becoming "their" table tucked away in the back of the restaurant. "I do not travel all this way from London—in commercial, no less—to sit amongst the plebes," he would bemoan to his elitist friends, not that this upset Celeste in any way. But every once in a while, his Anglo snobbery was over the top even for her. The well-heeled Per Se clientele could hardly be pigeonholed as "the plebes."

Once they were settled at their table, Celeste noted the bottle of red wine aerating, no doubt pinot noir, Omar's favorite. He refused wine pairings, no matter the restaurant. *Because who wouldn't be skeptical of the wine pairing at a Michelin three-star restaurant? Obviously, the sommelier would be an amateur, right?* Omar was not known for his depth or sophistication. He was known for being garish, always under the influence of some illicit substance, and wealthy.

"Celeste, you are so beautiful tonight!" Omar exclaimed, nuzzling her ear while the server looked on with a neutral expression. This was New York—the server was accustomed to drunk bankers and their treasure seekers—but Celeste resented that others saw her as one of those women. She had shared her frustration many times with Omar. "I have a brain," she would protest, "and you trying to fuck me at the table doesn't help the way your colleagues and serious women view me." "Who cares what they think?" he would banter. "They're merely jealous, my dear, because they are not beside me, and they are not as pretty as you." *Riiiight.*

When the server arrived at the table, Omar said, "Isn't she ... just ... the most ...?" Omar kissed her, almost licking her cheek and squeezing her hand. *OK. Apparently, he's not as sober as I thought.* Celeste looked for signs he had started early with the powder. His red nostrils and sniffling confirmed her suspicion. *Fuck you, Omar. This was supposed to be my night.* Celeste needed him to weigh in on whether the meeting with Stan was indeed a bust. Omar was a powerful hedge fund manager, and she trusted his expertise, at least in the finance world. *That's one advantage to having a financier as a boyfriend, right?* Unless he was too fucked up to pay attention.

"Omar, darling, I was hoping we could discuss the meeting I had today. After you reveal my surprise, of course," she added to placate him. He took her hand with a flourish and kissed it.

"I'm so glad you reminded me!" He reached into his jacket pocket and extracted a rectangular navy box. *Harry Winston and not a ring.* Celeste hid her relief. "I knew I had to get this for you when I saw that it rivaled your beauty." *Oh boy.*

Omar opened the box to reveal a diamond bracelet Celeste had been eyeing since she received her bonus. Despite her attempt to remain stoic, she let out a small squeal. It *was* a stunning piece of jewelry. "How did you know? It's gorgeous!" she exclaimed, watching him unhook the clasp and fasten it on her outstretched wrist. It fit perfectly. She admired the sparkle and met Omar's lips for a thank-you kiss. Her excitement faded when she noticed his shaky hands. *So much for good behavior,* Celeste thought, disappointed when he sniffled before responding.

"You're welcome, darling, and there's plenty more where that came from. I took the liberty of ordering for us—the chef's tasting menu." Omar cleared his throat, and the server rushed over to fill Celeste's wine glass. "Are you OK with the pinot noir? You know it's my favorite."

"Of course, that's fine. How was your day?"

"A bear of a day! I told Itsuki we'd meet him downtown for a nightcap. I suspect he'll have his lady friend with him." Itsuki was Omar's colleague who visited New York regularly for business and had a different woman on his arm every time Celeste had seen him. It seemed all of Omar's friends, married or not, had women in every area code they frequented. She suspected the same was true of Omar and realized she cared less than she would have guessed. *He's certainly no prize these days.*

"Oh, is that so? And to which of his women are you referring?" Celeste inquired. Omar grinned at her sarcasm.

"To each his own, I suppose. Itsuki is a trusted partner, and we're closing on a big deal."

"I love hearing about your deals! Details?" Omar and his friends were not accustomed to a woman joining in conversations about their work. But Celeste worked in finance and wanted to hear from the innovators in her field. It inspired her to think outside the traditional career trajectory at a time when everyone her age in finance was set on the same path. Omar was often vague with her about his work, but when he was around colleagues, he spoke freely, so Celeste always agreed to go when invited.

"No, no, there will be enough work talk later. Let's talk about our upcoming trip."

This was the first Celeste was hearing of any travel. She looked at him quizzically.

"I have to be in Paris for a week or so starting next week, and you and I can jet down to Nice or Amalfi coast for a few days after," he explained.

"I would love to, darling! But Savin and I have many meetings scheduled for the next month. You know how important this is to me. The most I could do is a quick getaway this weekend to Miami or the Caribbean before your Paris trip."

"Yes, I heard all about one of your meetings today."

"You did? But you and I didn't speak today."

"I do listen to you sometimes, Celeste. Stan's a good friend. He and I had coffee before your meeting, and he called me after."

"And?" Celeste's heart was pounding.

"He said you had an intriguing pitch and that you were the whole package—whip smart, witty, beautiful—a 'class act' in his words. He proceeded to tell me how impressed he was with your proposal and that he wanted to fund it in its entirety. All fifty million dollars. A first for him, he said. He rarely commits his own money to new ideas. I told him I would pass that along to you."

So this was why they had not heard from Stan yet and the reason Omar wanted to celebrate.

"Wait until I tell Sav! I have to call him right away." With lightning speed, she reached down to fetch her bag from the little bench beside her chair and withdrew her BlackBerry.

Omar started laughing then. "Oh, Celeste, you misunderstood! This is not a done deal. His feedback was flattering, yes, and I was proud to call you my girlfriend. In the end, though, I asked him not to fund it, and he agreed."

Celeste's face registered confusion at Omar's glee. She swallowed and said through clenched teeth, "Yes, I must've *misunderstood* what you're telling me. You just said Stan told you he would back us, and in the same breath, you're telling me you asked him not to? Forgive my confusion, because there is no way I could discern why my own boyfriend would sabotage what Sav and I have been working so hard toward."

"Celeste, dear, I already have to compete with your work schedule and friends as it is. I'm not going to allow you to go fifty million dollars deep with someone like Stan. You would be in over your head, not to mention the time it would take away from our relationship."

Celeste was not one to cause a scene, but lately, Omar's words and behavior were pushing her to the edge of keeping her cool. She sipped her wine and counted to ten, but black spots of rage blurred her vision (or maybe it was the tears she was holding back, willing them not to fall in front of Omar).

"Our *relationship*? There is no fucking relationship anymore if you destroyed this opportunity for me! And this ... this fucking bribery bracelet? A consolation prize? Hearing about your meddling, no one else will commit the funds either." Celeste fumbled at the clasp, her hands shaking with anger as she removed the bracelet from her wrist. Even in her rage, she held the glittering diamonds gingerly as she placed the bracelet on the table. She had to escape before the tears washed down her cheeks. She grabbed her bag and stood up.

"Celeste, sit down," Omar said sternly. "Think this over rationally. You're not ready to take on something like this, and Stan was only too happy to hand over a decent sum of money to someone who's just a hot piece of ass."

"Did Stan actually say this to you, Omar? Or did he say what you originally told me three minutes ago?"

"He spoke in a respectful tone, but I know why he really wants to throw money at you. He wants to fuck you, and I won't allow you to go into business with him."

"You won't *allow* me? I don't know who the fuck you think you are, Omar, but no one *prohibits* me from doing anything!" Celeste pushed her chair back and looked into Omar's eyes. "You and I are over. Fuck you, Omar. Don't ever call me again."

"Stop talking nonsense. Our next course will be here soon, and in the morning, you'll understand why I did what I did. You've probably just had one too many glasses of wine to think clearly." She watched in disbelief as he took a slow sip, seemingly unperturbed that she had just ended their relationship.

Celeste resisted the urge to throw her glass of wine in his face. She bent down to Omar and whispered, "We both know you're the one who's had too much wine and a little too much coke to be thinking clearly. Good night, Omar, and goodbye."

"Celeste, we'll talk in the morning when you're feeling better. Have James drop you off at my hotel," Omar said loudly to the room to save face.

"Fuck you," she said for only him to hear. She held her head high and walked out of the restaurant, leaving a smug, coked-up Omar behind.

WHO DID OMAR THINK SHE WAS? SOME PATHETIC WOMAN WHO COULD be placated with a piece of jewelry she could buy herself?

"Doyers and Bowery, please," Celeste told the cab driver who was waiting outside the restaurant. Savin had agreed to meet her for a nightcap at a speakeasy in Chinatown. She swallowed back tears as she realized the magnitude of Omar's treachery. How dare he sabotage her life! For what? Some limp-dick morning sex and constant insults to her intelligence? She was finished.

"Thanks, this corner is perfect." She threw a fifty at the cabbie and rushed to meet Savin in front of the bar. He was waiting to the side of a long line.

"Finally. The bouncer is being a dick even though I slipped him two hundo."

"Traffic was a motherfucker. Let's get inside."

Apotheke was known for its artisanal cocktails and experienced mixologists, but Celeste and Savin liked it for the anonymity. Celeste found a spot for them in the corner, while Savin went to the bar to order their drinks. He returned with Celeste's favorite—a rye whiskey specialty cocktail.

"OK, you're going to have to start at the beginning."

"He sabotaged our entire fucking deal, Sav. Stan was going to fund us, give us the entire fifty million dollars. Stan told Omar it was the first time he was ever willing to commit his own money for a startup. He told Omar we were innovators, sharp, prepared. Then Omar asked him not to fund our 'little project' because I'm too pretty to work or some shit. I'm seeing red. I have to get myself and us out of this. And who's to say he won't shut down all my opportunities form here on out? He could wreck my entire career, Sav! What am I going to do?" She took a swig of her cocktail and stood up, gesturing with her hands. "I'm going to fucking kill him. That's what I'm going to do. Stab him in the fucking neck. Or maybe I'll just report him to the Feds. I'm sure I have enough tidbits to make someone flip on him."

Savin looked thoughtful as he considered what she was saying. Celeste sat and continued.

"He bought me that Harry Winston bracelet I've been eyeing, did I tell you that? Thought that was an appropriate consolation prize for completely fucking up my life. I wish I could shove that bracelet inside his dickhole!"

"Celly, wait ..." Savin's pensive expression slowly transformed into a smile. "I think you're looking at this all wrong. Why not just find some dirt on him? Blackmail him? Fuck turning him in; that gets us fuck all. Extortion, baby! That's where it's at. Then, voilà, we've got our seed money."

Celeste took a deep breath, considering Savin's suggestion. "Don't you think he's smart enough to cover his tracks?"

"Well, I've never met the guy because he always bails on meeting your friends ... but he doesn't strike me as someone who covers his tracks. In most of your stories, he sounds ... sloppy. The opposite of the composed, polished woman you are. How many times have I heard of him being fucked up, loud, and obnoxious? He sounds like he thinks he's invincible, but in reality, he's just a messy motherfucker. I can't fathom what you see in him."

"An ultrahigh-net-worth slob kabob who cost us fifty million today. What the fuck are we going to do? We're powerless."

"Powerless, my ass. I've never seen a woman run more shit than you. How many women can hold their own as a trader? You're the most powerful woman I know!"

A server made his way over with another round in response to Savin's signal and set the drinks on the table.

"You can go ahead and put in another round, mate. These are going down quickly." Savin smiled at the server. Celeste was too distracted to notice he was handsome and built like an Adonis statue.

"Savin, I'm so sorry. I'll fix this somehow."

"Cell, seriously. Quit being such a downer. I can't believe you aren't seeing the upside here."

"And what upside is that? Should I have hawked the jewelry to pay for the rest of the year's rent?" She nearly dropped her empty glass as she set it on the table and reached for the full cocktail. She wanted to feel nothing, to douse her anger and humiliation.

"No, silly. Let's beat him at his game. Spend a few weeks digging around, see what you can find. If he's as sloppy as you say and truly believes you're a bimbo, I doubt he locks his phone and computer around you. We'll find something to take him down."

Well, I suppose this is a silver lining. Celeste perked up. "Sounds so Jason Bourne!"

Savin shot her a weary glance. "Get it together. I'm fucking serious. I know you have it in you, and I, for one, would love to fuck him over. He sounds like a grade-A douchebag."

"I fucking hate him. He ruined everything." Celeste downed her drink and stood up to dance, but stumbled back onto her seat. "Well, fuck him!" She rarely lost her composure; that evening was an exception.

After several songs and two more drinks, Celeste slurred, "Wait. You mean to tell me you ... want me ... to stay with that asshole? And pretend like nothing even happened?" Her face contorted in disbelief, and then she collapsed into the booth, shaking with laughter.

"Did I tell you he does coke every morning now? His dick doesn't even stay hard to fuck! Doesn't even hide the lines he's snorting at six in the morning." She hiccupped before continuing. "But ... I'm always up for a good scheme; you know that. Just tell me what we're doing."

"Well, I don't know exactly, but we'll come up with something. Play this being angry thing out; wait until he's begging, and then go back to him." Savin rubbed his hands together, his eyes alive with excitement. "This is going to be fun! Fuck the fifty million; I can't wait to make him lose a lot more."

They exchanged ideas until the booze and heaviness of Omar's betrayal hit Celeste all at once. "I need to go to bed. Let's talk tomorrow."

CELESTE AWOKE TO TWENTY TEXT MESSAGES AND THREE ENRAGED voicemails from Omar, in addition to a massive headache. *Not in the mood for this shit.*

She scrolled down her text list and opened Savin's.

"Don't forget what we discussed."

She smiled and typed a reply. "I won't. Drinks tonight? I have an idea."

"OK see you at 8 at our spot."

Celeste shut off her phone, leaving Omar's texts unread, determined to sleep off her disappointment for another hour or two before work. She was sure the Miami trip had already been booked for Friday, so she and Omar would have all weekend to talk. Plus, it was only Tuesday, so she could wait until the end of the week to reconcile with him.

Celeste buried herself in work once she got to the office, and despite her hangover, she managed to book a six-figure trade. Later that evening, Celeste and Savin met at their favorite place, a dark mahogany bar in the West Village with an excellent scotch selection, where they could be somewhat anonymous—or at least not risk being overheard by other finance types. To the clientele at the Hudson Street Tavern, they appeared to be a couple—a handsome, well-dressed Middle Eastern man and a supermodel. They sat huddled in a corner.

"Let's go over the game plan once more. You'll talk to your shady-as-fuck friends, and I'll play the pissed-off girlfriend for a little while to buy us some time until you get everyone on board. We touch base on our burner cells this weekend while I'm in Miami and talk to no one else who's not involved. Then world domination."

Savin nodded. "Yes, that sounds about right." It had taken Savin only a phone call or two to learn the lay of the land. Apparently, it was not so hard to take down a major financier if you had burners, some hacker friends who were morally flexible, and a father who had introduced you to his rich friends before he died. Depending on what they found out from Celeste digging through Omar's things, they were well positioned to do some damage.

"Don't forget what I told you about the burner phone, Celly. Pay someone fifty bucks to pop in a store and buy one for you. Cell phones are constantly pinging your location, so turn the phone on in Times Square, where you won't be traceable in the crowd, and then power it down—"

"Yes, I know, I know. I won't use it at the office, use it only in emergencies, yada, yada."

All at once, there was a commotion at the door as a loud, drunk man wandered in. *Jack.*

"God, he is literally the male version of you, Celly." It was true.

Jack stumbled across the room toward their table. "Hey, you fuckers! I've been trying to call you all day! When you weren't at the Penthouse getting lap dances, I figured I'd find you here huddled in a corner like criminals. What the fuck is up?"

"I'd like to think I'm a little more refined than him," she said so only Savin could hear.

Celeste and Savin broke into genuine smiles as Jack approached the table. Leave it to him to show up unexpectedly and lighten the mood. *This is how happy we're going to be very soon!*

"Another round for us, Winston!" Savin shouted to the owner who was bartending that evening. Winston was not one to be ordered around, but they kept a healthy tab running and were likely responsible for keeping the lights on. Plus, the British accent and all.

Winston stepped from behind the bar and brought the three of them the usual. Winston and Jack shook hands as a greeting. "Good to see you, bro," Jack said as he pulled Winston into an embrace and clapped him hard on the back. Jack was not the hugging type. *Well, I guess Jack is fucked up.*

The three downed several more cocktails while contemplating whether to get a Hamptons share this summer or do what they did last summer and bounce around their favorite European islands.

"I should just buy a villa. Puglia? Monaco? Capri? Sav, I'm sure your trust fund could withstand your extravagances. We could go in halvesies."

"You know perfectly well, asshole, that my buffoon of a father decided it would be better to leave his fortune to his mistress, and who knows what Mother has done with the rest. Not all of us can retire at the ripe old age of twenty-eight. *C'est la vie.* At least I have his Rolodex."

Celeste rolled her eyes. "You're a son of a bitch, Jack. But I guess

65

that's partly why we keep you around. Now how about some dancing?" Celeste's eyes twinkled as she stood up and attempted to put on her coat. Savin watched her tipsy struggle and held the coat so she could slide her arms in. She pulled away when she decided to go to the restroom.

"I need to stop by the ladies'," Celeste said and walked in that direction. She could still hear their heated discussion across the small bar. They had moved on to another meaningful debate, this time about gym socks.

"What kind of animal owns socks that aren't wool or cashmere? Americans are savages," Savin protested loudly.

"Wool is itchy, and cashmere doesn't adequately absorb wetness. My trainer explained it to me," Jack said with authority. Celeste rolled her eyes at their antics. They were not that deep; they were not even that kind; but they were hers. She loved these men as if they were biological family. More than she loved her family, if she were being honest. The guys were her chosen family.

The bathroom had always been dark and cramped, but Celeste was delighted that Winston had finally listened to her pleas to renovate. It was now spic and span, sleek, and modern with a new mirror, vanity, and light fixture. Fresh daylilies rested on a new addition to the room—a small cabinet containing toiletries. She opened it to find elastic bands, tampons, lotion, and a special treat—condoms. Celeste laughed out loud at Winston's interpretation of her response to his question of how to be more accommodating to women. "Winston, you need to make them feel at home in a clean space," she had suggested.

Before they could make it out the door, Winston insisted they take a shot of something dark and strong. Celeste was quite tipsy at this point and decided to use the shot to wash down half of a Molly from Jack's stash. She pointed toward the door and began swaying to an imaginary beat. "Time for some dancing!"

Savin held out her coat once more, and she shrugged into it. Then she locked elbows with Savin on one side and Jack on the other, and they headed out onto Hudson toward the Jane. They spent the rest of the evening dancing and laughing, and she left feeling happy and invincible. It was after 3 a.m. when Celeste walked into her building. She was exhausted from being awake for nearly twenty-four hours, but grateful for Jack's cameo that evening.

Celeste awoke some time later with a splitting headache. She turned over and was relieved to see she had not brought anyone home. She crossed the room to retrieve her phone and called Savin. It was only 5 a.m., so she was not late for work.

"Fuck! What did Jack do to us last night? Or, rather, two hours ago? I can barely stand up," Celeste said as a greeting.

"Well, you may have taken more than your fair share of Molly, but Jack and I were too fucked up to notice."

"Fuck, seriously? I only remember taking a small half. I suppose I can just befriend some other degenerates to not look after me, since my best friends don't."

Savin's tone was somber, as all the boys protected her as if she were their sister. "I'm sorry. I swear if I would've noticed you were going to take too much, I would've stopped you. Jack, too. But Jack and I weren't communicating, and we realized later we each gave you halves of some pure shit."

"It's OK, I'm safe in my bed. I suppose I can spare a few brain cells."

"Get in the shower, and then get your ass to the office. We have a lot to discuss to ensure Project Douchebag has a successful launch." *Click.*

A HAGGARD, UNSHAVEN OMAR MATERIALIZED IN THE RECEPTION AREA OF her Midtown office around midday. Celeste was peeved when the receptionist called her to the front.

"Hello, darling!" Omar said. He hugged her for effect, then leaned in and whispered in a threatening tone, "I need to talk to you. Without an audience. Now."

"You are unfuckingbelievable. Get your hands off me, and don't ever show up in my office again," she whispered back.

"Do you really want me to cause a scene, dear?" Loudly, he said, "I've flown all the way from London to see you this week and wanted to surprise you for lunch! You know how I hate being away from you." He kissed Celeste's pursed lips.

"You betrayed me in the worst possible way the other night," she said through clenched teeth while smiling for passersby.

"Well, you can tell me all about it over lunch while we plan our weekend in Miami."

The worst part of Omar's theatrics was that now people knew she was dating an older, established financier, and from then on, they would always discount her success and her intelligence. He was well known throughout her office, viewed by others in the finance world as a savant. Her colleagues had stopped to stare.

"Of course, lunch would be wonderful. Let me grab my coat," Celeste said for the crowd, then left Omar standing in the foyer, buying herself time to think.

Savin was waiting at her desk. "Lucky for you, I'm one step ahead. I knew he'd show up like this. Spend the day with him; I'll cover for you. I put a clean BlackBerry in your bag, same model as Omar's based on how you described it. Call me after he's had a few drinks, and I'll tell you what to do. Stay with him until we get the data we need."

Celeste kept her face neutral for onlookers in spite of the questions racing through her mind. "Sounds good; call you in a bit."

"You can do it," Savin encouraged.

"Celeste, when can you get us a meeting with Omar Santos?" Celeste turned around to see one of the bank's portfolio managers standing behind her (she and Savin referred to him as Ricky Dicky Douchebag, but she did not actually know his name). "I'm baffled as to why you haven't offered this up yet. Business development is part of your *job* here, you know."

I definitely don't have time for this shit right now.

"Duke, I can walk you through some of my ideas. Celeste has

been making a lot of progress with Omar, so I think we'll be able to set up a meeting very soon," Savin said, putting his arm around Duke's shoulder and steering him away from Celeste.

"Thank you," she mouthed to Savin and scurried back to the reception area where Omar was waiting before anyone else could stop her. *Let's get this over with.*

Once back with Omar, she discreetly squirmed out of his grasp while dodging another theatrical kiss on the cheek, and they silently walked to the elevator. She was glad to see others in it. She kept a safe physical distance from him and rejected his attempt to hold her hand.

James was holding the back door of his Suburban open for them when they got outside. Once in the car, Celeste crossed her arms at her chest and stared out the window, playing the young pouting girlfriend. After she rebuffed his attempt to hold her hand again, he launched into a lecture, berating her for ignoring him the past few days. *How long will I be able to tolerate this shit? This play had better work.*

"Celeste, I'm speaking to you. Give me the courtesy of paying attention."

She rolled her eyes and turned to look at Omar. He continued, "I've arranged everything for us this weekend in Miami as you requested. I'm putting a stop to our miscommunication."

As awful as a weekend with Omar sounded, Celeste realized it would be a good opportunity to snoop. Omar was always trashed on their getaways. Meaning full access to his laptop and BlackBerry: emails, documents, memos. "Omar, you royally fucked me over in business. That's not a miscommunication. How can you possibly think I want to go away with you right now?"

"Celeste, you're acting like a petulant child. I'm growing tired of it. When you're done thinking irrationally, you'll no longer be upset."

"I will most assuredly still be upset, Omar. And you know what I'm tired of? I'm tired of your sloppiness, blowing coke at six in the morning like you're Tony fucking Montana. Fuck off." Keeping him pissed off all week would make it more likely he would stay super drunk all weekend and leave her alone.

THE FOLLOWING EVENING, CELESTE AND SAVIN SAT ON THE LIVING ROOM floor in his Upper West Side apartment, reviewing the contents of Omar's BlackBerry.

"I can't believe what a shit bag he is, Celly. Everything he's involved in is illegal, immoral, or skirting the edge of decency." Following Savin's instructions, Celeste had successfully mirrored the contents of Omar's phone onto their look-alike after he had passed out the previous night, which Savin then uploaded to a server as backup. Omar had bought Celeste's story that she would accept his apology if he made significant changes in his behavior, but then the two had a volatile screaming match before he passed out. His behavior was making it clear that she needed to get away from him, but not before they got some dirt on him. She was relieved she had managed to pull everything off last night, despite his insane behavior. *Who has the last laugh now, asshole?*

As they reviewed his emails and learned more about his business dealings, a plan formed. They had moved on from the blackmail idea—that would be difficult to pull off without implicating Celeste. Rather, they would profit off their knowledge of an insider trading deal Omar had in the works—and would cause him to lose millions in the process. It was simple, ballsy, and just stupid enough to reflect their inability to fully realize the stakes.

"We need a portfolio manager who can help us pull this off," Celeste said. "Which opens us up to enormous risk. I don't know anyone I trust well enough."

"Celly, relax. I was ready for this, and I've worked everything out. My dad's mate is going to help us. Roberto. He likes to color outside the lines a little."

"You mean violate a whole suite of federal laws and regulations and potentially face life in prison." *I hope Roberto isn't going to royally fuck us.*

Celeste respected Savin's instincts about people's character (unless his dick was involved; then all bets were off), so she swallowed her concern. Over takeout Chinese and Sapporo, they outlined their next moves.

"The exciting thing is that this will all be over soon, Celly! It sounds like Omar's planning something big soon. We'll make bank, leaving him in the dust. And we'll have seed money. Then you can tell him to fuck off!"

"I already told him to fuck off no less than four times last night when he tried to fuck, but I get your point. Speak of the damn devil," Celeste said when her phone indicated a new text had arrived. *He can wait.*

"You have to keep up the wounded puppy girlfriend act, Celly," Savin cautioned.

"That won't be hard," Celeste said. She lifted up the sleeve of her T-shirt, revealing a large bruise forming on her bicep where Omar had grabbed her last night in his hotel room. "You will learn to respect me, Celeste!" he had shouted and jerked her arm when she had turned to walk out of the room. "Do not *ever* grab me again, Omar! Go fuck yourself," she had shouted back. Once he had fallen asleep and she had what she needed from his BlackBerry, she gathered her things and headed back to her apartment. His physical roughness was a wake-up call to the fact that Celeste had begun normalizing his emotional abuse. It was also a signal that he was more dangerous than she had anticipated.

Savin erupted. "What the fuck is that? He did this to you? How could you not tell me about this? You know I would've taken care of this for you." Concern lined his face.

"Taken care of it? Are you in the mob now? You going to have him killed?" Celeste laughed. "Besides, I want something more out of this than a police report and him spending the night in jail, if it even came to that. I want to hit him where it hurts. I want to destroy him for thinking he can ruin my career and play rough with me." Celeste had never thought of herself as a woman who would be a victim of a violent crime, so Omar's force opened her eyes to the fact that it could happen to anyone, even a strong, independent woman.

"Celly, I didn't realize he was violent. Has he hurt you before? You have to get away from him. We can't move forward with this."

"No, he's never grabbed me before, but his behavior has become more erratic with his cocaine mood swings. The sex has become bizarre, and he's getting sloppy. Snorting lines in the morning before the alarm goes off. Telling me to fuck off when I point out that he's using too much. I'm not sure if it's being in New York so often or if he was always this heavily into it; either way, it's gross. He can barely get a hard-on."

"Yeah, you alluded to that the other night, but I didn't realize it was this serious. I think we should call this whole thing off, Cell. None of this will matter if you're in the hospital ... or worse."

"Not a chance. He's not going to *kill* me, Savin. I'll just make sure I'm not alone with him again until all this is said and done. Believe me, once he's humiliated on the global scale, he won't show his face in New York again."

Savin was not convinced, and they spent the next thirty minutes debating.

"Celly, you're planning to be alone with him all weekend!"

"Savin, we're going to Miami and staying at the Fontainebleau, not going to a remote village with no cell service. It will be fine."

"No, no. We'll find another way to take him down."

"Enough, Sav!" Celeste finally said. "I understand the risks I'm taking. Believe me, it's worth it." *Why do all the men in my life think they can order me around?*

"Please don't go, Celly."

"I'm going. He'll get suspicious, and then our plan will never work."

Omar's mirrored phone buzzed with a text notification. "An unknown number," Savin said, looking at it. "Get this—they're arranging a time to meet. The other guy suggested next Thursday night, but Omar just insisted that it has to be Monday. The other guy suggested a shitty Midtown Irish pub. O'Reilly's. Eight p.m."

"That's odd. Omar just told me yesterday he was flying back to London Monday night. We arrive back in New York Sunday night from Miami. He planned an early dinner for us Monday before he heads back to the UK, then goes to Paris later in the week."

"It seems he's had a change of plans. This is the guy from the emails, I know it!" Savin's eyes shone with excitement.

"Well, if it's important enough to change plans for, it must be important. Safe to say, Omar is unaware we are reading his texts and emails, or he'd be a little more discreet, don't you think?"

Savin nodded in agreement.

Based on what they had read from Omar's correspondence with a suspicious alias, Celeste and Savin predicted that Omar would be receiving material nonpublic information sometime the following week about a newly publicly-traded company and that he would trade on the information shortly after. Insider trading at its finest.

The two confirmed their plan for the weekend. Savin would monitor Omar's phone and alert Celeste if anything interesting came through. He would also continue to lay the groundwork with Roberto for whatever their next steps would be once Omar's communications with the unknown person revealed more information.

"Please be careful. Hop on the next plane home if he seems off." *Omar is always off these days, but I'll keep that to myself.*

Celeste was too excited to sleep when she got back to her Upper East Side studio apartment. She looked around, longing to be able to buy a real apartment, a chic, grown-up apartment. *Maybe someday. And someday may be sooner than I imagined.* She responded to Omar's apology texts, providing the validation he needed that she still loved him with a perfunctory "I love you, too. I'm sleeping at home, though, because I'm exhausted and will see you tomorrow" text—it was surprisingly easy to stomach now that the end was in sight. Her mind raced with possibility. She and Savin as the giants of Wall Street, leaving everyone to wonder how they had pulled off such a play.

THE NEXT MORNING, CELESTE HAULED HER LUGGAGE DOWN HER building stairs to the car waiting for her outside. James would pick her up at 3 p.m. from the office, and she and Omar would be in Miami in time for a late dinner. The thought of staying with him after what he had done to her arm and her business prospects made her skin crawl, but she knew she could get through it. *Omar's days of shitting on my life are numbered.*

Savin was waiting for her at her desk when she arrived at the office.

"Don't you ever get tired of all these assholes yelling at you to get off the trading floor?"

"Not in the slightest," Savin replied. He loved to inconvenience people, especially the finance bros he disdained.

"I take it from your luggage that you've not changed your mind about going away with him," he observed.

"This again? If you came by to lecture me, I've got to get to work."

"OK, I'll stop. But I—" Celeste shot him a weary look. "Fine, I'll carry on as we planned."

"I'll message you later, Sav. I really do have some work to do. My psycho boyfriend requiring my unlimited availability is not making my boss happy." She gave Savin a quick hug then turned her computer on. "Now, go!"

Savin laughed and left her to get her work wrapped up.

OMAR WAS IN A FOUL MOOD WHEN CELESTE GOT INTO JAMES'S CAR THAT afternoon. Rather than saying hello, he began berating Celeste for being five minutes late.

"Omar, if you think I'm going to listen to this all weekend, you're sadly mistaken. So there are two options: Either I can have James pull over, and you can go on to Miami alone, or you can cut this bullshit and treat me with respect. I don't *owe* you an explanation as to why I was late. What'll it be?" James's face was largely impassive in the rearview, but she thought she saw the tiniest hint of a smirk when he caught her eye. *See, Omar? Even your staff knows you're an asshole.*

Celeste was surprised when Omar kept silent and turned to look out the window. His knuckles were white from clenching his hands together. *Just a few more days.*

After twenty minutes of silence, Omar turned to her and said softly, "I thought we would just do dinner tonight at Hakkasan in the hotel. You loved it when we came down for Art Basel."

"Yes, that sounds fine. I did enjoy the food." *When Omar plays nice, I will, too. But no more ignoring his abuse. This play is not worth my dignity.*

Celeste busied herself with work emails the rest of the drive to Teterboro, responding when Omar asked questions about the weekend, but otherwise remaining silent. Omar's pilot, Ken, was standing outside the plane waiting for them when they arrived, a huge smile on his face.

"And here's the happy couple!"

Omar shook his hand, and Celeste allowed Ken to kiss her hand.

"The prettiest woman in all of New York, isn't she, Ken?" Omar asked.

Celeste smiled at Ken, but inside, she bristled. *Yep, Omar, that's all I am. A pretty face.*

She pretended to fall asleep during takeoff. She needed to minimize talk time with Omar if she wanted to make it through the weekend without killing him. He busied himself with his laptop while barking orders to the flight attendant. After a few drinks, he began snoring. Celeste took the opportunity to go to the restroom and check whether Savin had sent her any information on her burner.

No new messages. She hoped that Omar was still on the aggressive timeline and that they would have some actionable information by Wednesday morning. She assumed no news was good news and went back to her seat to sleep for the last thirty minutes of the flight.

Omar had booked the penthouse suite with sweeping views of the ocean for the weekend. As soon as the bellman had dropped off their bags and left, Omar pulled a joint and lighter out of his jacket pocket and walked out to the terrace. Celeste helped herself to a glass of champagne from the bottle chilling on the wet bar and followed him outside.

"I didn't feel like listening to your bitching about powder, so I left it at home," Omar said. He took a deep hit on the joint and slowly blew out a cloud of smoke. He turned to her and offered the joint.

Is he actually conceding he has a problem? This is new. Celeste took a hit off the joint and handed it back to Omar. "What time is dinner? I'm starved but need to change."

Omar exhaled more smoke, then responded, "It's at nine. Can you be ready on time?" The usual warning tone was absent from his voice.

"Yes." She downed her champagne and left the glass inside by the bottle. After a quick refreshing shower, she put on a taupe satin slip that set off her sun-kissed skin, a neutral shrug to cover the bruise on her arm, and five-inch gold Aquazzura sandals. Omar would be pissed she was not wearing a bra. *Good thing I dress for myself and not for him.* She smeared a natural gloss on her lips, brushed her hair, and went out to the living room for another glass of champagne before dinner. Omar's eyes were bloodshot, meaning he had continued smoking while she was getting ready. *Can this man do anything in moderation?*

"Are you going to change before dinner, Omar?"

"You're not leaving this hotel room with your tits out. Go find something less slutty to wear."

Be agreeable. "Omar, can we please just enjoy each other and not argue all weekend? We've been fighting for weeks."

"No woman of mine—"

Nope, can't handle this shit. "I'm not going to be "your woman" much longer if you don't stop acting like a tyrant."

"Don't you threaten me!" Omar bellowed. He swept his arm across the bar, knocking the glasses and the bottle of champagne onto the floor. Celeste jumped backward to avoid being hit by the flying glass shards. Omar's eyes widened in shock, as though he had not been the person to cause the mess.

"I'll be down in the restaurant. If you haven't sobered up and fixed this little mess you've made by the time I get back, I'll be on the first flight tomorrow morning." She picked up her room key and bag and walked toward the elevator. She did not realize until she was alone that her heart was pounding and that she had nearly run out the door.

CELESTE SAT ALONE AT THEIR TABLE FOR TWO AND PULLED OUT HER burner from her McQueen clutch. Savin had sent her several texts.

"How's it going?"

"Celly! Tell me what's going on."

"Incoming text confirmed Monday. I'm researching the company, so we're totally ready this week."

"Why aren't you answering me? Now I'm worried!"

Celeste was not in the mood to convince Savin everything was OK —mostly because everything was most certainly not OK. She also couldn't share the truth, or Savin would hound her to come back home. Going home was not an option; she would not risk Omar missing the Monday night meeting.

Savin and I are so close. I can't just disappear into the shadows. That's not who I am. Omar can't get away with acting like this.

She rationalized it was only two nights and decided to spend the entire next day at the spa by herself, only meeting up with Omar for dinner. Which was not that much out of the ordinary, since he spent a lot of time working on their trips.

Celeste managed to calm herself down and redeemed the night over a leisurely, decadent meal and another glass of bubbles. Omar had not texted her since she left the room, which indicated he had passed out. *Thank God.* She charged the bill to the room, then braced herself to face Omar.

When she got back upstairs, there was no trace of broken glass. The lights were low, and the suite felt empty.

"Omar?" No response.

She walked into the bedroom to find the bed untouched other than the blanket being folded back from the turndown service and slippers placed beside the bed. Celeste decided to take advantage of the solitude and get a good night's sleep. Omar had probably gone looking for coke and a strip club. She went through her nightly bedtime ritual and was in bed before midnight. When Omar arrived home at 4 a.m., Celeste did not stir.

5

CELESTE FUCKING DONOVAN

Celeste awoke at 8:30 the following morning to find Omar asleep next to her. She left a note for him by the bathroom sink, explaining she would spend the morning pampering, then head to the pool for a few hours. She put her two phones and swimwear in her crossbody bag and went down to the spa, relieved she could spend the day away from Omar and sneak in a quick call to Savin later on.

Celeste had a three-hour treatment, including a deep tissue massage, seaweed body wrap, and rejuvenating facial, in an attempt to clear her head. Afterward, she had a light lunch and then bought *Vogue, The Economist, Harvard Business Review,* and *People* in the gift shop to read at the pool. As a whole, Miami was a bit cheesy, but it was so easy to travel there from Manhattan, which could not be undervalued. Plus, the views of the Atlantic from the infinity pool were breathtaking. Today was just what she needed to keep up the act with Omar. She switched on her flip phone, and it vibrated with a text notification.

"Status of Project D-bag?" Savin inquired.

Celeste laughed and typed, "I had dinner alone and spent the entire morning pampering myself. The less I see him, the happier I am."

"I've pulled some strings. Old Dad came through from the grave, that's for sure."

"Calling you now."

Celeste dialed Savin's number, and he answered on the first ring.

"Celly! You're never going to believe how well this is working out." Celeste could almost feel Savin's excitement through the phone. "Wait, more importantly, everything is OK, right?"

"Omar came home at four a.m. after he bailed on dinner and has been sleeping all day as far as I can tell. Believe me, it's been amazing." Celeste laughed. She was not going to give Savin any reason for pause.

"OK, good. So here are the details."

Savin broke down the plan for her. She had to admit she was impressed with its simplicity. Savin, who had never met Omar because Omar had repeatedly backed out of meeting with her friends and had to this day only met Mark, would impersonate the bartender at O'Reilly's, where the meeting was to take place. *Omar? At an Irish pub? Clearly something out of the ordinary going on.* When Omar and his unknown coconspirator arrived for their 8 p.m. meeting on Monday, Savin would monitor their conversation and get the information he and Celeste needed to provide to Roberto. Roberto, who had a low opinion of Omar, would take it from there, giving them a fair share of the bounty. ("He hates Brazilian men who put the reputation of Brazil in jeopardy," Savin had explained.) The owner, Doug O'Reilly, had asked no questions when Savin offered to pay him eight grand, four each to him and the bartender if they would let Savin bartend for a few hours. He had also arranged for the bar to be nearly empty for the evening. ("Hell, you coulda bought out the entire place for three grand, but don't worry, I'll take your eight grand and have a customer or two for show," he had told Savin in a brisk Irish accent.) Once Omar arrived that night, the bouncer would lock the door until Savin signaled he had what he needed. "Just don't piss off my customers" was the only instruction provided to Savin. The following day,

Tuesday, a chain reaction would begin in every major financial market, confusing Omar. Savin had also managed to investigate Omar's holding company. Apparently, Omar was not doing as well as he let on. He was leveraged, and his portfolio appeared to be controlled by some heavy hitters in the Middle East, Hong Kong, and London.

"Interesting. He's under someone's thumb," Celeste said slowly, processing the information.

"Celly, this is going to be so much fun! Our first real takedown!"

"Don't get too pumped. I still have to get through this weekend and ensure he doesn't run off to Europe without meeting his mystery contact."

"You can do it, Cell; I have faith!"

"OK, I have several very important magazines to read and some sunbathing to get back to. Let me know if anything else comes up."

"Toodles!" Savin said before hanging up.

Celeste's BlackBerry vibrated with the inevitable summoning text from Omar.

"Are you joining me for dinner? Or throwing a temper tantrum and leaving me alone again?"

Ugh. How did I ever find this man tolerable? "What's the plan for dinner?"

"Be ready by 6. We can watch the sunset, then head to dinner after."

"OK."

Celeste put her phone in her bag and dozed off to the sound of the breeze rustling through the palm trees around the pool. At 4:30, she walked up to their room.

"There's my beautiful angel in the flesh," Omar said from the terrace. He was sipping on a glass of scotch and smoking a cigar. He did not appear coked up.

"Hello. You're in a good mood," Celeste remarked.

"How was your day? Did the spa staff pass your muster?"

"Yes, it was a lovely day. I'm going to take a quick shower, so I can be ready on time."

"Did anyone hit on you at the pool?"

Celeste rolled her eyes. "No, Omar. No one hit on me."

Omar laughed and said, "You're such an obedient woman today."

"I HAVE A LITTLE SURPRISE FOR YOU, DARLING." CELESTE AND OMAR were tucked away a few hours later in the corner of La Côte, the rooftop lounge at the Fontainebleau. Omar was sitting close to Celeste, nuzzling her neck possessively. It was all she could do to sound interested.

"And what is that, Omar?"

"You'll have to come back to the room with me after we have another drink."

"I thought we were going to dinner?" Celeste questioned.

"Change of plans." Omar kissed Celeste's forehead and then slid his hand up her dress.

"People are watching."

"No one would mind watching me finger fuck you right here."

"*I* would mind that, Omar."

He laughed and summoned the server for another round of drinks and the check. After he paid and they downed the drinks, they took the elevator back to the room.

Let's get this surprise over with, so I can get back to New York.

When they arrived at their room, Omar insisted she close her eyes until he told her to open them.

"OK, but this seems a little silly."

"It will make me so happy."

Celeste closed her eyes and let him lead her to the terrace. She opened them on his cue to find an elaborate table setting, complete with candlelight, a bottle of bubbles chilling in an ice bucket, and an enormous display of magenta roses. He had been sending her magenta roses at least once a week after she mentioned liking them. Now she hated the sight of them.

"Please, please, sit." Omar played the perfect gentleman, pulling out her chair and pouring her a glass of champagne. After she sat, he laid her napkin across her lap and slid her chair in. He retrieved a glass of scotch for himself from the wet bar and rejoined her on the patio.

Please don't let this be a proposal.

Omar sat down holding his glass of scotch and stared into her eyes. "Celeste, I can't tell you how happy it makes me for us to be together. I want you, I *need* you, to be with me all the time. That's why I get so ... upset when we argue. I won't be without you."

The platitudes were making Celeste nauseous. "Yes, of course, dear. Hold that thought, though. If you'll excuse me, I need to go to the restroom."

"Hurry back, my love."

Once safely locked in the bathroom, she pulled her burner out of her clutch and rapidly typed a text to Savin. "He's going to propose."

Savin responded instantaneously. "WTF. What are you going to do?"

"I haven't the slightest. More later."

"Keep me posted." She went back onto the terrace.

"I missed you, dear Celeste. Let's eat while it's still hot." *I have to put a stop to this.*

Silver domed entrée plates had appeared at their places, and both of their glasses had been refilled. Classical music played on the speakers. Celeste heard the suite door close, presumably the room service staff leaving.

"The chef has outdone himself. This is excellent," Celeste said, trying to make conversation. It was true—the lobster ravioli was otherworldly.

"Indeed. We'll fly back to New York tomorrow afternoon. On Monday, we can have an early dinner before I fly to Europe."

He's sticking to his story.

"That sounds great." She faked a yawn. "I, for one, am beat after a long day."

Celeste downed her champagne, determined to pass out right after dinner and fast forward to Tuesday when she could rid her life of this man. She was quiet while Omar spoke of minutiae—potential vacation spots, his life in London, the latest restaurant opening he wanted to take her to. She mostly looked down at her plate.

"I'm thinking you'll move to London in the next month or so." Celeste's head shot up. "Well, don't look so surprised, Celeste. It's time for you to live with me. You've gotten spoiled with me always making the trips to visit, but that's coming to an end," he said, taking their glasses for a refill.

She took a deep breath. *Bright side is, it's not a proposal, I guess. But how can he think—*

Omar's return interrupted her thoughts. "A treat for the lady," he said, placing a berry tart dessert and more drinks in front of them. He babbled on for the next half hour about his vision for their lives in London—the gym she would go to and the clubs he expected her to join. "You'll need to keep up appearances, join philanthropy boards, et cetera, like a proper wife. And you'll stop working so that you can be around when I need you. Your little job is too distracting, and this nonsense about you and Savin going into business is absurd." She nodded. *Tuesday. This will all be over Tuesday.*

Despite her complacency, his mood darkened after he had finished two more glasses of scotch.

"Celeste, I'm happy you've decided to behave better. But your insolence lately has not gone unnoticed. I won't tolerate it any longer."

He took a hit off a joint and continued on, blowing smoke rings to prolong his words. "It's time to show you how things will work from now on. You will obey me. Always. There'll be no more temper tantrums, no more avoiding my calls."

After a few more puffs on the joint, he startled her, standing up and jerking her upright.

"Ow, Omar, you're hurting my arm!" Celeste said, attempting to twist out of his grip, but even with his intoxication, he was stronger than she was. He stumbled backward a bit but did not loosen his hold on her. Meanwhile, she could not seem to get her feet to work underneath her, helpless as he effectively dragged her through the living room and across the foyer to the bedroom. *How did I end up so tipsy?* She wondered if he slipped her one of his muscle relaxants he was always popping.

"I'm going to teach you," he slurred when they got to the bedroom.

"Omar! Are you listening to me? You're hurting my arm, Omar. C'mon, let's just go finish our lovely dinner."

He punched her in the stomach and pushed her onto her back on the bed. "Now you'll know what happens when you disobey me."

Her shock must have registered on her face. They'd had rough foreplay before where she and Omar agreed upon what she was and was not comfortable with. But she had never once consented to being hit. In fact, it was specifically a hard limit for her, and he knew it. This was a violation of the first rule of bedroom play—consent. She looked at him in disbelief, and he seemed pleased by his betrayal.

Despite his obvious intoxication, he moved quickly. He was on top of her straddling her before she had a chance to process what was happening. She tried to squirm underneath his weight, but he pulled her arms over her head and restrained one wrist and then the other with a rope. *A perfect sailor's knot.* He situated her so that her head hung off the side of the bed, and she had to lift her neck uncomfortably to see what he would do next.

"I had to make do since we aren't at my apartment," Omar said. *He bought rope when he disappeared last night?* Once her hands were bound, he stood over her lower body. Suddenly he jerked her by the ankles, pulling the rope taut on her arms. She winced in pain from the tension in her joints.

"Omar, please! You're really hurting me." She wanted to shout, but the words came out like a whimper.

He proceeded to tie her right leg with the same rope binding her right arm, further stressing her joints.

"I'll leave the other leg free. That'll make things a little easier." He ripped off her silk slip and thong. "You slut, this is what you deserve for dressing like a whore."

When she tried to kick him with her freed leg, he punched her in the abdomen again. She closed her eyes; this time, she saw white spots from the pain.

She winced. "Omar, please. You're scaring me," she pleaded.

"Shut up, you fucking cunt," he replied. "You brought this on yourself."

Celeste was terrified by the menace in his voice. He had been explosive around her before, but he had never gone this far, hitting her and with so much force, too. Her struggling and begging only seemed to make him more angry—and more violent. She did not recognize the man standing over her, and she felt a growing sense of unease that this was only the beginning of his punishment. *I have to get him to stop.*

"Omar, please look at me. What are you doing? I've asked you to stop. I don't want this. You're hurting me." He did not seem to hear. *Is he having a psychotic episode?* The confusion and dread were overwhelming, not to mention the physical pain in her midsection. She leaned her head back and tried to loosen the knots on her wrists, but they were too tight. She stretched her neck further so she could glance under the bed. A makeshift pulley had been set up.

Omar was now mumbling to himself. He turned his back to her and opened the nightstand drawer. She watched him pull out several things: a switchblade, duct tape, a silk scarf, and some sex toys, which she immediately knew would be used as torture devices.

"Can we just talk about this? Please untie me," she pleaded.

Omar erupted. "Shut up, shut up, shut the fuck up! You *will* obey me! If I hear another sound, I'll stuff your panties in your mouth and tape it shut." She flinched at the sound of duct tape being pulled off the roll. *I'll choke to death if he stuffs my mouth and tapes it shut.*

She gulped and pursed her lips.

"That's more like it. Not another sound out of you, or you'll be sorry." He walked over to her head, tied the scarf around her eyes, and then left the room. She heard him strike his lighter. Weed smoke wafted into the room and stung her nostrils. Then, she heard him pour himself a drink. After what seemed like an eternity, he returned.

"Now I'll have some fun with you, you dirty little bitch. You want to disobey me? Well, I'm going to fuck you like you've never been fucked. Then you'll learn this way, my way, is how things will work from now on."

Celeste braced herself for what was to come. She had seen him unhinging little by little, but it had never crossed her mind that he was capable of brutalizing her, of raping her. *I just have to survive this.*

"No licky licky for you. You've been very bad, you little cunt. You're going to feel this." She bit her tongue to hold back a yelp when he jammed the dildo inside her with no lubrication, yanking it out and pushing it back in, tearing her skin. The mattress moved, and she felt him close to her body. She moved her head almost imperceptibly and the silk scarf adjusted. She could see with one eye through a sheer bit of the silk. *His eyes. They don't look human.* Her blood turned cold. *He's going to kill me.* Tears rolled down her face. She hoped he would not see them fall, lest he grow angrier.

He began murmuring under his breath again, talking about Celeste in the third person. "She's mine. This will show her." He shoved all sorts of devices in her orifices, her body tensing in protest each time. The worst was a spiked dildo that he had saved for last. It felt as though it were cutting her raw insides. Then, he rammed himself into her, first vaginally, then anally. "Now she'll obey me." She blocked out his mumbling, his carrying on as if there were not another breathing person in the room.

It seemed like hours before he gave her body a reprieve. She no longer had any sense of time. "Where the fuck is my scotch? Goddammit." He must have swept his arm across the nightstand because she heard several objects crash to the floor. She involuntarily whimpered.

"I told you to shut the fuck up!" She felt him climb onto the bed and then tower over her body. He kicked her in the abdomen. "Not another sound! You understand me? This is your fault."

He left. She heard the sound of a blade against a mirror and Omar snorting several lines of coke. Then he came back in, and she heard him place a glass on the nightstand.

The pattern repeated itself over and over—objects painfully

inserted of objects into her body, Omar forcibly having sex with her, followed by breaks when he left the room, causing her to wonder if the next time he would come back in and kill her. This went on for what seemed like an eternity.

Survive. Just survive.

Her cheeks stung from the tears, and she gave up trying to free herself. Her wrists were raw from struggling against the rope every time he left. *If I managed to break free, what good would it do anyway?* She had no idea what sort of weapons he might have, and his temper was frightening, especially when he was this fucked up. Her body was exhausted from the abuse, and her mind could not find any way out except to stay as still and quiet as possible. She imagined herself floating above her own body to dissociate from the pain.

After another long session, Omar knelt next to her head, and she could tell he was jerking off. He came in her hair, the final "fuck you," then asked in a gleeful, pleasant tone, "There, now that wasn't so bad, was it?"

Finally, Celeste felt him untying her. When he had untied the last knot, she scurried off the bed in a rage, suddenly no longer fearing what else he may do to her.

"You fucking monster! I told you to stop! You tortured me!" She backed away from him toward the bathroom, clutching her abdomen with one arm, her other arm out to block him if he decided to come after her. "You stay away from me. Don't you ever come near me again!"

Omar seemed to be enjoying himself, leaning against the headboard with a self-satisfied grin. "Maybe you'll start thinking twice about disobeying me when I give you a direct order. Besides, you're not fooling anyone. You enjoyed it. I felt you come."

Celeste's skin crawled. She limped into the bathroom and closed the door, locking it behind her. She wrapped herself in the robe hanging on the back of the door and collapsed to the floor in tears. Her mind raced. Even if she could get past Omar, where would she go? She could go to an emergency room or a police station. There she'd be given a rape exam and submit to an evidence collection kit.

She'd be poked, prodded, judged, questioned. He was her boyfriend, after all, and he would insist this was how they had their fun. *Except this wasn't play; I didn't want this.* She gulped, swallowing the magnitude of her thoughts. *He raped me. And I was afraid he was going to kill me.*

No, she was in no shape to go through the process at a hospital or with the police. Her body simply could not withstand anything more. How did she live in a world where this was the only recourse, when mere minutes before, she had been tied up and brutalized? She knew she could not just let him get away with this, let him think this was OK. She would find a way to get even, beyond what she and Savin were already planning. And she would heal from this. This hideous act, this torture Omar had inflicted upon her, would not define her.

Violent sobs racked her body. The cramps in her abdomen were becoming unbearable, and she felt wetness underneath her as though she had urinated. She stood and watched the deep-red liquid seeping across the floor. She held back a scream. *So much blood.* She removed the robe and saw that the back of it was saturated. She grabbed towel after towel wiping the puddle and willing it to disappear. *Back and forth, back and forth.* She had used nearly all the towels before she was satisfied. She wondered what the housekeeping staff would think of the mountain of bloody towels, then realized Omar would make up some excuse and pay them to keep quiet.

Omar. Suddenly, she wanted to vomit at the thought of him, his stench, his cum, his sweat all over her body. She gingerly walked to the shower and turned it on to the hottest setting. She waited until steam filled the room entirely before getting in. Detached, she poured shower gel onto a washcloth and began washing her body. She would lean against the wall for support when the cramping was extreme, then power herself back up, intent on scrubbing away any remnants of Omar. *Rinse, repeat, rinse, repeat,* she thought dully. She watched the blood run down her legs, mesmerized as the water diluted it from deep red to light pink.

Celeste stayed in the shower until the bleeding eventually slowed.

She stepped out and wrapped herself in the one remaining clean towel. She was no closer to knowing what to do next. What did women usually do in these situations? Should she walk out of the restroom, get dressed, pack her things, and leave wordlessly? Would he try to stop her? Should she avoid eye contact and pretend to sleep next to him in bed, keeping one eye open? Should she wait until he slept and then call the police? Or should she make a run for it, hail a cab to the airport, and get on the next flight to New York? Confronting him in any way seemed dangerous—he would resort to more violence to stop her from leaving. Complacency seemed like the only way to survive the night with her body in such bad shape. She stifled a scream, frustrated at the limited options she had. She wanted him to pay for what he did, much more than he would during a quick interview with sympathetic cops.

She brushed her teeth and gargled with mouthwash, wanting to sanitize every part of her body. She combed out her wet hair, sat down at the opulent vanity, and turned on the blow dryer. Savin's excited words echoed in her brain. It was going to work, it had to work, it was the only way to make Omar pay; she and Savin were going to make him lose millions and millions of dollars. This was her only solace now, and she resolved to do everything in her power to get him back to New York, where he would have his Monday meeting. *You'll be hard-pressed to find someone to help you out of the hell I'm going to rain down on your life, you evil motherfucker. I am Celeste Fucking Donovan, and I am no one's fucking victim.*

Omar began calmly lecturing her the moment she walked back into the bedroom. He found her anger unattractive, he said, and in fact, her reaction quite disturbed him when after all, he was only trying to teach her how she had to behave, how their relationship was going to work. He was helping her, he further explained, so they could be happy. He seemed to buy her act when she swallowed her rage and apologized. *One more day.*

Celeste was silent while she packed her bags, and Omar was fast asleep by the time she got into bed. His face was peaceful, masking the monster she had seen earlier. She resisted the urge to run but didn't sleep. It was so confusing being raped by an intimate partner you had once wanted, cared for, and trusted. She now understood how a victim could be driven mad by the ambiguity of such an act. But she had no doubt about it—Omar was a rapist, a sociopath. She wept silently and wished the revenge she was plotting brought her more comfort.

———

OMAR WALKED OUT ONTO THE TERRACE THE NEXT MORNING, WHERE Celeste was pretending to read the *Times* and going through the motions of eating a light breakfast. He acted as she expected—as though nothing out of the ordinary had happened the night before. Celeste followed suit.

"How are you feeling this morning, my beautiful Celeste?" He kissed the top of her head and sat in the empty chair.

"It's a beautiful day, though I seem to be coming down with a bit of a cold." *Hell will freeze over before I'll ever spend another night with you.* "I'm going to hit the dry sauna for a bit before we leave. All this vacationing is catching up with me," Celeste said in what she hoped was a cheerful tone. She had dressed in black capri leggings and a long-sleeved running shirt to hide the rope marks on her wrists.

"I hope you're not thinking of doing anything stupid, my love," Omar said blithely, though there was an edge to his voice.

"Of course not. I just need a little detox after so much drinking this weekend. There's coffee over there if you're interested," she said, pointing to the bar in the living room.

"Thank you. What would I do without you taking care of me?" *You'll find out soon enough, you piece of shit.*

The rest of the day continued in a superficial, pleasant rhythm, both of them avoiding any talk of the night before. When they got to the private hangar, they boarded the jet like the happy couple they had played all day. Once on board, Celeste claimed she had a debilitating headache.

"This cold is hitting me hard!" she exclaimed.

"Maybe we should take you to the ER when we get back," Omar said.

He's not concerned in the slightest that I would turn him in, audaciously offering to take me to the hospital when I still have lacerations all over me. "No, no, I can see my doctor tomorrow. I just need a good night's sleep."

Celeste was dying to look at her burner phone to see if Savin had anything new to report, but she would have to wait until she got back to her apartment. She had been taking a pain reliever every few hours since last night to dull the throbbing all over her body, and it made her drowsy. She fell asleep before takeoff and woke up when the plane slowed to a stop in New York.

Omar was gazing at her like a devoted boyfriend when she opened her eyes. "Aw, precious, you're really coming down with something. I insist that you go to bed immediately when you get home."

"Yes, you're right. I do need some rest. You won't be too upset if I stay at my place tonight?" She batted her eyelashes in what she hoped seemed like a sweet girlfriend thing to do.

"Taking care of yourself is the most important thing."

"OK. I'll rest up tonight, so I'm able to meet you for dinner tomorrow night before you leave for Europe."

"Yes, dear, that sounds lovely."

When the flight team opened the door, Celeste and Omar exited the plane and walked over to the Suburban waiting for them. Omar did not seem to notice that it took all of Celeste's strength to walk upright. He grasped her hand and kissed it. "James will take you home, my love. I've got a few things to look after tonight."

Celeste was relieved. "OK, thanks, darling. See you tomorrow."

Omar hugged Celeste and whispered, "Isn't it wonderful how happy we are when you behave?"

Celeste stiffened. "Yes, of course, dear."

ONCE CELESTE WAS BACK IN HER TINY ONE-ROOM APARTMENT, SHE opened her burner to find several missed calls and messages from Savin. She dialed his number, wincing in pain when she sat down on the couch. *Time for more pain reliever.*

"Yo. You alone?" Savin said by way of greeting.

"I just got back. I'm, uh, sitting on my couch nursing a hangover."

"I'm coming over."

There's no way I can deal with Savin right now. "I'm exhausted and coming down with a cold. Can we do breakfast tomorrow instead? I just need ten hours of sleep."

In an un-Savin-like move, he relented and encouraged her to take care of herself. "Get some sleep. It's going to be an exciting week!"

They planned to meet at 7 the next morning at the Sarabeth's by their office. Celeste hung up, relieved to be alone. She got a bag of frozen peas from the freezer and sat on it, hoping it would dull the pain in her bruised genitals. Then she began sobbing, simultaneously sad, hurt, and angry. Omar had stolen so many things from her. Her dignity, her power, her sense of control. She had no friends or family she could share this with, so she crawled into bed, hoping for a dreamless sleep to escape the pain. But that was not to be. In her nightmares, Omar held a large knife. He thrashed about, making huge, painful gashes in her abdomen while shouting that no one would believe her. When she awoke for the fourth time that night, she resolved to find a therapist as soon as possible.

At breakfast the following morning, Savin was all nerves. "Celly, we're going to do it! We're going to make him pay for what he did to you." *If you only knew.* Celeste looked down at the sleeves of her white blouse to make sure the marks were concealed. *But you must never know, because I don't want you to end up in prison.*

She plastered on her best smile. "Yes, this is so exciting!"

Celeste spent the entire day going through the motions at work, with Savin stopping by her desk periodically to give updates from Omar's phone.

"He was totally out late last night, and it sounds like he was with a woman, Cell. He's a scumbag."

I wish he had gotten hit by a bus. Or better yet, that someone had tied him up and raped him, so he could feel how I feel.

"He confirmed tonight with the mystery guy," Savin continued. "So we are a go. Everything is in place."

"Thank you for the updates. Now leave me alone. Don't you ever work?" After seeing Savin's expression, Celeste instantly regretted her tone. "I'm sorry, Sav, I'm just a little jet-lagged and not feeling well. I can't wait till this is all over!"

Celeste was still in excruciating pain. The injuries to her abdomen were extensive, and her vaginal tissue was raw from all Omar's torturous poking and prodding. The heavy bleeding had subsided, but in its place was consistent spotting. On one hand, she knew she should go see a doctor; on the other, the thought of the sterile hospital lights and the questions—it was all too much to fathom. And she had to act as though everything were normal, at least until they finished this deal. Then she would figure out a way to get past all this.

As Celeste had anticipated, Omar canceled dinner with her that evening, so she went directly home after work to nurse her injuries and obsess about all the things that could go wrong, not the least of which could be Omar coming to her apartment unannounced. Savin's phone call finally came at 9:30 p.m. after Celeste had spent the evening limp-pacing her apartment.

"Celly!" Savin shouted into the phone excitedly. "I'm on my way! You're going to die!" *Click.*

He arrived thirty minutes later.

"OK, first let me say that Omar is exactly the real asshole you described. He didn't look at me once but managed to treat me like I was subhuman the entire time. What a jerk!"

"Sav, I already know he's a hideous person. Don't keep me in suspense! What happened?"

"Roberto will spread the trades out across PMs all over town based on the info I got tonight. No one will be the wiser." Celeste processed this with disbelief. Portfolio managers at all the major institutions would be on the hook now. Meaning there would be no way to claim insider trading with everyone involved.

"But it's happening? You definitely got the scoop?"

"Cell, relax. You act as though this is the first time you've been involved in a deal."

"Well, it is the first time I've gotten every bank in Manhattan to short my boyfriend's stock ten minutes before the market closes. We still have an entire trading day ahead of us. Any number of things could go wrong," Celeste hissed.

Savin was unruffled, clearly enjoying his role as the calm one. "Settle the fuck down. I'm starved; let's grab din. Tomorrow night we can celebrate for real! How about a dance party at Lavo? It's finally open!"

Celeste knew she had to go, even though a loud dinner was the last thing she needed. Savin would never buy that she was staying in because she had a cold, and she could not risk his prying. Over their Sushi Samba usual, several caipirinhas and yellowtail, Savin recounted the twenty-minute meeting between Omar and his mystery friend. The friend had given Omar material nonpublic information—MNPI, as the firm's lawyers called it in Celeste's training on insider trading—telling Omar about favorable clinical trial data that a small company called Biochrome was going to release the following week. If someone could prove that Omar had traded on the information, he would be in clear violation of federal law. However, Celeste and Savin wanted his money more than they wanted to turn him in. No one actually served time for one count of insider trading, but he would definitely miss the money if everyone shorted the stock tomorrow, causing him to lose everything he'd invested. Then Savin's hacker friends would hijack Omar's accounts and sell off all of his stock at the nominal value the following day, eviscerating his holding company's profit margins. Finally, before the clinical trial results came out, Roberto would buy up millions of shares, thus profiting on both ends of the deal. No one would be the wiser, because Roberto often did the same with low-value biotech stocks.

"But Celly, this isn't Omar's first rodeo. He does this sort of thing often. He threatened the guy's family, too, if the tip turned out to be bogus. He's a mean, manipulative, power-hungry piece of shit."

Oh, Sav, he's so much worse than you could ever imagine.

"We'll start our own firm, Cell! We'll be the people everyone else wants to be."

"But what else do we need to do? How can we know for sure this will work? We'll never have another opportunity like this."

"I've got it all covered." He eyed her suspiciously. "What's going on with you? You're so skittish. And you're never so paranoid."

"Nothing. I just don't want to jinx it." *Let's just say the stakes are a little higher than they were last week.*

Savin looked down at his phone and shot off a text.

"People like Omar always come out on top." Celeste was still worried. "What if something interf—"

Savin glanced up and put his hand over hers. "Enough. We're celebrating. Jack is meeting up with us!"

"His cameos are well placed these days, aren't they?" Celeste welcomed the distraction. Just then she got a vibrating text message notification. She glanced down at her phone to see that it was from Omar.

"My beautiful! Are you feeling better? The jet had some mechanical problems, but we're leaving in a few minutes."

"Yes, feeling a little better. Just took some NyQuil and am heading to bed. Safe flight!"

"OK, I'll call you after my meetings tomorrow. Love you."

Celeste reached across the table and handed her phone to Savin. He raised his eyebrows after reading the messages.

Celeste said, "I guess that gives us cover if he ever suspects ..."

"Which he won't."

Jack appeared and walked toward them. After scanning the room, he pulled up a chair and sat down at their tiny table.

"Some nice-looking ladies here tonight! I ordered another round.

Just picked up some Colombian shit, too!" He placed a small baggie of coke in Celeste's handbag and slid another into Savin's hand.

"Well, you know where I'll be," Celeste said, standing up and walking to the restroom. She snorted two key bumps in the stall, freshened her makeup, and washed her hands. *Fuck it, I've had a rough couple of days*, she thought, and went in the stall for two more bumps before rushing out the door.

"Oh, sorry!" she said, recoiling when she bumped into someone leaving the men's room.

"Why are you so jumpy, Cell? It's just me." Celeste looked up to see Jack standing in front of her. He picked up her hand, and her heart sank.

"Celly, what the hell is this?" He gestured to the marks on her wrists from Omar's rope. She pulled her hand away and pushed her sleeve back down.

"It's nothing."

"Celly. What the hell happened? Did that asshole hurt you? Savin told me he saw a bruise on your arm the other day," Jack said in a hushed tone.

"It's fine, I promise. Please don't say anything. Sav will freak out," Celeste begged. They were so close to taking Omar down, and she did not want Savin calling a halt to their plan.

"I'm freaking out, too, Cell."

Celeste looked at him with wide, pleading eyes. "Jack, please never mention this again. I took care of it. He's out of my life. Please tell me I can trust you."

"Celly, you're one of my best friends. Of course I'm not going to say anything if you don't want me to. But if I hear of you around that shitbag again, I'll have him killed." His tone was convincing.

She blinked back tears and embraced him in a hug. "Everything is OK. I promise. And thank you."

VERANDA, THE HOTTEST DANCE SPOT IN THE NEIGHBORHOOD, WAS

packed later that night. The last thing Celeste wanted was to be at a club around a bunch of drunks jumping on couches. Her body was aching, and she was exhausted.

"Guys, this cold is kicking my ass. I feel like shit. I'm going to call it a night."

Savin opened his mouth to protest, but Jack jumped in before Savin could begin.

"Angelo will take you home. He's waiting outside for you. My security. He's the best," Jack answered to Celeste's questioning eyes.

"OK," Celeste responded, relieved that Savin had moved on and was chatting up a woman, oblivious to their exchange. She sneaked out while he was distracted.

A tall black man in a dark suit approached her immediately outside the bar. He towered over Celeste, at least six feet eight inches of solid muscle.

"Hello, I'm Angelo," he said, thrusting his hand out to hers. She shook it.

"It's, uh, lovely to meet you, Angelo. This is unnecessary, but I appreciate you getting me home safely."

"No problem," he said, smiling. He led her to a black Lincoln Town Car parked on West Tenth Street and closed the back door after she got in.

Once Angelo was in the driver's seat, she said, "My apartment is at—"

"Actually, miss, I have strict instructions from Jack to take you to his suite at Le Parker Meridien. Well, first, I am to take you to Burger Joint in the hotel lobby and then escort you up. He said for you to make yourself at home and insisted you take the master bedroom. He also requested I book a doctor visit at the hotel very early tomorrow morning for you."

Celeste was touched. The speakeasy's burger was one of her favorite after-hours snacks. She knew a doctor visit was necessary and was relieved it could happen in the privacy of a hotel room before her big day tomorrow.

"OK, sounds good."

Once they arrived at the hotel, Angelo handed the keys to a valet, then helped Celeste from the back seat. They walked into the hotel lobby together, and she led him behind the enormous curtains to the hidden burger joint. The line was not long, so within five minutes, Celeste had her burger and fries. Angelo sat with her while she devoured her food. It was the first time she had been hungry since Miami.

"At least take a bite, Angelo!" She noticed his eyes lingered for a moment too long at the marks on her wrists. *This fucking shirt sure doesn't conceal anything.*

"No, thank you. I never eat while I'm working."

"I bet Jack keeps you busy these days, jet-setting all over the place."

"I'm not at liberty to share my client's whereabouts. Contractual obligations," Angelo said.

Celeste laughed, finding it humorous that anyone would actually care much about Jack's shenanigans. "I completely understand; didn't mean to put you in a bad position." *He's a barrel of fun.*

After she finished eating, Celeste followed Angelo up to the suite. He explained to her Jack's strict orders that he, Angelo, wait at the suite with Celeste until Jack arrived home. She wanted to be alone, so she escaped to the master bedroom, leaving Angelo to watch television in the living room. Men's pajama pants and a Balmain T-shirt lay folded on the bed. She changed, then retrieved a Xanax from her handbag and washed it down with the bottle of water on the nightstand. She longed for a dreamless sleep as she got under the blankets.

Celeste awoke to Jack softly whispering her name. "Celly, I got you some breakfast."

"What time is it?" Celeste opened her eyes to Jack holding a room service tray.

"It's early. Five thirty."

"Oh, wow," she said when she saw the spread he had ordered. "Thanks so much for this. It was lovely to have a good night's sleep and what a treat to stay in this elaborate room." Suddenly, she did not want to be alone. "Will you help me eat all this food?"

Jack placed the tray on the bed and closed the door before sitting down next to her. He gave her bruised wrists a cursory glance and then focused on her eyes. "Celly, don't worry. I'm not going to pry. But I need you to do a few things to make me feel like you're safe. I've been sick with worry."

"What do you want me to do?" *Please don't tell me to go to the police.*

"Let me loan Angelo to you. He'll make sure no one ever hurts you again, and he'll make sure you can take care of yourself. Also, I want you to stay here until you can get another apartment in a location where Omar can't track you down. You need to take this, whatever this is, seriously. Abusers never stop." Jack did not talk about it often, but his father had been abusive toward his mother. He was extremely sensitive about any sort of violence.

"He's out of my life, Jack. I promise," she pledged. But she knew she could not promise this, not really. Omar would not go away on his own.

"I didn't want to say anything at the time, but I saw him from across the room at that gala a few months ago, saw the way he looked at you. He isn't a normal guy, Celly. He's obsessed with you. He's dangerous. Just please say yes."

Celeste evaluated the idea and sighed. *After what we're going to pull off today, it wouldn't hurt, I suppose.* "OK, but I have three conditions of my own, and they are non-negotiable."

Jack laughed. "There's the Celeste we all know and love."

Celeste smiled. "You can *never* tell anyone else about this," she gestured to her wrists. "Also, Angelo and the doctor you guys arranged for need to sign NDAs, and I want to pay you back for his time when I can."

"OK, done. Except the paying me back. That's ridiculous. But we can discuss that later. Top priority is keeping that shitbag away from you."

"Jack. Thank you. Truly."

Jack smiled with dimples similar to Celeste's. "You're getting soft on me, Celly! Now get up. Big day ahead of you."

Does he know? Jack picked up a piece of toast and walked out of the room, closing the door before she had a chance to ask.

She forced down some yogurt with fruit, and then took as quick of a shower as she could manage. The pain from Omar's blows, compounded by the cramping, was slowing her down. She dressed gingerly. Would the doctor shudder as she herself had when she saw the bruises from his beating?

———

THE CONCIERGE DOCTOR KNOCKED ON THE HOTEL DOOR PROMPTLY AT 6 a.m., as Celeste had requested. She heard Angelo shuffle to answer the door.

"Hey, Doc, how are you?" Angelo seemed to know the woman well. They exchanged pleasantries. When they started discussing the weather, Celeste grew antsy. *C'mon already! I have so much at stake today.* She had to be at work by 8 a.m. at the absolute latest and still had to pick up work clothes from her apartment. The only clothes at the hotel were her club clothes and the pajamas Jack had left for her.

As though reading her mind, the woman's voice became crisp and businesslike.

"Is she here?"

"Yeah, Doc, she's in the bedroom."

Let's get this over with.

Angelo rapped on her door. "Are you ready for the doctor, Miss Celeste?"

Celeste smoothed her hair in its ponytail, suddenly aware of her shoddy appearance.

"Yes, yes, of course." She opened the bedroom door. Angelo moved aside, and a woman stepped into the room.

"I'm Dr. Simone. I hear you're in a rush to get to work, so let's get started." She closed the door behind her.

She was likely Pakistani or Indian, with dark features and long, dark hair, and her petite frame was dwarfed by Angelo's size. Her presence, warm eyes, and kind smile instantly calmed Celeste. In her hand was a doctor's briefcase.

Angelo chimed in from the living room, "Miss Celeste, I'm going downstairs for an espresso. Call me when you're ready. We'll stop by your apartment to retrieve some clothes, and then I'll drop you off at your office." She heard the main hotel room door close after he left.

Dr. Simone sat on the bed. She gestured to Celeste. "Please, have a seat." Celeste followed suit, sitting a safe distance away from the doctor.

Dr. Simone continued. "It isn't ideal to rush through this exam, but I know you're short on time. I completely understand wanting to stay out of hospitals, especially after what you've been through. In the event we do need X-rays or other tests, I have a discreet office a few blocks away where I can see you again. Today I'm here to assess the extent of your injuries and see whether you need further medical care.

"I'm not here to judge or ask questions you don't want to answer. But please know you can share any details you want, and everything you tell me will remain between us. If you ever want to share the information with a third party, you'll sign a release form.

"I also recommend to every woman in your situation that you see a therapist who specializes in domestic violence and sexual trauma. I have a list of recommendations I'll leave with you. I'm sad to say that situations like yours, where women are terrorized by their partners, are much more common than you think." She stopped for a moment and placed her hand on Celeste's arm. "You're not alone, and you'll get through this. There are so many people pulling for you. Tell me how you're feeling."

Maybe it was Dr. Simone's empathy; maybe the trauma was finally wearing her down. Celeste began spilling information she had not intended to share.

"There was so much blood, Doctor, and I'm ... I'm black and blue." Celeste began to sob. She lifted her shirt to reveal her bruises. "Everything hurts. It burns to pee. My vaginal skin feels like it's been scraped open, which I guess it has. It hurts to sit. Or stand. Or do anything, really. I have a job. I can't be limping around the office with no explanation.

"I'm a fucking disaster. It's all I've thought about since it happened. How sick is it that I keep making myself relive this? I've barely slept since it happened, and I'm afraid he's going to come back and do this again. He tortured me, and somehow, I'm the one who has to pay. All I can do is sit here and suffer in silence." She took a few deep breaths.

"Do you mind if I examine you a bit to see the extent of your injuries?"

"That's fine." Celeste lay back on the pillow, and the doctor moved over to the side of the bed. Her hands were warm and her pressure gentle as she lightly pressed in different spots on Celeste's midsection.

"I don't think there's any internal bleeding or broken ribs, but it would still be a good idea to get an X-ray. Do you have time later today?"

"Uh, today isn't possible for me. I have to be at work." *No way am I letting this keep me from watching him go down today. I'll go in a body cast and say I got hit by a bus if I have to.*

"I think the extent of your injuries warrants a sick day—or a sick week for that matter."

Celeste stared at her plainly, indicating she would absolutely not be staying home.

Dr. Simone continued. "OK, well, it's clear your abuser inflicted significant harm. I'm not saying this to be melodramatic—but you should hear it. He'll kill you next time. Rage like this doesn't subside."

My abuser. What if I never wanted an abuser? Why don't I have any say in this whole fucking train wreck?

"I think you're right. I'm not sure if Angelo told you, but his team is going to keep an eye on me for a while. Hopefully, there won't be a next time. I'll never voluntarily let him near me again."

Dr. Simone sighed. "Men like this are extremely dangerous, and often, pulling away provokes their anger even more. I'm glad you'll have Angelo around, but you still need to be on high alert for quite a while to ensure he has moved on from his obsession with you. He is a sick, sick man, and you did nothing to deserve this."

Celeste felt anger rising from the pit of her stomach. *This is so fucking unfair! This is his fault, not mine! He's the evil one, the sadist. And I'm the one with the bruises and the bleeding and the uncomfortable exams.*

"He tied me up for hours, and he kept hitting me in the stomach, even kicked me once. Then later, there was so much blood. All over the bathroom. And the cramping—it still hasn't stopped."

"I'm so sorry you had to experience this. Tell me a bit more about the bleeding." Celeste revealed more specifics of Omar's abuse and described her time in the bathroom. Dr. Simone asked clinical questions and seemed careful not to pry.

"Celeste, are you OK with me doing a vaginal and anal exam? I have a few things I can give you to relieve some of the pain, but I want to make sure we aren't missing any other injuries."

Celeste consented to the exam and removed her pants. She spread her legs a bit, feeling exposed and sad. The doctor put on latex gloves and then moved to the bottom of the bed to examine Celeste.

Dr. Simone confirmed that Celeste's genitals were in bad shape. The doctor removed her disposable gloves and reached into her bag. She pulled out two small prescription bottles and two tubes of cream. "There's not much to do other than allow everything to heal, but these will help a bit. Here is a mild sedative to help you sleep and some Tylenol to help with your pain. The topical pain reliever will help a little. Since the skin is raw, the antibiotic ointment will be protective."

The doctor recommended Celeste allow her to draw blood to test for sexually transmitted diseases and to check her overall health. Celeste consented, and Dr. Simone drew three vials of blood. "OK, this should cover it for now," the doctor said.

Then she sat down next to Celeste once again and began, "There's no easy way to say this ..."

How the fuck could there be anything else?

"My best guess is that the bleeding and cramping were due to a miscarriage, though I'd like the X-ray and more blood work to rule out other causes. The X-ray will allow us to see if you have internal bleeding and damage to your organs."

Celeste's face scrunched in disbelief. *Miscarriage? I was pregnant?*

"But that's impossible. He doesn't even stay hard half the time, let alone come."

"I'm sorry. I know this is difficult to process on top of everything else you've had to deal with the past few days."

Celeste's mind raced. "But ... but I don't even know if I would want to have a baby. Why does he get to make so many decisions for me?" *Pregnant. Woman who miscarried from being beaten up by her boyfriend. Rape victim. All phrases to describe a woman I never asked to be.*

The two women spoke a bit longer, but then Celeste grew antsy. She had to get to work. And she needed time to process everything. *But today is not the day for any of this.* Today was the day to make Omar pay for what he had done to her. *Please, God, let this play work. Please let us take him down. It's the only thing keeping me together right now.*

Dr. Simone must have sensed Celeste was reaching her limit because she was all business once more. "Why don't you get dressed? I'll just grab my list for you."

Once Celeste had put her clothes back on, the doctor was waiting with a list of recommended therapists and spiritual advisers. "You're going to experience a lot of really tough emotions over the next weeks and months. You'll need help to develop tools to manage the impact of what this monster did to you. Seek out help and support from your friends and family."

Well, telling them is not an option. Celeste felt so alone.

"I'd like to see you in two days. Can you make that work with your schedule? Angelo and I can arrange a discreet office visit."

"Yes, I can make something work. Thank you so much, Doctor."

"Hang in there. I can't promise this will be easy, but you're extremely brave and strong, Celeste. You'll get through this." Dr. Simone squeezed Celeste's hand and then saw herself out.

Two minutes later, Angelo texted that he was downstairs waiting for her. She put on her high-heeled boots (*Great look with Jack's pajamas*) from the night before and went down to the lobby. Angelo took her to her apartment where she got ready for work and packed. He stood watch while she gathered what seemed like two weeks' worth of clothing and stuffed it all in a suitcase. She felt as though she were moving through quicksand, everything much more difficult than usual.

At work, she was on autopilot. She kept her eyes glued to her monitors the entire day, obsessively refreshing her browser to make sure she would not miss anything. She stepped away from her desk only once, to use the restroom and get a snack. She was particularly tense right before the market closed. When the bell rang on the trading floor, it was official. Omar's holding company had lost over $1 billion in a day, the single biggest loss by a major financier in twenty years. The news coverage of the crushing blow would dominate at least a week of news cycles. Celeste had to find Savin. She went to the restroom and texted him from her burner phone.

"When can we talk?"

"Too risky here. Dins at Lavo at 8."

An evening of being manhandled at a nightclub was the last thing she needed, but she knew she couldn't say no without raising suspicion. "Don't keep me waiting that long!"

"Have to clear a few things up. And ... you're welcome!"

Ugh, he loves building up the suspense.

Celeste sneaked out by way of the back elevator a bit later and had Angelo take her back to the hotel. Truth be told, she could use a nap before a celebratory dinner with Savin. She was torn between a feeling of vindication from making Omar lose so much money and the heavy weight of sadness and fear his abuse had brought.

"Angelo, I'd like to nap for a bit. Can you knock on my door at six thirty?"

Angelo nodded his agreement, and she went into her room and closed the door.

Once in bed, so many thoughts swirled around in her mind. *Pregnant? How could I have been so stupid? I knew something was off with him from the moment I met him, and I ignored all the signs. Aren't I at least partly to blame?* She heard Dr. Simone's words replay. "You did nothing to deserve this." *But didn't I?* She shook her head back and forth with resolve. *No, no, I won't let him make me doubt myself. Dr. Simone is right. He's the monster, not me.* She finally dozed off.

Celeste awoke to Angelo's knock and began getting ready for dinner. She changed into a turtleneck dress with long sleeves. Her back ached from wearing heels that day, but Savin knew her too well. If she showed up underdressed, he would have many questions.

She walked into Lavo a little after 8. Savin was sitting next to an older man with dark features whom Celeste had not met. *Roberto?*

"Celly! Come join!" Savin shouted over the crowd. Celeste walked over to their booth and scooted in next to Savin.

"Celeste, meet Roberto Barbosa. Roberto, this is my esteemed colleague and business partner, Celeste Donovan."

"Lovely to meet you, Roberto." Celeste extended her hand. Instead of shaking it, he kissed the top of her hand.

"Ms. Donovan, you are the lovely one. Savin, you didn't mention that she is smart *and* beautiful."

Can a woman really ever escape dirty-old-man flirtations? She ignored him.

"Sav, what was I summoned here to discuss?"

"Roberto wanted us to be together when he tells us the details of our little arrangement. He wanted to meet you in person and was in New York today anyway."

Celeste ordered a dirty vodka martini from the server and then looked pointedly at Roberto. "Well, Roberto, do tell what happened today to make my ex's now defunct holding company lose all of its value."

"Oh, now that, sweetie, is not what I came to talk about. I came to talk about something I think you'll find much more interesting. Your future as a very rich woman." Roberto's Brazilian accent was thick, but his English was flawless. He kept the details high-level, intentionally avoiding implicating himself, but explained that he and others had profited much more than he had planned on the information thanks to Celeste and Savin. Further, he said, he was prepared to gift them $400 million dollars. Celeste tried but failed to keep a straight face. *Four hundred million dollars! That almost makes me want to forgive the "sweetie" thing. Almost.*

After Roberto explained the "vesting period," as he called it, he encouraged them to consult with an attorney.

"I have just the guy, Celly," Savin interjected. "He's not one for following the rules, and he won't ask a lot of questions."

"Well, I like to color outside the lines a little, too," Roberto said. "This arrangement worked out well for all involved. Except Omar, of course. We'll see to it that he stays out of the States and out of your hair for a while. He's a disgusting excuse of a Brazilian, so today was as fun as it was profitable for me." Celeste hadn't asked Jack, but she guessed Angelo had some "colleagues" in Europe who would "encourage" Omar to stay away from New York for a while. She hoped it was in the form of cutting his dick off.

"Well, Roberto, you're full of news I like to hear," Celeste said, revealing her dimples. Roberto had appealed to Celeste's two favorite things—large amounts of money and discarding men.

"Let's celebrate!" Savin said and left the table to seek out the server—to order an obscenely expensive bottle of champagne, Celeste was certain.

ANGELO WAS WAITING OUTSIDE THE BAR TO ESCORT CELESTE HOME. SHE had explained to Savin when Roberto had excused himself for the restroom that she was using Jack's security guard for a few weeks "just in case." Savin's face had spread into a big grin. "I'm ecstatic you finally recognize how dangerous Omar is."

She and Jack had finalized the details of their arrangement: She would stay in the suite until she found a new apartment and would take him up on the offer to train with Angelo. "Real self-defense, Celly, not that shi-shi boxing shit you do to get good triceps," Jack had told her. "You have to promise to do whatever Angelo sees fit—

learning how to shoot a gun, for instance. You need one in your apartment."

The enormity of what Jack was saying—that Omar could reappear and likely would—frightened her enough to take him seriously. Celeste had agreed to the generous terms, relieved that her secret was safe. She had considered again the prospect of pressing charges against Omar, especially now that she would soon be flush with cash to hire a team to protect her. After researching extensively what it would entail—the invasive rape examination, the badgering of the victim by defense counsel, the witness list Omar could call— she had decided to forgo involving law enforcement. It was too personal to discuss with just anyone, let alone deal with the headlines when one of the richest men in the world was charged with rape. *No, I made the right decision for me. A woman should be allowed to make that decision on her own.*

After Celeste arrived back at her hotel that evening, she found a note from Jack. "Off to my next adventure. Be safe, and call if you need anything. You deserve this." He had included gift certificates for the spas at the Mandarin Oriental and the Peninsula, as well as a pamphlet for a guru, Swami Shivarajananda. He had also included a manila envelope of cash, about ten thousand dollars by the looks of it, to "hold her over" the note said. She knew she had a long path to heal both her physical and emotional wounds from Omar. But tonight she would allow herself a hot bubble bath, room service, and a nice glass of celebratory champagne. Omar would not derail her life.

6

PLAYING GOD

Now, over a decade later, Celeste scrolled through the latest Ace special delivery on her iPad. Hackers came in many different forms. Some, black hat hackers or crackers, were the ones in the news, who maliciously created chaos by stealing bank information or money from weak systems. White hat hackers were the good guys, helping remove viruses from computer systems. Ace was somewhere in the middle, meaning sometimes he went on the offensive for D&C, like today. And sometimes he merely kept their networks secure. He was not the only hacker on the payroll, but he had quickly become the most important—and the most lucrative. Time and again, he delivered news stories above the fold, and each time, Celeste sat back and watched the market respond. Today it was a *Financial Times* article predicting a tightening of EU regulations on carbon emissions, a direct countermeasure to the flaccid "anything goes" US environmental policy—sure to result in a global tumble of energy stocks by market close.

She shot off a text to Ace from her burner phone (these hacker types demanded safety precautions): "Well played, my friend."

"I aim to please." She smiled at his response.

Quant investing relied on algorithms that predicted future occurrences in the market based on historical data. As a general rule, this worked well and yielded high returns, as evidenced by the massive shift on Wall Street toward quant. The current instability in the geopolitical market, though, only confirmed what Celeste and Savin had discovered a few years earlier—for the algorithms to work under any circumstances, you had to influence the external environment, not just sit around on the sidelines. They retained consultants and insiders at every level of government in most major financial markets and used nontraditional means of influence. They did not *make* things happen, not really; they used methods to expedite what was *bound to* happen anyway. D&C then built predictability into its algorithms—something others failed to do well. They went a step further to use machine learning, or artificial intelligence. In AI, the algorithms extrapolated rules from the data. So AI was a sort of quant investing based on the information quant investing derived from human behavior—computers analyzing data. Some would claim they were playing God, but both Celeste and Savin would argue to the contrary—they had merely taken advantage of the direction of the markets and the regulator crackdown on insider trading, not to mention the world's indifference toward facts these days. Whether their genius was evil was of little concern to them.

"OK, Celly, Ace is good, I give him that." Savin barged in unannounced.

"Do you ever knock anymore? I was enjoying a peaceful Tuesday morning ..." The two laughed, and Celeste continued. "And yes, Ace delivers an excellent product. I'm glad you finally agree we needed to pivot away from the crowd."

"Ha! That's one way to characterize it. By the way, what do you think Fred wants to discuss with you? It's odd he reached out to you, right?"

"It's strange for sure. He called me at nine last night. I accidentally answered instead of hitting ignore."

"All I have to say is Fred is fucking nuts and has had a vendetta against us since last year. Just be careful. I don't want a boiling bunnies situation ..."

"You're using the wrong metaphor, Sav. Boiling bunnies is single white female shit."

"Exactly." He grinned.

She rolled her eyes at this and went back to her monitors. One of her favorite ways to pass the time was to watch the tickers on her screens bounce—and in essence, markets move—because of media she had planted.

"Excuse me?"

Celeste and Savin looked up to see a twenty-something analyst standing hesitantly in the doorway. A sharp young woman, though meek. Celeste had hoped when they hired her that she would be more of a ball-buster. She made a mental note to have a development session with—*Damn, what is her name?*

"Yes?"

The woman stepped forward, looking from Savin to Celeste and back to Savin for encouragement.

"I noticed something this morning that I think you two should be aware of. Shall I find time with your assistant to discuss this? Brett suggested I bring it to your attention immediately."

D&C had an open-door policy—if the door was open, staff was allowed to come in—but both Celeste and Savin made it crystal clear from the beginning with each new hire that any interruptions had better be important and urgent. They envisioned an empowered, confident staff and trusted them to make the distinction between what could wait and what could not. Since staff did not abuse the privilege, they gave full attention when approached.

Savin, who was still standing over Celeste's desk, motioned to the woman to have a seat at Celeste's large conference table, and he and Celeste made their way over and sat down. "Now works for us, Lorraine."

Ugh, no wonder I blocked out her name. Lorraine? Her parents must have hated her.

Lorraine closed the door softly behind her and walked over to the table, shifting to straighten this season's Balmain blazer under Celeste's scrutiny.

"Love your Alaïa boots," Celeste offered. "Very *now*. I've been admiring them myself. So, tell us, what's happening that's caught your attention?" Celeste made an attempt to empower the next generation of leaders, though she generally found their "everyone gets a trophy" mentality misguided and insufferable.

Lorraine at once relaxed and began to describe what she had observed last week.

"Well, you always tell us to stay one step ahead of everyone else, so I often come in early to analyze political news to, you know, see if anything noteworthy is happening. As you may recall, I've been monitoring the African markets and impact of the political fluctuations. We are outperforming this quarter from what I can te—"

"As usual," Savin could not help but interject. Lorraine smiled and continued on.

"But I think we're misreading what's happening in select African markets and underestimating the potential impact. I think everyone else is, too. Our algorithms are not prepared for China's demands for repayment in South Africa, Mozambique, and Nigeria. My sources say there is chatter of China demanding repayment *now*. Our algorithms are built to look longer-term—quarterly rather than monthly or weekly."

Celeste interrupted, "You think? Or you *know*? And how confident are you in your sources?"

Lorraine sat up straighter and looked Celeste in the eye. *She's done her homework. That's more like it*, Celeste thought. Maybe there was hope for good, old Lorraine after all.

"I'm confident we're on the wrong side of this, that China's demands are imminent given there are elections sometime this month in nearly all the countries that are completely leveraged, which will further destabilize their markets. We need to adjust the algorithms before anyone else does. Code that is more granular, that looks for subtler signals and identifies the problem *before* anyone else notices it. Think more AI, more nimble." She opened her Louis Vuitton folio and pulled out two neatly stapled copies of a lengthy report, handing them to Celeste and Savin.

They each flipped to the executive summary and skimmed the high points. Celeste smiled in satisfaction to see that the report was on her preferred template and included the references and sourcing she and Savin demanded. Celeste had once fired an analyst for an unsourced prediction, complete with a measured "Get the fuck out of my office, and clean out your desk." "Really, Celly?" Savin had later asked. "He was one of our best." "Not if he cannot follow my instructions, he's not." Celeste had zero tolerance for incompetence. Lorraine, in what was her first presentation to the managing directors, had met and exceeded Celeste's expectations. *Now let's see if there's any substance to the report.*

"We'll take a look at this and get back to you within the hour. Is anyone on your team briefed in the event we need to act? Your timeline suggests we need to move before the market closes today."

"I wanted to keep it under wraps until I spoke with you two, so I only told Brett."

Brett was one of the senior analysts, retained for his performance but also for his discretion. He acted quickly, did not ask a lot of questions, and came to work to make money, not friends. Celeste and Savin tried to keep the finance bro culture to a minimum, so people like Brett did well at D&C.

Celeste nodded in satisfaction, and Lorraine, taking the cue that she was dismissed, stood up to leave.

"Nice work, Lorraine," Savin complimented her.

"Yes, great work," Celeste echoed.

Lorraine smiled and walked more confidently out of the room, closing the door behind her.

"Well, that hire wasn't for naught," Celeste commented. "Total domination this week once we get to Ace."

"Yup."

In silence, Savin and Celeste read through Lorraine's brief for the next twenty-five minutes. By the end of the report, Savin was nearly exploding with excitement, his energy buzzing. He began pacing. "Lorraine is on to something. If everyone is miscalculating this, then we should see results by the end of the day, once the market has time to react to the recall of the Mozambique election results."

"Shall we pull Ace in again?" Celeste asked, already knowing the response.

"Absolutely."

Celeste shot off her second text of the morning to Ace. "Call at 10:10."

They knew very little about "Ace," as Celeste and Savin had nicknamed him. At the outset of his hiring, Ace informed them that he would speak through a voice enhancer. Their calls were usually less than a minute and entailed information they did not want captured on tapped phone lines or elsewhere. The firm's private investigator suspected Ace lived in Germany, but they had no way of confirming. Despite not being able to validate his identity, they trusted Ace because his predictions were never wrong, and he used his network to strategically place what he called "earned media" in the markets they prioritized. In Celeste's mind, earned media was a savvy descriptor for media they dreamed up and then built algorithms around to beat the market.

Celeste and Savin positioned themselves in the soundproof war room in preparation for the call. Right at 10:10, the encrypted line rang. Celeste placed Ace on speaker and sat back. Their office floor was regularly swept for bugs, and they took many safeguards to ensure no security breaches. These days, the FBI routinely wiretapped hedge fund phone lines, thanks to the Steven Cohen scandal in the 2010s, treating fund managers with disdain traditionally reserved for the mob or big tobacco. If someone rolled over on you, that provided enough probable cause to get an activist judge on a high horse to agree to a wiretap, reason number 327 that Celeste and Savin trusted few people but each other.

"Tomorrow's news: China demands Mozambique and Nigeria repay by Friday and the market is further destabilized by their election results."

"This is hardly news. Analysts have been anticipating this all quarter. It's not time to short the debt yet," Ace opined.

"Au contraire, my friend. The algorithms are built based on the fallout and repayment demands happening in four weeks."

"Got it." *Click.*

Sav turned to Celeste and asked, "Are you joining Mark for din tonight?"

Mark was in town for business and had gotten them a table at Eleven Madison, which had been named yet again as the best restaurant in the world on the World's 50 Best Restaurants list and was one of Celeste's favorite restaurants in New York.

"Yes, after my quickie with Fred," Celeste joked, winking as Sav made a gagging hand gesture.

"Gross visual. Do you ever feel bad about what we do? Playing God, I mean?" Savin asked.

"No. We've been through this—we aren't playing God, we are playing time."

"Phew, I thought you were going soft on me," Savin said and laughed. He walked to the door, opened it, and bellowed for Rani, their overworked assistant, to retrieve Brett and Lorraine.

"Ugh! You have to stop being so barbaric to her, Sav. She's going to quit, and she's the best office manager we've ever had!" The firm's office manager also had taken on the role of executive assistant after Celeste and Savin had gone through a series of incompetent ones. They overworked her, for which they compensated by overpaying her, but no amount of money in the world made Savin's abuse OK.

Lorraine and Brett walked in with their laptops. Celeste gestured for them to settle around the table. They had to work quickly to finish by lunch.

CELESTE SPOTTED FRED AS SOON AS SHE WALKED INTO BEMELMANS BAR on Manhattan's Upper East Side for happy hour. It had recently been renovated from a stuffy bar to a modern, chic lounge. Fred was seated in the back with a half-drunk highball of scotch in front of him. He seemed oblivious to the activity of those milling around him but looked up at her when she arrived at the table. His mouth was twisted into a frown, probably still holding a grudge about their panel at the London conference a few months before, and he did not stand to greet her.

"This isn't a social call, Celeste. Sit down. I don't have a lot of time."

Celeste glided into the booth across from Fred and stared back at him blankly.

Fred looked over his shoulders, and once satisfied no one was within earshot, he began. "Celeste, I've made it no secret that I don't give a fuck about you or Savin after the shit you pulled last year. That said, I have some information about you, and I wouldn't be able to live with myself if I could've stopped it by warning you."

Try as she may, Celeste could not keep the surprise from her face. "Well, darling, I must admit this is not what I expected to discuss after your cryptic phone call last night ..."

"I don't have time for niceties, Celeste. Listen to me because we can never speak of this again. I have good reason to believe that someone means to harm you."

"And here I thought this was about the UBS deal."

"Something is happening, Celeste, and you're in danger. You need to get serious about protecting yourself."

"Our security team would never let anything happen to me."

Fred downed the rest of his scotch as a server approached, a pretty, petite woman in her mid-twenties. Fred, the ultimate womanizer, did not give her a glance. "Two more of the same and charge it to my room," he barked, waving the woman away.

"Well, there's certainly no reason to be rude to the staff, Fred! And why are you staying here? Trouble in paradise again?" Celeste scolded. Poor manners mortified Celeste.

Fred, frustrated, said, "I'm not here to discuss another failed marriage of mine, Celeste. I'm trying to do the right thing, but I need you to fucking listen to me." He pounded his fist on the table.

"OK, OK, let's calm down a little. You have my attention. What's going on? Some whistleblower bullshit again with the Feds?" Celeste inquired, confused about Fred's angle.

He leaned in close to her, his eyes wide. "I can't tell you why or how I know this, but someone means you harm. Not harm to the fund or Savin or Mark or Jack, Celeste, my intel points to harm to you personally."

Not one to overreact, Celeste felt a shiver in spite of herself.

"Can you tell me anything more about this threat? I'd appreciate any info you can give and would of course make it worth your while."

The server placed the drinks in front of them with a smile and walked away. Fred stared into his drink and then abruptly downed it, slurring an order for another round to the server while she was still within hearing distance.

"I've never seen you waste a nice scotch! What's going on with you?" Celeste's attempt to soften the tone was unsuccessful.

"I'm not fucking around, Celeste. This is real, and it's happening. I recommend you take the normal precautions, alias passports, cash, the like, and get your affairs in order in the event you need to get the fuck out of town quickly. Which I suspect you're going to need to do."

"You're freaking me out, Fred. Is this about the steel stock again? I expected you to fuck me on the UBS deal, but making up some story is beneath even you."

"I'm most definitely *not* fucking with you. Do you think I would be sitting here right now *with you* if this wasn't fucking serious? You and Savin have been nothing but a thorn in my side for years. This is real. It's not just you; I'm fucked as well. I fear we'll both be six feet under in the next month." Fred stared into her eyes as a fleeting expression of panic crossed his face. He regained composure, though the air remained charged with his urgency. "And don't think I haven't noticed the little games you and Savin have been up to lately. I see the headlines, see what you're doing. Right now, I don't even care, though you need to keep a lower profile. Get your shit in order, so I don't have your blood on my hands."

Celeste swallowed slowly, torn because, on the one hand, her mind was racing with questions, and on the other, she felt certain he was lying. "Who gave you this information? Who do you think is after us? And why are the two of us targeted? I doubt we have a common enemy. The only overlap you and I have is deals where we've fucked each other over."

Fred downed his scotch and stood up. He leaned down to her until he was uncomfortably close and said under his breath, "I don't trust you as far as I could throw you, so you won't get anything else from me. I hope you take heed, Celeste, and move quickly. If I were you, I wouldn't share this with anyone. There's no one who can help and no one you can really trust. Get outta town ... and don't leave a trail."

With that, Fred walked away, leaving Celeste to process what little information he had provided. She was startled out of her reverie as her iPhone clattered against the table to indicate a text. *Savin.*

"What did Fred say? Tell me you're not going to be late!"

"Same old Fred. Some bs about the UBS deal, but it's clear he's trying to set us up. Such a dick!" She rarely lied to anyone, and especially not Savin, but she needed time to look into whether Fred's claims had merits.

Sorry, Savin, I was just told by our mortal enemy that someone wants to kill me, so excuse the fuck out of me for being a few minutes late for dinner, she wanted to write. Fred had gotten under her skin. Cryptic warnings, mistreating the waitress, no veiled threats. Very un-Fred-like.

The server returned. "Excuse me, shall I still bring another round? He seemed to be leaving."

Celeste smiled at the woman. "No, another round is not necessary. We're both late for another event and have to dash."

Monty was waiting outside with the car door open for Celeste. He smiled at her, and she willed herself to smile back. Once settled in the back seat, she freshened up her makeup while Monty maneuvered in and out of the evening Manhattan traffic. It would be a late night—extensive chef's menu, wine pairings, and nightcaps at The Lobby. There was no reason to let Fred's theatrics ruin a wonderful evening.

The maître d' at Eleven Madison, Javier, recognized Celeste when she arrived, kissing her cheeks before offering to pass her coat along to his staff. He walked her over to the premiere table in the center of the dining room. Everyone at the table stood as she approached—Savin; the firm's lawyer, Johnny Carolo; his wife, Demetra; Mark; and to her surprise, Jin. She had never met Jin in person and had only seen photos. The photos did not do her justice. Jin was stunning, with a petite frame, long shiny black hair, creamy skin, and a sparkling smile. Celeste plastered a smile on her face and sat down after greeting everyone with a kiss on the cheek. She introduced herself to Jin, gushing that she was positively radiant. "It must be all the pregnancy hormones that give you such a glow!"

Jin blushed and explained ... well, Celeste lost track of what she was explaining as her mind wandered. The extent of her appropriate engagement with pregnant women was complimenting their glow. Pregnancy was so sci-fi, and after Omar, she'd never again considered having children, so she had no curiosity about the experience. *Omar.* Was he behind Fred's warnings? Was Fred working *with* Omar? No, that was impossible. Fred's fear was genuine, afraid for his own safety and Celeste's. Plus, Omar had been off the radar for years.

"Excuse me," Celeste said to the group and walked to the ladies' restroom.

In a stall, Celeste withdrew her burner cell. She texted a code only Ace would understand. She could not risk pulling Savin in on this without any intel—his hysterics would distract her. Fred's warning echoed. *There's no one who can help ... and no one you can really trust.*

"Just you?"

"Yes, just me."

"K."

Back at the table, Celeste forced herself to stay present and enjoy her friends' company, even though she was antsy to speak to Ace. It wasn't every day they were all together, so she made an effort to learn more about Jin with champagne-fueled questions about Mark and what it was like to live in Shanghai year-round. It was a herculean effort, but by the end of the evening, she could tell Mark was happy they had embraced his fiancée.

––––––––

ACE CALLED HER BURNER PROMPTLY AT 7:10 THE NEXT MORNING. Celeste hadn't slept the entire night, considering different scenarios: Fred's warning was sincere, Fred was lying, Omar was trying to destroy her. *But why would Omar want to kill Fred?* The two didn't know each other. And why come back now, after all these years? She locked herself in the war room to ensure Savin and their staff could not eavesdrop.

"Look, you know I'm not one for overreacting, but I need you to do a little digging nonetheless. One of our mortal enemies blindsided me yesterday with news that I'm in danger. I need you to determine whether there are any security threats on any of my accounts and ..." she trailed off, nervous to even say the words. "And can you also look into what Omar Santos is up to these days? I can't imagine he'd have access to me after all these years, but you never know." Celeste continued, thinking aloud. "I mean, we're so thorough. There's no way anything could be awry, but I have to admit Fred has gotten into my head. I should probably be prepared for whatever happens. Get me a new passport or three, credit cards, and the rest. European. You know the drill."

"You're finally taking my advice with a go bag. What exactly did this mortal enemy say?"

"Basically that someone wants to kill me or something of that nature. Just look into it and tell me it's unfounded, so I can move on."

"OK. Will be in touch. In the meantime, take extra precautions and consider getting out of town. The last thing I want is for something to happen to you on my watch."

Click.

For the first time since she had seen Fred, Celeste exhaled.

On Wednesday, Savin was riding the high of their headlines expediting the loan defaults and had forgotten to grill her more about her meeting with Fred. His short attention span was one of his wonderful traits, at least in situations such as these. Wall Street buzzed with confusion as to how D&C, and only D&C, knew of China's repayment demands, its entire strategy upended. Lorraine possessed a new air of authority when she walked through the office, and Celeste had come to trust her more than the other analysts. Perhaps Celeste's instincts had been right about her all along—she had raw talent and cunning, both needed to dominate in a man's world.

Ace followed up on their secret session with disturbing confirmations: unusual activity, someone accessing her phone records and bank statements, tracking her travel, but the access points were not traceable. "This isn't the work of some script kiddie or neophyte. This is a black hat," he relayed in a somber tone.

Celeste, frustrated, said, "In English, please."

"This is the work of a very bad guy, someone who wants to harm you. There are only a few hackers sophisticated enough to hide from me, and you'd turn the other way if you saw them walking down the street. It's time."

It could only be one person. Celeste took a deep breath. "OK. And what did you find out about Omar?"

Ace reported that Omar was leaving quite a trail and likely was not the culprit himself, splitting his time between London and Dubai with hookers, scotch, and cocaine. She had to hand it to him— despite his addictive personality, Omar was a mastermind. His ability to manipulate anyone about anything was what had kept Celeste around for so long while they were dating. Omar was a narcissist, a sociopath, but he was also adept at anticipating market behavior by modeling off the predictability of human behavior. Ace had provided her with records of Omar's dealings in the past five years, and his holding company had recovered and was doing well. Quite well; he seemed to be playing by the oligarch handbook.

Later that evening at home, Celeste sat at her desk in her home office reviewing files from the disc that Ace had FedExed to her with specific instructions to destroy after review. She was hoping to figure out what Omar was up to. She inserted the disc in the special drive Ace had provided. *How is this literally the safest way to get me this information in this day and age?* She moved through the files, trying to digest the information quickly and figure out what Omar's angle was.

Celeste looked up from her work when she heard a light knock on the door. Dina, Celeste's nutritionist and chef, stood in her office doorway, smiling warmly.

"Celly, you work too hard. You need some antioxidants to keep up your energy."

"Ugh, I can't believe it's so late," Celeste groaned as she glanced at the clock on her monitor. Dina had been holding Celeste's dinner for several hours now.

"I am in the thick of a big deal and lost track of time. Please forgive me!"

Dina chuckled. "Truly, no worries. I just finished a telephone interview for the *Times* 'Well' column! Apparently, your championing of my nutrition program has generated some interest in the wellness world, which, by the way, I can't thank you enough for." Dina's excitement lifted Celeste's spirits.

"Well, if there was ever a way to ensure your new cookbook would sell, a quote in the *Times* will do it. Your concoctions are divine, and my ass and skin have never looked better—so this recognition is well deserved."

Celeste saw to it that those she employed were the best of the best —and to ensure that they, too, were flush with cash, she sang their accolades to anyone who would listen and paid them well. Patrick was in the process of launching a makeup line backed by Celeste, and Tyler had his own product line. Her investments had only one condition—that they would still be available when she needed them.

Celeste followed Dina into the dining room. Under normal circumstances, Dina may have joined her for dinner and a glass of wine, but tonight, Celeste had indicated she would be tied up with work. Dina said she would wait until Celeste was finished to clear the dishes.

"Dina, darling, that's completely unnecessary! I'm capable of putting a dish or two in the dishwasher and starting it. Get some rest! I insist!"

Dina smiled, knowing she was fighting a losing battle. "OK, OK, I'll go and leave you alone with that pile of work. Are you still dining out as planned tomorrow evening?"

Oh, shit. Theodore had emailed her midday yesterday and asked if she could have dinner with him Thursday. Buried in Omar's transactions, she had forgotten. Plus, she was still salty it had taken him three weeks to contact her after their first date, so she hated being available when he asked. Is this what other women did? Wait by the phone?

"Oh, yes, that's correct! I have a dinner tomorrow night and another dinner the next. Enjoy a few days without my insanity!"

"You're a delight—you aren't fooling anyone!" Dina said over her shoulder as she retrieved her handbag from the mirrored sideboard in Celeste's foyer and closed the front door behind her.

Celeste reviewed the files for another hour and realized two things: she was going to need some help, and she would need to do some traveling if she wanted to get to the bottom of whatever Omar and his deputies were up to. *Fuck.*

After another sleepless night, Celeste knew she needed a reinforcement. "Rani, will you send Lorraine in?"

"Sure thing."

Within moments, Lorraine appeared in Celeste's doorway. She was wearing a tan wool midi pencil skirt, white silk blouse, and Saint Laurent pumps, accented with tasteful diamond studs and two Cartier Love bracelets. Her hair had the sheen of a fresh keratin treatment, the transformation from mousy analyst to glamorous financier complete.

"You can close the door behind you. Do have a seat." Celeste gestured to her conference table. "Would you like some water or tea?"

"Still water would be wonderful." Celeste handed her a bottle of Evian.

"I see Meredith has connected you with all the right people in Manhattan. You look so chic!" Celeste said.

"Thank you. Coming from you, that truly means a lot."

Celeste nodded her approval. "But I didn't call you in here to discuss your blowout. Your work lately has not gone unnoticed. Savin and I see real promise in you. Your ingenuity and instincts have served us well, and we hope you feel appreciated at D&C."

"Well, if I may—the bonus was too much, Celeste. I was just doing my job."

Celeste laughed. "Darling, a man would never turn down money and would in fact have stormed into my office demanding twice as much for the market discrepancies you caught. You earned it. We notice that you're first in and last out, highlighting how useless some of the bros can be. Now enjoy the money in whatever way you see fit.

"I'd like for you to do a special project," she continued, "reporting your findings to me and only me. I want you to know it is highly unusual that I keep something from Savin and the rest of the team. In this case, however, I need someone I can trust to do some research and not ask questions. I'll approve any resources you need. All I ask is that you work alone, and it will require a few late nights for a week or so. You and I can download at my apartment early next week. We are not to discuss this in the office, in writing, or by phone. This is the last time we'll discuss the matter outside of my apartment."

This was a first for Celeste, letting an analyst into her home. Yes, Lorraine was newly in Celeste's good graces, but Celeste believed she was the only D&C analyst with the skill and discretion to complete the task. Lorraine had not told anyone about their readjustment of the algorithms, though she surely had noticed the headlines appeared *before* the default. And Celeste's apartment was the only venue where the meeting would go undetected.

Of course, Celeste could have had Ace or another of the

consultants she had on retainer do this research for her, but she needed someone inside D&C to be up to speed in case of an emergency, someone capable of doing this sort of work for her if Omar or whoever was meddling was going to complicate her life. Besides, she was uncomfortable trusting only Ace with this information and wanted someone to validate his findings. She was not blind to the fact she had given him an enormous amount of power by letting him in on this. Especially with Savin in the dark.

"Thank you for thinking of me. I'd love to help! Anything you need."

"Rule number one—never, *ever* agree until you know what the project entails, Lorraine."

The two laughed, and then Celeste grew serious again.

"I have a special laptop for your project that cannot be hacked." Celeste walked over to her mammoth desk, removed a laptop, and placed it in front of Lorraine. "It looks just like your D&C laptop, so no one will be the wiser. I keep two extra laptops on hand for this very type of situation. I'm not one to micromanage, but you'll need to use this laptop only in the office on the network and VPN I'll provide or in my apartment. *Not* a coffee shop or your apartment or your boyfriend's place. The security risk is too great otherwise." Ace was not the only cybersecurity person she employed, and she was losing confidence in his abilities with the latest news that someone was hacking her undetected.

Celeste walked Lorraine through the project, providing her with the accounts and passcodes she had created. "I mentioned this may require some late nights this week, so I've asked Angelo to send someone here to walk you out in the evenings and drive you home. And you're probably not going to like this—but one of his guys will sit outside your apartment in the evenings until we're finished with this project and make certain you're safe. I don't want to frighten you, but I believe in taking precautions." Celeste would not let Omar hurt anyone else.

Lorraine's face shone with excitement, reminding Celeste of her younger self, bursting with enthusiasm, drive, and complete naïveté about how dangerous this world could become.

"Finally, I want to be clear. No one must know about this project. Absolutely no one. I wish I was being melodramatic, but it could get you and me both killed."

Lorraine's eyes widened, then she regained composure. "You have my word."

Celeste nodded and continued. "Savin doesn't monitor your work, and most of the others will be in external meetings all week. If anyone asks, you have a new potential client who is curious about business opportunities in Central America and East Africa. Or better yet, tell them I said to fuck off. We'll meet next Tuesday evening. Please do exactly as Rani and Angelo say with regard to security. They aren't away of any specifics on this project, though, so please don't discuss with them."

"Thank you for trusting me with this, Celeste. I won't disappoint."

Celeste hoped this was true, though given her current predicament, she knew she had no other options. The finance bros of the office were a necessary evil but could not be trusted with anything confidential, and the math nerds were antisocial. *It's nice to be able to work with a woman who has discretion and competence.*

7

STEAL AWAY WITH ME

Time passed in a blur of late nights with Lorraine and secret calls with Ace. Celeste was convinced Omar was behind the hacking, but the information coming in from Ace was a slow drip. There was no more news from Fred, either, who was rumored to have left Manhattan to escape the embarrassment of divorce number three, though Celeste knew the real story. Keeping secrets from Savin was becoming more and more difficult, and Celeste found herself avoiding him for fear she would blurt out the truth. "Omar's in some deep shit, and I think he's building a case to put me away forever!" she wanted to tell him. But that would make him vulnerable, and she would not have D&C suffer from Omar's shenanigans.

Theodore was a nice distraction. Since their first date in March, he was on his sixth visit to New York, and they had also sneaked in some quick weekend trips. He was always hassling her for an extended holiday. "Steal away with me for a few weeks," he would say. "We've been dating for months, and all I ever get is a weekend here and there." She tried to be at least *occasionally* unavailable because she feared she would lose her intrigue if available all the time.

"Darling, you do know I'm a working woman, right? I cannot just 'steal away' for a European rendezvous," she would say.

128

"You're so *American*. Europeans have a much better philosophy. Work comes second to *living*." It *was* tempting. He was a dream to fuck, and her schedule had been freed up a bit, since she was entrusting Lorraine with more work. More importantly, the stress of her cyberthreats and what they could mean was getting to her. Ace's constant harassment to get the fuck out of dodge, claiming he could not protect her now and she was a sitting duck for whatever the black hat was planning, was not helping her stay her usual calm self.

"I've been thinking, Theodore, and I've decided I'll go away with you for a week or two," she said resolutely. It was 5 a.m. and they were intertwined in her bed, having been awake all night talking and having sex.

Theodore's face broke into a grin. He propped himself on an elbow and looked her in the eyes. "Wait, really? I can have more than a day or two with you? I was beginning to think you weren't that into me! How about now? I have to bounce around Europe next week and would love nothing more than to have you with me."

She had never seen him so animated, and she felt undeserving of his affection. *What will happen when he finds out my elusive ex is trying to take me down?* She shook off the worry.

Theodore began nibbling her neck and then whispered, "Can you imagine weeks of this?" He caressed her breast, still having the ability to make her wet on command after all these months.

She sighed happily. "You're relentless!"

"It's the perfect time of year to explore the French countryside, with the Christmas markets and such. We can do that if you like! Amsterdam is also beautiful this time of year. You don't have to answer now. You can tell me yes tonight at dinner to everything I'll have planned. Paul wants us to try his new wine pairings." Paul owned one of the six Michelin three-star restaurants in New York. He and Theodore had a long history, though Celeste did not know the specifics.

"We'll discuss tonight, but if you'd like to fuck me before my spin class, you'd better get busy. I should also note that if you don't fuck me before my spin class, I'll be pissed." Theodore may have had a unique ability to make her soften her commitment to her disciplined life, but she never missed her morning workout.

Theodore laughed and tucked his head under the covers, scooting his face down to her abdomen.

"I aim to please, Celeste."

Celeste lay back and let Theodore's hands and mouth bring her to two orgasms before her alarm went off.

"Now get to your workout, gorgeous," he said, "and try not to think about two weeks of this during your meetings today."

"I hate to leave you in bed with a hard-on, but I do have to get up."

"I can wait until tonight."

He kissed her with a hunger unrivaled by other men and gently pushed her to standing.

"Go! I won't have you skipping dinner over protests that I kept you from your workout!"

Celeste knew she would think about Theodore's hard dick the entire day.

———

"Fred Warren is on line one for you, Celly," Rani's voice boomed from the speaker phone. Celeste was scouring numbers in her office that morning, anxious for her meeting with Lorraine in a few hours to discuss Lorraine's latest findings. "Put him through," she said.

"Fred, darling. I haven't heard from you since you stormed out of Bemelmans. To what do I owe this pleasure?"

"Take me off speaker," Fred grumbled.

"And here I was hoping you'd be in a better mood this time. I'll call you from my cell," Celeste said into the handset as she held it up to her ear. She dialed his number on her cell, and Fred picked up on the first ring.

"You don't seem to be taking our last conversation seriously, Celeste. It's been weeks, and you're still gallivanting around town. What the fuck is wrong with you?"

"You'd have to discuss that extremely long list of my shortcomings with my therapist, dear, but I do appreciate your thinking of me."

"Goddammit, Celeste, this isn't a fucking joke. Get out of town for a bit. I don't care where you go, but take some time away. I'm doing the same."

"Oh, I wondered where you've been!" Celeste switched tactics. "Why the mystery, Fred? Why do you refuse to give me information if I'm in so much danger? It sounds like it's all smoke and mirrors to me. But what I can't figure out is why you give so much of a shit or what your angle is."

"I have word the timing is fast approaching."

Celeste would not let Fred know she was feeling a knot of fear in the pit of her stomach. She hoped her nonchalance would infuriate him, and he would inadvertently reveal more details.

"Oh, so now there's a hit on both of us? This sounds like a bad made-for-TV movie plot, Fred!"

"Yes, and I won't be able to contact you again. Do whatever the fuck you want. I've done what I can."

Celeste's burner phone rattled in her desk drawer just as Fred hung up on her.

"911," read Ace's text.

Ace wasn't one to sound the alarm for nonsense. *But what? Omar? Won't he ever go away?* What also still wasn't clear was why Fred was involved.

Fuck. Couldn't Omar have just given me chlamydia and skulked into the shadows like a normal finance douchebag? Why won't he just go away?

Celeste walked to the war room. "What's up, Ace?" Locked in the war room speaking with Ace while Savin was out to lunch was becoming the norm as she sat on edge waiting for the news.

"I'll reiterate what I've told you—it's time. Now. At least for a few weeks." *Ugh, not Ace, too. What the fuck?* Since day one with Ace, he had been coaching her and Savin in the art of disappearing in case things ever got hairy for them, though she had been much more prepared for a knock from the Feds on their questionable media practices than a crazy ex.

C'est la vie.
Click.

CELESTE MADE IT THROUGH THE DAY WITHOUT ANY FURTHER interruptions from Ace, which was more disconcerting than comforting. It meant he was going full on with their plan. She wouldn't disappear completely for an undefined threat, but she was going to get out of New York for a while, and she had just the motive and travel companion. She could do more digging on the ground while in Europe than she could with all eyes on her in New York. As she sat down for another delicious dinner with Theodore, she agreed that Amsterdam and the Christmas markets sounded lovely, disguising the fact that her decision to leave Manhattan was out of necessity, not a sense of adventure.

"So, the answer you've been waiting for ... drumroll, please ..."

"Don't keep me in suspense!"

"Europe sounds wonderful!" She paused to take in Theodore's ear-to-ear grin. "But don't get too excited. I still have to work and will need to arrange a few meetings while you're doing whatever it is you do during the days."

"Of course. I'm thrilled to have you all to myself and will agree to most any demand you have. Except separate bedrooms, that is. I plan to fuck you four times a day."

"That is perhaps the best news I've heard this week," she said with a laugh. On an impulse, Celeste leaned over to kiss Theodore's lips before backing away. She was still unsure how to handle affection outside of the bedroom, though Theodore never pushed the issue.

"I've got it all planned. Our first stop is Amsterdam, then we'll explore a bit of France—Strasbourg, Colmar, maybe some champagne tastings in Epernay. I need to make a quick stop in Luxembourg at some point, and then we can spend a few days anywhere you like to relax!"

"Luxembourg? So money laundering's your specialty?

Theodore winked. "You've always seen right through me, baby."

She continued. "And I pick Saint-Tropez or Marrakech, easy flights from Paris after our countryside tryst, for our last few days. Well, I suppose Marrakech could be rainy ..."

The evening was one of the nicest Celeste could remember, the imminent threat far from her mind. She fell asleep in Theodore's arms with a smile on her face.

A FEW DAYS LATER, ON TUESDAY EVENING, CELESTE AND LORRAINE SAT in Celeste's home office in front of her three enormous monitors, and Lorraine walked her through the research findings on Omar's trading. Ace had reported back as well, reinforcing Celeste's intuition that Omar was involved in some shady shit. His company had contacts on every continent. It appeared from the outside to be a multinational holding company, but once he dug deeper, Ace found ties to nearly every major drug cartel and terrorist organization across the globe. Lorraine's findings supported what Ace had uncovered. Omar's publicly traded company had become a safe harbor for an extensive global criminal network.

He's no longer just an oil man. He's so much more dangerous than he was a decade ago. How has no one on my security team uncovered this?

"It may be inappropriate to ask questions, but I'm dying to know —who is this man? With all the crackdown, I can't believe he hasn't been caught yet."

Celeste turned to Lorraine. "He's my ex-boyfriend."

"Oh, fuck."

"Yeah. I knew a lot of his dealings were illegal, but until recently, he'd stayed out of my business, so I stayed out of his. Now, though, it seems he wants something from me, and I have no idea what that could be. He's a monster, yes, but why come back after all these years? These aren't your problems, though." Celeste took a deep breath. "However, I do need to be up-front with you.

"Lorraine, I'm sure it's become evident how dangerous Omar is—

but I didn't ask you to do this research with the belief that you'd be in harm's way. I'm confident no one knows you've looked into this for me, and you're the only person I trusted to do this. Based on what you've shared tonight, Omar is more connected—and far more dangerous—than when I knew him. I'm worried about my safety, but I'm more concerned about yours.

"I'm doing something I never do—taking a two-week trip with a man I'm dating. I'll be meeting with a few colleagues on the trip and will do a bit more fact-finding. Once I have more evidence, I plan to come back and find a way to hold Omar accountable for his crimes. It's the best way I can think of to guarantee my own safety and the safety of those around me."

"Where do I sign up to help?" Lorraine asked, face flushed with excitement.

"Slow down, lady! Much of this is out of our hands. Obviously, law enforcement should be involved … but I'm afraid I don't yet have enough evidence to blow the whistle on all this. Also, I couldn't live with myself if you or anyone else at D&C were harmed. Once I'm sure everything is in place, you'll get your time to shine. Here are the terms if you agree to stay on this case. I need to be able to trust that you will keep this all to yourself. To reiterate—you can't even tell your parents or best friends. As I mentioned the other day, both of our lives could be in jeopardy if anyone finds out you're in the know. And until I'm back with answers, you'll have one of Angelo's men with you at all times, more invasive than of late—sleeping on your couch, standing guard outside your apartment, watching you in the gym, and escorting you to work. They'll continue to be discreet, of course, so none of the guys here will know. And I'll have my chef deliver food to you, so you don't have to food shop or order in. We can't risk a stranger showing up at your door with malicious intent. That's two and a half weeks of all work and no play. Sorry I didn't clear all this with you earlier, the security, the quarantine, and such, but I feel it's a necessity. Is this acceptable to you? Please know there'll be no repercussions if you decide to say no. You have to be sure you want to stay in this."

"It's OK. I don't have much of a personal life, given our hours, so it's not an imposition. I do understand the risks as well. I can commit to two and a half weeks of discipline—only work, exercise, and sleep. I also have no problem with the extra security," Lorraine said in an excited tone.

She has no idea what she's getting herself into. Celeste was confident Angelo would keep Lorraine safe, though, as he had kept Celeste safe in the past. *But what if? What if Omar somehow got to Lorraine? Could I live with myself if he hurt her like he hurt me?* Celeste shook off her worry. *No, it's me he's after.*

"Outside of you and me, only one other person knows of our little project. I will put you in touch with him only if necessary."

The main reason Celeste felt she could trust Lorraine was that Ace had been monitoring her. Lorraine was a regimented woman and had had little communication with anyone outside of work since the project began. Ace would continue to keep an eye on her while Celeste was away. He had his own sources but agreed with Celeste's assessment that she had to bring in someone inside D&C—and that it should not be Savin. Another partner would be too high profile in a way that an analyst would not. Besides, a project of this magnitude would set Lorraine up for life. Best to pay it forward in hopes that Lorraine would do the same for another young woman at the height of her career.

"I'm already excited for your return to hear what you find out!"

"I've never had a romantic getaway with a man for two weeks, so I may be excited to return as well," Celeste said, and both women laughed.

MEREDITH HELPED CELESTE ZIP HER FINAL LOUIS VUITTON CASE AND stood back to admire the pile.

"Voilà! You'll be the best-dressed woman in all of Europe."

Celeste could not hide her anticipation and had an uncharacteristic nervousness in her stomach. "Two weeks is a long time to spend with a man. What if I find out he doesn't like to fuck a lot? What if he doesn't floss twice a day?"

Meredith wrinkled her nose in disgust at the possibility of a man who did not floss, then perked up. "Celly, you'll have a fabulous time with a man who loves you. Don't overthink it."

"Love? Now he loves me? What the fuck! Do you want me to have a heart attack?"

"Stop! Get out of here! Your car is here."

Her buzzer chimed, and on her video cam, Celeste saw Theodore's driver standing at the front desk with Jonah. "Send him up, dear." The driver loaded her bags on the luggage cart and left to take them to the car.

Celeste took one more deep breath and promised Meredith to be present and enjoy the moments with Theodore. *And I'll set aside thoughts of Omar and Fred as much as possible. I deserve this time away.* Meredith helped her into her coat, a gorgeous floor-length sable fur, and Celeste left, blowing her stylist a kiss on the way out.

Downstairs, Theodore stood at the back door of a black Rolls Royce while her bags were loaded into the trunk.

"Nice wheels," Celeste said.

Theodore smiled and bent down to kiss her. "It's time I had a real car in New York," he joked. "My apologies for not coming up, darling. I had to wrap up a work call. An angry investor."

"Oh, you have those also? Occupational hazard."

Theodore embraced her, thrusting his body against hers.

"Theodore!" Celeste blushed as she pushed him away and got into the car. Jonah had witnessed her drunken nights strolling in with hot male models, but never intimacy. Theodore walked around to the other side of the car and climbed in.

"Embarrassed, huh? I think someone has a crush on me!" They laughed. When they pulled away from the hotel and were on their way, Theodore got down to business, walking her through their agenda.

When he was finished, she said, "It all sounds magical, Theodore. You've thought of everything, and the timing was perfect for me to escape. I managed to set up a couple of meetings during our stays in Amsterdam and Luxembourg, so I'll feel like I'm being productive."

"Don't think you'll get through this with all work and no play!"

Theodore's driver dropped them off at the South Street Seaport heliport where a helicopter awaited to take them to Teterboro, the private airport servicing the greater New York area. Celeste, ever the control freak, allowed herself to exhale once they were seated in the helicopter and accepted that Ace and Lorraine would have to hold down the home front. She was relieved she had the excuse of Theodore whisking her away to distract attention from the investigation she was doing abroad.

———

THEODORE SPARED NO EXPENSE FOR THE SIX-AND-A-HALF-HOUR FLIGHT from Teterboro to Amsterdam's private terminal, booking a G700 jet for them at God knows what cost. Not that Celeste cared much for commercial flying, but she especially liked flying private when she was not footing the bill. A chauffeured Maybach waited for them at Schiphol's VIP terminal. The traffic was light at this hour, and Theodore went into planning mode once more, since they had spent the entire flight fucking in the enormous bed.

"I thought we'd relax tonight. Explore the city a bit tomorrow, then try my friend's restaurant tomorrow night. Spend a few days here, and then heli to the countryside for the weekend. Sound good?"

"I only have one meeting tomorrow and one in Luxembourg when we make it there, so I'm at your mercy."

Theodore kissed her forehead and squeezed her hand. "I'm so happy you were able to come!"

The car slowed in front of the hotel.

"Hotel TwentySeven?" Celeste said. "It received the Best Small Luxury Hotel in Europe award before it even opened! It looks incredibly well done in the photos, and I'm a tough crowd. I can't wait to see inside!"

"Yes, it's quite a magical place. I'm looking forward to showing you around."

"You've stayed here?"

"I stayed here before it opened. A test guest, if you will."

"Are you ever going to tell me who you are, mystery man?" Celeste asked, laughing as the driver opened her door, and Theodore escorted her inside.

It was rare for Celeste to be impressed, but Hotel TwentySeven lived up to the hype. Theodore had booked the most decadent suite for the week and had it stocked with her favorite things—Perrier sparkling water, Dom, fresh fruit, full-size versions of her expensive toiletries.

"You called Meredith!"

"Well, I wanted to think of everything, but I'm smart enough to realize I'd need help with this."

Celeste walked into the enormous living room and sat on the luxurious velvet sofa, fingering the silk pillows. The storybook window framed with burnt-orange velvet drapes looked out over a bustling city, the evening aglow with city lights.

"I think you'll like the artwork. My curator helped with the collection."

God, this man. It was rare to meet a man who appreciated everything in life that she did—fucking, fashion, food, and art.

"I'm fairly certain I need this piece in my apartment," she said, eyeing a gorgeous painting.

The butler, who had introduced himself as Alfred, appeared from the bedroom.

"Miss Celeste, on the bar, you'll find a book of our extensive art collection. If there's something you'd like to take home for your collection, we can arrange that."

"Thank you, Alfred."

While Theodore and Alfred were discussing logistics and

preferences, Celeste explored the two-story suite. A round Jacuzzi-style tub upstairs in the master bath was placed in front of another picture window with a city view. The showers were equipped with steam, and the toilets had computerized bidets. Most Dutch hotels prided themselves on a bare aesthetic, but not this one. No expense had been spared, from the textured wallpaper to the artwork to the Dom in the wine refrigerator.

"Alfred, I must say—I'm hard to impress ... and I am dazzled," Celeste said. Her dimpled smile was contagious.

Alfred grinned in satisfaction. "We're happy to hear this meets your liking, Miss Celeste. Please let me know if I may be of service." He left the suite soundlessly, and Theodore handed her a glass of champagne.

"Cheers to the first of many times I whisk you away to have you all to myself!"

"I suppose I can toast to this—but only because I admire your taste in just about everything ... especially women. *Salud.*"

They clinked their glasses, and before they could have a second sip, their clothes lay in a heap on the floor, and Theodore was carrying Celeste into the guest bedroom off the living area.

"It's closer," he said with a wink.

"Let's go check out the rest of this place," Theodore said when the two had finished making love. Still nude, he lifted her naked body over his shoulder. She laughed at his silliness while he carried her up the stairs.

As though on command, soft jazz began playing over the speaker system. Theodore collected the robes from the wardrobe and held one out for her. After she was swaddled in the sumptuous terry cloth, he rang for Alfred. "Stay right here, gorgeous," he said and went downstairs to discuss whatever else he had in store for her.

Celeste lay back on the bed, marveling that for the first time in a long time, she wasn't overcome with worry.

"Celeste, darling, your phone is ringing in your handbag," Theodore called to her. "I wouldn't disturb you, but I know you've had a lot going on at work." *And ... back to reality.*

"Yes, I have. Thanks." She pulled herself up from the bed, where the mattress had molded to her body, and walked down to the living room. She pulled out her burner phone discreetly, took a quick look at it so Theodore would not notice, then stuck it back in her bag.

Three missed calls from Savin, one from Lorraine, and several texts from each.

"Excuse me, I have to make a few calls. Will you run a bath and keep it warm for me?"

Theodore handed her a fresh glass of champagne and kissed her forehead. "Of course. Do what you need to do."

She retreated into the guest bedroom and closed the door.

"Savin, what's going on? You do know it's the middle of the night in Europe, right?"

"Celly, I wouldn't have called, but ... Omar's in town. He stopped by the office looking for you. Rani didn't say where you were, of course, but he was stoned and angry. Shouting at her and causing a scene. Rani was very shaken up. Any idea why he's in New York?"

Celeste was enraged. "Jesus fucking Christ. How the fuck did he get into our building? I was hoping he'd at least keep a continent or two between us while I figured everything out. After all these years, I don't know why I'm surprised at how arrogant and stupid he is. I can't believe he's resorting to terrorizing our staff."

"Wait, what? Figured what out? What don't I know here? Why do I feel like you're not surprised he's resurfaced after a decade?"

Fuck, fuck, fuck, now I have to tell Sav. She took a deep breath. "OK, Sav, are you sitting down?"

"Tell me what the fuck is going on, Celeste. Is this why you gallivanted off? Start at the beginning." He never called her by her full name.

"Hang on." She opened the door and yelled up to Theodore.

"Theodore, darling, something has come up with work. I'll be up in a few minutes." She closed the door and sat on the bed.

"Calling you back now." She hung up and called Savin on his secure line. She told him most everything, from Fred's repeated warnings to Lorraine's research. She knew Savin would be extremely worried about her, so that he exploded was no surprise.

"How could you keep this from me, Celly? *Have you lost your fucking mind?* Omar is dangerous! Have you thought this through at all? No one can keep you safe while you're playing around in Europe with no security. Does Theodore even know that you're in danger?"

Being accosted by Savin was foreign to Celeste.

"Not exactly. And I'd prefer he not know. Security is such a drag, Savin! I'm tired of Omar ruining everything. If you recall, he's the reason I got to know Angelo so well—because I needed round-the-clock security for years." She sighed and continued. "I'm sorry for not keeping you in the loop. I was trying to protect everyone, and I screwed up. But we are here now. What do you think is the best path forward?"

Savin made her promise to check in with him every day after she persuaded him not to tell Theodore. To her surprise, he moved away from the topic of her betrayal quickly and began scenario planning with her. They tossed around several ideas and arrived at an agreement for what came next. If necessary, Celeste would stay in Europe until they fully understood the landscape, especially now that Omar was poking around the city. Savin would oversee Lorraine's continued investigation. "Make sure Angelo doesn't let her out of his sight," Celeste warned.

"We have to get Ace involved. What if this is bigger than Omar?"

"Ace is monitoring Lorraine's progress, and we're using scramblers with our burners."

"OK. At least you're as thorough as you are deceitful. Now go get your brains fucked out again by my old mate, and let me take care of some of this. I'll see Fred this week—apparently he didn't go far—and find a way to bring this up. See if he'll give me more than what he's shared with you."

The two agreed to talk again the next day when she was able to sneak a call. After she hung up, Celeste wandered upstairs to the

master bath to find candlelight illuminating the room and a relaxed
Theodore in bubbles. It was surreal to be able to compartmentalize
work and play, but Theodore's presence brought out this new side
of her.

"Thanks for waiting! Now where were we? I believe I promised
you a blow job in exchange for your superb performance earlier?"
She shed her robe to the floor and sank into the hot water with
Theodore.

"Not if I get to you first." Theodore pulled her close, and the two
of them kissed. Telling Savin the truth had taken a weight off. She
laid her head on Theodore's shoulder, and they sat in comfortable
silence.

CELESTE AND THEODORE FELL INTO A RHYTHM THE NEXT COUPLE DAYS
—morning sex, parting ways for meetings (or shopping and museum
hopping when Celeste needed to clear her head), and coming
together to share meals at one of the myriad Michelin restaurants or
in their private dining room. Celeste enjoyed the solitude of walking
through the streets, following the twists and turns of the canals,
allowing herself to get lost in thought. What could Omar want from
her? This question burned through her, and she was growing
frustrated that she was unable to answer it. He had wanted her back
from the minute she left him, but his sense of urgency now was
apparent. What could she have that he needed? Was it business? Was
he spiraling out of control with his addictions again? She was not
sure she wanted to find out. She was also concerned with the
disturbing data and algorithm outputs Savin had discovered. Before
she knew it, it was dusk. She ducked into a quiet cocktail lounge in
the red-light district for a call to discuss further with him and Ace.

"Ace, are you any closer to figuring out what he wants from
Celly?"

"No. It's good that you stay under the radar, Celeste. Enjoy some
time away from New York while I keep digging." *Click.*

"Would it kill him to say goodbye just once?" Ace's telephone etiquette, or lack thereof, bothered Savin even more than it did Celeste.

"He's a rude son of a bitch, but who else could help us with this?" Celeste reasoned.

"True, true. You were right, by the way. Lorraine is a savant. She's the only one with the patience and intelligence to dive into the web of Omar's holding companies. I can't believe his ties run so deep in so many places. How could such a fuckup make all this happen? The fact that his cocaine use hasn't blown out at minimum one of his heart valves is in itself a modern medical miracle."

"Who knows? Maybe he was cryopreserved for a few years or something. The best thing for us now is to keep doing things as we always have. Tell everyone I'm scoping out plans for a new satellite office in Europe. It's probably not a bad idea anyway."

"Agreed. But Celly, I'm worried. We've alerted security not to allow Omar into the building, but how did it happen in the first place? And what if he gets to a janitor or someone else with open access to our office? Let's think through relocating for a bit to Greenwich and decide later this week."

Celeste shuddered at the thought of Omar reigning over Manhattan, forcing her to skulk away to the suburbs in fear. "No fucking way. He's not scaring us off the island. *My* island. Fuck that. Besides, I'm not exactly Connecticut material, Sav."

"It wouldn't be forever, Celly, and we may have no choice if he shows up unannounced again. You know more than anyone how dangerous he can be. We have an obligation to keep our staff and investors safe."

Celeste digested the magnitude of what could be happening. Leaving her Manhattan office to run to Connecticut with her tail between her legs. *No fucking way!* She wanted to scream.

"OK, I have to dash," said Savin. "I have to wrap up a few things, then I'm off to lunch with Jack. He popped in again—from Seychelles this time, I believe. Oh, and get this—he managed to obtain a pilot's license. He's been flying all over East Africa, in and out of remote beach towns."

"That is terrifying! Who the fuck would find him fit to fly a plane?"

"Well, in what world is Mark fit to be a father? Stranger things, I guess."

Celeste laughed. "On that note, I'll let you go. Since you've decided to take care of everything, I think I'll spend the day dropping a wad of cash to stimulate the Dutch economy." They both laughed.

"Till tomorrow. Same time."

CELESTE RETURNED TO THE HOTEL WITH SEVERAL SHOPPING BAGS— Chanel, Balmain, Gucci, Manolo, and some gifts for Theodore from Agent Provocateur and a local sex shop. Alfred materialized with a luggage cart for her bags and held the elevator door open for her. He hit the sixth-floor button with a promise to be right behind her with her swag.

She found Theodore in the alcove office at the desk, puzzling over a legal pad with indecipherable scribbles on it. He looked up at her and smiled, pushing his notes aside. Celeste closed the door and began taking off her layers—gloves, Max Mara trench, Hermès scarf —placing them neatly on a vacant chair. She was horny and in need of Theodore's flesh against hers. She removed her blush cashmere sweater, boots, and leather leggings to reveal a black balconette bra with nipple cutouts and a garter belt with a slit in the crotch. She walked to Theodore, who was aroused from watching her little striptease, sitting with his legs spread and his hard cock poking out of his track pants. She stood above him, twisted her nipples until they were hard, and then placed her fingers inside her.

"Now it's your turn, dear. No touching. Only watching." She continued pleasuring herself to the groans of Theodore, who nearly had to sit on his hands to refrain from touching her. When his breathing was as fast as hers, she knelt before him, removed his pants, and stroked his pulsing cock with her tongue. She took the length of him in her mouth, hollowing out her throat to account for his size.

"Cele—oh God, Celeste! You ... are ... fucking incredible."

When he was close to climax, she sat on his dick, gyrating against him while his mouth sucked on one nipple and then the other. Her G-spot responded to his cock, and she threw her head back in pleasure.

"Your cock ... oh, it fills me up comple—completely." She was breathing deeply, struggling for words.

They climaxed in unison, and Theodore caressed her cheek as he thrust his tongue into her mouth for a steamy kiss. When his dick began to harden again, he stopped and locked eyes with her.

"I'm falling for you, Celeste." Celeste's eyes widened in surprise, intimate moments like this foreign to her. She resumed her stoic facial expression and climbed off of Theodore, pushing down panic.

"You are too kind and quite possibly the most wonderful man I've had the pleasure of fucking."

Theodore laughed at her evasion, then stood up, pants falling to the floor. "What do you say we shower off and start again?"

AFTER A DECADENT EVENING OF MORE SEX, A BOTTLE OF A PREMIERE Chablis, and lobster, Celeste and Theodore lay together in the master suite staring up into the tower above the bed. The skylight at the top glowed with candlelight from well-placed candles.

"This is perhaps the most perfect bed in the most perfect hotel at the most perfect moment," Celeste said.

"And I am lucky enough to be here with the most perfect woman." He turned to her. "Hey, what do you say we leave a few days early? Thanksgiving in Paris could be fun, and Friday is the last day of white truffle season. My friend swears his white truffle menu at 1741 restaurant in Strasbourg is the alpha and omega. We could go to Strasbourg Friday morning, enjoy the Christmas markets for the weekend, and indulge in everything wonderful about life. Back to Paris for a few days, and then, of course, Saint-Tropez as promised."

Celeste would have agreed to anything if it meant not discussing the words Theodore had muttered earlier. "Ooo, white truffles! How can I resist?" Her dimples puckered in playfulness as Theodore ducked under the covers, spread her legs, and began fingering her again. After another session, they collapsed in bliss. Celeste rolled over and closed her eyes. Theodore, thinking she was already asleep, caressed her face and whispered, "I love you, Celeste. I hope you never question this."

THEY DRESSED FOR WINTER WEATHER THE FOLLOWING MORNING. SHE wore brown leather pants, a camel cashmere sweater, and over-the-knee low-heeled Stuart Weitzman boots to navigate the treacherous cobblestone streets. Theodore donned an ivory sweater, dark jeans, a caramel tweed sport coat, and Ferragamo loafers. The two were oblivious to the gawks of the staff wondering about the identity of this radiant couple as they exited the hotel into the waiting black Mercedes that would take them to the airport.

"Strasbourg is one of the few places I haven't explored in France," Celeste said. "After living here for a year in college and having an apartment in Paris the past few years, you'd think I would've gone at least once. Speaking of which, shall we stay at my apartment in Paris?"

"I've already booked us a suite at the Hôtel Plaza Athénée. I never have anyone to share Paris with, so please indulge me!" Theodore responded and kissed her cheek.

"Well, since you ask so little of me, I suppose I can make this sacrifice. I am a giver, after all."

"That you are, and it's been incredible giving and taking this week," Theodore whispered into her ear, pulling her close and cupping her breast just as the driver raised the privacy window.

"You're incorrigible!"

After Theodore checked them in to the Plaza, he and Celeste went to Le Bar, the chic hotel lobby bar, for a glass of wine.

"What shall we do for your very American holiday tomorrow? We, well I, rather, have a lot to be thankful for." He kissed her forehead and continued. "We may have a hard time finding turkey, though, my love."

"I haven't had a proper Thanksgiving in as long as I can remember. Let's just do our own thing."

Theodore beamed. *He's so easy to please.* "I was hoping you'd say that! Because I have a surprise—Natalie Bisson agreed to cook for us!"

"The World's Best Female Chef recipient? Where? Wow. How'd you swing that?"

"So many questions," Theodore responded, laughing. "Yes, that's her. I've invested in a few pet projects of a friend of hers. As for the where ... well, I hope you're not upset with me ..."

"OK, now you have to tell me! Where?"

"Your apartment. Savin said you always brag of the ample dining room and underutilized kitchen fit for exquisite dinner parties. Is that OK?"

"Of course, sounds fun!" Celeste retrieved her phone to call the concierge of her building and request that the staff prepare for her visit.

"Nope, no need to make calls. I've already taken care of everything. Rani is extremely resourceful by the way."

Celeste should have been angry about the imposition, but instead, she was relieved someone else had taken the reins for a bit.

"She's the best!" Celeste said. "So, she took care of everything with the concierge? Shall we stay there tomorrow night before we leave?"

"Yes and yes. We'll leave straightaway from your place for the countryside on Friday very early. Does that work?"

"Of course. Though I am sad to cut our stay at the Plaza short, since you were so excited to enjoy it."

"No, it's fine. Don't worry about me. I'm enjoying every minute of this time with you. I only wish we could do this every day."

"Mm. Would be nice, wouldn't it?"

The bartender came back by with the bottle of Beaujolais Theodore had ordered, filling their glasses. When she left, Theodore grew serious. He looked Celeste in the eyes.

"Celeste, I want you to know that no matter what happens, these last few days have only cemented for me that I love you. I've never felt this way about anyone before."

Celeste squirmed, uncomfortable with this display. Theodore picked up on it and said, "What do you say we cork this bottle and enjoy the room?"

"Perfect."

The bartender came over and said, "Mr. Prescott, I've already had a bottle sent up to your suite. On the house for one of our favorite guests," she said, smiling.

"Thanks, Stacy."

Celeste didn't even ask this time, having become accustomed to Theodore's mysterious ways. *He probably owns the land the hotel is on,* she mused.

THE NEXT DAY, CELESTE MARVELED AT THE NUMBER OF PEOPLE BUSTLING through her apartment.

"I had no idea it took so many people to prepare a meal for the two of us," Celeste said. She and Theodore were lounging on her sofa, watching no less than a dozen people shuffle in and out of the apartment. "I don't know that anyone's ever used the kitchen, so let's hope the oven works," she quipped.

"It's going to be an exquisite meal!" Theodore said, taking a pull of his scotch. "So tell me what's going on with work. Don't think I haven't noticed you sneaking secret calls in the middle of the night."

"Guilty as charged," Celeste admitted. "Sav and I are getting ready for a few big plays. We're expanding into some new markets, and finding people on the ground is becoming extremely difficult. It's hard to tell who we can trust." *This is actually all true*, she reasoned. Though her work was technically none of Theodore's business, or anyone's for that matter, she was starting to enjoy getting closer to him. But she could never tell him everything. She couldn't, she wouldn't put him in danger by telling him about Omar, the dark cloud. Especially because Theodore had known Omar back in the day. If he knew the truth … *Well, he'll never know the truth.*

"That doesn't sound so urgent. You're sure there's nothing else going on?"

Dammit. She'd never been great at hiding things. "Well, I suppose it's a little more complicated than that." *How could I ever explain that I think Omar's trying to kill me? No, I mustn't say anything. What's one little white lie?* She continued, "You see, we've got a new analyst, Tim is his name, and we think he's a double agent. So we're funneling false information to him to determine if he's working for a competitor—or worse, the Feds. Anyway, Sav is feeding me daily updates on our burner phones, you know, in case this kid has infiltrated our system." *Shit, I most definitely should not have mentioned the phones. A little sex and scotch, and apparently, I'll tell anyone anything.*

Theodore was nodding. "Sounds like you two are taking the right precautions. I know it's a tough time in the US with the Feds trying to crack down on anyone and everyone. It'll become clear soon enough who is after you, and I'm sure you'll all be fine."

If he only knew who was really *after me.* "Well, fortunately and unfortunately, we know it's Tim. Now it's just a matter of keeping our enemies closer and all that."

A nondescript man in a chef's apron, white dress shirt, and black bow tie came over to them.

"Dinner will be ready in approximately ten minutes," he said and quietly walked back into the kitchen.

Theodore stood up abruptly. "Need a quick restroom break."

"Yes, I should probably freshen up a bit before dinner as well," Celeste said. "I'll be back in a moment." She walked into her office to her desk, where her handbag was perched. Her regular phone had three texts—two baby photos from Mark and one of Jack enjoying a fruity cocktail on a beach somewhere. The burner had much more activity.

"Call me."

"Right away."

"Hello????"

"OK, fine. I guess I won't tell you what the 911 is."

Celeste rolled her eyes. *Typical Savin. This was less stressful when he wasn't involved.* Which was only partially true, but still.

She dialed his number. "What's so urgent, darling?"

"Hang on," he whispered into the phone. She could tell from his quickened breathing that he must be walking quickly to the war room.

"*Everything* is so urgent, Celly. I'm freaking out."

"OK, start at the beginning."

"Ace thinks Omar's working with the Feds. That he turned after he got busted."

Celeste's eyes widened. This was a plot twist she hadn't anticipated, even though she had joked about it. She tried to think rationally. "Well, that's not necessarily bad for us, right? What's he going to do to us?"

"Celly, think about it. You're trying to find something to hold him accountable ... but he's already got protection. Now who's going to protect you? And what if his plan is to uncover ..."

"Don't," Celeste warned. *Don't you dare say Biochrome when our lines could be tapped.* "Sav, we confirmed he never knew anything about it at the time. I do agree Omar is a monster, though, and any Fed who is working with him is a fucking idiot. I have to know. Why are you blindly believing Ace, anyway? Do you have any other intel? You know we always find more than one source. And finally, why are you at work on Thanksgiving?"

"Lorraine and I are here following up on a few leads."

"Jesus Christ! You're making our star analyst work on a holiday, Sav?"

"It was her idea. And if you must know, none of us want you caught in the crosshairs of all this."

Celeste softened. "OK, but please give her another bonus. She's doing too much."

"Fine, Celly, but she's not doing it for the money. We all actually care if you're safe. If we can just get to the bottom of what Omar's angle is ..."

"Please be careful, Sav. Take Angelo and Lorraine out for dinner tonight, please. Enjoy yourselves. Have some wine!"

"OK, OK, I get it. I'll try to be less doomsday, but it's really difficult. I mean, what if we could be put away? Or what if?"

"Enough! Now go have some fun! This can wait until tomorrow."

The two hung up, and Celeste wandered into her bedroom to find Theodore sitting on the bed, looking defeated. "Oh, no, not you, too. Savin was down in the dumps. What's going on?"

Theodore straightened up. "Mum just called, and our family dog, Cheryl, an old chocolate Lab with the enthusiasm of a puppy, just passed away. Cancer."

"Oh, doll, I'm sorry to hear that." She sat next to him on the bed and put an arm around him, kissing his cheek.

"Whaddya say we turn this day around, have a delicious meal, and fuck all night?" Celeste laughed at Theodore's phrasing because he usually used terms like "make love" instead of "fucking." This was more her crass style.

"That sounds wonderful!"

Meeting Natalie was a treat, and her creations lived up to the hype. After everyone had left and Celeste and Theodore were alone, they sat together on her chaise, their limbs intertwined, talking and idly kissing. Celeste had never experienced this casual intimacy with a lover, and she found Theodore's presence intoxicating. She was beginning to understand why people liked relationships when they found someone tolerable.

THE NEXT FEW DAYS WERE A SEAMLESS CONTINUATION OF THE TRIP. They passed through Luxembourg on the way to Strasbourg. Celeste stuck to her story of a business meeting. In reality, she was actually retrieving a file from a man Ace had found. This man had allegedly hacked a video surveillance company and retrieved video footage that implicated Omar in a host of crimes, including murder. Exactly what she needed to take to the Feds.

The man had contacted her the previous night on her burner phone.

"I've left something for you with the hotel concierge. Do not show T." *That's all the info he's going to give me? A text? And why the fuck does this person know who Theodore is?*

Nonetheless, she gave Theodore an excuse and met with the concierge that evening.

"Hello. I hear you have something for—"

"Ah, yes, Miss Donovan. Wait right here." The concierge, a woman in her thirties, left her for a few moments. She returned with an envelope with *Mlle. Donovan* scribbled across the front and handed it to Celeste.

"Please let me know if you need anything else—anything at all, Miss Donovan."

"Yes, of course, thank you!" Celeste said, clutching the envelope and hurrying to the lobby restroom.

Once in a stall, Celeste tore open the envelope. It was a piece of paper with a rough map of the neighborhood drawn on it. There was a star on one corner of an intersection. The paper had no other writing on it. She committed the location to memory and then ripped the map into tiny pieces and flushed them down the toilet.

When she returned to their hotel room, Theodore was sitting at the dining table with his laptop, a pensive look on his face. When he saw her, he smiled widely.

"That was quick!" he observed.

"Turns out the front desk had a fax machine after all, and it was easy peasy!" Celeste fibbed. She sat down next to him at the table.

"What are you in the mood for this evening, gorgeous?" Theodore asked.

"Do you mind if we stay in tonight? Maybe a massage and a bubble bath? I need some rest."

"I anticipated we may need some rest. Two massage therapists will be here in an hour or so. Why don't you take a bath and relax?"

"Brilliant, thank you, handsome." She kissed him and walked to the bathroom.

The truth was, her nerves were shot. Being on the run was taxing. She would not admit it out loud, but she was extremely anxious for her meeting tomorrow. Best-case scenario she would receive the files. She had not ruled out foul play. What if this was a setup? What if Omar had infiltrated Celeste's network? What if Ace had malicious intent? She had not been in touch with any of her cybersecurity gurus other than Ace for weeks, and she felt as though she had a target on her back. Still, she refused to discuss this with Theodore.

The next morning, she stood on the agreed-upon street corner, taking in the scene. Visibility was low, with snowflakes as far as she could see. The Christmas lights illuminated the city center, and the spirit of the crowd was bustling with excitement. She was quite taken with the beautiful scene, allowing her to briefly forget the reason she was waiting there. The moment passed, and the realization she was likely being followed by any number of known or unknown villains came back to the forefront of her mind. The phone in her mittened hand vibrated with a text.

"Go inside pharmacy next to bank." The text had come from an unknown French number.

Celeste looked over her shoulder and identified the drugstore. She walked over and entered. *Not creepy at all that this guy is watching my every move.*

"Go straight back to cosmetics. Security camera blind spot in front of the Evian spray water. Envelope behind fourth bottle back."

Are you fucking kidding me?

She walked nonchalantly to the back of the store, removing her mittens but leaving her hat and sunglasses on. The small, white envelope was exactly where the person had described. She looked around, and when she had confirmed she was alone in the aisle, she slid the package into her bag. She nearly jumped backward in surprise when her phone vibrated again.

"Good. You drew too much attn to yourself on street. Leave."

Celeste rolled her eyes. *Having all these hacker types following my every fucking move is really fucking annoying.* She checked the time. She had about five minutes before she had to meet Theodore. She dropped her phone into her handbag, put on her cashmere mittens, and left the store. Once on the street, she spotted a street vendor selling hot chocolate. Her mouth watered. She walked in that direction.

"*Deux chocolats chauds,*" she said. The vendor looked at her with alarm. He moved quickly, muttering under his breath in French as he made the drinks. Celeste leaned in, curious as to why he was so angry. A chill ran down her spine when she heard him say her name, and she listened more intently, noticing in her peripheral vision that there was now two men behind her.

"*Idiote,*" he muttered. "*Ce n'est pas le moment de traîner! Ils veulent l'enveloppe.*" Didn't she understand the importance of what she was holding? Why was she stopping for hot chocolate when there were others who wanted what was in that envelope?

"*Vas-y! Fiche le camp!*" he said as he handed her two cups of the steaming beverage. *He's telling me to beat it! Well, he doesn't have to be a dick about it.* She nodded once to him in acknowledgment, pulled her bag close to her, and grabbed the cups. She turned to leave, but the men were much too close. Dressed in all black with black stocking caps, they were much taller than she was, with broad shoulders and angry scowls. One of them moved closer and grabbed her arm. Her heart dropped and her breathing quickened. *Think, Celeste.* Angelo's voice rang in her head. *Run! Now!* She looked left and right, hoping a law enforcement officer would be close by. The sidewalk was suddenly empty, except for her, the two men, and the vendor.

The vendor shouted something in what sounded like German, and all three instinctively turned to stare at him. Celeste ducked out of the way just in time to miss a huge bucket of water being thrown at the men. She dropped the cups and begin running toward the meeting spot.

Thank God I wore snow boots and it's only a block. As she turned the corner, she nearly ran smack into a man's chest. She looked up at him, fearing it was one of the men in black. *Theodore.* He stood there smiling.

"Well, hello, there," Theodore said. "You're late, so I was coming to look for you."

She was breathing heavily from her mad dash. "Yes, I'm sorry, darling. My friend was running behind, but we were able to have a quick chat. I hope you haven't been waiting too long."

"Just a few moments. Let's get out of here so we can enjoy the Capital of Christmas. You know that's what they call Colmar, right?"

They walked to the car at an idle pace, Theodore with his arm around Celeste's shoulders. She looked behind them, but there was no sign of the rough-looking guys. Once they were inside the car and the driver put it in gear, she sighed in relief.

"Are you OK, Celeste? You seem a bit rattled," Theodore said, his brow furrowed in concern.

"Oh, yes, no worries. Just more of the same on the home front—wondering what that little shit Tim is up to and if the Feds are going to show up on our doorstep tomorrow."

"I hadn't realized things had escalated. Let me know if I can help. I happen to have some of the best lawyers at my disposal."

Celeste grinned, letting herself enjoy the moment. "Of course you do," she said, her dimple flashing. Theodore leaned over and kissed her.

"You're irresistible in that adorable hat," he commented.

"And you're always irresistible," she replied, resting her hand on his chest and kissing him back.

"Well, there's nothing you can do about the Feds now, so let's enjoy our last few days of leisure together."

"Leisure" is a laughable word choice, but it has been a wonderful trip, minus the narrow escape and attempted kidnapping. She needed to

connect with Ace. She was dying to know if the file would have what they needed to implicate Omar. It was too risky to reach out to Ace today—she didn't want to have to lie to Theodore again.

AFTER A TWO-HOUR DRIVE, THEY ARRIVED IN COLMAR, A QUAINT LITTLE town, with Christmas beckoning from every street corner.

"We'll stay at my friend's apartment tonight in La Petite Venise, Little Venice. The hotels here are shit, and he has an incredible place with great views. Shall we start out there, freshen up, and then go on a hunt for food?"

"Yes, sounds wonderful!" Celeste said excitedly. This was just what she needed to take her mind off of everything else. *The impending doom and gloom that awaits my return to New York will still be waiting even if I have a good time today. Omar, I won't let you ruin my last few hours of vacation.*

Little Venice was a charming neighborhood consisting of canals and narrow streets. Her favorite part was the canal lined with a rainbow assortment of half-timbered houses. The houses all had multicolored Christmas lights that illuminated the canal, and the snow began to fall again. She looked to Theodore and marveled at the scene.

"What a delight! I'm not normally one for the Christmas spirit, but even I can appreciate this."

Theodore beamed. "I'm so happy you like it. I was worried your work drama would ruin your time here."

She still had not had a chance to look inside the envelope. When they had arrived at Theodore's friend's pied-à-terre, they had made love, showered, and dressed, Theodore not leaving her alone for a minute. She kept the envelope tucked away in a zippered pocket inside her small Chloé crossbody bag for safekeeping. The enchanting scene was the perfect distraction. She kissed Theodore and whispered, "You're wonderful, you know that? Thank you for making this so special." Theodore eyes shone with that foreign look again, and she said to lighten the mood, "Oh, and I'm starving. Can we eat now?"

Theodore laughed. "Yes, of course. It's only a short walk from here to the markets." He looked down at her feet to assess whether she was wearing walkable shoes.

"I can walk, darling. These are my special cobblestone-streets-in-Europe boots."

"Phew, that's a relief," he said, kissing her forehead.

They wandered from booth to booth at the Colmar Christmas markets, debating which one had the best mulled wine. "The nutmeg-to-cardamom ratio is perfection in this batch," Theodore said, licking his lips.

"Well, I know nothing of such things, but I can say the booth over there was my favorite."

"We'll have to agree to disagree, then," he replied.

Celeste felt the day was magical—the perfect end to a perfect trip. They gorged themselves on French delicacies and exchanged stories of their childhood Christmases. Celeste's were some of her fondest—before her parents died and her brother became an idiot. Theodore's childhood wasn't as carefree, with his father's philandering and his mother's self-medicating, though his parents had redeemed themselves once he reached adulthood. "I'm pretty sure I have half-siblings all over London," he joked.

Celeste purchased a few gifts for her friends and staff, even finding an adorable sleeper and stuffed reindeer for Mark's baby. Satisfied with the day and a little tipsy from the wine, she held up her bags and turned to Theodore. "OK, I've bought them all out of house and home. What next?"

"Tonight is something special. Jean will take us to 1741 in Strasbourg for what is promised to be the most decadent meal of your life."

Theodore wasn't exaggerating. Their server, Gabriel, encouraged them to order the ten-course white truffle prix fixe menu. "Today is the last day of white truffle season. It would be criminal to miss out on it!" he said, presenting them with a wooden box of the largest white truffles Celeste had seen.

"We'll do the white truffle and the white pairing," Theodore told Gabriel.

The meal and the exquisite wine pairings left them both satiated and giggly.

"OK, OK, you were right. This is the best meal I've ever had," Celeste admitted.

"Yeah, it was great, but I'm really looking forward to dessert," Theodore said.

When they had finished the final course, Theodore nuzzled her neck. "It's time for me to have you all to myself," he whispered.

"No complaints on my end," she responded. A few moments later, they stumbled onto the twilight street and headed back to the car, hand in hand, drunk with desire. She could not remember a time she had been happier, thoughts of Omar and the envelope far from her conscious mind. *If only this moment could last forever*, Celeste thought as she kissed Theodore on the cheek.

8

SHE'S UNRAVELING

"I don't understand what's happening to me. I need to fix this ... this entire situation."

A panicked Celeste sat in her therapist's Manhattan office, a chic, minimalist space, concentrating on the barges moving slowly along the Hudson River to avoid looking Anne Marie in the eye. The afterglow from the magical European vacation was fading, and Celeste was struggling to learn how to fit a relationship into her lifestyle. Theodore had yet to reveal any flaws, which annoyed her because it made her countless flaws more apparent. It didn't help that the disc she'd gone to great lengths to obtain in Luxembourg had not contained the intel Ace had hoped it did—so all of her work there had been for naught. Omar was still after her, and no one knew who had sent the street vendor thugs. All she knew was that Ace and Angelo were growing more vigilant, and she was trying to find outlets for her frustration. Instead of being a distraction, thoughts of Theodore were becoming her main source of anxiety.

Anne Marie looked at her inquisitively. "OK, let's explore this a little more. What do you think needs 'fixing'?"

"All of it! I skipped my morning workouts twice last week, did I tell you that? And I turned down a speaking engagement, so that I could be free for dinner with him tomorrow night. Dinner! I'm a forty-one-year-old woman in the throes of an adolescent crush."

Anne Marie caught her eye and stared, calmly waiting for her to continue. Celeste pursed her lips stubbornly.

"Let's look at this another way. Perhaps having a relationship with someone you like is changing the way you view activities you once considered obligations. Is it accurate to say you're feeling agitated? Maybe because your priorities have changed a little? And that you're still getting used to your new view of your priorities and fitting them in while still spending time with Theodore?"

"A man should not be a priority! My entire life is Theodore, Theodore, Theodore. When I'm with him, there's nowhere else I'd rather be. And when I'm not with him, I'm mostly just thinking about seeing him again. I'm sleep-deprived because I've stayed up late the last two nights talking to him on the phone like a lovestruck adolescent. I have to break up with him. I can't live like this."

Anne Marie laughed heartily, then straightened up when Celeste glowered at her.

"Apologies, Celeste, I don't mean to make light of your concerns. But it doesn't sound like what you really want is to end your relationship with Theodore. From what you've said over the past few months, it sounds like you quite enjoy spending time with him."

The two continued their usual back-and-forth, Celeste admitting yet again that she cared for Theodore but refusing to relax into the changing lifestyle. She left the session frustrated. Once in the elevator by herself, she removed her phone from her Birkin and skimmed over her new texts.

"Can't wait to see you tmrw, baby," Theodore's text read. *Ugh, this mushy stuff is getting a little out of hand.* Celeste looked at her reflection in the mirrored elevator wall, annoyed to see the goofy grin spread across her face. She sighed and distorted her face into a grimace.

"Yes, doll, excited to see you, too!"

Theodore's just going to have to understand I'm a very busy woman and can't be expected to send flirty texts all day.

THE FOLLOWING DAY, LORRAINE AND BRETT PRESENTED THEIR FINDINGS on China's exploitative financing in Kenya and Sri Lanka. Celeste and Savin were obsessed with exposing vulnerability in China's strategy and had charged Lorraine and Brett with outside-the-box brainstorming.

"Don't we have an ethical duty to ... I don't know ... protect the people living in these countries? It hasn't worked out well for Sri Lanka with China taking possession of its ports. Why isn't the UN stepping in to protect these low- and middle-income countries from predatory lending practices?"

Celeste and Savin had been clear about D&C's mission from the beginning—they were in the business of making money. However, the world was evolving, and they wanted to be nimble. They exchanged a glance, and Savin nodded almost imperceptibly.

"OK, let's tweak the assignment a little. If you two can design an algorithm for us to win in the East African market over the next two months, we will reinvest whatever amount we clear. If you want to get really creative, you can outline the case for a country of your choosing as the investment target," Savin said.

A huge smile crossed Lorraine's face, while Brett looked confused.

"So, like, philanthropy?" Brett asked.

Celeste nodded affirmatively. "It's a bit of a shift, yes, but Bloomberg doesn't get to be the only one getting positive PR for commonsense investing." The truth was, Celeste had challenged Savin to identify a philanthropic focus area because they were inching up to the point where amassing more fortune was fruitless. This fit perfectly with their developing-world strategy.

"Let's touch base tomorrow after market close."

Later that evening, Celeste and Theodore sat at the bar at the bustling Beatrice Inn, neither noticing the eager patrons on either side of them clamoring for drinks. Holding her left hand in his, Theodore idly stroked her ring finger with his thumb. "Someday," Theodore said, his eyes mischievous.

Celeste's eyes bulged in surprise, and she gulped.

Theodore laughed. "Don't look so terrified! You and I wouldn't be so bad together, would we?"

As if I have any idea how to respond. "Well, I suppose we do enjoy each other," Celeste said noncommittally, relieved when Theodore seemed satisfied with her response.

"How do you feel about a weekend gallivant? I could use a massage and some time in bed with you."

"Things are a bit busy at work. Could we do something quick and easy?"

"Miami? Carillon Spa? Let's go somewhere warmer; this weather is a downer." Celeste nodded affirmatively. "Easy. I'll book tomorrow. Next Friday to Monday work?"

"Perfect," she said, relieved they had moved on from the marriage talk.

"Told you we make a great team, Celeste!"

Celeste smiled shyly. *He never fails to throw me off my game just a little.*

"You haven't talked about work much lately," Theodore continued. "What kind of chaos have you and the elusive Savin been bringing down on the finance world?"

"Ugh, he's had some new lady move in, so of course he's MIA. Don't worry; it'll be over in a month or two. D&C's going to become a little more involved in infrastructure investment."

Theodore beamed. "Philanthropy in the developing world? You? You rebuked the thought when I brought it up two weeks ago. Hmm ..."

"Sav made me read a book about managing millennials. It seems that my most promising analyst is motivated by do-gooder causes. And when she's motivated, I make money. Besides, Bloomberg and Buffett shouldn't get to corner the publicity on causes. I can do causes, too, you know."

"Well, it sounds as though you've found all the ways to justify this as a business case. Your motivations don't matter; just happy you're joining the bright side."

"As bright as you may be, Theodore darling, you're a little too ... cheeky, in your words, to convince me of these pure intentions you're always trying to sell."

"Never pure where you're involved, baby." He nuzzled Celeste's neck, tickling her, and Celeste squirmed.

"Now, where is that bartender? I could really use another glass of bubbles!"

After another round, the two moved to a table for a feast—côte du boeuf paired perfectly with two bottles of Remelluri Rioja.

"Are you sure you haven't had sommelier training? The wine was incredible!" Celeste gushed after dinner while they walked to Monty's waiting car. She stumbled a little, entering the back seat. "I'm afraid I may have been a little overserved," she said, laughing with Theodore as he slid in on the other side. As Monty started driving, he rolled up the divider, allowing the two privacy for a heady make-out session on the way home. They then stumbled up to Celeste's apartment, both of them exhausted from the heavy meal.

Once they were tucked into bed, Celeste's head rested on Theodore's chest, listening to his steady heartbeat. He caressed her hair, then traced her lips with his index finger.

"I meant what I said tonight, darling. About wanting you all to myself one day," Theodore said.

"OK," Celeste said while yawning. "Sweet dreams, sweet man." It was the best she could offer.

When she thought he was asleep, she rolled over to the cooler side of the bed. Theodore turned on his side and slid closer to her, his body cradling hers. "Good night, love you," he said sleepily, his breathing slowing in her ear as he fell back asleep. Omar's voice popped into her mind, echoing the words Theodore had murmured, followed by his ominous laugh. *But Theodore isn't Omar*, Celeste coached herself with Anne Marie's words over and over, until she finally fell asleep.

The following morning, Theodore and Celeste showered.

"You're sure you can't come with me to London?" he said, thumbing her clit.

"Stop taunting me when you know I can't get away! Plus, Miami is next weekend, so you'll have plenty of time with me."

Theodore enveloped her in an embrace, his hand in her hair, gently pulling her head back to kiss her. "You still have ten more minutes for me to ravish you, though, right?"

Two can play at this game, she thought, lowering to her knees and taking the length of him in her mouth. He picked her up, and she squealed in delight, wrapping her legs around his waist. He pressed her back against the shower wall, entering her. *This is how I want to begin every day*, she thought, submitting to a quick climax before work.

LATER THAT MORNING, CELESTE'S PHONE VIBRATED WITH A TEXT notification.

"I'll be back for you in less than 72 hours. Don't miss me too much!" Theodore's text message read.

"Can't eat, can't sleep LOL," she typed and hit send, then placed her phone in her bag.

She dialed Rani's desk. "Rani, let's run through my schedule," Celeste said.

"Sure thing; I'll be right in." Rani entered Celeste's office, and they sat at her conference table. Rani called Meredith to streamline Celeste's logistics for the rest of the week.

"I've decided I'll be skipping Christmas dinner with the Goldman guys Saturday evening. Savin can handle it. Theodore gets back that day. Can you make us reservations at Milos at Hudson Yards? I'm dying for some dorado, and they do it so well. Meredith, can you find something for me to wear?" Celeste ignored Rani's raised eyebrows. She could almost hear Rani's wheels turning—this was the second event she had skipped in as many weeks to spend time with Theodore.

Once the three had coordinated Celeste's meetings, work dinners, and weekly appointments for the next few weeks, Celeste dismissed

Rani to prepare for her follow-up meeting with Brett and Lorraine. She read through the memo Lorraine placed on her desk, impressed by the depth of the analysis and proposals. She mentally committed to the strategy in advance of their presentation. Then she dialed Savin in his office.

"Lorraine strikes again!" Savin said as a greeting.

"Let's meet in the war room and discuss."

They settled at the table in the war room moments later. "I'm one hundred percent in. But I'd like them to sweat a little," Celeste offered.

"Wholeheartedly agree!" Savin exclaimed.

"It's time we promote Lorraine. In a big way. She's outgrown Brett, and she's consistently one of our top earners."

"I agree. Let's work out details over dinner tonight. When they hear our enthusiastic support today, I guarantee good old Brett will suddenly stand behind Lorraine's do-gooder ideas," Savin joked.

"It was wonderful to be able to commit to a cause, wasn't it?" Celeste said later over martinis at Cipriani's downtown.

Savin chuckled at Celeste's comment. "I fear Theodore's influence is making you a bit soft," he said.

"Fuck you. But yes, he did plant a seed. Especially with Omar bringing his dark cloud over everything lately, it feels nice to do something bigger than ourselves."

"And there you have it, ladies and gentlemen. Mark this day—the day the Ice Queen's minuscule frozen heart defrosted for love."

"Ha. Ha. Ha," Celeste responded sarcastically. Theodore had influenced her; whether she was going to openly embrace it was a different story.

"What's the latest on Omar?"

"Well, Ace is looking into the leads I got in Luxembourg, though he seems convinced they're dead ends. I'm still hopeful we can find some way to take him down."

"Darling, you look delicious," Theodore's baritone voice crackled over FaceTime on Celeste's laptop. She lay in bed naked, enjoying how easy it was to tease Theodore. "I can't wait to see you Saturday."

"Likewise," Celeste said.

Theodore chattered on about his day, recounting a hilarious story of mistaken identity.

"I was supposed to meet the broker to discuss that apartment I'm thinking of buying, and after we talked for twenty minutes, I realized he was trying to sell me a two-hundred-thousand-dollar condo, not show me the vacant unit in One Hyde Park."

They laughed, then Theodore turned serious.

"The things I'd like to do with your body right now," Theodore said in a low growl.

"Mmm, do tell," Celeste said, reaching into the bedside table for her bullet vibrator. She turned it on and moved her hips as she massaged her clit.

"First, I'd run my mouth from your head to your toes, stopping at your delicious wet pussy to nibble on your clit. Then I would massage your G-spot with one hand while I stroked myself with the other."

Celeste's breathing quickened, mesmerized by Theodore's hand stroking his cock. "Yes, and then?"

"Once you climax, I'd pull you on top of my cock and thrust myself in and out," Theodore said while firming his grip and quickening his hand movement. Celeste looked into his eyes, his lust mirroring hers.

You're the perfect man, Celeste thought as her eyes rolled back. Her body tightened in orgasm and then went numb. When she opened her eyes again, Theodore, too, had climaxed and was cleaning himself with a towel.

"Celeste, you're incredible."

"On that note, handsome, I've got to get some shut-eye."

She dozed off happily that evening.

CELESTE AWOKE EXCITEDLY THE FOLLOWING MORNING AND RUSHED through her morning workout and breakfast.

"Good morning, Rani," she said breezily. "Sav here yet?"

"Yep. He's sulking again," Rani replied. The two rolled their eyes, both knowing it had something to do with a woman.

Celeste walked down the hall to his office, prepared to discuss a new strategy for Roberto's portfolio.

"Morning, darling. Tell me why you're sulking, then we can get down to business."

Savin looked up at her with a sad frown. "Nothing big; just another breakup. Same old story," he said, smiling weakly.

Celeste sat down at his conference table and motioned him to join her. "I'm sorry, Sav. I know you really liked this one," she said in an attempt to be comforting.

"Yeah, yeah, I know that means you don't even remember her name. What's it matter anymore, anyway? I'll be single forever. Speaking of, what are you so chipper about? Don't tell me you and my best mate are having phone sex again. Gross."

Celeste chuckled. "It was FaceTime sex, thank you very much! I am a lady!" she said.

He laughed and his typical morning focus came back. "OK, OK, I'm cheered. Now what's up?"

She walked Savin through her ideas, and the two agreed they would present the plan, packaged very nicely thanks to Lorraine and Brett, to Roberto over lunch in a few hours.

"Where we going?" Savin inquired.

"Some midtown steakhouse. You know Roberto." The two laughed. Roberto's diet consisted exclusively of red meat and scotch, from what they'd observed over the past decade.

CELESTE KNEW THE MOMENT THE BLUES WALKED INTO HER OFFICE after lunch that something was wrong, terribly wrong. The two nondescript men in NYPD uniforms exchanged somber glances.

The shorter one, Greek by the looks of his nose and bushy eyebrows, cleared his throat and began talking, but his words sounded muffled. She struggled to make sense of what he was saying. A sharp pain shot through her abdomen, and she doubled over, lowering to the floor as though someone had sucker punched her.

"Ms. Donovan ... listed as his emergency contact ... accident while flying in the Berkshires ... rough patch ... plane down ... body badly burned ... next of kin identified him ... truly sorry for your loss, ma'am."

The officers stared at her, stoic.

No, no, no, this can't be possible, her mind screamed. *This doesn't make sense.*

"I ... I don't ... I don't understand. Plane? Theodore didn't fly planes."

"He does, er, did have an active pilot's license, ma'am. We were able to track down the paperwork he signed at the airport yesterday. It's a tiny airport, so it didn't take long." He beamed, proud of his sleuthing.

"Well, yes, I know he has a license. But he didn't just steal away to the mountains to go for a spin. Plus, he's in London this week. I ... I spoke to him last night. You must've incorrectly identified the person in the accident."

"Ma'am, I'm so sorry. We know this is unexpected, but we have confirmed the—the body—"

"He's a person, not a body!" Celeste nearly shouted.

"Yes, yes, I'm sorry. We've confirmed the *person* in the accident was Theodore Prescott, who your secretary informed us is ... well ... *was* your boyfriend."

Celeste's mind raced with questions, but none these men could answer.

"Please. Just go."

"Ms. Donovan, here's my card. Let us know if there's anything you need." Celeste took the card.

"Officer ...," Celeste looked down at the card for his name and continued, "Officer Mykos, I need you to either tell me this is some sick joke or get the fuck out of my office."

"Yes, ma'am. Well, we're real sorry for your loss." With that, they turned and left, closing the door behind them.

Celeste reached for her iPhone and shot off a text.

"Monty, please pick me up at the office in 5."

"NP." No problem. *If only Monty knew how many problems there actually are.*

Celeste calmly gathered her handbag, iPad, and phones, then donned her oversized Thierry sunglasses. She called Rani at her desk.

"Rani, please cancel my day. I have some things to take care of," she said to her right-hand woman.

"Of course, Celeste. Shall I send dinner to the house?" Rani's voice was tinged with concern. *She knows.*

"Yes, that's a good idea. Have Savin call my cell when he returns from his meeting."

"I asked Monty to meet you at the back entrance."

"You read my mind as always, Ran." Celeste ended the call, then hurriedly walked out of her office and down the hallway toward the back elevator. *The last thing I need is to see the facial expressions of all those nosy kids whispering about why the police showed up at my office.*

Monty had the door waiting for her when she got outside.

"Hello, Miss Celeste," Monty said, wearing a sympathetic expression. *Goddammit, can't anyone keep a secret?*

"Hi, Mon." She slid into the car, and Monty closed the door softly behind her.

Once he was in the front seat, he met her eyes in the rearview mirror. "It's all over the news. I'm so sorry."

Fuck. Celeste had not even processed what had happened to Theodore, let alone how to deal with news coverage.

"Thanks, Monty." She pressed a button and the divider went up.

She dialed Savin, and he answered on the first ring. "I was just getting ready to ring you. Rani said you're on your way home. I'll meet you there."

"OK," was all Celeste could muster before she hit end call. Savin's tone was the reality check she hadn't asked for.

None of this is real. Theodore's in London, and he's coming over tonight as we planned. This is just a bad dream.

Celeste declined Monty's offer to walk her up to her apartment. "My boyfriend died; I'm not crippled," she said snidely, instantly regretting her tone. "I'm sorry, Mon. I just need some time."

"Of course. Get some rest."

"I don't need rest; I need a month's supply of Xanax and a bottle of scotch. Luckily, I have both upstairs."

Monty hugged her in an unusual display of affection. "Please let me know if you need anything at all. I can run errands. My wife can cook for you."

Celeste, touched by the kindness, nodded and said, "Sure, I'll let you know." She walked to the door held open by Jonah, who was wearing his usual ear-to-ear smile. "Long time, no see, Miss Celeste," he joked. *Well, at least lower Manhattan hasn't received the memo yet.*

"Hi, Jonah. I'm not feeling well. Savin will be arriving soon. Please send him up."

Her walk to the elevator was labored, like struggling through quicksand, and she steeled herself against the tears pooling in her eyes. *We just spoke last night. How could this happen?*

Once in her apartment, she tried to change into something more comfortable. As though she had two left hands, it took several attempts to unzip her dress and slip out of her heels. Removing her thigh highs and garter belt proved an even bigger challenge. *Why did I wear these fucking things in the first place?* She tripped while standing on one foot, landing in a heap on her closet floor. She lay there curled in a ball and finally let the tears fall. *Dead.* The word was so heavy. Just like that, the man she loved had disappeared. His good-night text the night before was the last she would receive from him, the hastened kiss as he rushed out the door to the airport the other day the last he would ever give.

I love you. She fantasized about all the times she could have told him. Walking along the beach, after the countless times they had made love, when he returned from Paris with her favorite croissant (complete with an insulated cooler and handwritten note from the pastry chef at her favorite café). *"I love you," I would say. "You mean more to me than anyone ever has. If I ever lose you, I won't know how to go on," I would tell you. And I would make sure you understood and remind you all the time, like you did to me.* Now she wouldn't have the chance, for she had squandered the opportunities time and again because of her own shortcomings. *I deserved to lose him. I never should've had him in the first place.* She waffled between berating herself and trying to rationalize ways this could be a mistake. *Shit, Sav will be here soon.*

She pulled on a blush cashmere tracksuit and padded into the living room. Savin was there, already sitting on the sofa with a drink in hand, scotch from the looks of it.

Taking one look at her face, he rushed to embrace her. "Oh, Celly, I'm so sorry." The tears came without her permission, streaming down her face, sobs wracking her body. The two stayed like that for what felt like hours, roused by a knock at the door. Savin smoothed her hair, saying, "I'm so sorry," over and over.

"I'll get it," Savin said. Celeste wiped her nose and tears on the sleeve of her sweatshirt, trying to appear presentable before realizing she did not care who was there. *Theodore is dead.*

And then Jack was there embracing her, wearing the same concern as Savin, Rani, and Monty. After what seemed like an eternity, Celeste pushed Jack away.

"OK, please stop with the pity. I'll be fine once I ... once I get used to all this."

"Celly, it's OK to be upset. I'm so sorry."

"It's so senseless. Theodore rarely flew, and he told me he was in London, not Massachusetts, this week. Why would he lie to me?"

Savin and Jack exchanged a look.

"He was supposed to come over for dinner tonight, straightaway from the airport."

"Have you watched the news coverage?"

"No. I have no desire to see what kind of circus the media makes of this," Celeste said dryly.

"Good. Wait for all this to die down. D&C released a statement immediately after we heard. We'll take care of the aftermath."

Celeste heard her iPhone vibrate with a notification. "Can you hand me my phone? It's in my bag."

Jack retrieved her phone. A *New York Post* headline taunted her on the locked screen. "Mystery Financier, Dating Ice Queen Celeste Donovan, Dead in Fiery Plane Crash." She unlocked her phone to view the article and saw herself with Theodore, all smiles at a gala a few months prior.

Jack and Savin looked over her shoulder, both fuming.

"Insensitive pricks. I'll make a call and get this pulled."

"He fucking *died*. Do they not have any ... any humanity?" A sob escaped her lips, and Celeste threw her phone across the room in a rage, satisfied with the crashing sound it made as it hit the hardwood floor.

Jack handed her a glass of scotch, a three-finger pour by the looks of it. She swallowed the drink in one gulp, letting the warmth tingle through her body.

"Another," she demanded, handing the glass to Jack. He obliged, filling it halfway. She fished out a Xanax from her pocket, washing it down with the scotch.

"What the fuck, Jack?" Savin scolded. "Trying to put her in a coma?"

"It's only Xani," Celeste said.

"Just dulling the pain a little, man. Settle down," Jack replied.

Celeste wept silently, not registering the guys talking. "I'm going to lie down. I'm fine, really. I just need sleep. Please go. No sense in me ruining your day. I'll call you when I wake up."

"Sure thing, Celly."

She walked to her bedroom and closed the door behind her. *The sunlight is deafening.* She pulled the blackout drapes closed. The light from her closet shone under the door. She entered the closet, Theodore's clothes drawing her attention. A few weeks ago, she'd had Meredith clear some space for some of Theodore's things. Meredith had been shocked at the request.

172

"Yes, of course, I can consolidate some of your things ... to, uh, make space for Theodore's, but, uh, I guess I just never thought I'd see the day that you moved things around for a man. I mean, you've always said you never wanted your Birkens and Chanels to know about each other."

"Thanks for your commentary, Meredith, though it was unnecessary. It's not a big deal. Can you have it done by tomorrow when Theodore gets back from Shanghai?"

"Absolutely."

Celeste shook herself out of the memory. *Sleep.* She took an Ambien out of its bottle in her medicine cabinet and swallowed it. Then, she climbed into bed and cried herself to sleep.

CELESTE WATCHED THEODORE'S BODY WRITHING IN PAIN. HE WAS ALIVE, but barely, his breathing uneven and raspy. His face—his beautiful, kind, open face, the face she used to lie awake at night admiring— was scrunched in agony, his body parts distorted at unnatural angles, indicating multiple broken bones. His white button-front shirt was soiled with dirt. The smell of rotting flesh burned her nostrils.

A pool of blood haloed his head, seeping across the filthy cement floor. So much blood. She heard a door slam, but she could not tear her eyes away from him. Shadows danced across the walls as a creaky metal lamp swung from the ceiling. And then they were no longer alone. The intruder strolled across the room slowly, methodically, reveling in the suffering of his prey. She immediately recognized the gait. *Omar.* She let out an audible sob as she choked back her pain, though Omar seemed unaware of her presence. The light illuminated Omar's smiling face, pure evil grinning at her lover's tortured body. Omar bent down and spoke after first landing a right hook on Theodore's bruised and bloody face.

"I'm giving you one last chance, motherfucker. Where is she?"

"Fuck you," Theodore spat, blood running down his chin.

Omar laughed maniacally, then his face distorted in fury. "I'm losing my patience!" he bellowed. "Where ... is ... Celeste?"

"I'll never tell you where she is. Kill me; I don't give a fuck." Theodore was weak, his words measured.

Omar's rage was reflected in his wide, darting eyes, a rage all too familiar to Celeste, while delivering blow after blow to Theodore. Celeste winced at the sound of skull being smashed against the concrete.

Then it came, that final blow. Theodore's body went limp, his face unrecognizable from the blood and bruising. Satisfied, Omar stood up and calmly strolled out of the room. "Clean up that mess," he barked. She was too late.

Celeste awoke to the sound of her own sobs, her pillow soaked with tears. She rolled over groggily, reaching for Theodore to tell him about her nightmare, but the bed was empty. Once she opened her eyes, everything came rushing back—the cops, disbelief and confusion, sadness, an emptiness she had never experienced. She walked into the bathroom and splashed cold water on her face. Her face was puffy and tear-streaked, and a feeling of dread and self-loathing washed over her. The prophetic dream told her all she needed to know.

Omar killed Theodore to get to me. How naïve I was to believe all those years ago that Omar wouldn't resurface and take everything I've built, everything I've become, and destroy it.

HOURS, OR MAYBE DAYS, LATER, SHE AWOKE ON HER SOFA, THE SUNLIGHT burning her eyes. Her apartment was empty now. There had been a steady stream of visitors coming through for a long time: Savin, Jack, Dina, Lorraine, Meredith, Roberto, Sam, Patrick, Tyler. Mark had called her. Business associates she hadn't spoken to for years sent her flowers and emails. Even her brother phoned in an "I'm so sorry" call. She was relieved no one was around right now.

Celeste looked down to see she was wearing the same cashmere

sweater and sweats she had put on the day she found out Theodore
was dead. She had no recollection of how long she had been sleeping
there. Was it the next day or a week later? Her skin was tight from
dried tears, and at the moment, her sadness was gone. In its place
were emptiness and the realization that this was all her fault. Omar
had to be behind Theodore's death; the timing and circumstances
were too suspect for anyone else to be responsible. She berated
herself. If only she'd been honest with Theodore, had shared Fred's
warnings with him, he would still be here with her. *But I didn't know,
Theodore; I swear I didn't know. How could I have known?* What she
could not let go of, would never forgive herself for, was that she *should
have* known Theodore could be in danger. She understood Omar's
jealous tendencies better than anyone. Of course he would swoop in
to destroy any chance she had at happiness. She recalled Ace's intel
on the extensive hacking of her accounts and whereabouts. Fred's
warnings. Lorraine's research. The rough guys she'd escaped in
Luxembourg. She'd had countless occasions to share any threats to
her safety with Theodore, to warn him he needed to be vigilant and
take extra precautions.

Her head pounded, and her mouth was dry. She walked
trancelike into the kitchen and poked her head into the refrigerator.
Ignoring the food Dina had prepared for her, she grabbed a bottle of
Perrier. She scratched her head and was startled to find her hair in
knots. *How long have I been holed up like this? Savin would know. And
where's my phone?*

Back in the living room, she found her iPhone perched on the
cocktail table. *One hundred fifteen unread texts.* She was tempted to
delete them all and go back into the Xambien coma from her Xanax
and Ambien cocktail.

She heard the front door open. "Who's there?" she asked without
conviction. *Maybe it's someone who's come to put me out of my misery.*

Savin rushed into the living room from the foyer. He stood over
her. "Celly, I've been worried. We haven't heard from you today. How
are you feeling?"

"What day is it?"

"It's Friday."

"Where's my housekeeper? She always comes on Fridays."

"Meredith put a hold on her so you could rest."

"What have I missed? My hair's in knots, and my tongue feels like it's covered in fur. Get me something to drink, please. Something strong."

Savin headed to the kitchen and returned with a glass of water.

"I have water. I need something to forget."

Savin shook his head no. "You've been having nightmares. Calling out to Theodore. Shouting warnings about Omar. I've been stopping by every day, as have a few others. You're either sleeping or sitting up staring into space. Celly, you've gotta lay off the pills. Jack and Mark disagree, think I should let you grieve, and by that they mean letting you pop pills and remain in this coma. But I can't watch you crumble like this. Theodore wouldn't have it. And his parents want you to be involved in the ... planning. I think you'll regret not being a part of it."

So many regrets.

"When's the ...," she paused and choked up. "When's the funeral?"

"Thursday. The autopsy is taking a while," Savin explained. Celeste's face fell. "Celly, I'm so sorry we have to discuss things like this."

She shrugged, unsure how to respond. "Onward to the funeral," she said.

The funeral of the only man I've ever loved. Whose death I caused. Fred had been telling the truth all those weeks ago—Celeste was in danger. What she had failed to realize was that Theodore had also been in danger. Grave danger.

THE NEXT TWO DAYS WERE A BLUR, AND CELESTE WAS DRAINED. SHE had overcommitted—planning the funeral meal, responding to inquiries, coordinating their friends. It was all too much, but it took her mind off the booze and pills she had promised Sav she would stop. Even choosing an outfit was exhausting. *Why doesn't anyone realize I don't give a shit about any of this? Theodore is gone, and therefore nothing, absolutely nothing, matters to me anymore.* Theodore's mother, Poppy Prescott, called Celeste on Sunday night after the two had been texting back and forth about the arrangements.

"Theodore Senior and I, well, he goes by Teddy, we're looking forward to spending some time with you. We'll arrive in New York tomorrow morning. Would you be available sometime early this week? I'd love to have some time with you before ... before the events," Poppy said.

I can't bear the thought of going out. "Would lunch tomorrow at my place work for you? Dina is a wonderful chef."

"Absolutely! Teddy will be tied up, but I wouldn't miss it!" The two had only met briefly in London a few months earlier, but Poppy seemed to know a lot about Celeste.

"Theodore talked about you nonstop, darling. He loved you so much, Celeste. I've never seen him like this about a woman. In fact, he never really talked to us about any woman before. We kept begging him to bring you around more, but he always claimed you two were much too busy. I'm so glad he found love, even if it was ...," she paused and inhaled sharply. "Even if it was cut short."

"Mrs. Prescott, that's so nice to hear. I fear I never deserved him, but I loved him so much—do still love him so much."

"Well, dear, that's a silly thing to say. Of course you deserved him. I look forward to seeing you. Savin said you were sick. Please take care of yourself. Theodore certainly wouldn't want you growing ill. And please call me Poppy."

They said their goodbyes, and Celeste hung up relieved. She had not left her apartment for a week and still was not ready to face the public yet. The security in her building was solid, but she knew the paparazzi were just around the corner, waiting for the "Ice Queen" to emerge. Was it too much to ask to allow a woman to grieve?

The following day, she and Meredith were in her bedroom before Poppy arrived. "You look incredible, Celeste," Meredith said. Celeste had been too distraught to even shower since she'd heard the news, so she'd asked Meredith to come over and help her look presentable for Poppy. *My dead boyfriend's mother. I wonder how she'll feel when she finds out Omar was behind it.*

Celeste looked in the mirror. Her hair was silky from her blowout, her makeup flawless. Meredith had chosen a pussy-bow burgundy cashmere sweater, cream slacks, and nude Manolo pumps for Celeste. The transformation from a few hours before to now was remarkable, but Celeste could still see the emptiness in her reflection.

"Let me take your coat, Mrs. Prescott," Celeste heard Dina say.

"It's Poppy, and thank you, dear."

"I'm so sorry for your loss, Poppy. We all loved Theodore. Such a magical soul."

"Wish me luck," Celeste said under her breath to Meredith, then went out to greet Poppy. Dina had been bustling about all morning, preparing an elaborate lunch for them. Celeste would have to force the food down; the only food she had been able to consume since Theodore died was one of Dina's Vitamix concoctions.

Poppy was as beautiful and polished as Celeste remembered. She was dressed in slim-fitting navy wool slacks and a blouse that matched her eyes, eyes the exact shade of Theodore's. *Eighty-five-millimeter Jimmy Choo pumps at her age. Impressive.* Her hair was the same raven shade as Theodore's, though hers was clearly from a colorist. When she saw Celeste enter the room, her eyes lit up and she smiled that easy, familiar smile that was all Theodore.

Poppy walked over to Celeste and embraced her tightly. The kind of full-body mom hug that was always held several beats too long. The kind of hug Celeste had not had since her parents died. The kind of hug Celeste avoided because it made her cry.

Poppy released Celeste after what felt like thirty minutes. "Hello, dear. So lovely to see you. It's startling how much he resembles me, isn't it? Ever since ... well, ever since we found out about Theodore, his father regards me with the same haunted look you have on your face. Teddy says it's like seeing a ghost."

"It's uncanny." Celeste choked up. "I miss his face, Poppy. I miss everything about him," Celeste stammered before she could stop the words from tumbling out. "I've never been so sad, not even when I lost my family. Today's the first day I've showered in I don't know how long, and Meredith had to help me because I was too weak to stand. I feel so empty." She stopped herself, mortified. "Oh my God, Poppy, I'm so sorry. How selfish of me to go on and on, as though you're not grieving the loss of a child."

"No apology necessary. I miss him, too, dear. God, how I miss him. Every second of every day, I still can't believe my only child is gone. And it was preventable! If he were still here, I might have killed him myself for doing something so dangerous as flying during a winter storm. He always was a bit reckless." A tearful smile crossed Poppy's face. "Well, let's see what feast Dina has prepared, shall we? My mouth was watering from the aroma all the way down in the lobby!"

Celeste's heart sank. What if she could not keep up the charade? She lowered her eyes, lest they give away her shame, and her mind raced. *Poppy, what if you knew it wasn't his fault? That he was in London when he was killed, not flying a plane in Massachusetts. And that my ex-boyfriend murdered him. Would you still greet me warmly with a smile? If you ever did find out, how could I survive the shame, seeing the disappointment in your eyes, Theodore's eyes? Did he know I was behind it all when he was kidnapped? Did he resent me?* Then her mind asked the question she had been avoiding. *Did he stop loving me?* Tears fell, but then Celeste realized she was missing this moment, this rare opportunity to be with Theodore's mom. *No more self-pity. Today is not about my guilt journey. Today is about getting to know Theodore's mother.*

Poppy was as compassionate, charismatic, and lively as Celeste would have expected from a woman who raised such a phenomenal son, and once Celeste got out of her head, the two had an easy rapport. Poppy chatted on and on, telling story after story of Theodore's youth.

"You poor dear. Theodore told me you lost your family, and at such a young age. He considered you his family." Poppy's face darkened for a moment, and then she continued. "It's truly so magical you two found each other."

Poppy kept up a happy chatter over their Nicoise salads and fruit tarts. As the meal was coming to a close, Celeste needed some liquid courage. She motioned to Dina to refill their wine glasses. "Poppy, um, this is awkward to discuss ... but we expect there will be a lot of media types and photographers at the funeral. It's just the way New York is, and ..." *May as well be honest about this at least, Celeste.* "Well, people love to gossip here, and about me in particular, so the press has been tormenting me with headlines all week. I haven't left the building since the day I found out he died."

"Oh, my! That sounds terrible, dear, and while you're grieving, too. I'm so sorry. Teddy and I will provide a statement to spare you in all of this."

I deserve to suffer. Out loud, Celeste replied, "A reprieve, even for the funeral, would be amazing." Poppy's face lit up, and she retrieved her phone from her handbag.

"Good, it's done then. I'll call our publicist, and we'll hold a brief press conference tomorrow."

Celeste's energy was depleted by the time Poppy left that afternoon, but only because she had enjoyed herself for the first time in a long time. Poppy was a delight, the perfect balance of motherly and fun. Celeste wished the two could have spent more time together while Theodore was alive. She knew he would have been thrilled to see how well they got on.

CELESTE HALF EXPECTED OMAR TO SHOW UP AT THE FUNERAL, MOSTLY because Ace's paranoia was getting to her. Ace did not approve of her attending the funeral ("You're a sitting duck, Celeste") and had demanded that Angelo hire extra staff to man the door. Not only were they all wary of an Omar cameo, but the statement issued by the Prescotts and picked up by Page Six had hardly called off the paparazzi. Still, Celeste was touched by the gesture and had read her favorite part several times:

> Our son Theodore would be shocked and enraged by the
> lack of respect and humanity shown to the woman he loved
> and with whom he wanted to spend his life, Celeste Donovan.
> In fact, he intended to ask her to marry him before we lost
> him in a tragic and untimely accident. Out of respect for Ms.
> Donovan and our late son, we urge the press to stop making
> a circus of our pain.

He wanted to spend his life with me. See, Omar? Theodore was a man who loved, who built people up, and you are a man who destroys everything you touch. Including me.

Monty stopped the car at the corner of Fifth Avenue and Fiftieth Street in front of the recently renovated behemoth church the morning of the funeral. Celeste was surrounded by Savin, Mark, Jack, and Angelo's crew as they rushed her inside, dodging the journalists shouting questions. She did not relax until they were in the church, where the security was strategically placed to check people in.

Celeste hugged her friends and walked alone toward the altar, stopping at the front row, where Poppy and Teddy were seated alone. When Poppy saw Celeste, she rushed to her and embraced her. Theodore's father gave her a kiss on each cheek. "You'll sit with us; we insist. You're family," he said.

"OK. And thank you for your beautiful statement yesterday." She sat down next to them.

"We meant every word. You were our son's favorite person. We only wish you'd had more time together," Teddy said, smiling sadly. He was a handsome man, a full head of silver hair, a tan evidencing a leisurely life of traveling well, and laugh lines. Theodore got his height from his father, who was a head taller than Celeste.

Celeste was relieved she did not have to watch the hordes of people entering the church behind her. Poppy was weeping silently, Teddy's arm around her slim shoulders. Celeste struggled to hold back her own tears while she stared numbly at the silver casket on the altar. All of Wall Street seemed to take pleasure in her mourning, and the *New York Post* had been posting daily polls over the past week, including what the Ice Queen would wear to the funeral and whether she would even show at all. It was humiliating, and even though she did not want to let them see her cry, she could no longer hold it in. She retrieved a handkerchief from her handbag and blotted her tears.

She went through the motions of the service but had no recollection of what it entailed, not even realizing it was over until she saw the casket being carried down the aisle to the back of the church. Savin was a pallbearer, along with Edward and Triston, both of whom she had not seen since the night she met Theodore, and three other men whom she presumed were Theodore's friends from London. Her body was racked with sobs when it hit her that this was the last time she would be in the same place as Theodore's body, which would be flown to London for the burial.

When everyone but her closest friends had retreated outside, Celeste went to the bathroom, pulled a flask out of her handbag, and washed down a Xanax.

"She's unraveling," she had heard Patrick whisper to Tyler that morning. *He's right. I'm merely a shell of my former self, and I need to get my shit together. Tomorrow I will. I'm just too sad today.* But Celeste had been telling herself the same thing all week—she would stop the pills. *Soon.*

She had already given herself permission to make only a brief appearance at the funeral meal and head straight home. Savin had promised to entertain Poppy and Teddy when everything wrapped up, though if they felt anything like Celeste, they would prefer to be alone.

Celeste walked outside and stood in an awkward receiving line with Theodore's parents. The New York winter temperature was at a record-setting low, and Celeste was grateful she could flee shortly after the service was over. She promised Poppy and Teddy she would meet them in an hour at the restaurant for the funeral meal, and then Monty and Angelo rushed her to the car in an attempt to dodge the media types still hanging around. Savin and Jack sat in the back seat waiting for her.

"We sent everyone away so you could have some time to yourself. Here," Jack said, holding a flask in his outstretched hand. She brought it to her lips and took a long swig.

Later, Celeste sat next to her friends—Jack, Savin, Mark, Jin, Roberto, and Sam—for an early dinner at Cipriani. She could not force herself to put food in her mouth or participate in conversation, especially because everyone was treating her with kid gloves. After two dirty martinis, she'd had all she could take. *I can't bear the crushing weight of sadness any longer.* She texted Monty to pick her up, and Jack, noticing she had decided to leave, stood up and accompanied her to say goodbye to Theodore's parents. "Poppy, Teddy, I'm so sorry to leave early, but I'm not feeling well. Savin said he'd happily escort you back to your hotel."

Poppy looked at her with concern lining her face, though she had probably taken as many sedatives as Celeste. "Yes, dear, I understand. Get some sleep. We're staying the week, so perhaps we could have dinner again before we head back to London. We'd love to spend more time with you." Poppy stood up and embraced Celeste warmly. Celeste awkwardly returned her embrace.

Teddy nodded in agreement and shook Celeste's hand when Poppy released her. "I haven't had a single conversation with Theodore in the last year where he didn't mention you, Celeste. I'm glad we've gotten to meet, but I wish it could've been under different circumstances." Tears pooled in his eyes.

"Thank you for that, and yes, dinner later this week sounds lovely. Good night."

Jack silently walked her to the car where Monty was waiting, his somber expression weighing on Celeste. *Theodore, why did you have to go? Why couldn't it have been me? That's who Omar really wanted.* Jack hugged her, and she got into the back seat before she started crying again. Monty closed the door, and Jack turned to walk into the restaurant.

"One last thing, Jack," she called to him. "Tell the press to fuck off." Jack smiled because he was walking right past the entire press corps of the gossip rags in New York and knew she intended them to hear.

"I'll see what I can do," he said, winking. Celeste rolled up her window and closed her eyes in relief that the funeral was over.

PART II

AFTER

9

HE WILL NOT HURT ANOTHER PERSON
I LOVE

I t felt like an eternity had passed since Celeste had spent those
wonderful weeks with Theodore in Europe. Her memories with
Theodore were some of the best of her life, and she felt cheated to
have lost him so suddenly and so prematurely. *Who will Omar take
from me next?* She thought of her brother and his family, Savin, Mark,
Jin, and the baby. Her enemy had plenty of resources and played
dirty. Violating international law, murdering innocent people, tearing
families apart—none of it mattered to Omar, a formidable enemy
paying her back for what she and Savin had done a decade prior.
That had to be what Omar's revenge was about—the Biochrome
short.

How the mighty have fallen. Celeste scowled as she surveyed her
surroundings. A third-rate fetid motel room in Frankfurt paid up for
two weeks in cash. Ace had warned her to be careful, and she was not
taking any chances. She surprised herself with her commitment to
fight for her life. She hadn't realized she had so much to live for, so
many people to protect. As tempting as it was to find Omar and beg
for mercy, she doubted that would solve anything. Her loved ones
were in danger until she finished him off.

She recalled her last conversation with Sav before she fled New York, and a wave of sadness overwhelmed her.

"Celeste, I can't let you do this. It was my scheme that caused us to cross Omar in the first place." She had stood at the window in his office, her back to him, eyes glued to the Manhattan skyscrapers. As much as she loved New York, it seemed an ugly and cruel place lately with its overcast sky and decrepit buildings, her overwhelming melancholy a dismal overlay. She had no energy to placate Savin, nor was she going to change course. She had made her decision. She massaged her temples, hoping it would prevent her from exploding in rage.

"I'm the one Omar is after, and I'm the only one who can fix this. He wants something from me, and I'm going to find out what it is without putting anyone in danger."

"Celeste, Omar won't hesitate to kill you. Celly! Look at me. We drove him out of town years ago without him discovering your involvement. We can take care of it again through our network; it does *not* have to be you." The fear in his eyes was disconcerting, but Celeste refused to back down.

She turned to face him and laughed at the irony of his words. "Savin, we clearly didn't take care of it before. I put my guard down with Theodore's ... death and the funeral, but I can't ignore this any longer. Omar's probably alerted his entire network to try to find me, putting a price on my head or whatever else he wants. The only way he'll spare everyone I love is if I do what he wants. I have to go to him once I get a little more information. Besides, what do you propose is our alternative? Shall we call NYPD?" She mimed holding a phone up to her ear. "Yes, officer, my ex-boyfriend who has an explosive temper and a disgusting coke habit told his criminal network he is after me. Oh, and he's also involved in arms dealing, wire fraud, insider trading, murder, and the list goes on. Proof? No, I have no proof, except Fred told me. Oh, who is Fred? Well, until recently, he was our mortal enemy. No, I don't know how Fred knows."

She rolled her eyes and addressed Savin once more. "What does alerting the authorities get us? A few dead officers when they try to investigate him? Should we call the Feds? Maybe Omar will harm their wives and children. Wait, maybe the Ghostbusters can help us, since he moves in and out of the country undetected by anyone. Hmm ..." She straightened up and decided to deal head-on with this nonsense. "Let me be clear, Savin," she said with an ominous intensity that frightened even herself, "I'm not asking for permission. I told you only because I didn't want you to worry."

She softened as she saw the tears in his eyes, his face twisted in a distraught frown. "You have to trust me, Sav. I'm the only one who can do this, the only one who can handle him, the only one who can get rid of him. Deep down, you know this. And you know that I, and I alone, started this years ago. I saw with my own eyes what he was capable of when he was spiraling out of control, and I still proceeded with our idiotic scheme. It was fortuitous that he never found out back then that we were behind Biochrome. I won't put anyone in danger. It's settled. You'll carry on as though I am away on business, and I'll be in touch when I can. In the meantime, you'll keep everyone, Angelo, Lorraine, Rani, Jack, and Mark, in the dark to the extent that you can. Please do this for me. Please do not let me be the reason Omar hurts someone."

"Celly, you know I would never do anything to put you in danger. But please reconsider."

"I've made up my mind, Sav. Please try to understand." She walked over to him and hugged him tightly, then turned and walked out of his office with feigned confidence. Sav relied on her calm, always had, and she needed to ensure that he knew only enough to stay grounded and not do anything rash while she was away. She was playing to his instincts to keep her safe, for he recognized that meddling would only endanger her. She hadn't shared with Savin or the others that she was sure Omar was behind Theodore's death. There was no way they would let her leave if they knew. Keeping everyone in the dark, at least for the time being, was much better.

Celeste walked down the hall to Rani's desk. "Rani, I'm stealing away for a few weeks. A spa in St. Moritz and then maybe some hopping around to end up in Paris. I've been so out of sorts with the funeral and all the craziness around here. Can you keep Sav in line while I'm gone?"

"Celly, Savin will be fine; he always is ... eventually!" The women laughed. "I'll book your flight and accommodations now. What's the name of the spa?"

Rani had been telling Celeste to take some time off for weeks now and seemed happy with the development. Celeste smiled convincingly, her dimples puckered. "No, darling, I've got it covered. The spa staff took care of my arrangements. I'm paying a fortune, so they ought to!"

Rani did not appear to suspect anything was amiss, even with the round-the-clock security at the firm, or at least she was polite enough not to let on that she knew something was awry. Celeste opted to get out while she was ahead.

"I'm going to my apartment now to ensure I have time to pack. I have no idea what to bring. At least at Canyon Ranch, I knew to dress for dinner. I'll err on the safe side like I usually do and overpack to make sure I'm prepared for all scenarios."

Rani laughed, and then rolled her eyes as Savin summoned her. "Ran, get in here ..."

That was Celeste's cue to get out before Rani began asking more questions ... or before Sav lost it again and barricaded her in the office. She had scrambled to the elevator, relieved she did not have to lie anymore.

Celeste shook herself out of the memory, sweating from the damp heat sputtering out of what she imagined was supposed to be an air conditioner circa 1930. She had left New York over three weeks ago and was no closer to ensnaring Omar. She sat on the lumpy bed and frowned at the yellowing, faded flower print of the bedspread. The smell of mold and stale semen stung her nostrils and made her eyes water.

Ace had not contacted her again since he helped her leave the States without a trace. It was disconcerting, and she had begun to wonder if Ace were working with Omar. *Or is the solitude just making me paranoid?* Either way, it meant she was on her own this time and could not count on any of his intel. She pulled her newly purchased iPad Pro and Apple Pen out of her duffel and sat down on the bed once more. Ace had provided her with an impossible-to-hack dinosaur Lenovo laptop, but she could never be too sure that he or anyone else she employed was trustworthy.

CELESTE LOOKED OVER HER SCRIBBLES AND TRIED TO FIND THE COMMON thread. She had listed every major deal she thought Omar was involved in over the last seven years. He had bet against the market every time—yet had made billions. It was not above Omar to be involved in insider trading or Ponzi schemes, but deals of this size should have attracted the attention of regulators somewhere. Yet even after she and Ace had called in favors and offered bribes, they could find no trace of audits or investigation. She heaved her pen against the wall, sighing heavily. She was running out of time; she could not be on the run for much longer before Omar tracked her down. *And then what?* She had no idea what would happen when she saw him. She closed her eyes, fighting tears, and lay back against the lumpy, wilted pillows.

As she often did these days, Celeste indulged in the saccharine memory of Theodore whispering "I love you" to her in the twilight glow. It had only been a couple of months before that they had stolen away for a long weekend in St. Barth's, though it felt as if a lifetime had passed since then. She could almost feel the warm evening breeze rustling her golden mane and could see his almost-black hair waving around. For the first time in a long time, or perhaps ever, Celeste saw a pure, sincere love in a man's eyes. His clear blue eyes twinkled with mischief, as always, but this time they also shone with vulnerability, pleading her to say the same, as always supremely patient with her shortcomings.

"Celeste, I don't intend to pressure you, but know that I'm sticking around for a while. You're the most intoxicating woman I've ever met." How she longed to feel his arms around her once more, to feel him nibbling her ear and caressing her nipple through her sundress, taunting her with his hardness against her back as she stood against him that night. But her carelessness had destroyed him, and for her sins, she had paid dearly. Now it was someone else's turn to pay. *Omar, I will destroy you, or I will die trying.*

She could not stay in Frankfurt any longer. She was hitting dead end after dead end, and pretty soon she would run out of regulators to bribe, stalk, and entrap, not to mention how quickly one misstep would blow her cover. Yes, it was time to move, but where would she go next? Some of the top financial epicenters—Brussels, London, Frankfurt—had left her empty-handed. If she were in Omar's position, where would she turn? *No*, she corrected herself, *where would he turn to blackmail, strong-arm, deceive, even murder, to unleash his rage about me slipping past him?*

Celeste walked herself through several scenarios, but the only one that actually played out in her favor was the last-resort plan she had come up with in New York. She had hoped, wished, prayed even, that she would uncover something, anything, with which to trap Omar so that she would not have to deploy this dangerous plan. How was he getting by without any authorities anywhere intervening? The money was real, and yes, it was buried in a string of LLCs and overseas accounts, but if she could trace the money, then surely someone else was monitoring what he was doing, the trail of cryptocurrency transactions he used for arms dealing, his involvement with human trafficking and cocaine trade organizations. But they were all dead ends—nothing seemed to motivate law enforcement to pursue charges against one of the richest, most powerful men in the world. Celeste had to take matters into her own hands, if for no other reason than to avenge Theodore's death and protect everyone else she loved.

Her plan was modeled on the media manipulation tactics she and Savin had employed at D&C and on a bust that had happened a few years earlier. In a desire to cut down on corruption in Saudi Arabia, the new king had indicted hundreds of men on corruption charges. The market responded dramatically, and one man had lost billions of dollars in a single day. It was going to take something on this scale, something that regulators could not ignore, to take Omar down. She had to act on her plan in a market that would respond, and she had to do it without Ace or anyone from home discovering what she had planned.

Celeste would fly to Dubai to pick up supplies—money, new passports (she had already used the two Ace had given her), suitable clothing—from someone she had trusted for many years, Zari, who would then arrange for a helicopter to transport Celeste to Riyadh, Saudi Arabia. Once there, she and a man who looked like Omar, Hadid, would stage having sex in public, a crime punishable by death in Saudi Arabia. Hadid was Egyptian, but he looked nearly identical to Omar. He was a businessman who had ties to Saudi law enforcement and knew how to clean up messes. She had no idea how Zari had found someone who looked like Omar so quickly and in the right place at the right time, but then again, she did not need to know. Hadid could guarantee her safe escape from the country. Once she was safely on her way out of Saudi, Hadid would facilitate the release of edited video with Omar's face on it to every major media outlet across the world. He confirmed that the video release would be swift and coordinated. The market would respond accordingly, understanding that Omar's imminent death would render his holding company meaningless, and the value of his holding company would tank before he could do anything to stop it. Hadid had urged Celeste to hire another woman to be on the ground, but she refused to put someone else in harm's way. She could not risk Omar hurting another woman.

After spending several hours arranging for the wire transfers and ensuring that everyone was in place, Celeste was satisfied that she had an infallible plan. She smiled a genuine smile, the first in a long time, and hopped off the bed to prepare for her next trip. She was going to focus on this game of cat and mouse as a meditation in motion, as her guru was always saying, and once it was all over in a few days, she could finally return to New York, where she would no longer have to wonder when Omar would strike next. Knowing he would be stripped of his influence and money and would end up behind bars, if not sentenced to death in Saudi, made the past few weeks and the next few days ahead of her tolerable.

After a quick shower, Celeste wiped everything down to conceal any fingerprints she may have left, humming to herself. Finally she had something to focus on besides Theodore's death. She was going to pull this off and ruin Omar's fortune and life. *Your number is up this time, Omar.*

Her enthusiasm faded, though, when she saw her reflection in the smudged mirror hanging crooked on the wall by the flimsy, cigarette smoke-stained door of her motel room. Gone were the long flaxen locks and gleaming skin of a woman routinely mistaken for a supermodel; gazing back at her was the sallow, emaciated face of a stranger with lackluster brown hair. She had already suffered so much, and now she had to endure this hideous disguise. An image of Theodore's body writhing in pain as Omar tortured him leaped to the front of her mind in that moment, and she resolutely swallowed her longing for her old self. In its place rose a protectiveness for her loved ones. *He will not hurt another person I love.* With that, she strode out of the motel room, closing the door silently.

FLYING PRIVATE FROM THE US TO PARIS WAS ONE THING, BUT SWOOPING in and out of Western European countries in a Gulfstream was sure to call more attention to Celeste's travels than flying commercial, so she decided to depart from the Frankfurt airport.

"Whatever you do, do *not* fly commercial," Ace had warned her a few months ago when they were discussing precautions after Omar returned.

Well, Ace, I don't have much choice now, do I?

Celeste knew she was unremarkable now in her dumpy clothes (her attire was gray and baggy these days with a ball cap and sunglasses to hide her face), so blending in at the airport would be simple. She exited the subway doors of the S-Bahn at the Frankfurt Airport stop. *The subway to the airport,* she mused as the doors opened. *I guess this is still how the other half lives. Not that I was ever curious to experience being poor again.* Just then, a tall, hefty man startled Celeste, shouting unintelligibly in German and shoving her aside. She stumbled and nearly toppled over her duffel bag, which had slipped off her arm and onto the ground, but rather than engage in a screaming match with the asshole, as the old Celeste would have done, she rolled her eyes and kept moving, determined to remain inconspicuous. She wove in and out of the crowd, careful to keep her head down so no cameras could capture her face.

Moving at a calculated pace toward her gate, she cleared security and customs. Hunger pangs distracted her, but she could not stomach food these days. Her formerly lithe, feminine body had transformed into a rack of skin and bones from starvation and lack of her usual toning and cardio activity. As she walked through the behemoth airport, she took mental inventory of what remained in her safe deposit box in Paris. Two more passports, meaning only two more identities; the equivalent of $1 million in cash, with a quarter each in US dollars, euros, yen, and shillings; and credit cards in each name. What she needed the most, though, was in Dubai, and it was not a thing, but a person, some information, and indirect access to Saudi Arabia. She ran through her plan step-by-step in her head as she had been doing all morning. *You can never be too prepared.*

As she veered left to her gate, a man walking at a cautious distance behind her caught her eye. He looked vaguely familiar, and now she remembered he was the aggressive man getting off the S-Bahn. *A coincidence?* No, she did not believe in coincidences, especially not when Omar was involved. What if this man who was seemingly following her was on her flight? *How stupid I was to fly commercial.* She realized the danger of being trapped on a plane with someone who wanted to kill her or, at the very least, was tasked with kidnapping her. She would have to find another way to Dubai.

GRATEFUL SHE HAD NOT SKIMPED ON PACKING MAKEUP, SHE SAT IN THE bathroom stall and finished her handiwork using her compact mirror and a concealer palette. *Voilà!* She pulled the burner phone out of her duffel and searched for what she needed. She memorized the airport layout and reminded herself to move more intentionally this time.

She was certain the man would be waiting for her outside the restroom and was hopeful that her clothing change and hoodie would be enough to throw him off for a few minutes. Just long enough to get a head start. She ducked out of the restroom and turned away from the man, who had looked in the other direction for a moment. She exhaled when she realized he had not noticed her. *Perfect!* She broke into a run toward the German airport security department, praying that he would not catch up to her before she could plead for help.

Celeste explained in rough German to the sympathetic guard behind the security desk that she was in grave danger. You see, she explained, her ex-husband had followed her here and was likely to harm her as he had done just a few days before, which explained the "bruising" of her eye and cheekbones she had skillfully created. "Is there any way, kind sir, that you could help me?" Though she was not pretty like she used to be, she was still charming enough. The guard relented and offered to call for help.

Satisfied that he would cooperate, she accepted his gesture to walk behind the counter and enter a closed door into a tiny room, her eyes glued to the security monitors inside. Luck was on her side, as the giant man was easy to spot. He was on the move again, no doubt realizing she was no longer in the women's restroom. Celeste heard the security guard convey her situation over the radio to his fellow *Bundespolizei*, describing the man as potentially armed and dangerous. He poked his head into the closet to assure her that the man would be caught.

"We've got it under control and will have him in custody momentarily. No need to worry, Miss ..."

"You can call me Bobbi." She gazed up through her long lashes timidly. "You've saved my life. Thank you so much." *One henchman down, who knows how many to go.*

In English, the security guard introduced himself as Lars and promised to let her know when the man was detained. "Bobbi, is there someone you can call to arrange for a safe transfer?"

"I wish we had met under better circumstances, Lars. Is there an exit that's not publicly accessible? I fear that this man ... er, my ex," she gestured toward the monitor, "is not working alone. If there is any way I could leave undetected, well, I'd be forever grateful. And yes, I do have someone I can call if I can get to the private hangar." She flashed her smile.

She was too spooked to fly commercial at this point. She had one resource in Europe that no one knew about. She would have to contact him and arrange another means out of the airport. She feared her life depended on it.

"I'm not supposed to tell anyone about this, but ... see this little door over here? This takes you into a stairwell that is not on the building blueprints for this very sort of situation." *Celeste 1, Omar 0.*

Her disguise was blown, maybe, but not the fake name on her passport. Omar had the resources to put an alert on her real name, expecting her to be stupid enough to use it. Still underestimating her. It must be driving him crazy not knowing where she was or what she was doing. Her brother's pregnant wife popped into her head, and concern for the safety of everyone she loved flooded her thoughts. Though she and her brother had never been close, there was love between them nonetheless. Celeste realized that if she failed at this attempt to frame Omar, the body count would mount—her sister-in-law, her brother, Savin, Mark, Lorraine, anyone close to her—with bizarre but believable causes of death like sailing accidents or overdosing from drug addictions they never had or being hit by a bus. *Or crashing a plane into a mountain.*

Lars provided her with a police escort down the stairwell, and another officer was waiting at the exit door to escort her to the private hangar.

TWO HOURS LATER, SHE WAS SAFELY TEN THOUSAND FEET IN THE AIR ON a luxury G550 to Dubai, leaving no trace of the disappearance of Bobbi, the woman being hunted by her "ex-husband." Only then did Celeste allow herself to exhale. She would not make the mistake of going to a public airport again and felt comfortable with the flight attendant and pilot, who were paid handsomely to keep her identity hidden. She would stay in a safe house in Dubai for a day or so to pick up the things Zari had arranged, and then she would move on to Riyadh.

Celeste could not afford to make any more mistakes. Of all the places she could have chosen to pull off a media scandal, Riyadh was one of the most dangerous. Since 2006, commercial developers had aspired to make Riyadh an influential financial hub and invested billions to that end. However, there was still much to be done to overhaul the Saudi regulatory system to provide an environment as favorable as Dubai for financial institutions. Cultural changes would also have to occur to attract expats, as women were still marginalized, required to wear long black robes called abayas and not allowed to travel alone or speak to men in public. They were only recently granted the right to drive. Blasphemy, which could be interpreted broadly by the judiciary, was punishable by death and could include petty crimes. This tension between the conservative Saudi culture and the desire to diversify the economy to reduce reliance on oil made it the perfect location for Celeste's revenge against Omar to play out.

Celeste twisted the top off a bottle of Evian water and washed down an Ambien. *Please, if there is a God, let me sleep.* The nightmares about Theodore seemed more vivid with each passing night, assuming she was able to sleep at all. They came again, flashing behind her eyes with painstaking detail that left her sobbing aloud in her sleep. Rani's call to her that two NYPD officers were at the reception desk for her, asking if Celeste wanted them in a conference room. "No, have them come to my office." Afterward, she struggled to find the words, how she knew in that moment that Theodore was dead, how she doubled over, clutched her abdomen, wincing in pain, unable to catch her breath. She remembered thinking, *So this is what a panic attack feels like. Being strangled from the inside.*

She did not know that day that Omar was behind Theodore's "accident." No, it had taken her a few weeks to put it all together. Once Omar's involvement became clear, it was only a matter of hours before she understood the extent of his destruction.

THE SOUND OF THE WHEELS HITTING THE TARMAC STARTLED CELESTE awake. Groggy, she looked around to see the female flight attendant walking toward her. They had not exchanged names. "Miss, we've arrived in Dubai. Is there anything else I can get for you?" Thin and well dressed, the woman wore her hair in a sophisticated chignon, and her bone structure was flawless.

Celeste stood up to stretch, embarrassed about her sloppy attire. "No, no, thank you. You've done so much already." *Understatement of the year, since she saved my life.*

The pilot came out to greet Celeste once again, a tiny, fierce woman with eyes that sparkled when she smiled, reminding her of Theodore. "I hope you had a chance to sleep on the flight."

"Thanks to you both, truly. Your kindness ...," Celeste swallowed back a sob as the enormity of the events of the past several weeks hit her, then continued, "... well, it means the world to me." *Keep it together, Celeste.*

"Our pleasure. Your driver is outside. Are you ready?"

Celeste imagined this was not the first time these women had delivered someone to safety undetected, their nonchalance a tell.

"One more thing, honey ... this may be a man's world right now, but you're right to fight. Whatever it is you're fighting, keep going."

"It's not easy taking on—" She stopped short, realizing this was not a normal conversation between two women commiserating about how they made seventy-six cents for every dollar a man made. "Well, I must be going. I can't thank you enough." She shook the hands of both women and placed the duffel over her shoulder. She walked out of the plane and down the stairs to the armored Maybach that was waiting to drive her to the helipad. Zari stood by the car. He was a Persian man in his late twenties, tall, thin, with chiseled bone structure and a wide smile. He walked toward her and took her duffel. He grinned briefly when she smiled in recognition, but then replaced the grin with the somber, sexless gaze required of men in this part of the world.

"Hello, Miss Celeste," said Zari. He furrowed his brow, peering closely at her face. "Has someone hurt you?"

Celeste had forgotten about the makeup. "Oh, no, no, Zari, I'm fine! It's makeup."

Zari smiled with relief.

Celeste was in unfamiliar territory these days when she had control over so little. Her only option, if she could even call it an option when she had no other choices, was to trust that this man she knew from her old life would keep her safe and not reveal her presence in Dubai to Omar.

"It's so great to see a familiar face these days. I trust you've received instructions."

"Yes. Pardon for rushing you, Miss Celeste, but we do need to hurry. The chopper is waiting."

"OK." She slid into the back door he opened for her and caught a glimpse of a Caracal pistol with a silencer on the front passenger seat. The implications of the handgun sent a shiver throughout her body. She situated herself in the car, and they drove across the tarmac to the helipad in silence. She remembered a simpler time when she and Zari would banter on drives, before her life took on this somber tone.

Tomorrow it begins ... or ends, as it were. She walked through the plan mentally once more, realizing for the first time its myriad shortcomings. She had no choice but to rely on sheer luck and her own memory of Riyadh from a previous visit to pull off what would be the biggest media manipulation since Qatar accused the UAE of financial warfare by releasing false news stories about its currency, the riyal, a few years prior.

10

HIDING IN PLAIN SIGHT

Once Celeste and Zari were buckled in with their helicopter headphones in place, Celeste relaxed a bit. Too late to turn back now. May as well enjoy the ride.

"It has been a long time, Miss Celeste! I have news! My wife and I are taking the children to America to visit the family of my brother-in-law in a few months."

"Wow, I'm so thrilled to hear it! You've been planning a visit for a long time. Send me the dates, and I'll have Rani, my right-hand woman, plan everything. I insist. Take it as a thank-you from Savin and me for all your kindness over the years. Maybe we could meet you for lunch one day if you have time. I'd love to meet Nasrin."

Celeste trailed off as she realized it was entirely possible the lunch would never happen—or at least may happen without her there. As was typical these days, her happiness switched to melancholy, reminding her why she was here. This was her new reality—life as a ghost, drifting from continent to continent without so much as a faded passport stamp to prove her existence.

She turned away from Zari and gazed out the helicopter window as the high-rises whizzed by below. The Burj Al Arab, a futuristic building designed to resemble the shape of a sail, glowed in the distance, fading from blue to purple and back to blue, and the half moon was mirrored on the calm Persian Gulf. Glittering at a stunning 2,722 feet in the air, the Burj Khalifa more than doubled the tallest of the other high-rises, awe-inducing by its height-to-thinness ratio if not its sheer magnitude. The Burj Khalifa was the world's tallest building, at least for the time being. In typical Dubai style, the ground was already broken and construction under way for the next world's tallest building, the Kingdom Tower, which would surpass the Burj.

"Yes, Miss Celeste, I will certainly provide the dates when we will be visiting America. My son is counting down the days to finally see the USA!"

"How old is Shah now?" Celeste and Savin sent lavish gifts every year for the children's birthdays, but that was actually Rani's doing, not hers—she would not know what to buy for a child.

"He is five years old but acts like an adult—already wants to learn how to drive, even has a girlfriend in his class. And our daughter, Samar ... we will have trouble with that one! In fact, she reminds me of you. Strong, knows what she wants and wants only that, even at two and a half years old." The two laughed. The last few times she had been in Dubai had been a whirlwind trip with Theodore, and she had not seen Zari. They had a lot to catch up on.

The ride passed quickly, no more than fifteen minutes, with stories of Zari's children, Celeste allowing herself to set aside worry for a moment. They descended to the well-lit helipad on a high-rise adjacent to the Burj Khalifa. In any other city, Celeste might have been fearful of detection, but she knew that Dubai kept arrivals and departures tight-lipped. Thanks to the short list of useful wisdom Omar had imparted to her, and unbeknownst to the rest of the world, there was not even an official aviation record of comings and goings in Dubai, allowing Celeste to take full advantage of her phantom status. It was ironic that she was using so much information gained from Omar in an attempt to beat him at his own game.

Once safely on the ground, Zari helped Celeste climb out of the helicopter. Celeste nodded to the pilot, then followed Zari to the doorway into the building. She knew Zari had tended to all the details and that the security camera reels had stopped rolling while they descended into the apartment that would harbor her for the next few hours. She would use the space and safety to finalize details.

The best time in any given week for breaking news to impact the global financial markets was Wednesday around 10 a.m. Greenwich Mean Time, the local time in London. Riyadh was three hours ahead, so the "event" she was planning would have to occur at precisely 1 p.m. Wednesday Arabian Standard Time. Celeste had little over forty hours to meet with her contact in Dubai, pick up the materials, make her way to Riyadh, and get settled into the safe house. All without raising alarms that she was leaving UAE and entering Saudi Arabia as an American in a time of chaos in the region. She had gambled that Omar was looking for her in London and hoped her Plan B bait and switch in Frankfurt had been successful. She banked on his men searching the train routes and private hangars all over Europe, assuming she would not set foot in Dubai, that Dubai would be too difficult a place for her to hide. *Hiding in plain sight is always best, they say.*

Celeste followed Zari down a fluorescent stairwell to the parking garage. Lambos, Ferraris, Maseratis, Rolls in all shapes and colors. The apartments in this building were cost-prohibitive, even for someone with Celeste's net worth, and usually available only to those who had made fortunes from criminal activity such as illegal arms trading or harvesting opiates. The morals of whoever was loaning her their place were of little concern to Celeste, though, with so much at stake. The garage appeared empty as she followed Zari to an elevator bank. He was reading something on his phone with a frown.

"Is something wrong, Zari?"

"Let's get inside where we can talk freely."

Zari took Celeste's duffel and led her to the elevator. He scanned the key fob in front of the sensor and then pushed ninety. The express elevator reached the destination in seconds, and the doors opened into the most beautiful apartment Celeste had ever seen. Under normal circumstances, she would have contacted the building owner and put a bid on something in the building. But these were not normal times, and she barely noticed the panoramic view of Dubai. Two black duffel bags caught Celeste's attention, out of place in the opulent, immaculate apartment. Zari walked over to the bags and carried them to the enormous dining room, nodding to Celeste to follow.

He opened the bags and began placing their contents on the table.

"What do you have for me, Zari?"

"Everything we could think of to keep you safe, Miss." There were two burner phones, two US passports and a German passport, and large stacks of cash in euros, Emirati dirham, yen, and US dollars.

"I've been asked to stay here with you tonight. Are you comfortable with this? I have also had the refrigerator stocked. I will prepare dinner for you. I remembered your preferences." Zari looked at her shyly, unaccustomed to being alone with a woman other than his wife.

Her stomach rumbled at the mention of food, reminding her she had not eaten since—well, she could not recall when she had last eaten. Her hunger had now overtaken her grief, and she was not sure when she would be able to have a decent meal again. "Thanks, Zari, I would love something to eat." She smiled, taking a phone from the table and excusing herself to one of the bedrooms.

No one to call. Ace would stop her. Savin would completely lose his shit, and it was not fair to bring anyone else into this probable death sentence. The only other people involved were paid handsomely in cryptocurrency for their discretion, faceless saviors who had volunteered with a full understanding of the risks.

Zari rapped softly on the door. "Come in."

"I have prepared dinner, when you're ready."

"I can't tell you how long it's been since I've had a home-cooked meal, Zari. You are wonderful. I'll freshen up and be out in five."

Unpacking was futile at this point, so Celeste pulled out only her toiletries and walked into the attached bathroom. The bathroom was modern like hers, with a Jacuzzi tub the size of a small backyard pool.

This could be her last night to enjoy such luxuries if anything went awry, but she was not feeling indulgent. *Who knows where this little scheme will take me? Life sentence in a Saudi prison? More likely an unmarked grave.* She mostly tried to avoid mirrors because her facial expressions had no depth anymore, empty from a life much sadder than that to which she was accustomed. She pledged that when this was all over, she would escape to a spa for many weeks, maybe escape forever. Celeste exhaled a forlorn sigh. *What I wouldn't give for a day of Savin's breakdowns or an awkward phone call with my sister-in-law. Hell, I'd even babysit Mark's baby for some normalcy. This face is not mine; this life is an impostor's.*

Celeste relished the feeling of the plush Turkish cotton washcloth as she wiped away the remnants of the bruising she had painted on earlier in the day. She leaned against the vanity, weak from exhaustion, her frame of mind teetering between panic and relief. It felt as though weeks had passed since Frankfurt. Even though her disguise was blown, her location was not. Omar's henchmen may have known she had planned to stop in London, but he would not expect that she had contingency plans. There were men like Zari waiting in a few cities, men Hadid had prepared, in the event she needed an alternate escape route. She had to believe Omar was unaware she had options—people who knew the rules of Omar's dark world. Celeste stared into the stranger's eyes in the mirror and imagined it was her old face staring back. She tried to recall how the old Celeste, the one not defeated by the murder of the man she loved, would have handled this situation. *I may not look or feel like her right now, but I am still Celeste Fucking Donovan. Omar won't take anything else from me because I am smarter, savvier, and better prepared. It's his turn to sweat.*

Celeste donned a cashmere jog suit that had become her uniform. She walked out to the dining room to find that Zari had prepared a feast. On the table were two place settings of exquisite china, and Zari had included a glass of white wine at hers.

"Zari, this looks divine!" Celeste shoveled the precisely prepared steamed scallops and wild rocket into her mouth, hunger overpowering her manners. "And it tastes even more wonderful than it looks! I had no idea you could cook." Zari beamed at Celeste's praise, as she thought, *This may be my last supper.*

"Miss Celeste—may I ask you a question?"

"Sure."

"Do you think whatever you are planning is going to work? You are in extreme danger, it seems. Is it worth it?"

"I have no idea, Zari. I can only hope my instincts are on target. Otherwise, I'm fucked."

AFTER DINNER, CELESTE REARRANGED HER BAGS TO ACCOUNT FOR THE costume she would wear the next day, as well as the money and passports. She perused the clothing she had requested: a sequined dress, a Victoria's Secret push-up bra and matching thong (this was no time for restraint; the added two cup sizes made it the perfect bra for the job), bright-pink 120-millimeter Louboutin spike heels, a long brunette bombshell wig, and a makeup bag full of garish goodies. A lambskin Chanel clutch topped off the look she had planned. She would have this outfit on underneath her abaya, which she would take off at the opportune time.

This will be the end of Omar. Avenging Theodore's death was finally within her grasp. She pondered whether Theodore would have tried to dissuade her from going through with her haphazard plan and decided that he indeed would have found another way.

Well, he shouldn't have left me to my own devices, then, should he? A rhetorical question, since it was her fault he was gone.

Celeste awoke to sunshine peeking through the heavy drapes, momentarily forgetting what daylight brought. She stretched her long limbs, grateful for a good night's sleep in a sprawling bed. She reached over to the nightstand to retrieve her flip phone. *Six a.m.* Getting out of bed, she walked to the window and opened the curtains. It was a clear morning with visibility for miles. Celeste was struck by the minutiae below, small boats moving freight in the

Dubai Creek, people on their morning commutes. It all seemed so foreign to her. *No turning back now.*

Despite her nerves, she was still confident she had made the right decision to do this herself. She should have handled it more effectively many years before and rid the world of his destruction much sooner. She dressed in a fresh cashmere tracksuit, socks, panties, and bra that had been placed in the closet for her by some person she would never meet. She slung the bag over her shoulder, opened the door, and walked into the living area to ask Zari to prepare a quick breakfast before she left to meet the pilot on the helipad.

"Zari, darling, can I trouble you for a poached egg and some fruit?" she said.

Silence.

Celeste placed the duffel on the sofa and crossed the enormous living area to the closed bedroom at the other end of the apartment. She rapped on the door.

"Zari, are you awake, dear?" She put her ear to the door. Nothing. She reached to turn the doorknob but stopped short when she heard a noise by the front door.

"Zari, is that you?" she asked, walking toward the sound she heard.

Celeste frowned when she found no one in the foyer. She strode back over to the bedroom door and knocked again.

"Zari? I'm coming in." She entered the room and looked around, then let out a scream.

"No! No! No!" Celeste shouted to the empty apartment. She knew she was alone, felt it; whoever had done this had slipped out the front door mere moments earlier.

Not Zari. Not him. A man who is nothing but goodness, who represents what is right and good in the world. Celeste fell to her knees with a sob, dry heaving at the sight of his supine body. A clean bullet hole punctured the spot between his bushy black eyebrows. A puddle of blood oozed around him, staining the pristine travertine floor, and his lifeless chocolate eyes remained open in surprise. Celeste took in the scene. Zari was dressed in jeans and a T-shirt, less formal clothing than she was accustomed to seeing him wear. The drapes were open, the floor-to-ceiling windows showcasing a view of Dubai similar to the view from her room. The bed was made, and nothing was out of place in the room. Celeste knew she had to move, knew that it was dangerous to remain here if for no other reason than that she could be framed as a suspect. She had to move, but she was frozen in shock. She had never seen a dead body before, outside of a casket, and the shock of it all was not easy to digest.

AFTER CELESTE VOMITED IN THE TOILET, SHE DID THE ONLY THINGS SHE could think to do—she placed a towel over Zari's face and careful not to get any blood on herself, she fumbled in his pants pockets for his phone and wallet, cognizant that it was time to leave for Riyadh. Her cover was blown, and whoever had done this could be waiting for her on the other side of the door. She recalled that Zari had placed the handgun in a drawer in the kitchen. She stuffed the phone and wallet in her bag and grabbed the gun on the way out. Her fingerprints were all over the apartment, so it would be a waste of time to attempt to wipe anything down.

She took the elevator up to the helipad to wait for the ride Zari had arranged. She kept looking over her shoulder, terrified this was a trap, that the murderer was up here, ready to attack. But there was no sign of anyone. Celeste withdrew Zari's phone from her bag. It had seemed morbid to use Zari's still-warm but lifeless finger to unlock the phone and change the settings, but it had been necessary. She texted herself Nasrin's contact information and scanned his emails and texts for anything unusual. Unless Zari had deleted any useful contacts, nothing appeared out of the ordinary. *Wait a minute.* There was a series of texts with a UK phone number that had not been saved into his contacts:

"I have her."

"Does she know?"

"She knows nothing."

Had Zari been part of a ploy against her? Had he told Omar her whereabouts? No. She knew Zari was good at his core. The only reason Zari would flip on her was if Omar had threatened his family, and she could not blame him for that. She would have turned on most anyone if she could have saved Theodore.

She ran to the trash bin at the other end of the roof to get rid of the SIM card before the helicopter arrived in case Omar could geotrack it. She removed the SIM card, stepped on it, and threw it into the can. Then she stomped on the phone to shatter the screen and put it back into her bag. If she made it through this situation alive, a hacker could recover everything on Zari's phone and perhaps provide clues to the identity of his text friend.

The chopper appeared then, and a blast of air from the rotors nearly knocked Celeste over. She stood back as far as possible, waiting for it to land. Once it was on the ground and idling, Celeste walked over. She could see the pilot smile at her, even through his helmet; then he went back to flipping switches and such, seemingly unaware of the dead husband and father a few stories below.

"Hello! I'm ready to go. Zari won't be joining us," she shouted over the engine, choking back a sob. She hoped she had made the correct calculation to address Zari's absence up front.

"Yes, he mentioned he may not be with you," the pilot shouted back. *Interesting.* He climbed out and assisted her into the seat behind him. He buckled her seat belt without making eye contact.

"I'll put my abaya on once we land," Celeste said. Saudi Arabia was the most gender-segregated country in the world. Though a burqa, a headpiece that completely covered the head and had a net over the face, was not mandatory in Saudi Arabia, Celeste would wear one to take advantage of being able to disguise herself completely. Unless they were expats in an expat compound, visitors had to abide by Saudi laws, and ignorance of the law was no defense. Celeste was not ignorant of the law, though, and knew that her little plan, if it went awry, was punishable by death. *A little too late to let reality interfere.*

She fished her Nokia out of her bag, her hand brushing the Caracal. Still no communication from the outside world. She had no answers and no options but to move forward with the haphazard plan that had left Nasrin widowed and Zari's children fatherless. The helicopter ascended, Dubai shrinking, but the distance between her and Zari did not allow her to escape the vision of his lifeless body or the knowledge that Nasrin would soon feel the way Celeste had been feeling since the day Theodore died. Empty. Numb except when the overwhelming anger took over.

"We have about a two-hour flight, ma'am, and it looks to be a spotless day for flying. Sit back and relax." *Well, it's clear he doesn't know what I'm in for.*

"This is Riyadh below. We will land on the outskirts of the city, undetected in the sand dunes, where a driver will pick you up and take you to your next destination. You won't see me again." Celeste gazed out her window to see a cosmopolitan city, the construction site and shiny new high-rises of the King Abdullah Financial District visible from the air. As they began to descend outside the city, she pulled on and straightened her garb. Celeste noticed one lone car in the dunes. She was not a religious woman but offered a quick plea to some higher power, the universe, a god or goddess—she would take any divine intervention at this point—for a swift and successful mission.

Hamid was awaiting her landing and retrieved her bag after holding out a hand to help her exit the helicopter. *My life and the lives of everyone I love rest on this man's moral fortitude and whether he is competent and loyal to only me.*

"Miss, we'll go directly to the safe house, an apartment in the middle of town. I cannot guarantee your safety if you are in public. You do not have access to an expat compound, so you must follow the laws. I cannot stress enough the danger you're in as an unaccompanied woman."

"I'll decide what's best for my safety," Celeste snapped. *My nerves are shot.* She said in a softer voice, "Sorry, yes, you're right. I need to get to the safe house, eat a decadent meal, and prepare for tomorrow."

"We must get going," he responded. Celeste climbed into the back seat. Her true mistakes in life had been falling in love with a dangerous man who killed and falling in love with a man who got himself killed. It was time to take matters into her own hands. Tomorrow she would do what no else could seem to do—she would take down Omar.

11

I'M A PROBLEM SOLVER

Men ran toward Celeste from all angles, scrambling to detain her. She locked eyes with a woman whose look urged her to run. Celeste could see pity in the woman's eyes, for the woman knew that what Celeste had done would likely get her killed. Celeste braced herself as the blond man who reached her first threw her over his shoulder and began running, weaving in and out of the chaos as the crowd struggled to understand what had happened.

Celeste curled her fists and punched the man's back again and again, hoping he would loosen his grip and put her down. She felt him wince slightly when she resorted to pinching him, yet he never slowed. He ran through the streets, keeping close to the buildings and moving through alleyways. The running was jarring, and she had to hold her head up to ensure her jaw did not crash into his back. His sweat soaked into her skin. Or maybe his sweat mixed with hers. *If he would just slow down for a minute ... I could get away.* With Zari gone, there was no one to call. She had not told anyone else the details of her Middle East detour, and though Ace may have suspected she was scheming, he could not have known the specifics. Lorraine had instructions to monitor the fallout and an untraceable email address to send Celeste the information, but she never would have been able

213

to keep it a secret from Savin if she had known Celeste's full plan. Celeste squeezed her eyes shut and willed herself not to cry when she realized her unusual predicament—she was helpless ... and hopeless. The money, the passports—they were all back at the safe house. She let out a sob, unheard over the sirens and the stomping feet of men chasing them.

The man turned down an alleyway, then entered an apartment building and ran up five flights of stairs. He stopped in front of a door, withdrew a key from his pocket, and unlocked the door. Setting her down, he gestured for her to enter. He followed behind her, closing and bolting the door. "You are fucking crazy with the stunt you pulled. You're lucky you aren't being publicly stoned to death right now!" he bellowed with a Norwegian accent and then rubbed his arm. "And I'm going to have bruises all over from your abuse. This is how you treat someone who rescues you? Fucking crazy lady!" She looked at his face for the first time. He was enormous, solid muscle, blond with a strong jawline. He looked furious and winded.

"Fuck you. I had it under control, and I won't have another opportunity like this. You ruined everything." Celeste was terrified that everything had escalated too quickly and her guys had not had time to get the media coverage they needed to frame Omar. Which would have rendered the dangerous scheme useless.

She could no longer contain herself. Tears fell, smearing her heavy costume makeup. She sank back in exhaustion. She did not have the energy it would take to admonish this meddlesome man, though she resolved to try.

But he turned the tables. "Do you have any idea what you just did? You risked your own life and that of the man you were fucking in a public square in the center of fucking Riyadh in Saudi fucking Arabia ..." He raked his hands through his hair and turned away from her. "I lost everyone who was tailing us, but he was captured from what I can tell."

"He wasn't captured, and we weren't actually fucking," Celeste explained in a condescending tone. "And what's your plan now, knight in shining armor? You ruined the one shot I had to save the people I love. Oh, wait, let me guess. Your plan is to take me to Omar. Well, go ahead. You've wrecked my plan because now I have no money, no passports, no phone. I have nothing to lose."

The man left the room without further notice of Celeste.

"Aargh!" Celeste yelled in frustration. She had to move, but her body was glued to the only piece of furniture that looked clean, a sofa along the back wall.

Who was this man? Maybe military stationed in Riyadh? Celeste was sure she had never seen him before. She doubted the shithole apartment was his, and there were no family portraits or other personal effects to clue her in on his identity. Her tears continued to fall as she realized the gravity of her situation. The room was filthy, with a sunken-in couch someone had found at the curb on trash day and plastic blackout blinds covering the small single window. And the smell—body odor with an almost tangible stench.

The man returned. "Here."

Celeste was startled out of her reverie by the duffel bag flying at her face. She looked inside and confirmed it was all there—money, passports, clothes, phones, laptop, and iPad. *I must have a guardian angel somewhere.* Relief washed over her, and she relaxed despite her current predicament.

She tried a different tactic with him. "I appreciate that you ...," she swallowed her ego and continued, "...rescued me. But now what? I have no idea who you are, where we are." She gestured at the space. "I can't figure out who sent you after me. No one knew my location or what I was planning. Why aren't you turning me in?"

"I can't give you my name, strict orders. Your employee? Lorraine, is it? Well, she couldn't keep a secret when she realized your reckless, idiotic, dangerous plan. She did the right thing by contacting Ace. Didn't take long for him to figure out what was going on."

"How do you know Ace? Does Savin know?" *So much for my assessment that Lorraine was trustworthy.*

"Never mind all that. We need to get back to the helicopter. The car is waiting. Change out of that hideous outfit and put the abaya and burqa back on. We no doubt have every Saudi looking for us right now."

The asshole has a point, but ... "There's no way I'm coming with you. I have no idea who you are, and I've made all my own arrangements."

"Hadid won't be of any help to you now. Your only option is to come with me."

Celeste felt panic spread throughout her body. What if he were telling the truth? Hadid and his crew were the only connections she had in Riyadh, and she could not risk being discovered there. She looked at her phone and saw no missed calls. She quickly dialed Hadid's number and frowned when she heard a message that it was disconnected. *Fuck.*

Ding. An incoming text from Ace. "Stop this insanity, Celeste, and go with him now. You're in grave danger."

She looked up at the man, who was smirking. "Now do you believe me? We have exactly nine minutes to leave so we can make it to the helicopter before we are stranded here."

"Fuck you. I need to go change."

Celeste went to the bathroom, slamming the door behind her. She changed back into her tracksuit, scrubbed her face, removed the brunette wig, and tied her hair back in a ponytail. She slid the abaya and burqa into place, relieved to have a disguise on top of a disguise.

"Voilà."

"Took you long enough. Let's go," the man said without looking at her. Celeste noted a handgun tucked in his waistband and a backpack slung over his shoulder as she scrambled to keep up with him, her bag slowing her down. *Chivalrous fuck, isn't he?* They ran down the five flights of stairs and out into the scorching sun. An empty armored Jeep waited outside the door.

"Get in."

The man knew about Ace and Lorraine, so either he was here to rescue her or he was one of Omar's men. She looked left and right down the empty street and considered running for a moment, then resolved herself to her current situation and got into the back seat, since the car Hadid had arranged was not there waiting for her. *What happened to Hadid? Please, please let him be unharmed.*

The man slammed the door behind her, got into the driver's seat and, before she was settled, squealed the tires as he floored the gas pedal.

"OK, now that we are on our way—would you mind telling me what the fuck is going on? You're taking me to the helicopter to go where?"

"You've got a lot of nerve, lady. You aren't exactly in any position to make demands. Did you really think you would get away with this whole thing by paying off a few of the *hay'ah*? And you also thought they were actually going to help you get out of the country after you pulled this stunt? Fucking nuts." The Commission for the Promotion of Virtue and the Prevention of Vice, known in Saudi Arabia as the CPVPV or the *hay'ah*, was the religious police charged with enforcing Sharia law in the country. *So much for my plan.*

"I have orders to give you no information, take you to an undisclosed location, and leave you there," he continued. "If I don't get you there alive and unharmed, Ace is going out be furious with me."

"I had one shot to destroy Omar, and Ace's intervention ruined it. I couldn't care less about what Ace wants. In fact, I'm convinced he's working with Omar."

He looked back at her, his expression clear. If he could have, she was certain he would have wrung her neck at that moment. She held back a laugh. Even she knew there was little humor to be enjoyed in a high-stakes getaway in the desert.

"Are you going to tell me where you're taking me?" Celeste was bored. They had been driving for hours, she was sweating through her cashmere under the black traditional garb, and the man still refused to answer any of her questions, turn on music or air-conditioning, or let her use his cell phone. To any question she asked, he stubbornly stuck to the party line: "Ask Ace when you talk to him."

Celeste kicked the seat in front of her, and the man leaped forward in pain. "I demand some answers. How the fuck am I supposed to ask Ace on the phone when I have no cell service? You kidnapped me, and now you won't even let me use your phone!"

"Kidnapped you?" he bellowed. "I saved your life—not to mention risked my own—to get you out of the dumbest scheme I've ever seen anyone attempt."

"We're in the middle of the fucking desert! Not a car in sight. Not even a fucking camel. How do you expect me to believe that you aren't just taking me to Omar?" She decided to nickname him "Todd"—she and Savin called everyone they thought was a douchebag Todd.

"Lady, if anyone attempted to kidnap you, they would immediately release you once they realized what a pain in the ass you are. And I don't work for Omar."

"Why, thank you for the kind words, asshole."

Todd scowled and stared out the window.

"I'm thirsty."

Without turning around, he responded, "There is a cooler in the back. Can you grab me a drink? Coke."

Celeste opened the cooler to find a host of goodies. She grabbed a water (*Who told him I only drink Evian? And where did they find Evian in Saudi?*) and a glass bottle of Saudi Coke, along with two energy bars.

"Thank you," Celeste said dryly.

This was Celeste's first road trip in the Saudi desert. The scenery was beautiful, if she had the capacity to take it in, with intricate sandstone formations all around.

"So, we're going to Bahrain? Qatar? Oman? If Ace demanded you keep me safe, you wouldn't dare keep me in Saudi. Those motherfuckers are out to find me, I'm sure!"

Todd rolled his eyes and then relented. "You are correct; we're getting out of Saudi along the least populated path. The plan is to get you to Jordan, and then you can fly out of there."

"Why didn't we just go to UAE? In case you haven't noticed, what I need is a plane, not a tour of the Middle East."

"Too risky. Jordan has its own chaos right now and won't be monitoring Saudi alerts, whereas UAE would take great pleasure in getting in the Saudi king's good graces."

"So can I use your cell?"

"No," Todd said with his jaw set.

Celeste was growing comfortable that there was at least a plan. Maybe she would not have to use the Caracal, not yet.

"OK, then tell me, what time is it in London?"

"Don't worry, your insane little plan worked."

Celeste rested her head back on the seat, willing her mind quiet. She could not shake the empty stare in Zari's eyes or the image of Theodore writhing in pain after a beating from Omar. And what had happened to Hadid? He had agreed to her scheme for a handsome fee, framing himself for the very public and very illegal (punishable by certain death) display between him and Celeste. She decided that he must have escaped and that the *hay'ah* bribe paid off. He had been too collected before and during their brief encounter to have been concerned for his life.

Celeste fell in and out of sleep for the next hour or so. As soon as there was a safe distance between her and Riyadh, she was going to kick Todd in the balls. He was correct, though; she had no alternatives right now. How she longed to wake up from this nightmare, to call Rani, have her arrange a magical helicopter rescue, and sleep in her own bed with a day of pampering ahead. *Someday.*

THE JORDAN BORDER PATROL STOP WAS A BLUR—THE UNIFORMED officer shining his flashlight in the Jeep, startling Celeste awake; the officer pointing a rifle at Todd's head; Todd slamming the door into the officer, knocking the man off his feet. Before Todd could get to the officer's rifle, a second officer ran over, shouting in Arabic at Todd. Todd rushed him, smacked the man with his own rifle, and then snapped his neck. Satisfied the man was dead, Todd ran over to the officer on the ground and shot him with his handgun.

Todd got back into the car and sped off. "Don't try anything stupid, Celeste."

Celeste lay across the back seat, too stunned to speak. Thoughts came and went, brief and nonsensical. No more fantasies of jumping out of the car and running free—this man was too dangerous. She was trapped in a hell of her own making, her arrogance that she could pull off the stunt in Riyadh sealing her fate.

"You ... I don't ... you just killed those men. That puts us in even more danger. What do you propose we do now?"

"While you were sleeping, I got word that they were under orders to take you. Which I couldn't allow. It was the only way. I'm not allowed to share any further information with you. But you may want to consider the possibility that Omar and Ace are not the only people involved in your little game of cat and mouse. You'll be able to talk to Ace soon enough, and he will explain everything to you, I'm sure."

"Can I at least use your cell phone? People are worried about me."

"No phones. No more questions. Your phone can be traced if you use it. You're lucky I even let you keep it, because you've risked both of our lives. It is up here with me."

"Lucky? You think this is lucky? Yes, I'm fucking lucky."

Celeste was furious. She picked up her duffel and began sifting through its contents. The Caracal was still there. She weighed her options and decided killing him without having any assurance that he had indeed kept her cell phone was a bad idea. She would be lost in the desert without a map.

CELESTE WAS NOT SURE HOW IT WAS POSSIBLE, BUT THE DESERT WAS even darker now. Todd pulled over and turned off the car headlights. He turned to look at Celeste. *And here is the part where he kills me.* She kept her finger on the Caracal trigger.

"I don't think driving through Jordan is a good decision after all, and you certainly can't go anywhere else in the Middle East. By this point, Europe is probably out, too, because your face will be plastered all over the news. But we have a Gulfstream waiting for us about an hour away with a pilot given orders to take you wherever you want to go. The deal, though, as per Ace, is that you don't try any more funny business and that I accompany you."

Finally, I can make a decision!

"How far can we get without refueling?" It went without saying that the United States was out of the picture, and any major financial market like Shanghai or Hong Kong was too risky.

"Egypt? We have easy access in and out of Cairo, and I have a secure apartment there. You can freshen up, touch base with Ace, and assess the fallout. Don't worry; your plan worked. A little too well, actually, because there are at least a dozen men who will stop at nothing to see you dead and a government with a hit out on you and Omar."

Celeste shuddered at the memory of how swiftly he had killed the two men, something she had not yet digested.

"Cairo works. I'll evaluate then what I should do."

"It's done, then."

CELESTE STILL FOUND THESE CLANDESTINE FLIGHTS IN AND OUT OF secret desert airports thrilling, this time perhaps more than she normally would since she was stifling all her other emotions at this point. No amount of ayahuasca she could ingest on a retreat in Peru would cleanse her of the trauma she had been through the past few days. Celeste had to find a way to get her old life back—when flying to a glamorous locale on a private jet was what she called an uneventful Tuesday.

"Incredible, isn't it? Civilians aren't normally allowed to fly out of here," Todd explained. They climbed the Gulfstream steps to enter a luxurious jet, where they were greeted by two flight attendants, a man and a woman. The cockpit door was closed.

"Hello, Miss," the woman said with a welcoming gesture. "I've heard you've had a rough few days. You'll find a change of clothes in the bedroom, as well as some toiletries."

"Go on. We have plenty of time. About six hours in the air," Todd relayed with a kinder tone than he had used all day.

"Thank you," Celeste said, relieved she could scrub the past few days from her body and have some space to gather her thoughts.

She walked slowly so she could hear the murmurings of the three as she retreated to the back of the plane.

"What does she know?" the male flight attendant inquired.

"Can't tell," Todd responded. "She hasn't stopped talking for hours, but she's not letting on. Just keeps demanding to speak to Ace."

"Which we all know is impossible," replied the woman.

"Right. It's not time."

Then they fell silent as they busied themselves for takeoff. *Goddammit.*

CELESTE CLOSED THE BEDROOM DOOR AND COLLAPSED ONTO THE KING-size bed. She felt calm, but she supposed she was in shock from the past few days. That or she was a sociopath—if she ever made it back to New York in one piece, she needed substantial time to explore what was going on in her mind. It was infuriating to be kept in the dark. She left the bedroom to speak her mind to these strangers, whoever they were.

"Excuse me? Can whoever is kind enough to bring me new clothes at all these locations please bring me something more flattering next time? I think it's time to change my look a little, too. Perhaps some hair dye? A blow-dryer? A curling iron?"

The three seemed startled to see her, and it was clear they were still discussing what she may or may not know.

"I told you," Todd said to the other two with a grin. His demeanor was disconcerting, considering what he had done in the past twenty-four hours. She shuddered as the image of the dead border guards flashed in her head, but she recovered quickly. *No more letting them see you lose your cool.*

"Told them what? That I am a demanding prima donna? Well, I am, and it seems that you've been paid to ensure I make it somewhere —who knows where or why, because you won't give me any information—so it would behoove you to keep me happy. I need better clothes next time. I'm tired of looking like an old maid. And I want to know all your names."

"We've already discussed this," Todd interjected.

"Well, your answer was inadequate. You kidnapped me, killed two men in front of me, stole my phone and my other electronics ... the list of your crimes goes on and on. So you *will* tell me—at the very fucking least—your names, why you are all together, and for whom you are all working. You seem familiar with each other."

She examined them. The woman was a tall brunette with sharp features, perhaps Eastern European. She had to admit Todd was handsome (*Couldn't Ace or Omar find any ugly handlers for me that I didn't immediately imagine fucking?*). The male flight attendant had dark features, likely Italian or Spanish. Their faces were impassive.

Todd cleared his throat and began an explanation. "We've worked for Ace for many years. He's been like a big brother to us, and we help him out whenever he needs it. It's critical that our identities are not compromised, so I'm afraid we cannot share our names or our stories."

This was going nowhere. Celeste was going to explode in frustration. "Can you just give me some tangible information? This cryptic bullshit is not working for me. I—I've been through a lot, and ... well, just put yourself in my shoes for a moment." Tears threatened to fall, but she resolved to remain stoic.

Todd sighed. "I'm sure this is scary for you, but it's almost over. Once we get to Cairo, you can speak to Ace, and he'll tell you everything. I know you have no reason to, but try to trust us. Or at least, trust Ace."

"Whatever." Celeste stormed back to the bedroom, attempting to slam the pocket door but failing. She would have stayed to argue, but there was no way she would let them see her cry.

———

THE ORDEAL SURROUNDING HER LANDING AT A PRIVATE AIRPORT IN Cairo was consistent with all her travels lately. After goodbyes to the mysterious pilot and attendants, she and Todd were transferred in an armored SUV to a private apartment building, where she found herself in Todd's sleek, modern apartment with a wall of windows looking down on Cairo.

"Make yourself at home. I can't let you leave, but I had the refrigerator stocked to your liking. I can cook."

Celeste was famished. She dropped the duffel on one of the sofas and nosed around the kitchen. Fresh fish, vegetables, even a few decent bottles of wine. Cookware and utensils.

"Would you like some fish?" she offered. Celeste was still assessing her escape options now that she was out of Saudi Arabia. Kill Todd and then escape? Kill Ace for all the mystery surrounding her "rescue"? *Could* she kill someone? Her days at the shooting range with her self-defense trainer might come in handy. She was not clear yet which path would best serve her; she needed time to assess the situation further.

"No offense, lady, but you don't seem like you know how to lift a finger, let alone cook a meal."

Careful. He was right, she was better suited for the bedroom than the kitchen. But she had watched Dina and Theodore often enough to know that she could pull something together. She smiled.

"Well, how about I give it a try? Sea bass and steamed veggies? And if you don't like it, you can have something delivered. Sound good?"

"Sure."

Once he had a few glasses of wine and a meal, she would grill him about Ace and get her phone and laptop back. Men were simple.

—————

Todd set the table while she was preparing dinner, but they were otherwise silent. After she had heard the three talking on the plane, she could not afford to slip up.

Celeste plated the meal and brought the two plates over to the table. She had chosen a bottle of white Bordeaux, which would pair well with the fish. *Now for the awkward dinner.*

"You have an impressive wine collection."

Todd grunted and returned to his food.

"I guess there's not much to talk about if you can't even tell me your name."

"Ace's orders."

"Fuck Ace. He should've never gotten involved. I was perfectly capable of getting myself out of … out of my predicament. All he did was fuck everything up and lead to you killing two men." She could not be sure how much Todd knew.

"I'd prefer we didn't discuss that again. And you would've never escaped with your harebrained plan. I can't believe you thought you would get away with it."

"Am I allowed to turn on the news? I haven't even seen the coverage to know how bad it is."

"I will say this, lady. As reckless as you are, it was probably the only way to take down Omar. Many of us have been trying for years, and you pulled it off with a short skirt and a wig."

"Oh yeah? What have you tried? I mean, I at least want to know what won't work if he doesn't kill me this time."

"We've tried framing him for entrapment, insider trading, war crimes, international arms dealing. Nothing sticks."

"Hmm. I dated him for some time, so I guess my advantage was that I knew him a little better."

"I heard."

"I'm probably the talk of the town with you undercover types these days, huh? Are you a hacker?"

"I'm a problem solver."

"Ah, I see. You've given me so much to go on; I feel like we've really gotten to know each other intimately over the past few hours," Celeste said sarcastically. She poured each of them another glass of wine. "Could you at least give me a name to go on? I've been calling you Todd in my head. An inside joke between me and my best friend. We call every guy we think is a douchebag Todd." And just like that, the sadness was back. She missed her friends. *Poor Savin. He is no doubt a wreck.*

The man chuckled, then straightened up. "How about you keep calling me Todd?"

"OK, Todd, who works for Ace. Creative. Am I to presume we will be here at least another day or so?" she continued innocently.

"Yes. We need to get a handle on the situation outside before we allow you to be in public again."

"Good. Then I see no reason not to open another bottle of wine."

Receiving no protests from Todd, Celeste found another wine that she paired with macaroons from the refrigerator. She filled both of their wine glasses and bit into a raspberry macaroon. It tasted like heaven.

"So tell me, why Cairo? It's an unusual place for a Scandinavian to choose to live."

The wine had loosened Todd up a bit. "I was in the military and was stationed here for a time. Fell in love with the culture." *That explains the broad shoulders and rough hands.*

"You had to be special ops or something, right? With your proficiency for uh ... disposing of people."

"They were bottom feeders. Bad guys. If you knew some of the things they'd done, you wouldn't think twice about the situation."

And so the evening went on, with Celeste trying to work information out of him, but despite the wine, Todd proved he was too smart for her tactics. He did, however, let one critical puzzle piece slip when she grilled him on how Ace knew where she was.

"How do you employ hackers for a living and not know about the WiFi Pineapple?" he asked her.

"Of course I know about the Pineapple," she said. "We have

sweeps for any abnormalities in our web traffic all the time. Plus, I always use a VPN, and we have our own servers. In fact, Ace had a new server set up for me on my dinosaur laptop."

"I hate to tell you, but you've been a victim of the oldest trick in the book. Actually, several. It's one of the ways we discovered your many locations and how we narrowed down your plan. We think Omar's guys have some sort of tracker on you as well, but we haven't narrowed down exactly what. We're hoping he lost you by now."

The WiFi Pineapple, a platform that operates much like a normal WiFi access point through a device that looks like a router, allows a hacker to create a network and name it as though it is a legitimate WiFi connection. While the hacker impersonates a legitimate connection, he or she can steal information from the user's computer, known as a spoofing attack. Celeste was schooled on web security and took all the precautions to prevent anyone from hacking into her system, in addition to retaining the best in the industry to regularly test for abnormalities that expose vulnerabilities, called penetration testing.

"No fucking way. I've always been vigilant about such security breaches, especially while I've been traveling, always using virtual private networks and such. I haven't used a single public WiFi network, only the hot spot device Ace tested for me." The truth dawned on her, as Todd sat back, smiling.

"So, you see, you're not invulnerable to security breaches."

How could I have been so stupid?

"Ace only did it to protect you. As long as we knew your whereabouts, we could get you out of trouble. You would be dead in Riyadh if he hadn't. You Americans and your entitlement to privacy."

Ugh, defending Ace again. Celeste was losing her patience, the camaraderie fading. "What is the real plan here? What happens when I'm 'allowed' to leave Cairo?" Celeste felt her temper rising. "You know what? I want my fucking laptop and my fucking phone right now."

They both knew her demands were fruitless—Todd had her by the balls. Sure, she could shoot him, but it didn't feel right, at least not yet. The apartment could be monitored, and law enforcement could know of her presence in the country. It was best to wait until she had more information. But her patience was wearing paper thin.

"OK, let's take a step back and calm down," Todd said. "I wasn't trying to anger you."

Celeste had not earned the nickname "Ice Queen" without reason, but she could no longer contain her emotions—or her temper. She swept her arm across the table, knocking off glasses and dinnerware to shatter on the floor. "I want the truth, all of it, and I want it now. It seems you've all underestimated me to this point, but I won't be fooled again. I want to go home!"

And then Todd was against her, all of her, lips against lips, his tongue swirling in her mouth, his hips pressing against hers. As if on command, she was aroused. They tore at each other's clothing while they stumbled over to the couch. She removed her remaining clothing just as Todd shed his jeans and boxer briefs. In the dim light, she admired his muscle definition and bone structure, and her carnal need to be fucked took over.

Todd grunted in appreciation, his dick erect as he scanned her naked body. It had been so long since she had felt wanted, connected to her own body and to someone else's. So long since the weight of a man's body left her breathless in anticipation. *Much too long.* They lay together intertwined on the sofa, tangled limbs and sweaty torsos, bodies slipping against each other as he entered her.

12

WHERE DO I GO FROM HERE?

It turned out that fucking Todd in every room of his apartment was not a salve. Her grief for Theodore had dulled her orgasms, and she mostly lay there merely going through the motions when she and Todd had sex. Memories of Theodore's body against hers, his hand caressing her cheek, his lips on hers—it all haunted Celeste. In an instant, she felt repulsed by this stranger on top of her, this man she had watched take two others' lives. She pushed Todd off and rolled over, squeezing back tears.

"What's wrong?"

"I'm sorry, I can't do this. Too much has happened, and I ... I can't be intimate with you anymore." She stood up. "I'll sleep in the other bed. I'm exhausted, and it's all hit me at once. I need to be alone."

Todd recovered and transformed into her handler once more, all business. "No, you take this room, I insist. Ace will—how do you Americans say?—have my balls if you are upset."

Not long ago, Celeste would have found his formal manner while still naked sporting a hard-on hilarious and would have shared the entire story with her friends at brunch. Now, her mind was reeling as she wondered if he had taken the bullets out of her gun and how she could pirate the WiFi.

"Please make yourself at home. I'll update you on the Omar fallout after you've had some sleep. The dresser is stocked with some clothes, and there are books on the nightstand. See you in the morning," Todd said as he began closing the door behind him.

"Wait. What's the WiFi password?"

"Let's do all that tomorrow. Get some rest tonight."

She opened her mouth to protest, but then realized she needed the sleep. "OK, it can wait. Do you have any idea what happens next?"

"We'll talk tomorrow. Ace has taken care of it but insisted we do not talk business tonight."

Under normal circumstances, Celeste would have made demands. Instead, she waited quietly for Todd to leave and shut the door. The carefree Celeste Donovan had died along with Theodore, and in her place was this stranger with the unrecognizable face. Fucking all the Todds in the world would not change that.

Celeste sat parked in front of the TV the following morning, watching the cable news reporters relish in Omar's downfall. The edited video had succeeded in framing him for the Saudi crimes of adultery and blasphemy, punishable by death. The Saudis were out to get him, oblivious to the fact that he had not set foot in Riyadh for many years. Omar's holding company had lost several billion dollars in an investor panic after the news broke that the Saudi government was charging him with a crime punishable by death, and a fatwa ordering his execution was proclaimed. The file she had prepared for Ace had apparently been leaked to the US DOJ and the European Union authorities. Each government was racing to respond to the news that Omar's holding company had been the financier for nearly every powerful transnational criminal organization—and that he was profiting from destabilizing democracies everywhere. Omar was on the hook for all of it. He was painted as an evil genius, and the world, in solidarity, wanted him to pay. Todd was right—her plan had worked almost too well.

When Celeste had left New York, she expected Lorraine and Ace would continue adding to her file on Omar. But this ... She was in awe of the breadth and depth of the evidence against Omar and how many crimes were attributed to him—insider trading, jury tampering, arms dealing, Ponzi schemes, murder, kidnappings, and on and on. She hoped to someday ask Ace how he had done it, how he had all this information released in concert with the Riyadh charade, but right now, she had to focus on keeping herself and those she cared about safe from Omar's rage. The silver lining was that there was little mention of the woman accompanying Omar's look-alike in the video, and the Saudi government announced that it could not identify her, hence admitting that it would not pursue charges against her. Celeste was in the clear, while Omar was destroyed. Her hideout in Cairo would soon be over.

"Celeste, you'll want to see this," Todd said. He motioned to Celeste to sit next to him at the dining room table.

Celeste strode across the room. She looked at his black laptop screen with the DOS prompt as he typed indiscernible code next to the blinking yellow cursor.

"Ace thought you should know about this before you head back to New York."

Celeste hoped she recovered quickly after her jaw dropped in awe. As Todd scrolled through trades inside the D&C electronic trading records, it was clear that Savin and perhaps others had known what she was up to. The records indicated D&C had been quite busy the day before the Riyadh video was released. D&C had gained what Omar's holding company had lost—and then some. Billions of dollars now sat in a restricted fund, according to the D&C system. Todd exited the system once Celeste had digested the activity.

"And this," he said, pulling up trading records from Roberto's accounts. Based on the trading activity, Roberto and other colleagues had also taken advantage of the knowledge that Celeste had framed Omar.

"How did they know anything about Omar? And the timing? There's no way anyone could've known what I had planned."

"Ace knows everything before it happens."

Celeste frowned.

"Never underestimate him, Celeste. You left a trail he could find; everyone does."

"I have resources not connected to Ace."

"You sure about that?"

The truth was, Celeste had been questioning Ace's motivations since Zari's murder, but she would never let on to Todd. She changed the subject to hide her rising frustration at Todd's discretion. He still had not revealed anything useful to her during their hideout—no chink in his professionalism.

"Let's discuss tomorrow's plan."

"We'll fly nonstop to Teterboro, leaving here around ten a.m. You'll arrive at night and head straight to your apartment, where your security team will be in place. But there's one more thing—the Feds will want to talk to you. Johnny Carolo will meet you the day after you get back to prep you."

"Why? Has Savin been questioned? Is this about Omar or the trades?"

"I'm not sure, but Ace said you are not to speak with anyone until you talk to Johnny."

"Unlike you, I don't take orders from Ace. I'll speak with whomever I damn well please. He's on my payroll, not vice versa."

Todd smirked.

Celeste swallowed the nagging feeling that she was missing something. *Think, Celeste, think.*

"If I'm in the clear, can I speak with Savin? Access my email? Reach out to Angelo to make sure everything is in order?"

"Ace would prefer you wait until you are back in the States. He wants to take extra precautions. It's only one day. He asked that you please give us the time to keep you safe. You will need a passport stamp to indicate a return to the States. As far as anyone knows, you have been staying at your Paris apartment, looking at real estate for the D&C Paris satellite office. Your house staff in Paris will provide your alibi."

The plan was brilliant in its simplicity, but one thing remained. "How do I explain that I look like a completely different person? No one will believe that I chose to look like this."

"That's apparently taken care of as well." Todd opened a new window with an encrypted message board and read from it. "Here's what a woman named Meredith sent." He squinted at the computer screen and cleared his throat. "Tyler and Patrick will come to your apartment once you've spoken to Johnny and Savin. Meredith arranged for your plastic surgeon to stop by, too, for—" He frowned and rolled his eyes, then read directly from the screen: "Dr. Smythe will come by for Botox and filler. You'll be as good as new before anyone sees you. XOXO Mer." He shook his head in disbelief. "I can't believe this is your life."

Celeste ignored the insult and sighed in relief. "Wow, they've thought of everything." *Can finally be back to my old self.*

"Don't thank me, thank your New York team."

"Oh, darling, I wasn't thanking you. I find you to be insuffer—" Celeste stopped herself and switched tactics.

"Have you been involved from the beginning?" Celeste read Todd's expression to say he wanted to prevent another outburst. He sighed and responded.

"Yes, I was tasked with tracking you as soon as you began working with Ace."

"You've been spying on me?"

"More, uh, fact-gathering, really. And if I hadn't been around, your little stunt would've never worked."

Sleep did not come that night. She tossed and turned, contemplating different scenarios. How had Savin managed to coordinate trades across many of their accounts? How much did Ace know? Did Omar know she was behind Riyadh? What did Zari's texts about what she knew mean, and who had killed him? Why did the Feds want to talk to her? Where was Omar? And most important, could she keep everyone safe with Omar still on the loose? It had all transpired so quickly, and she had yet to process it.

CELESTE WAS LIVID THE NEXT MORNING WHEN TODD HELD FIRM THAT she could not communicate with the outside world until she was back in New York.

"You promised, you motherfucker!" she said and kicked the coffee table. "Ow!" she yelled, grasping her toe. She sat down on the sofa, momentarily defeated. She had awoken at dawn in a panic at the thought of getting on a plane again with this man about whom she knew nothing. Last time it had been out of necessity, but this time she had options. She was in a metropolitan city, after all, not the middle of the desert. And even if she did not really have options, with all the unknowns, she was going to act as if she did.

"I'm not getting on another plane with you until I speak with someone I trust. I'm finished feeling like a prisoner. I want to use my fucking phone," Celeste said, taking a deep breath to prevent another tantrum.

But Todd disappeared, seemingly unconcerned, leaving Celeste to pick at her breakfast of poached eggs and fruit he had prepared. Tears of frustration burned her cheeks. *Where do I go from here?*

Todd sauntered back into the room. "Here," he said, jamming a flip phone in her face. It appeared he had someone on the line already. Celeste took the phone from his outstretched hand and held it up to her ear.

"Celly! I'm so glad you're OK! We've been so worried!"

"Savin, oh my God! It's really you!"

"Celly, Alexsandr is good people. You can trust him. Now get your ass back to New York!"

"Wait, don't hang up, please!"

"You'll see me in just a few hours. I'll be at your place tonight to catch up. Get some rest on the plane. Everything has been taken care of. Your Queen of Manhattan throne awaits."

Celeste could not remember when she had last laughed. It felt good. She shut the phone and handed it to ... Alexsandr, apparently.

"Thank you," she said with a smile. And for the first time, he smiled back at her.

"I told you I'm not one of the bad guys. Savin's right—we need to leave soon. Do as he says—pack your stuff so we can get your ass back to New York!" It was his first attempt at a joke in their time together.

Celeste went in her room to shower. She felt lighter, and she even smiled at her reflection in the mirror while she was getting ready. She searched the dresser Alexsandr had stocked for her and settled on a pair of L'Agence jeans, a Wolford turtleneck bodysuit, and Chloe ballet flats beside the bed. There was even a pashmina shawl and a leather jacket, so the outfit was not far off from her usual travel uniform. *Well, I suppose this makes up for being spied on.*

WHEN THEY BOARDED THE PLANE ALEX HAD CHARTERED, SHE SAW THE same crew who had dropped them off in Cairo a few days prior.

"Hello, again," Celeste said. She was going back home, and she could not contain her excitement that this involuntary confinement was coming to an end.

Once she was settled in her seat, the male flight attendant asked if she would like anything to drink. "A glass of bubbles would be delightful." Yes, there would be some hurdles to clear once she was home, and Theodore was still gone, but for now, even if just for a few minutes, Celeste was allowing herself to be happy.

"I'll have one as well," Alexsandr said and turned to Celeste. "What are we celebrating?"

"My rebirth back into the land of the living in the only place that matters—New York."

It was difficult to have much of a conversation with the crew after their initial awkward encounter, so after a glass of champagne and light chitchat with everyone, she retreated to the bedroom. She collapsed on the bed and slept hard, waking twelve hours later to wheels on tarmac.

Celeste leaped out of bed and retrieved her duffel bag from the cabin. She was elated. She shook hands with the flight crew and thanked them. *It's time I learn what form of thank-you is appropriate for people who have saved your life.* She descended the stairs to the tarmac. *Thank God it's nighttime, so no one sees me like this!*

Monty was waiting for her at the bottom, and she noted his Mercedes was close by.

"Monty! I'm so happy to see you!" This man had become like a father figure to her, and she hugged him tightly.

"Miss Celeste, it's wonderful to have you back," Monty said, his voice muffled until Celeste released him.

Alexsandr walked over to Celeste and leaned in so that Monty would not hear. "It's time for you to head home. We still don't know where Omar is, so precautions must be taken. Monty is to take you directly to your apartment."

"You're not coming to my apartment, are you?" Celeste hissed.

Alexsandr laughed heartily. "Well, I hadn't realized our time together was so bad. But no, I will not be coming to your apartment. I just need to make sure you arrive there in one piece—"

"Or Ace will have your ass, yes, I know." Celeste shook Alexsandr's hand, mumbling a thank-you so that Monty could not hear. As far as Monty knew, she had been in Paris.

"OK, Monty, let's take me home! How I've missed everyone."

She slid into the back seat of his car, startled to see Savin inside. "Surprise!"

"Savin, you scared the shit out of me! If I wasn't so happy to see you—"

"But you *are* so happy to see me, so stop right there."

Celeste laughed. "Touché," she said while half hugging him. Monty entered the car, rolled up the divider window, and began driving.

"OK, I'm not even going to get into my 'What the actual fuck were you thinking?' line of questioning right now," Savin began. "That will come later. Here's what you need to know right now: Monty knows nothing. The staff, with the exception of Lorraine, has no idea what's been going on. There are murmurings, according to Lorraine, that you had some connection to Omar in your past, but there's no way for them to confirm their suspicions. We even had a Celeste doppelgänger going in and out of your Paris apartment building. All bases covered."

"And Omar hasn't surfaced in all this?"

"Nope, not since he came into our office when you were still in Europe with Theodore. His passport was scanned the day after that in London, and he apparently has not used it since."

"Well, he could have used others—or may be traveling by boat or train."

"Yes, that's possible, but for now, let's just enjoy that you're home safely, and that we are a few billion dollars richer than when you left!"

"I saw! Alexsandr showed me. Said it was on Ace's orders."

"Celly, we were all so worried."

"What do the Feds want with us, anyway? And how does Ace know Johnny?"

"We'll explain everything at your place tomorrow."

"So Johnny is prepping me as a precaution?"

"Something like that. Our trades are safe from federal scrutiny, though. We have documented Omar intel—backed by analyst reports, and we made other big moves those two days, also backed by research. I gave a believable pep talk the day before the trades, outlining the new plan that you and I had decided on: to ramp up our earnings by taking on higher-risk trades. I had no idea the payout would be that big ..."

"I figured you would be nimble enough to cover our tracks. I'm sure Roberto appreciates the gift."

"Yeah, let's say he was made whole after divorce number three drained him."

"My final question: How did you know what I had planned?"

"Well, for one, you're an arrogant narcissist of a woman, so it was obvious you'd think you could pull off something of this magnitude."

"Go big or go home."

"Yes. And second, Ace knew all the details, down to the name of the Omar look-alike."

"Impressive." *Fuck. I'm going to need some distance from Ace moving forward to figure out his intentions.*

"Everyone in the office thinks you've been nursing a broken heart in St. Moritz and then Paris. I wish that *was* what you'd been doing. But you're in the clear, as long as Omar doesn't come after you."

"OK. Now I'm going to sleep for a day. I hope I have some Ambien at home."

"Meredith and Rani have been hard at work to make you comfortable. I'm sure they thought of everything."

"You haven't mentioned my hideous disguise. How am I ever going to explain this to Ty?"

"You look great. A little thin and tired, but it turns out you can pull off being a brunette. But do put this on." He handed her a baseball cap. "Don't worry about Ty. Meredith made something up about you wanting to try a new look in St. Moritz."

Celeste laughed lightly, but her eyelids were heavy. She leaned back on the headrest, dozing for the next hour during the drive home.

"We're almost home, sleepyhead," Savin said when they pulled up to her building. "We've got a lot of stuff to cover tomorrow, but first, get some rest. And for God's sake, don't speak to anyone unless we clear it."

"Fuck off, Sav! I got the message! Wait, what day is it tomorrow? Do we have work?"

"No work, it's Saturday. After the glam squad comes through, I'll stop by with a few others to get you up to speed. Meredith insisted that's how you would want it."

"She knows me well. And whom should I be expecting?"

"Johnny and Roberto. Mark may call in. Fred may make an appearance as well."

"I'm too tired to care about why Fred is coming over. And I guess he sort of saved my life, so ..." she trailed off when she realized she had to thank Fred. "On that note, I'm going to bed. What time will you make an appearance?"

"At five p.m. Dina is preparing a feast."

"I'm glad you feel comfortable mooching my staff all the time. Can't we go out to dinner? I've been cooped up for so long."

"Whatever works for you—after you're fully briefed on what's going on," Savin said.

"OK, sounds good. I'll let Dina know. Good night."

She put on the baseball cap and opened the door to find Angelo standing outside. "Inside, now. We only have a minute to get upstairs," Angelo said.

She rushed inside, handing off her duffel bag to Angelo when he insisted.

Once in the elevator, Angelo said with a grin, "You're traveling light these days."

"Ugh, you have no idea. I've been wearing *tracksuits* for as long as I can remember now. All I want is to attend an A-list event and wear a custom Ralph Lauren gown and some Saint Laurent strappy heels. Well, after a spa day and seventeen hours of sleep."

Angelo laughed, and they walked into Celeste's apartment. "Sounds about right." He straightened up and got down to business. "Meredith arranged for me to sleep in one of your guest rooms for the next few days. I've had everything swept. We have eyes and ears on the entrances of the building and your office as well for the foreseeable future."

"What's the likelihood of Omar showing up again?"

"Knowing what we know about him, and knowing that his ego has suffered a serious blow, I'd say very likely."

"Gotta love a man not deterred by a death sentence."

"He's Omar. He doesn't give a shit."

"Yeah. Listen, I'm heading to bed. I need some time to clean up and sleep. What's my schedule tomorrow?"

"Ty will come over around eleven a.m., and the others will be here around one p.m."

"OK. Good night, and thanks for everything you've done." She walked into her bedroom and closed the door before he could see her tears.

She looked around her room to see everything just as she'd left it —a place for everything, and everything in its place, as her mother used to say. There were so many emotions she thought she should be feeling. Relieved, victorious, powerful. After all, she'd won! She was safe, she'd destroyed Omar in retribution, and she'd emerged a bona fide billionaire. The realization that none of this brought Theodore back, that none of this took away her pain, was too much to bear. He was gone because of her, and her penance was to have everything she thought she ever wanted but to live without the one thing she never thought she would have a taste of—true love. Celeste still had not shared with anyone what she knew about Theodore's death, and truth be told, she still hadn't come to terms with it herself.

13

THE ILLUMINATI OF WALL STREET

Celeste awoke after a night of terrifying dreams, relieved to open her eyes and realize she was in her own bed. After a quick shower, she wandered into the kitchen. Someone had stocked her refrigerator with fresh melon, eggs, and vegetables. Dina was not there yet, so she decided to cook for herself. She combined several ingredients and prepared a fluffy omelet. *Yum*, Celeste thought as she polished off her omelet and fruit. *Maybe I can take care of myself after all.*

Ty would be showing up soon and would no doubt be shocked at her appearance.

"Knock, knock. Anyone home?" Angelo, who had left a note that he was sitting outside her apartment, had let Ty in.

"Speak of the devil! I was just thinking about the expression on your face when you saw what I did to my hair."

"I'm not even gonna ask what happened. I have to be discreet with the clientele I keep, ya know. But I wish you had consulted me before you went all Britney in your mourning. We'll need to get busy fixing it right away if you don't want the others to see it. First color, and then some keratin-bonded extensions. No one will be the wiser until your natural hair grows back, but I will be charging a premium for having to reverse this disaster."

"You're a lifesaver!"

Ty trailed behind Celeste into her dressing room with his equipment case. As he unpacked, he said, "Oh, my God! I can't believe you're back! You have missed so much! I can't even remember how long you were gone, but it seemed like a forever vacation. Was Paris amazing?"

"It felt like forever. Paris is always wonderful, but you know how it is—lots of work. Almost settled on a space and interviewed several candidates to run the office."

Ty gestured to Celeste to sit down in her vanity chair. "I expected you to come back with suitcases full of Dior's fall line! What gives?"

"Oh, it's all in my Paris apartment, since I'll be back and forth a lot in the next few months to get the satellite office up and running. Less to transport this way." *Well, it certainly sounds believable,* Celeste admitted.

"Are you still sad? We were hoping this time away from New York would turn your frown upside down! We miss seeing your TG!"

"What's TG?"

"Your Theodore Glow. I can't take credit—Patrick came up with it."

Celeste's smile did not reach her eyes. "Oh, got it. Funny! Tell me what's been going on with you."

"So much! You wouldn't believe it! I'm still dating THE guy—remember? Before you left?" Celeste nodded at Ty's prompt, though she was having trouble staying focused. She wanted to look like her old self as soon as humanly possible, but more importantly, she needed to get an update on Omar's status and any intel the hackers or Lorraine had been able to dig up, as well as to figure out what the Feds wanted. Instead, she had four more hours of hair coloring and extension insertion.

Angelo lightly rapped on the door to Celeste's bedroom suite. "Come in, Angelo! We're decent," Celeste said.

"Dr. Smythe is here for you."

"Oh, thank God! Ty, we can finish the extensions once Dr. Smythe plumps me up. When you come back in, I'll look like myself again."

"Sounds like a plan. Hey, Doc!" Ty walked out to the bedroom to greet Celeste's plastic surgeon. He lowered his voice to a half whisper. "She needs a lot more than usual. She looks haggard—a shell of her usual self."

"I heard that! Get out of here!" Celeste laughed despite herself because she knew he was right.

"Ty couldn't be more wrong. You're gorgeous as always," the doctor said when he walked into her dressing room. He was a mousy man with sallow skin, about Celeste's height. But he was the best. He reserved the energy he did not put into his own appearance for his patients—and Celeste was grateful for his talents.

"I know you're lying, but thank you! So great to see you! Let's get down to business."

Dr. Smythe got to work, first numbing Celeste, and then poking, prodding, and plumping her back to normal.

"Oh, thank you so much!" Celeste nearly cried tears of joy when she recognized the face in the mirror. The hyaluronic filler had lessened the impact of her gauntness from not eating, sleeping, meditating, or otherwise doing anything healthy for many weeks. The chemical peel sloughed off and resurfaced her skin into a dewy glow. *Maybe looking like my old self will help me feel like my old self again.*

Patrick arrived a few hours later, just as Ty inserted the last extension. "Celly, you look fantastic! Ty, she doesn't look as bad as you said."

"You didn't see her before Dr. S. got to her."

"You're lucky I love you so much!" Celeste said.

"Don't worry, I'm only kidding! Well, sort of. She was *brunette. From a box*," Ty said in horror.

Celeste stuck her tongue out at Ty and turned to Patrick. "Can we do an organic airbrush tan and some makeup?" She looked at the clock on her phone. "Savin et al. will be here in an hour. Can we make that work?"

"Sure thing!"

An hour later, Celeste was coiffed and made up as if the Riyadh detour had never happened. She shooed Ty and Patrick out of her apartment, scarfed down part of the lunch that Dina had left for her, and changed into a pale-pink cashmere sweater, jeans, and nude Jimmy Choo pumps. She had canceled Dina's feast and informed Savin they were going out to dinner. Once this briefing, whatever it would entail, was over, she fully intended to enjoy a well-deserved night out on the town.

Angelo escorted Savin, Mark, Roberto and his chic girlfriend Sam, Johnny, and a man she did not recognize into her living room.

"I can't tell you how happy I am to see some familiar faces," Celeste said, hiding her bewilderment as to why everyone seemed to be in on the scheme. She hugged each of her friends.

"Mark, I've missed you! Glad you could make it in person. How's the baby? I bet she's adorable!"

"You've missed a lot, Cell. Don't ever disappear on us like that again. And she's perfect."

"And Sam, Roberto, all the way from Brazil! I appreciate the visit."

"Well, we were going to be in town anyway. We were ecstatic to hear you were safe."

"Johnny! I was hoping I could stay out of trouble a little longer, but you know how it goes."

"You're a magnet for danger, but all the best clients are. Glad you're back safely."

"I've already seen you, so hi again," Celeste taunted Savin.

"But you missed me, nonetheless!"

"Of course, darling. Thanks for holding down the fort while I was away."

She stuck her hand out to the stranger. "I gather you know my name. And you are?"

"Yes, Ms. Donov—er, yes, Celeste, I know who you are. You had a lot of people worried back here in the States with your little multicontinent tour. I work for the FBI, but I'm here in an unofficial capacity. I have been, shall we say, advising behind the scenes on how to get you home safely in partnership with my friend at the CIA."

Celeste, a quizzical expression on her face, asked, "Why on earth would you need to be involved? And I appreciate your help, but clearly I made it home safely on my own."

Savin chimed in. "Easy, now, Celly. These guys work with Ace."

"And where *is* the elusive Ace? The man with all the plans who failed to respond to any of my urgent messages." She lowered her head, turned to Savin, and whispered, "We should revisit our contract with him. He's become quite lazy."

Savin laughed and said, "OK, Cell, we can discuss later."

"Let's all grab a drink, and then we can get started." For confidentiality purposes, Angelo had stepped out of the apartment after sweeping it once more, and Celeste had asked Dina to go home after preparing a few hors d'oeuvres. Celeste gestured for everyone to help themselves at her wet bar, where two scotches, several reds, and two whites were sitting. Once the drinks were flowing and everyone was seated, Savin cleared his throat.

"So, as you know, Celly, your little plot succeeded. In fact, it worked better than any of us could have expected."

"Is it safe to assume that everyone here has been briefed on all my, er, whereabouts while I was away?"

"Yes," Savin answered.

"OK. So how did you all know in advance what I was up to?"

Savin and Mark exchanged looks. Mark said, "Ace. He set up your devices with encrypted trackers only he could access. The duffel bag you picked up in Dubai was bugged, so he heard most of your interactions those next few days and pieced it together from there." Celeste reddened in anger at the invasion of her privacy. *That motherfucker*, she fumed. *At least Alex wasn't completely full of shit.*

She thought of the nights she'd cried herself to sleep, afraid of what Omar was capable of, but also overwhelmed with sadness from losing Theodore. Zari's murder and her subsequent sobs. Fucking Alexsandr for three days. *Ugh! My life is none of his fucking business.*

Savin seemed to anticipate her mounting fury. "Don't worry, we weren't listening in on you. It was only for your protection."

Celeste forced a neutral expression. "We can discuss that later. Just get to why you two keep exchanging glances."

"We can't find Omar, Celly," Mark said, voice tinged with sympathy. "After he came to your office, he used his passport to return to London, and then disappeared into thin air."

We still don't know where Omar is, so precautions must be taken, she recalled Alexsandr saying the previous night, but it hadn't fully registered until now.

"And there's another thing you should know—Fred has been missing for at least six days. No trace of his passport and no credit card usage. We have reason to be concerned."

Celeste swallowed. "So, basically, you're telling me I'll be looking over my shoulder for Omar for the rest of my life? What else? I can tell there's more."

"Well, the good news is, our trades stayed under the radar. All of them. We are the envy of Wall Street, and our records are airtight." Savin nodded to the FBI agent and took a deep breath before continuing.

"Get to the fucking point, Sav. I know when you're hiding something," Celeste said.

"Omar killed Theodore," Mark said. "Well, we think he did. Theodore's mom, Poppy, reached out to Savin. Celly, she didn't identify his body. She didn't even receive a call."

Savin picked up the story. "The hospital in Massachusetts—"

Celeste interrupted him. "Guys, I knew all this before I left. Theodore was in London before he died, like he told me. He had an argument with two men, and two witnesses reported he was overpowered and pushed into an SUV. Then the trail went dry, so Omar must've ... must've taken care of Theodore. Then he paid off a few people to orchestrate a plane crash, make it look like an accident." She kept her cool but bit her lip to hold back the tears. *Ouch.* She had forgotten about the fresh filler injections.

To Celeste, it felt as if everyone breathed a collective sigh of relief that she knew Theodore had been murdered. "I appreciate you getting to the bottom of this. Where Theodore is concerned, I want to know everything there is to know. But next time, tell me immediately. Please don't treat me like a child. I am devastated. Devastated. My heart has broken into a thousand pieces because Theodore is gone. However, I'll be OK again someday. Soon. I will. Because I have to. I won't let Omar take anything else from me."

"There is one more thing about Theodore, Celly," said Savin.

God, what now?

"His mum found something at his apartment with a note that she was to give it to you." Savin reached into his satchel (*Oh, that's why he's carrying a man satchel*) and pulled out a small, wrapped gift box. An envelope with *Celeste* written in Theodore's handwriting was affixed on top. Celeste was taken aback.

"Poppy said you haven't returned any of her calls," Savin commented without judgment. "Celly, everyone just wants to be here for you. And you seem to forget we're all grieving Theodore's death, too."

Celeste looked down at her feet. *Well, what was I supposed to say to her? I'm framing my ex to avenge your son's death? I'm convinced your son was brutally murdered, and I could've stopped it?*

"She flew here to hand deliver it, Celly. Don't worry, I covered for you and stuck to the Paris office story to explain your absence. I said you needed some time to grieve and hadn't returned anyone's calls."

"Wow, that was extremely kind of her. I'll open it a little later, after dinner. What else do we need to cover? I need several more cocktails!" Celeste hoped they were buying her blasé attitude. The truth was, she was not ready to face what Theodore had to say. He was gone. What did it matter?

Sam and Roberto exchanged glances. "This is where we come in," Roberto said. "I'll just cut to the chase because I, too, need a cocktail, and we've been through too much for me to start sugarcoating things for you. We've been working with the FBI and some of the European regulators for a while. We're helping them take down some pretty bad guys."

Celeste let out a laugh, then covered her mouth to hold back another. "Sorry—but aren't we the bad guys? I mean, I just framed someone for a crime punishable by death, and we all made billions of dollars as a result. Am I missing something?"

"Celeste, we're talking about cutting off major funding sources for terrorist organizations around the globe, with stunts similar to what you and Savin have been doing with your fake headlines."

She recalled how vague Sam had been about her law practice when they had met so many months ago. *Or was it just last week?* There was only before Theodore and after Theodore. She had no concept of time anymore.

The FBI agent spoke up. *Why can't I remember his name?* "I've been on to you and Savin for some time, and frankly, what you're doing is brilliant. Effective. Swift. We want to replicate this, handicapping organizations all over the world. Think of the good we could do."

"I'm assuming this isn't within the purview of your day job," Celeste said sardonically.

"Well, what Chet isn't saying, Celly, is that his wife also worked for the bureau and was murdered by men who worked for Omar. She was investigating an arms dealer who was shipping automatic weapons through Miami to Central and South America and was in the wrong place at the wrong time. So this is personal for him. Kindred souls, as they say," Savin explained.

So much death. So much sadness. Her heart went out to Chet. "I'm so sorry for your loss, Chet. Omar has caused so much destruction."

Chet nodded but remained silent.

"Johnny, what's your role in all this?"

"Sam and I have been working together behind the scenes to make sure you guys are protected for a while now," Johnny explained. "Our ears are to the ground to discern what Justice and the SEC are focusing on, and we have a global underground network of hackers, lawyers, traders, intelligence. The illuminati of Wall Street, if you will."

"Is this a recruitment?"

Chet jumped in. "We're impressed with your research, your

ingenuity. You've demonstrated a commitment to the higher good, to ridding the world of one more bad guy. You, Savin, Lorraine, all of you we need more of you."

Celeste suddenly felt as if she were at an Amway conference. She was hesitant to commit to something this life-changing without serious consideration. "I'm a simple woman, really. I like to win. I like to make money, enjoy my money, and live a semi-stress-free existence so that I can look twenty-seven when I'm fifty-five. I didn't sleep, fuck, or relax—my three favorite pastimes—for an entire month." *Well, two truths and a lie, right?*

Mark picked up on Celeste's reluctance. "All right, enough for tonight. This can wait. Let's celebrate the Queen's return!"

"Did they ever change that fucking headline? It should read 'Queen and King of Wall Street.'"

"Sorry not sorry. The journalist must've known I'm of superior intelligence to the likes of you," Savin joked.

Everyone laughed, probably because they knew she would decimate Savin in a ball-busting contest. "I'll let this one slide. Where are we going for dins, by the way?"

"Il Mulino."

"Mmm, I haven't been there in ages. I'll grab my bag and we can go."

The box with the card—Theodore's last words to me. She picked up the box gingerly, carried it into her bedroom, and placed it in her top dresser drawer. Too much information was swimming around in her head; she could not read his last words to her just yet. She needed to connect with the living for a few hours. *I'm sorry, darling. I'm drowning in sadness from missing you, and I just need to feel light tonight. For once.*

Could she really disrupt her old life for the thrill of taking down criminals like Omar? She was no heroine, but something about it did entice her. It could be a reprieve from her overwhelming sense of loss, if nothing else. Maybe she could corner Sam to learn a little more of her perspective. Why choose this insanity when they could afford stable, luxurious lives of leisure?

"Let's go! I've been holed up like a prisoner for a month!" Celeste said when she walked back out into her living room, and everyone headed toward the door. Mark hung back and waited while Celeste switched out the lights.

"You OK, Celly?" Mark asked. "This is a lot to take in."

"Yeah, it is. But it's time to move forward and not let Omar hurt anyone else. I have to know, Mark. How long have you been involved in this ... game?"

"About two years, but I'm even more committed now that I have to worry about Jin and our baby."

Two years. Life before Theodore.

Mark continued. "Celly, we're on the right side of this. It gives my life meaning I've never had before. You wouldn't believe what we've been able to accomplish in such a short time. We've all been waiting for the right time to bring you and Savin in. You sort of forced our hand with your appetite for vigilante justice." Celeste was astonished that Mark had kept a secret, especially one of this magnitude, for so long.

"I couldn't let him die in vain, Mark." She fought back tears.

"He didn't, I assure you. I can't bring him back, but I can promise that working with us will give you a sense of purpose beyond what you've ever imagined."

"This meal! I should've worn an elastic waistband!" Savin said, and the others laughed. Celeste was managing to have a delightful evening with some of her favorite people. The group was buoyant after a few bottles of wine, and Savin was rallying everyone (except Chet, who was more the buttoned-up DC type than a late-night guy) to step out to a club on the Lower East Side called et al. for a little dancing. Normally, Celeste would have been game, but the envelope from Theodore beckoned her. Plus, she had an early start the next morning. She had a two-hour massage planned and had asked Swamiji for a consultation on some new mantras that would bring to the forefront some of her pain so she could process it. She texted

Monty to pick her up at the restaurant while the others arranged for their next destination.

On the ride home, she was quiet and fidgety. Since the moment she had found out Theodore was dead, she had wondered what his last thoughts were. Would his card give her any insights? Monty interrupted her thoughts.

"Miss Celeste, we're so happy to have you back. My wife has been asking when you're coming over for dinner!"

"Oh, that's so sweet! Let's arrange it soon." Monty's family was warm and loving, just what Celeste needed right now.

When they pulled up in front of her building, Celeste was ecstatic to see Jonah holding the front door for her.

"Jonah!" Celeste embraced him with a warm hug.

"New York is whole again!" Jonah exclaimed. "We've missed our favorite resident!" He walked behind the concierge desk. Celeste went over to her mailbox to get her mail from the past few days. *I'll get the rest of the mail the post office held tomorrow morning.*

"These were delivered this evening for you. Shall I carry them up?"

Celeste was only half listening while she waited for the elevator to arrive. She nodded over her shoulder. "Sure, darling, can you bring them up in ten minutes?" That would give her time to read the card in solitude.

"Of course."

Angelo was waiting at Celeste's front door for her. "Everything is secure, Celeste. Your housekeeper came by to tidy up, but other than that, no activity."

"Fantastic! Thanks, Angelo. Come on in. Jonah will be up in a few minutes. I'm going to change into some sweats and then pour myself a nightcap. Would you like one?"

"No, thanks. I'm going to call it a night."

"Sounds good. Sweet dreams!" Celeste nearly ran to her room, closing the door behind her. She retrieved the envelope and box, sat down on her chaise lounge by her floor-to-ceiling window overlooking the streetlights sixty stories below, and began reading.

My Darling Celeste,

 If you're reading this, things likely did not turn out as I intended. Please know that whatever happened is not your fault. In fact, it was destined to happen all along. I hate to admit that I did not always have the most honorable intentions. But you made me a better man. You showed me what it was like to love and be loved. And yes, I've always known you loved me. Even if it wasn't easy for you to say it in words, you said it to me a thousand times a day with your eyes, your touch, your smile. You are without a doubt the most magnificent woman I've ever met, and I wanted nothing more than to spend the rest of my days waking up next to you. Our time was cut short, though, and perhaps a love like ours is not meant to last. Know that we were the lucky ones. And if I were sitting beside you today, I would have asked you to be my wife. I saw you admiring this when we were shopping on the Champs-Élysées. Nothing shines as brightly as you, but it comes close. I love you now and always.

 Love,

 Theodore

Tears streamed down Celeste's cheeks as she slowly unwrapped the box. Inside was an impeccable diamond—perfect clarity, perhaps eight carats, cushion cut. An engagement ring. She slid it onto her left ring finger and was overwhelmed with sadness. She sobbed uncontrollably, mourning the life that had been ripped away from her. She curled up on her chaise and fell asleep, tearstained and snotty.

 Her dreams were disjointed, troubling. First there were happy memories with Theodore, the warm sea air on their skin as they dined by the water. And then images of a wedding. Her wedding. Savin, Mark, and Jack stood behind Theodore at the altar at St. Patrick's on Fifth Avenue where Theodore's funeral had been, and she stood at the back of the church looking at them. She was radiant with happiness. Theodore slowly turned to look at her, and she felt the excitement build to see him. But instead of his face, it was Omar's. His mouth twisted into a sinister smile. "Hello, Celeste."

The sound of Omar's voice in her dream startled her awake. She slowly opened her eyes to the sunshine beating down on her. Her sweater stuck to her skin, wet with perspiration. Her sinuses were dry. Once she realized she was at home, she went into the bathroom to splash cold water on her face and rinse off in the shower. She was starving and hoped breakfast was ready.

She opened her bedroom door and went to look for Dina or Angelo.

"Good morning, Celly!" Dina called out from the kitchen when she heard Celeste walk into the room. Dina walked over to Celeste and hugged her firmly. "Don't ever leave us again for that long. New York just isn't the same without you."

"Thanks, darling, though I just saw you yesterday and don't plan on leaving any time soon. It's always fantastic to see you, and today I'm famished, so I'm even more excited than usual!" Both women laughed.

"Well, you're in luck. I've prepared an antioxidant-rich meal for you. Ty said you were looking unwell, so I ramped up the nutrients."

Celeste was too hungry to care about Ty's dig. "You're wonderful. Thank you so much!"

"Go sit! I'll bring everything out. Oh, I saw your special delivery! Gorgeous!"

"Delivery? Oh yes, Jonah mentioned something about it last night, but I fell asleep."

"It's in the foyer."

Curious, Celeste padded in to look. She stopped dead in her tracks when she turned the corner and registered what was sitting on her console table.

Roses. Magenta roses. At least a hundred of them. "Welcome back, C," the card taunted.

14

CANDY-RED CFM BOOTS

"The audacity of this motherfucker! Can't we track down the flower shop, find out who placed the order and from where? What about your building's cameras?" Savin fumed.

Celeste shot him a withering look. "Of course we looked into all this yesterday," she responded. "Angelo was freaking out. A man whom no one can describe paid cash at a flower shop down the street that conveniently has no camera security system."

It was 7 a.m. on Monday, and she and Savin were seated in the war room. Celeste was tired of this mess, not to mention still jet-lagged and drained from the energy it took trying to acclimate to her old life as though nothing had happened while she was away.

"And what on earth happened to your hand?" Savin inquired.

"Once I realized Omar had sent the flowers, I did what any rational woman would do: I hurled the vase at my front door. Turns out flying glass can get lodged in your hand. Spent an hour or so getting scolded and then sewn up by my concierge doctor, who came to the apartment."

Savin's face screwed up in concern. "I'm worried about you, Celly. You're under an enormous amount of stress, and you still haven't discussed much of what happened while you were gone."

"Trust me, you don't really want to know. None of it was pretty, and I've never been so low in my life as I was for those few weeks. I'm trying to find a way to keep my head above water. But I still—" Celeste choked up and took a deep breath to hold back her tears. "I miss him desperately, Sav. And all this was for nothing, because Omar is still out there, probably somewhere in New York watching my every move. What the fuck does he want from me, Sav? And why now? He's free and alive, and Theodore is dead. It's not fair, goddammit!"

Savin walked over to Celeste and hugged her. She collapsed against him, and her resolve evaporated. She sobbed into Savin's chest, grateful for his friendship. They stayed like that for a while until a knock on the door interrupted them.

Rani, the only other person in the office with a keycard to the war room, stuck her head in. Consummate professional that she was, she pretended not to notice Celeste's tears. "Hey, guys, staff meeting in twenty minutes." They had two staff meetings per week, one on Monday at 8 a.m. and another on Thursday at 2 p.m. Today they would update everyone on the (fabricated) progress of the Paris operation.

"I need to freshen up. See you in a few." Celeste retreated to her office. *Ugh, my first day back, and of course I break down in tears.* She cleaned up her eye makeup, added some foundation to cover her red cheeks, then walked down the hall to their large conference room.

Lorraine was the first one to arrive. "Celeste! I'm so glad you're back!" The two women hugged, and Lorraine discreetly avoided mentioning Celeste's puffy face. Savin and Ace had kept Lorraine on a need-to-know basis regarding Riyadh, and she had proven trustworthy. Celeste was worried for her, though, now that she was involved so deeply. This was a lot to put on the shoulders of a person under thirty. Hell, it was a lot to put on the shoulders of a forty-something, and Celeste hoped she herself would be able to stay strong on her road to healing.

Once everyone had filtered in, Celeste called the meeting to order at two minutes before 8 a.m. (she despised tardiness.) In anticipation of her return, Savin had divided the analysts into teams and asked each one to present Celeste with a new pitch. The members of the team with the best pitch would each receive a generous cash bonus and the funds to invest as they pleased. With so much time to think during her hiatus, Celeste had developed this new strategy to motivate the analysts. She wanted each person working at D&C to embody an entrepreneurial spirit, thinking more along the lines of ownership and accountability. And she had always found that money was one of the best motivators, as was respect. She and Savin fired off questions to help the teams flesh out their pitches. The end goal was to identify the strongest members of the firm, who could take on more responsibility for business development.

Four hours later, the final team wrapped up its presentation, and Rani and the caterers brought in lunch.

In a rare display of earnestness, Celeste addressed the staff. "I'm impressed and energized by the dedication you've all demonstrated in identifying some viable new opportunities for D&C. I think I can speak for Savin as well when I say we truly have the best people in the business. Thank you all for the late nights spent researching and modeling. You should be as proud of yourselves as we are of you. You inspire us to do the best we can to help each of you develop to your maximum potential. Let's give everyone a hand. Thank you!"

The bros all exchanged high-fives, while Lorraine clapped.

"I don't even need to confer with Savin on this one because I know we're on the same page. For once!" she added. Everyone laughed, then quieted down as she continued.

"It was too difficult to pick one winner, so we've decided to give each of you the bonus—and to fund all the pitches. You'll each manage the project you've identified, and we'll have a competition to see whose project gains the highest percentage by the end of this quarter." She meant what she said—the teams had all risen to the challenge. But she also noticed a change in herself—she was more understanding of the staff's development and more appreciative of each one's unique talents. *Who am I and what have I become?*

Everyone in the room cheered with genuine smiles. It was the best Monday morning meeting she could remember.

Savin jumped in. "Now don't get too excited, because you still have to do your day jobs! You know what a whip cracker this one is!" he said, pointing to Celeste behind her back.

"I see that, and you are so inappropriate" she responded without turning around. "Now, let's eat!"

The rest of the day passed in a flash, the entire office electric with excited chatter. She was thrilled with the results of their competition and had been telling the truth when she said she felt inspired. It was a nice reprieve from her dark thoughts. Theodore's death had driven her to retreat into herself, and the Omar situation compounded her isolation. Swamiji had encouraged her yesterday to spend more one-on-one time with those she cared about and to confide in them about how alone she had felt since Theodore's death. *This warm fuzzy shit is so annoying ... but I do feel a little better.*

Later that evening, after Celeste and Savin had sent everyone home, the two sat in her office. She popped open a bottle of bubbly and filled the champagne flutes she kept for times like this. They toasted to the successful culture they had built at D&C.

"Our little experiment went over better than I could have imagined!" Celeste said.

"They were all excited to connect with you. They're intimidated by you and, you know, see that you can be cold at times." Savin's standard lecture was met with her typical eye roll.

"I've never claimed to be a warm fuzzy, but I'm happy they're happy. We make more money when they're happy."

Now it was Savin's turn to roll his eyes while he poured them another glass.

"Fred Warren is on line one for you," Rani's voice came over the speaker phone.

"At this hour?" Savin asked.

"Says he's in Europe and that it's urgent."

"Finally, he lets us know he's OK," Savin muttered under his breath. "Put him through. And get your ass home. No working late tonight, Rani!"

"I'm just wrapping up a few things. Will be gone in about twenty."

Fred's voice boomed on the line. "No time for polite conversation; don't want this line traced. I know what Omar wants. Celeste, you had an impressive head start, but we need to finish him off. I need you guys in Europe by midday tomorrow. Sav, I'll send instructions."

Click.

"He calls you Sav now? I take it this is his resurfacing after his hiatus?"

"A lot happened while you were gone. We called a truce after we learned Omar had beef with Fred as well. And yes, this is the first we've heard from him in a while."

"But what overlap do Fred and I have? Why can't we just ask Fred? We've been on opposing sides of deals for as long as I can remember," Celeste said, confused.

All of a sudden, Savin was gathering his things, his energy frantic. "This isn't about work, and we've got to leave. You have to run back to your apartment for your passport, I presume?"

"I need a lot more than my passport. And are we really going to hop on a plane just because Fred told us to?"

"Yes. I'll fill you in on the way. We developed contingency plans and escape strategies while you were away. We weren't just sitting around twiddling our thumbs, you know."

"How will we make arrangements this quickly?"

"Easy. Jack left his jet at Teterboro for just this purpose. His pilot is on standby."

Savin typed furiously on his phone and simultaneously told her the plans. "Monty is outside ready to run us by our apartments. We can leave by nine or ten tonight. Let's go."

Celeste followed Savin but continued her protest. "Savin, this is insane. I just got back."

"Tough shit. Believe me, this will all be worth it in the end."

"Fuck. I can't believe I'm doing this."

They grabbed their things, stopping at Rani's desk. "We have a last-minute investor meeting in Brazil," Savin told her. "You know how demanding Roberto and his crew are. Will keep you posted on our return."

"Can I come?" There stood Lorraine, looking as energized as always. *I hope she gets laid soon. This place should not be her only source of excitement.*

"No, we need you here," Celeste said. "But I promise we'll get you to an investor meeting soon. Look through our client lists and write up a pitch. Get creative! Look into the Philippines. I'll personally escort you, and then we can have a spa weekend!" *That should appease her for now.*

"I can't believe you talked me into this," Celeste said to Savin. After quick scrambles at their apartments to pack, they were speeding along the New Jersey Turnpike in Monty's Mercedes. ("The tunnel is a disaster," Monty had said.) "Since when are we at Fred's beck and call? And do we need to bring all those new guys in? The Feeb and his secret CIA friend?"

"No, Ace will take care of it."

"What the fuck does Ace have to do with this?" Celeste lowered her voice and continued. "He had me kidnapped and almost jeopardized the entire thing. You know I watched someone get murdered? Two men actually. And I had to be the one to find Zari dead and leave his body, did I tell you that? Ace isn't exactly at the top of my list."

"Celly, he's the only reason you weren't stoned to death in Riyadh. Literally. And rescuing you isn't exactly kidnapping. We need him if we're to find Omar, if we're ever to avenge Theodore's death."

"Whatever." As Celeste watched New Jersey whizzing by outside her window, she wondered what Fred had in store. She was shocked by Savin's cooperation with Fred and the illuminati. (Celeste still rolled her eyes at the name. *They're not fucking rap royalty!*) But he was right about one thing: she wanted Omar behind bars—or dead. *That's the* only *reason I am tolerating this insanity.*

"Zari is dead? I hadn't heard."

"Yes. I found him in Dubai just a few minutes after he had been shot. He and his family had a trip planned to America. I was going to meet his wife." She choked up at the memory of his vacant eyes.

Savin patted Celeste's arm. "I'm so sorry, Celly. I can't imagine. If it's any consolation, you're holding up much better than I ever could. I promise that when we get back, we'll send our condolences."

"Let's talk about something else. I'd really rather not have a tearstained face when we arrive in Paris. Where is Jack these days?"

"He's been hopping around Southeast Asia the past few weeks. He's worried about you. He said he'd call you soon, but in the meantime, I'm supposed to give you a hug."

"Is he still swooping in and out with a tiny plane? That's a terrifying thought."

"It really is. But, no, I think he's chasing down the perfect opium or the perfect woman or something. Or maybe a yoga retreat. He mentioned vipassana meditation, too. Who knows?"

"Has Mark brought the baby to New York yet?" She tossed her hair back, grateful to again have hair that could be tossed back. *Short and brunette wasn't a good look for me.*

"Whoa! What the fuck is that rock on your left hand? I was so distracted by the bandage on your other hand that I didn't even notice! Did you bed and wed Alexsandr in East Las Vegas?"

"No, of course not!" Celeste took a deep breath. "I forgot to mention in all the chaos today. This was the gift from Theodore in the wrapped box Poppy gave you. I grabbed it while I was packing. I struggled yesterday with what to do—it's probably so strange and tacky to wear it. But it's my only connection to him now. He proposed to me in the letter. Figures my only real proposal happened in writing. Posthumously."

"I'm not sure wearing it is the strangest part," Savin said. "It's more the 'you saying yes' part ..."

"Well, whatever. It's a breathtaking piece of jewelry. And he wanted me to have it. Once I tried it on, I never wanted to take it off."

Savin held her hand up into the light streaming in and whistled. "Flawless. What is that, about eight carats?"

"Yep. But more than the size—it's just so *me*. It's exactly what I would have picked out, had I ever been interested in getting engaged. Anyway, I need to focus on anything besides being sad about Theodore."

"OK. Here's what you need to know. Fred is on our side now. Enemies of your enemies are your friends and all that jazz."

"But why are Omar and Fred enemies?"

"I'm not exactly sure, but I do know that Fred wasn't particularly shocked to find out that Omar had a vendetta against him. Apparently, he's had some dealings with Omar over the years."

They chatted on, speculating how Fred and Omar could be connected, until they arrived at the airport, where Monty delivered them to Jack's plane. Monty handed off the luggage to the crew and walked over to Savin and Celeste.

"I don't know what you two are up to these days, but please be careful. My wife knows something is up and has demanded to see you. It's been a while, and she's worried."

"We'd love that, Mon. See you very soon!"

Celeste and Savin ascended the plane stairs, saying hello to the pilot. "Thank you for being available in under an hour," Savin said, shaking his hand.

Once they were settled in their seats and the flight staff had brought their drinks, Celeste asked, "Are you going to give me any of the details Fred sent you? Like where we're headed?"

"That's the easy part. We're going to your apartment in Paris."

"We're sitting ducks there."

"That's the point, isn't it? Omar was baiting you by letting you know he's watching you. You're responding as though you don't know it's him. We're all afraid he knows you were involved in Riyadh, but there's still the off chance he had someone monitoring your Paris apartment and thought you had just gotten home from France."

"Who are 'we,' and why am I not part of these conversations? Since when am I the little woman shielded from the men's grown-up talk? If it involves me, I need to be included. Period." Celeste had lost her footing in her old world, but she would not let this become the new norm.

"Relax. No one is plotting against you. It was just a few of us—me, Mark, Ace, Johnny, Chet. Roberto and Sam are also beside themselves with worry, but they don't know the extent of Omar's insanity. For the record, you were skeptical about working with the FBI. They can't bring you into the fold until you agree to participate."

"Sav, you're really doing this? It wasn't long ago we were in the DOJ's crosshairs, and in case you haven't noticed, you just committed one of the biggest insider-trading scams in history. Again. In the past two weeks."

"First of all, Omar's drug use is out of control. He's getting sloppy. We have documented sources who provided airtight rationale for why we would pull out of his investments—the day *before* you were in Riyadh. His activity there is consistent with the picture we've painted of him—imploding under his drug addiction, acting out irrationally. There was Page Six coverage of him in Saint-Tropez and Dubai recently showing his erratic behavior. Plus, D&C is protected because of our arrangement. The Feds view our contribution as more valuable than taking us down for making a few hundred million off of Omar. We can teach them how to catch the bad guys—the oil men, the oligarchs, the people taking from their countries and keeping their citizens impoverished.

"Celly, this is why I came to the West," Savin continued. "You can't imagine the world I grew up in in Lebanon. Spending evenings in bomb shelters. Afraid that at any time I would be separated from my family. And now I have an opportunity to make it better for other kids. Besides, although you and I sometimes operate in the gray areas on the edges of the law, we aren't destabilizing entire regions or preventing people from getting an education or feeding their children. We're doing quite the opposite—we're investing in the developing world's infrastructure; we're gambling to make these countries and regions stronger, not weaker. When the United States assists a country moving toward democracy, it is us and our friends investing."

"Oh, is that what we did, Savin, when we reported that China was seeking repayment in Mozambique and Nigeria? No. We were actually cutting off their opportunities with potential future investors. And we focused on the developing world to make money—not to be heroes. We aren't the worst guys here, but we certainly aren't the good guys."

"Celly, I'm on your side. You and I both know that it wouldn't be good for Mozambique to be in bed with China for long. Plus, Roberto and I just matched two hundred million dollars, earmarked for both countries. Anyway, we can talk business later. It would be good for you, for your soul, to be involved. But you can decide another time. Let's talk about where we're going to eat dinner."

Savin was trying to stimulate the old Celeste, but her mood had darkened again. There was no going back to her breezy, fun self. No diamond was going to bring Theodore back, either. So here she was, stuck in this hell of repugnant options—working for the Feds, going up against Omar. In her attempt to break off all ties with Omar, she had managed to make her entire life *about* Omar, the monster who had raped her and murdered Theodore. Her very real fear of taking him on yet again, when he had slithered away before, was that she would destroy herself and more people she loved in the process.

"Hmm. I could use a good meal. Alain Ducasse?"

"What about L'Arpège?" L'Arpège had been voted the eighth-best restaurant in the world and had maintained three Michelin stars since 1996 in an exceedingly competitive market.

"That works." Celeste was deflated now by Savin's recruitment, a reminder that life would never be "normal" again. *Omar. All the time Omar.* "You know, I broke up with Omar so many years ago because I was tired of thoughts of him consuming me, sick of his demands that I put him first, not wanting to be involved with his rage. Now, a decade later, after all we've managed to build, he still has me by the balls. Only this time, he's more dangerous, more unstable, and more enraged." She rubbed her temples, hoping it would prevent the onset of images of Theodore being tortured by Omar.

"I watched our security tape of when Omar came to the office," Savin said, seemingly reading her mind. "He looked like shit. He has aged a thousand years, while you've gotten twenty years younger, but he still has the same beady crazy eyes. You're going to be shocked if you see him, though I hope it doesn't come to that."

"Let's piece together some sort of plan. Consider this for a moment. Let's say we could lure Omar somewhere, entrap him, capture him. What then? Could our CIA and FBI buddies get him to Riyadh? Is that our best shot at ridding the world of him—getting him to Riyadh for his public trial—or do you think he could bribe his way out of it?" She had purposely stopped watching the news but was confident the Saudis were still on their jihad to find him. They didn't let go of these things easily.

"I know where you're going with this, and we are *not* making you bait. We've already decided against it. Of course, it was the FBI's idea, echoed by the CIA with a promise to facilitate the meeting overseas and keep you safe. But no. Ace agreed with me. No way in hell."

"Savin, what the fuck! Why are you or Ace or anyone making decisions for me? I am *fully* capable of assessing risks myself." *No man makes my decisions!*

"Are you, Celly? Your judgment is poor where Omar is involved; it always has been. You're operating on emotion and ego, but we need you clearheaded and logical."

"Are you suggesting that I'm just a hysterical woman?"

"No, I'm suggesting that you've been through enormous trauma at the hands of Omar, things you've never disclosed even to me, and you're too close to it. We're not going to let the Feds use you as bait in their own vendetta against him. So here's what I propose: we arrive in Paris and find out why Fred sounded the alarm, enjoy a few meals, have a few meetings. Make this satellite office seem real so that you always have an escape overseas with a hub to get anywhere you like. Security will escort us everywhere we go, obviously."

Celeste was only half listening. They all meant well, but they had let Omar slip through their hands too many times. He had been in her office, for God's sake! Where was Angelo then? Why hadn't Ace stopped it? Why weren't the Feds watching, ready to spring into action? There were no satisfactory answers.

"Fine, let's do L'Arpège for din tonight. After dinner we can check out that lounge we love. The dark, swanky one with the cheesy French jazz? Close to the Place Vendôme?"

"Perf," Savin said. He was on to his next task, already buried in emails.

"OK, I'm going to try to work through some of my forty thousand emails that piled up while I was away, then grab a few hours of sleep." Celeste made her way back to the plane's bedroom with her iPad Pro in hand. Once comfortable in the bed, she connected to the WiFi and opened her email application, but her eyelids were heavy.

She slept through the landing and awoke only to Savin's hand lightly shaking her. "Celly, it's time to go!"

RAOUL, CELESTE'S USUAL DRIVER IN PARIS, WAS WAITING FOR THE TWO of them. A severe-looking man, she guessed French by his scowl, stood next to Raoul, a gun on his hip. Her self-defense training had taught her to scan for weapons; she also noticed a holster at his ankle.

"Per your request, Miss Celeste, Victor will be joining us and escorting you around town."

"Thank you, Raoul, and lovely to meet you, Victor."

When they were settled in the back seat, Celeste leaned over to Savin. "Per *my* request? I seem to have forgotten that I requested an *armed guard* for our quick, *safe* getaway to Paris."

"Perhaps I had a little something to do with that. But we can't be too careful with that rock you're sporting. Someone will cut off your finger for it."

Paris was grumpy, overcast, with heavy rainclouds hanging low. Savin kept the tone light with a story about his latest SoHo shopping experience. "So I asked her, 'What's stopping me from wearing a white tux to a black-tie event, anyway?' You know what she had the audacity to say? Guess!"

Celeste was only half listening. "That you need a healthy dose of self-restraint for these grandiose ideas of yours?"

"She said I was much too handsome to make such a giant fashion mistake."

"When is she moving in?"

Savin laughed. "Fuck off. I didn't even ask her to dinner."

"Progress! See? Maybe you are exercising that self-restraint I mentioned!"

They arrived at her apartment building in the chic 8th Arrondissement, and both men escorted her and Savin into the building. Once their luggage was stowed and they were safely inside, Raoul excused himself. Victor explained in rough English that they would need to keep the front and back doors locked at all times and could not open the windows. Then he told them their schedule for the day. They were to spend the day working inside her apartment until it was time to meet Fred for dinner. Victor and his team would scope out the restaurant to ensure their safety.

"Thanks, Victor," said Celeste.

Victor nodded with a stoic expression and left the apartment to station himself outside the door. They spent the morning on conference calls and answering emails from their staff until they broke for lunch. Celeste's housekeeper had arranged for a Guy Savoy delivery.

"Mmm, this looks delicious!" Celeste remarked when she walked into the dining room with Savin.

"Can you smell that truffle? Tantalizing!" Savin said.

The two caterers busied themselves serving Celeste and Savin, while Savin gushed about her apartment.

"This place is incredible! And the view of the Champs-Élysées … to die for!"

"That's right, you've never stayed here before. My designer has impeccable taste, so I would fully expect you to love it!"

"I thought you 'handpicked' everything," Savin said, confused.

"Exactly," Celeste said, winking.

Once the staff had retreated to the kitchen, Celeste murmured, "It will be interesting to hear what Fred has to say, won't it? And to hear what his plan is?"

Savin looked upset. "Celly, I'm worried about continuing this vendetta against Omar. He's proven to be more dangerous than any of us could've ever imagined a decade ago. We've all agreed: we can't let anyone, especially you, get hurt by Omar again. It was a mistake to let you leave last time. When I think of what could've happened ..."

"Savin, we've been through this. I can take care of myself. I don't need all of you protecting me all the time."

"But don't you?"

"Sav, can we please change the subject to something more pleasant? I don't have the energy to debate this tired issue again. All will be well, and we'll find a way to take down Omar, albeit more slow-moving and with the involvement of the authorities." Celeste rolled her eyes and pursed her lips, indicating she had said all she was going to.

"Fine, we can shelve this for the time being. But this isn't over. Your reckless behavior has got to stop."

Just then, the caterers came in to clear the remains of their lunch. Celeste was relieved the conversation was over for now.

It wasn't reckless; it worked! Omar has resurfaced because of my little Riyadh scheme, and this time, he won't get away. I'll see to that! Aloud, she said, "Wasn't this meal amazing? I never get tired of Guy's creations."

They spent the rest of the afternoon working, making calls to their team and to investors.

By early evening, they were both getting antsy. "Ready for a cocktail? Your scotch collection is enticing."

Celeste shook her head no. "I'm going out to one of my favorite restaurants in one of my favorite cities with one of my favorite men. I need to get ready!" She went to her bedroom for a shower, blowout, and fresh makeup. She was unusually calm, more relaxed than she had been in months. The weather was shit tonight, so she would have to get creative.

She strolled into her walk-in closet, eyeing everything through a critical lens. She could make do with a dangerously low-cut ivory sweater that was virtually see-through, a black miniskirt, and over-the-knee boots. She would not wear Theodore's ring, though, in case Omar was watching her. No need to get him too enraged yet. She opened the small wall safe in her closet, reluctantly removing the ring and placing it on the crushed velvet jewelry tray. Images of Theodore's tortured body flooded her thoughts. She withdrew her small Glock 30S from the safe, a subcompact handgun that could be easily concealed in a handbag, and turned its smooth surface over in her hand, careful not to wrinkle her bandage. Her self-defense trainer's words echoed in her head: *Never carry a gun unless you are prepared and willing to use it.* She checked that the magazine was fully loaded and snapped it back in, flipping the safety on. She decided to bring it and an extra magazine, knowing that Omar had already slipped past her security before. Now, what handbag to carry to conceal it? She fingered several of the bags on her shelves, settling on a buttery leather Bottega hobo that would allow her to easily access the gun.

Celeste dressed carefully, sat on her bed, and pulled on her candy-red come-fuck-me boots. Once satisfied with her reflection in her full-length mirror, she grabbed a long, gray Max Mara coat and went into the living room. Savin had found the speakers to stream soft jazz. He was seated on her couch with a glass of scotch in his hand, watching the headlines on the BBC.

"I see you found your way around the liquor cabinet just fine."

"You're ready early! This is a first." He turned to look at her and started laughing. "A, I love the red boots, and B, I love the statement they make—that you give zero fucks."

"Hey, I've been holed up for months. I gotta step up the spiciness a little!"

Celeste took another glass of scotch from Savin's outstretched hand and gingerly placed her handbag on the end table.

"So, Fred is meeting us at the restaurant? Why doesn't he just come over here and tell us his big secret?"

"I suggested that, but he thinks it best to be seen out in public. When have you ever stayed in when you were in Paris?"

"You make a good point. Cheers!" Celeste took a long pull on the scotch. "Yum, you broke into the good stuff."

"Everything you have is the good stuff," Savin said, laughing.

"All right, I'm hungry. Let's go!" Celeste lowered her voice. "Is the serious guy in the hall joining us for dinner?"

"Ace insists Victor stay with us our entire trip."

Celeste rolled her eyes. *As if a Frenchie is actually going to be able to protect anyone against an evil mastermind.*

THEY ARRIVED AT L'ARPÈGE TO FIND A RED-FACED FRED, A FEW cocktails in. He gave Celeste an awkward hug, whispering in her ear, "We were so worried about you, Celeste. I kept thinking I could've done more."

"Great to see you, Fred! I'm starved! Let's get to our table."

Over countless decadent courses, Fred explained that Omar had been keeping an eye on Celeste for many years. "According to our intel, what really made him lose it was seeing you happy with ... what was his name?"

"Theodore."

"Yes, Theodore. Once he saw you happy with someone else, he started digging up things we all thought were buried for good. Imagine how he viewed your Biochrome short through his cocaine-filtered paranoia. He was blind with jealous rage and then discovered that, to top it all off, you were behind his most crushing trade blow. Couldn't stand seeing you happy with Theodore. I assume you know what happened next."

This was the most concerned Celeste had ever seen Fred. Whatever peace offering Savin had orchestrated had been effective.

"Makes sense, Fred. But what I don't understand is where you fit in. And I also don't understand the urgency of this trip."

"Well, there's something else you should know. I was the other guy at O'Reilly's." Celeste looked at him quizzically, then turned to Savin. He raised his eyebrows, indicating this was the first he was hearing of this, too. "Oh, that O'Reilly's," she said slowly as it all came rushing back. O'Reilly's was where Savin had played bartender the fateful night that had changed the trajectory of their lives. They had not known Fred back then, so Savin had taken no notice of the nondescript financier with whom Omar was speaking. He only had his eye on the prize, the information Fred provided to Omar about the Biochrome stock.

"Omar was the only person I conferred with on that arrangement," Fred continued. "Once I realized what'd happened, I looked into who had been at the bar that night. At first I thought Omar had orchestrated the entire thing to play me. Once I realized he lost bigger than I did, I knew something was awry. Of course, it didn't take long to figure out that Roberto had been on the good side of the deal, and then, magically, you two fresh-faced kids had seed money."

"So you've known all along? All these years you've known we fucked you?" Savin asked. Celeste was speechless.

"Yes. But I'm a pragmatist. I let it slide for a few reasons. One, I couldn't go after you without Omar figuring out what had happened. Didn't want to deal with it. Also, I had played both sides of the deal like anyone involved with," he cleared his throat and lowered his voice, "such situations would have done. Unbeknownst to her, wife number one was as deep on the short as I was on the long—so I was positioned to win either way. I set it up that way because I didn't trust Omar as far as I could throw him. Omar didn't catch my wife's gain but only saw my loss, so he had no reason to suspect I was involved in any way. We parted ways after that, and I vowed never to get involved with him again."

"So, the hostility you've always had toward us—I guess you got it honestly," Celeste said.

"Look, I'm no martyr and I'm no victim. I made a lot of money off your fuckover of Omar. I'm worried about me and mine in all this, too. Omar is unhinged. I understand he surfaced at your office recently. I have three ex-wives, seven children, and twelve grandchildren. I'm not particularly interested in getting in his crosshairs. Celeste, what you did in Riyadh was fucking admirable— but also reckless and suicidal. I understand you're heartbroken, but I'm not going to lie—I'm shocked you're still alive. I guess we can thank Ace for that." Fred looked around the restaurant, lowering his voice. "Omar is a cockroach. It's easier to get rid of cockroaches in Europe ..." he trailed off.

Celeste took a swig of her wine.

"Fred, let's think through the situation. Omar is after me. Why involve all of you? I can draw him out with you guys behind the scenes, and we can squash him." She knew it would work, but her skin crawled at the thought of being alone with Omar. *I wish there were another way. But there isn't.*

"Celly, cockroaches are impossible to kill," Savin said, the concern back in his voice.

Celeste ignored him and turned her attention to Fred again. "I need one more question answered. Why is this imminent? It's now apparent Omar has been dodging my security safeguards for years. He's known what I've been up to. I need to understand why you wanted us to fly here today and arrive by tonight. What am I missing?"

"We can thank our illuminati friends for the urgency. They've hacked him more closely than any of us can ..."

Celeste shot Savin a dirty look. She hadn't known this would be another recruitment. "Oh, please, Fred, just tell me what the fuck is going on. And for the record, we all survived just fine before those guys started snooping around."

Fred pulled out his phone. "My sources sent me this today. Right before I contacted the two of you."

Celeste and Savin leaned in to look. Fred scrolled through his photo library: Celeste and Theodore, hand in hand in Gustavia, St. Barth's. Celeste walking to Theodore's apartment in London. Celeste, yoga mat in hand, in Union Square. Celeste with brown hair in Riyadh. Celeste in Dubai. Celeste and Theodore skiing. Celeste with Jack and Savin brunching. Celeste walking out of Pilates class. Photos of a room with walls of photos of Celeste, all pushpinned into place chronologically. Celeste's life chronicled for over a decade with the latest photo just two days before in New York.

"Fuck." Celeste was not one to overreact, but she was uneasy. "Fuck," she said again and took another swig of wine. *Creepy. But not surprising.*

"The Feds made a recent sweep of one of Omar's properties overseas yesterday. These were on his hard drive. Don't worry, he was none the wiser. We think he's getting closer to executing whatever it is he's planning. I understand he had contact with you this weekend?"

"Yes," Celeste said, sighing in frustration. "He sent me flowers with a cryptic message. Of course, there was no trace of who ordered or delivered the flowers ..." She looked sheepishly at her bandaged hand. "I sort of broke the vase in a rage."

Fred glanced at her hand and continued. "And we know with certainty that Omar is in Paris today, which is why I urged you to come. I think we should connect with the embassy here tomorrow. Find out who is on the ground. Figure out a way to ensnare Omar."

"Agreed," Savin said. "We go about this the right way and turn it over to law enforcement to handle. Omar will be in jail for a long time, based on what he's done. And that's if they don't extradite him to Saudi."

Outwardly, Celeste was agreeable, but her mind was racing, poking holes in their plan. Omar would figure out what they were up to tomorrow and would disappear. She needed her own plan to ensure Omar didn't slip away again. "This is the right path forward," she said. "Now that we've gotten all this settled, let's enjoy ourselves a little. Omar will still be here to ruin our day tomorrow. Fred, where have your travels taken you lately?"

"I enjoyed a few weeks in Belize. Turns out it's not such a bad place to hide out. The diving there is incredible, too!"

"Oooo, that's one place I haven't been yet. Once things settle down a little, I'm going to need some major downtime. Guess who's going to have to hold down the fort?" Celeste pointed at Savin. "You!" He did not look concerned in the slightest.

"Now that our team is a little more independent, I may take a few vacations of my own!" Savin said.

15

MINE AND ONLY MINE

After dinner, the trio went to Buddha Bar, one of Celeste's favorites. She excused herself to go to the toilette to freshen up, lost in thought. Savin and Fred had been having a friendly disagreement on whether South Africa or Kenya had better safaris, but she had bigger things on her mind. When she walked past the front door of the lounge, she saw Victor in place, alert and scanning the street.

Once in the restroom, Celeste reached into her bag. She tensed when her hand brushed against the Glock, reinforcing yet again that her life had forever changed. Omar's obsession with her was unnerving, and she could focus only on weighing her options. The young woman inside of her who carried the trauma from Omar's brutality urged her not to do anything stupid, begged her not to poke at him, but the woman she had grown into, the invincible woman with unlimited resources, refused to shrink from him. She was going to take him down, and this takedown was going to be on *her* terms. She'd already made it so far. Just look at what she'd pulled off in Riyadh. It would be simple to find someone who would kill Omar. Or deliver him to Saudi. But why could she not shake the nagging feeling that this was too risky? She could not get comfortable with the only risk she feared. *What if he comes after Savin or Jack or Mark? How would I feel then?*

She recovered and pulled out her makeup bag, reapplying her highlighter and lip gloss. *Ugh, I need some time away,* she thought as she noted how haggard she looked, despite Dr. Smythe's work. Life on the run was not for her and being in Paris made her miss Theodore all the more. *How did I end up here?* She pasted a smile on her face, determined not to cry, and returned to the table. Her two friends were engaged in another friendly debate, busting each other's balls about recent trades where each had lost. Celeste ordered another glass of scotch and attempted to participate in the conversation. Her mind wandered to the "Celeste wall," as Fred called it, and she shivered. Savin noticed.

"Are you cold? Shall we move closer to the fireplace?"

"No, no, I'm OK. I'm just not feeling well. Do you guys mind if I call it a night? Victor is right outside. I'm sure he and Raoul can handle escorting me home."

Savin looked at her with a warning in his eyes. She laughed.

"Sav, stop! I'm not going to do anything stupid. I'm exhausted and upset and just want to take a bubble bath and sleep in my bed. Is that so wrong?"

Savin considered whether she was telling the truth and seemed to decide she was.

"Fine, but I'm walking you out to the car."

"Unnecessary, but OK." Celeste stood up and turned to shake Fred's hand. He grabbed her in an awkward embrace with another weepy "We were so worried about you" statement. *Awkward.*

"Good night, Fred. Let's regroup tomorrow over brunch at my place. I assume the Feds plan to make an appearance?"

Fred nodded in confirmation. "Good night."

Savin walked Celeste out to Victor, who promised to deliver her home safely. Victor escorted her to Raoul's waiting car and helped her into the back seat, then climbed into the passenger front seat. Both men were silent on the way home.

When they arrived in front of her building, Raoul wished her a good evening, and once she and Victor were close to the entrance, she heard the car pull away. She entered her security code, and the two walked inside the building. She prepared to greet her doorman but noticed the desk was vacant. *That's odd.* The building staffed concierges and doormen all hours of the day.

A movement behind her caught her attention. She watched in horror as two large men soundlessly rushed over to her. She retreated back into Victor, but instead of shielding her, he cupped a hand covered in cloth over her mouth. Then everything went dark.

Ow! What the hell happened? Celeste awoke and noticed the massive headache before she even opened her eyes. She groggily tried to recall where she was and opened her eyes to investigate. Her heart sank when she realized she was blindfolded. She struggled to remove the blindfold, then realized her hands and feet were tied. *OK. A minor fucking inconvenience.* She inhaled a sharp breath. *Focus, Celeste.* She scanned her other senses.

OK, I'm on a mattress. Her ears were popping. *On a plane? What the fuck?* Light was coming through the bottom of her blindfold. *I'm not in the dark.* She again attempted to loosen the rope on her wrists. *Omar.* She fought back tears. *Freaking out is not going to solve anything.* She willed herself to believe her internal pep talk that she could get out of whatever this was. *Yeah, right. He has you on an airplane.* She had convinced herself long ago that Omar could never hurt her again, *would* never hurt her again, but now she realized how naïve she had been to think so.

"She's moving around back there, boss."

"Oh, my darling always was a fighter. I'll handle her." Omar responded.

She heard his footsteps walking toward her. *I must be in the back bedroom of the plane.* The door opened, confirming her theory. Omar's cologne filled the room. "My sweet Celeste. We finally meet again, my love. Who knew I would be so lucky to have you back in my life again, my dear."

"Can you untie me and take this blindfold off? You know how I feel about being restrained and not being able to see." *You of all people should know this.*

"Of course, dear. My apologies for the theatrics, but it's quite hard to get to you these days."

"First things first, Omar. Please untie me. Then you can tell me what's going on."

"Only if you promise not to do anything stupid. My men are in the cabin, and I won't tolerate your disobedience."

"Fine, I promise. Just untie me. This is undignified."

"Oh, my darling. I hate that we had to start our little adventure under these circumstances." Omar untied the rope around her ankles and while she was stretching out her legs, he rolled her over onto her stomach and untied her wrists.

She removed the blindfold and widened her eyes when she saw how awful Omar looked. She had not seen him in person since the day after he had terrorized her, though she had seen news coverage of him. His eyes were bloodshot, he was unshaven, and his face had aged two decades. He appeared to be rotting from the inside out. She sat up.

"Ta-da! It's me in the flesh." He pulled her in a stiff embrace. "How I've missed you, dear."

"What's going on, Omar? You had my own security guard kidnap me?" *You really don't have a shred of humanity inside you.*

"I needed to see you." *And kidnapping is the rational way.*

"The flowers were a nice touch," Celeste said wryly.

Omar laughed. "I thought you would appreciate that. You and I always did share the same sense of humor."

Celeste nodded and kept her expression neutral, then smiled. "Yes, we did. It's been a long time."

"I've missed you terribly, my darling." He scooted much too close to her and brushed her hair back. He attempted to lightly caress her cheek, though it came across as a rough pat. She resisted the urge to pull away. His touch, his proximity, and his stench from one too many nights of chasing lines of blow with a shot of scotch made her stomach turn. *How could the younger me have been so blind?*

"So, what can I do for you, Omar, dear? And where are we going?"

"I want to make things right, Celeste. I've never stopped loving you, and if you'll let me, I'll prove to you that we should be together. I was immature back then, but I'm ready now."

Immature. That's one word for it, Celeste thought sardonically.

Outwardly, she smiled and said, "Well, you probably weren't the only one to blame. I, too, wasn't my best self back then."

"Darling, do you remember that magical weekend we shared together in Turks? I felt like the luckiest man alive on that trip! Making love to you all day and relaxing on the water with you for a sunset sail at night. And the food! Let's get back to those days."

"Oh, yes, of course. Such a lovely trip." Celeste tried to recall a telling detail that would indicate any of it was actually special to her, but she came up with nothing but vague memories of broken glass and shouting. "Where are we going, Omar?"

He stood up and pulled Celeste close to him in an embrace, his hard-on poking into her. He did not seem to notice her body stiffening in repulsion. He could never be bothered with things like consent. His philosophy was that if he wanted it, it was his for the taking—a predator in every sense of the word. She looked over his shoulder for her handbag and saw it sitting close by.

"I came to the office to see you, Celeste, but your receptionist said you were away in Paris, launching a satellite office. It wasn't hard to discover that that was a lie, but I figure you had your reasons. I'm just so happy we were able to get Ted out of the way. Now we can be together again. You still have such an effect on me." His hand slid inside her sweater to cup her naked breast. "I never could keep my hands off you, beautiful."

Celeste inhaled in disgust but hoped it was imperceptible. *Tread carefully, Celeste. He is clearly fucking insane.* Her nipples perked up from the chill in the air, which he mistook for arousal. He pushed her back down on the bed and forced her legs apart with his other hand, sloppily rubbing her clit. A familiar fear came over her. *I have to get control of this situation.*

"I'd forgotten how strong our connection always was," she said. "But let's slow down a bit. Maybe you're right. Maybe we could try again, for real this time. Our relationship wasn't always so bad. We had so many good times, didn't we?" *Get him talking, and maybe he'll give me a clue to where this plane is taking us.*

Omar pulled back and looked in her eyes. He seemed to be assessing her sincerity. His posture relaxed. "You're right, darling. We'll have plenty of time for this."

He picked up her unbandaged hand and brought it to his lips. "What happened to your other hand, my sweet?"

"Oh, you know me, never did know my way around a kitchen. My housekeeper was late the other day, and I tried to load the dishwasher myself. Dropped a glass right on my hand."

"You always were so clumsy when it came to household tasks. I wish you'd have let me properly take care of you, so you would've never had to lift a finger again. I can't believe you've had to work all these years. It is so unbecoming of a woman of your beauty."

"Maybe it was a mistake to end things all those years ago. Something I have regretted for some time now." She gave him what she hoped was a convincing, sweet kiss.

"Celeste, I've run into a few wrinkles with my business. You've likely heard about a bit of it. I'd like for you to come away with me. I've got the perfect spot for us. We can start fresh, new identities. I have some money tucked away, the yacht, etc. We could finally have a real shot at making things work. And of course, both of us could put all that unfortunate Riyadh stuff behind us. We both know how it could jeopardize your safety and that of Savin, Mark, Rani, Lorraine, Ace, and who knows how many others if your recent trip were discovered. I would never want anything to happen to them, and we both know you can ensure it doesn't. A shame about Ted."

There it was. The veiled threat. *Impressive. You felt me up against my will and delivered your threat to me in under ten minutes. And his name was Theodore, you rotten motherfucker.* The faces of everyone she loved flashed before her, and she knew that she would do whatever he wanted. At least, in the short term.

She had to conjure her old self. *I can't believe I ever rolled over for this man.* "You're right—I have been working too hard. And for what? A gray hair or two? You seem to know just what I need. An adventure! How exciting! Where shall we go?" She knew before he spoke that he wanted to get her off the grid as quickly as possible.

"The yacht is docked in Monaco. I was thinking we would set out to sea tonight after we land."

"Tonight? Oh, darling, couldn't we wait until tomorrow evening? I'll have to go shopping. You know how I love Saint-Tropez and the like. And I want everything to be just perfect for our first romantic getaway in so many years!" She pouted her lips and batted her lashes.

"No, no, it must be tonight. You understand, don't you, dear? I can't, I *won't* risk losing you again," Omar said. Celeste hesitated. It had to be late; by now, Savin would have discovered she was not at her apartment. *Please let there be security tapes for Savin to give the Feds.* She sighed when she realized tapes would only reveal what they'd already know but would provide no clues as to where Omar was taking her.

Omar grabbed her arm. "That's not a problem, is it, Celeste?"

Celeste flinched at the pressure he used, then said carefully, "Of course not, dear. A quick getaway will be romantic."

"Now, dearest, I don't want to have to restrain you again. Can you behave? Don't worry about a thing—I had clothes and such delivered to the boat for you. I just have to get my darling to the boat, and we can be on our way. Let's go so I can introduce you to my staff. We'll be landing very soon."

They walked together into the cabin to meet the others. She recognized the men from her apartment building foyer. She recalled the larger one had nodded to Victor before he put the chloroform rag over her mouth and nose.

"This is my perfect girlfriend that you two went to such great lengths to bring here." The two henchmen remained stoic. *You mean the woman they drugged and kidnapped to bring to you.*

"We haven't officially met yet. I'm Celeste. And you are?"

The shorter one looked her in the eye and said, "Leif. And this is Bjorn."

Leif lowered his eyes when Omar kissed her, slid his finger inside her sweater once more, and fingered her nipple, clearly marking his territory. "You're finally all mine now," he whispered in her ear, squeezing her nipple until she had to bite her lip from the pain. *Just what I've always wanted*, she thought, nauseated.

Omar motioned for her to sit down after he dismissed Leif and Bjorn to the back row. "Darling, I need to use the ladies' room before we land."

"Of course. Don't be long," Omar said.

Celeste hurried to the back, closing the pocket door to the bedroom behind her. She scrambled to her handbag, long forgotten by Omar. Celeste drafted an encrypted SOS for Savin and Ace on her burner. *Fuck Ace.* But Ace *had* found a way to magically scoop her out of Riyadh; she could use a little magic right now, even if she didn't agree with his methods. She had no illusions—she was in dire straits. She could only hope her texts would send once they landed, since she did not know when she might have a chance to pull out the phone again. She would have to continue to be agreeable. *I can do this.* Any dissenting behavior from her could cause trouble for Savin and the others. *He is more dangerous than I could have imagined.* She tried to find a way to conceal the contents of her bag, which would inevitably be taken from her, but with such a scant outfit, her options were limited.

She was back in her seat within minutes to ensure that Omar did not become suspicious. "Omar, do you know if Leif and Bjorn brought my coat?"

"No need for a coat in February in the French Riviera. The weather this time of year is perfect." He smiled at her, then continued, "I can't tell you how happy I am, Celeste, that we can start a life together without the distraction of your friends. They've always come between us. You'll grow to want the same thing I do."

"We can start over fresh. Tell me more about this romantic

adventure you're taking me on. I presume we'll fly into Nice if we're leaving from Monaco?" *I may as well be amenable while he is sober.*

"Yes. We never had a chance to be together on the boat, did we?" *I wasn't exactly in the mood to be alone with you after Miami.*

"No, but it sounds remarkable from what you've told me. Tell me more. Will your crew be with us? And these guys? They both seem wonderful, by the way." *Maybe if I get him a little jealous, he will call off his armed pit bulls and leave them ashore. Doubt it, though.*

After a smooth landing, they exited the plane, both of them continuing the charade of the happy couple living a life of excess, leisurely watching the sun rise as they walked toward their waiting car, en route for a relaxing week spent on their yacht. Once they were settled in the limo, Omar spoke happily of their next steps. The means by which he had gotten her there seemed long forgotten.

"You'll love the boat, darling. It is magnificent, and it's so peaceful on the water. There's a helipad in case we get bored, but it's hard to tire of the open sea with plenty of time for us to enjoy the pleasures of life."

"It all sounds divine, and I so appreciate you packing everything I need for the trip, dear. What would I do without you?"

Omar beamed.

The ride was much too quick, and Celeste prayed again—to a God she had never believed in but hoped could intervene to save her and her people—that her texts had been delivered. Once they were out at sea, it was hard to tell whether she would ever surface again. She had no delusions of grandeur—one misstep, and she and everyone she loved were done for.

They exited the car and walked to the pier. The henchmen and two porters appeared out of nowhere, carting the many pieces of luggage.

Omar said, "You know, Celeste, once we're married, this life will all be yours."

Wow, you nutso motherfucker. Yes, please, let me share in all your fortunes that you obtained by stealing from others. She was growing increasingly concerned about his state of mind—he seemed unaware that the last decade had happened, seemed to think that she was still the young woman he had known in the mid-2000s.

He stopped in front of a dock and pointed to his yacht, its size dwarfing the other boats. *You always did need to overcompensate, didn't you, Omar?* Celeste had to admit it was a beautiful boat. Under any other circumstances, she would have been ecstatic to stay there. "It's breathtaking, Omar. Truly."

"I knew you'd love it! And take a look at this." He took her hand, walking excitedly toward the other end of the boat. *Celeste* was scrolled across the back.

"Oh, uh, wow, what an honor! I've never had a boat named for me."

"Your beauty inspired me, and I knew we'd be together on it someday, so it made sense," Omar explained, as though they were discussing something that actually made sense.

"When did you name the boat?" she asked nonchalantly.

"Just a few years ago. I was waiting for the perfect time to show you."

Celeste kept her face neutral.

"I've taken care of everything—chef, masseuse, yoga teacher, everything you could want or need at your disposal for our little boat ride." As if on cue, the captain, from the looks of him, stepped out onto the deck.

"Everything is ready as you asked, sir. Let us know when you would like to leave."

"We'll leave immediately."

After a tour of the yacht, Celeste claimed she needed to change. "I'll be back, darling."

"Don't take long. I thought we could plan out the rest of our trip tonight."

She was surprised he was letting her out of his sight, maybe an indication that he was buying her enthusiasm. She could only hope.

Once in the master suite, Celeste got to work, hiding everything she had been able to keep on her person in strategic places around the room. She searched for anything that could be used as a weapon —a Mason Pearson hairbrush, T3 hairdryer, not much to choose from. The closet was full of beautiful couture. In another life, she would have spent hours playing dress-up. Now she was looking for anything that would repel Omar. She settled on a long Etro caftan and the least revealing one-piece swimsuit she could find. Her stomach turned at the thought of Omar touching her again. From what she could tell, her message had been sent to Savin and Ace, but they had not responded. She could not risk sending anything else in the event that Omar had someone monitoring outgoing cell signals, so she turned off the phone and removed the SIM card with a disappointed sigh.

Not for the first time lately, Celeste was out of options. She could hardly jump overboard and swim to shore. She ruled out poisoning Omar because his henchmen would notice and probably had orders to execute her for such transgressions. She had no way to communicate with the outside world, at least not from one of her devices.

She walked back up to one of the decks where Omar was sitting, typing away on a laptop. A feast with fresh fruit, soft-boiled eggs, croissants, and tea had been laid out for them, but Omar wasn't eating. His nostrils were a telltale red, and he was sniffling. Celeste's heart sank. He would be quick to anger if he was fucked up, and that was dangerous for her. She would have to be careful.

"I feel so refreshed. How thoughtful of you to have all of my things stocked!" Celeste said, sitting on the bench next to Omar.

"Of course. I want you to be comfortable." He kissed her forehead and then looked back at his screen.

"Omar, in all the rush, I didn't have a chance to grab any magazines or books. Without work to keep me busy, I'm afraid I'll get restless, darling. Do you have an iPad or Kindle? I could download a few things, maybe a Netflix movie or two. The beauty of a vacation is the downtime to catch up on such frivolous delights, right?" She smiled, showing her dimples.

He glanced over at her, assessing her in silence. She kept her expression neutral, though her heart was racing. If he had any inkling that she would try to communicate with the outside world or attempt to escape, the threats would begin again.

"Lucky for you, my staff thought of everything." Omar snapped his fingers, and a previously invisible cabin boy dressed in all white jumped to attention.

"Sir, how can I be of service?"

"Celeste would like to take a look at the books and magazines you stocked. And where the fuck is my drink?" The boy disappeared.

"Dear, you're looking awfully thin. Shall I make you a plate?" Celeste asked.

Omar grunted in response, turning his attention back to his screen.

Celeste nibbled on some fruit, then moved over to the pool. She sat on the side and dipped her feet into the water, staring out at the expansive sea. The contrast of the crisp white of the yacht against the spectacular Mediterranean was stunning. But the beautiful scene could not disguise what was happening here. Another, smaller boat passed them, three socialites sunning topless on the bow. Celeste wished she could signal to them that she was trapped, that she needed rescued, but that would only result in some sort of punishment from Omar.

It had only been a few days earlier when she had thought this was all over and that she could finally focus on grieving the loss of Theodore. *How could I have been so stupid, thinking the flowers were the finale?*

Once Omar passed out this morning, Celeste would scope out the boat a little more. Find out where the armed guards were, how many others were here, and what the communication capabilities were. She could hardly contact the authorities and claim to be a missing person. That would mean a death sentence for everyone at home and possibly for herself as well. *Omar will have no more casualties.*

The cabin boy returned and stood in front of her with a stack of books and magazines. "Thank you. *Merci beaucoup.*" Celeste looked up at him and realized she had misjudged his age—he was likely in his early twenties. He was rail thin with a pleasant face. Blond bangs hung down into his light-blue eyes.

"*Je m'appelle Celeste.*"

"*Moi c'est Léo. Je suis désolé, je ne parle pas très bien anglais.*" If the boy couldn't speak English, that meant Omar, who did not know French, would not be able to communicate much with him nor understand what Celeste was saying when she spoke with him in his own language.

She lowered her voice and thanked him for the books, adding that she had been forced on the trip and hadn't had a chance to pack anything. To lighten the tone, she smiled and gestured at the books. "*Au moins j'aurai quelque chose à lire en attendant de pouvoir m'échapper.*" There was no question about that: Celeste fully intended to find a way to escape.

Léo looked at her sympathetically. He told her in a roundabout way to let him know how he could help, then returned to his concealed perch. *Sweet and innocent enough to be useful.*

"*Merci, Léo.*"

Out of the corner of her eye, she saw Omar swallow the last swig of his scotch. "Celeste, you know how I hate it when you befriend the staff. You Americans and your equality soapboxes."

"Sorry, darling, I was just thanking him for the books."

"Well, tell him I need another drink. A double since he took so long with the refill."

"Sure thing, dear."

"Léo?" she called. Léo appeared once more, and she relayed Omar's request.

"*Oui, mademoiselle.*"

The day passed slowly, with Omar barking orders at Léo and the others. Celeste walked around a bit when Omar dozed off. She found the two henchmen, still wearing all black, sitting on another deck in the shade. Sweat glistened on their faces.

"We meet again. How are you two doing today?"

Bjorn replied, "The boss has been clear—we aren't allowed to talk to you, lady."

Leif smiled at her. "What he means to say is, please don't get us in trouble." *Leif could be an ally, perhaps?*

"Oh, of course! No worries. I just wanted to meet the people that I'll be living with for a while. Any idea how long we'll be out here? Omar is sleeping, so I can't ask him. One too many cocktails this morning!"

Both men nodded in acknowledgment. They knew his habits. Celeste wondered how long they had worked for him. *Was it one of you creepy bastards who snooped around in my apartment?*

Celeste kept the conversation light and was able to discern that the plan was to stay out at sea for at least five days. The rest was up in the air, but Omar had mentioned stopping on the Amalfi coast.

"Basically, he wants to keep me off the radar," Celeste said.

Bjorn responded, "That's enough for now. Great to meet you, lady, but we can't get caught talking to you. We have families."

So I'm not the only one Omar has threatened. She suddenly felt sorry for them and for everyone else on the boat. The Omars of the world treated them like commodities, blackmailing them to keep their secrets, threatening their loved ones if they didn't cooperate. But she wasn't naïve—she knew these men would hurt her if it came down to it. She sized up their weapons: each had at least two handguns on his person. They had replaced their facial expressions with the glazed-over look she had seen on Angelo when he was in work mode. *That's all I'll get from them for now.*

OVER THE NEXT FEW HOURS, CELESTE DETERMINED THERE WERE AT least eleven people onboard, including her and Omar. Everyone else regarded her with the same caution as Leif and Bjorn. It was clear Omar had promised punishment if they interacted with her. The only progress she had made was with Léo, and that could hardly be called progress.

Omar had informed her midday that they would be dining on the top deck for dinner and that the chef was preparing her "favorite." She had no idea what Omar was referring to (who knew what he recalled as her favorite, since he had liberally rewritten history?) but expressed syrupy gratitude nonetheless. She sat in a chaise lounge opposite him, pretending to read *Vogue Paris*. Omar had gotten into his coke supply again and was now openly snorting lines. From what she could tell, he would spend a few minutes looking at the market, wire money, drink scotch, and snort a rail. Then repeat. At some point, he dozed off again, though she wished he had finally blown out that heart valve and OD'd. *If only I could be so lucky.*

In the early evening, Celeste was in the master bathroom getting ready for dinner when Omar walked in. If he were the only person she had to worry about, she could have taken him out then and there. He was unstable on his feet from the drinking, and he was sweating from the blow. She had a glimmer of hope that her self-defense training would come in handy. But at the forefront of these thoughts were the very real unknowns—whether Omar was armed, how the henchmen would respond, who else Omar had watching her, and what the repercussions for her loved ones would be. She had no way to ascertain the stakes.

"Take your clothes off. I want to fuck you." Omar came toward her, loosening the belt on her kimono.

Celeste stayed the course of being agreeable, hoping that it would stave off any violence. "Oooo, I'm already turned on by the thought. But can it wait until after dinner? I was really looking forward to the sunset. You made it sound so wonderful when you described it earlier."

Omar grabbed Celeste's arm with a surprising amount of force. She had hoped his intoxication would weaken him a little. "Celeste, don't make me say this twice. Get on the bed. I want to fuck you *now*." He jerked her arm and pushed her so that she stumbled backward onto the bed, her kimono falling open to reveal her nakedness.

He was fucked up and drunk, but he could still overpower her. She had to make a trade-off decision that was familiar, one she had hoped she would never have to make again. She could lie there silently while he raped her, she could plead with him not to hurt her, or she could fight him. The last two options didn't seem viable because she would have to give up the charade that she was lovestruck. And no amount of screaming would motivate his staff to rescue her—they were all too afraid for themselves.

"Spread your legs. This pussy is mine now. Mine and only mine. I'm going to teach you how to obey me, for real this time, something you've still never learned. And you'll do what I say so that no one else will get hurt. Disobey me and you can watch as I dispose of everyone you care about. Think of Zari's kids—they'll grow up without a father now because you tried to fight against our love. Think of how sad your brother will be when something happens to his pitiful excuse for a wife." He removed his polo shirt, pulled down his golf shorts, and lay on top of her. He tried to push his flaccid penis inside her, but it was too soft.

He rolled off of her. "Get on your knees."

"Please, Omar, can we just wait until after dinner? You seem angry with me. Let's make love after we've watched the sunset and had a few glasses of wine. It will be fun!" Celeste stood up and backed away from the bed, tying the wrap to close her kimono. Just then, someone began knocking forcefully at the door. "Boss, it's time for dinner."

Celeste took advantage of the opportunity and opened the door to peek her head out. Leif was standing there. "Thanks for the reminder, Leif. Can you tell me what we'll be having?"

Leif looked at her with an odd expression and then rattled off, "Lobster, vegetables, and panna cotta." She asked a few more questions to buy some time, hoping that Omar would move on to something else.

"Sounds lovely. We'll be right there."

Celeste closed the door. Omar had put his clothes back on and was glowering at her. She walked toward him, trying to come up with words to defuse his anger. With lightning speed, he raised his hand and backhanded her cheek, knocking her off-balance. She fell to the floor, a single tear rolling down her face. Omar stepped over her and bent down, pulling her by the hair to bring her face close to his.

"This isn't over, Celeste. I'll deal with you later. This won't be like last time. You *will* do as I say, or you'll suffer the consequences. Now get cleaned up." He walked into the bathroom and began humming while he cut up and snorted two rails of coke. Celeste went into the closet and stayed in there until Omar left a few minutes later. When he was gone, she went into the bathroom to look at her face in the mirror. She'd never been hit in the face, not even in self-defense class. Her face burned, and she could tell she would have a bruise. *What the fuck is he planning? To turn me into his personal punching bag?* She retrieved the Ambien she had hidden in the closet. When he looked away, she would dissolve two in his drink. It would buy her a little bit of time.

She went upstairs to the rooftop deck and found an elaborate candlelit setting, Omar sitting at the table with a relaxed smile. She noted several members of the staff looking on. "There's my beautiful woman now, speak of the devil." It took a Herculean effort to remain stoic while managing his mood swings.

Celeste sat down in the chair Omar was patting. He pulled her chair closer to him. "I'm not going to let you out of my sight again," he said quietly. And he didn't. For the entire dinner, he had a laser focus on her, and Leif and Bjorn were seated on the periphery of the table, hands on their weapons. *No sneaking Ambien tonight.* The staff milled about with the various courses and kept their wine filled.

"You are perfect, my love." He leaned over to kiss her, his tongue forcing its way to hers. She swallowed her repulsion.

"Why, thank you, Omar. What a lovely thing to say."

She kept up the act of the doting girlfriend for the rest of dinner as Omar babbled on about their upcoming wedding, where they would travel next, and how excited he was to share their future together. She wondered if anyone else on the boat noticed that her face was bruised and swollen.

That night, he raped her again. It triggered memories of the last time. *How much more pain can I take from this man?* After he rolled over and fell asleep, she quietly donned her robe, grabbed a glass of water, and went up to the top deck for some air. She sat down and tucked her feet underneath her. The abundant stars illuminated the sky. There were city lights far in the distance, but no boats nearby. They were alone in the middle of the Mediterranean. Celeste wept silently for all the things this man had caused her to lose and had a sinking feeling that today had only been a preview of how bad it would get. She was trapped.

16

THIS IS THE END, BEAUTIFUL FRIEND

H er respite from Omar was short-lived. She heard him thrashing about downstairs, shouting her name. There was nowhere to hide.

"I'm up on the rooftop deck, admiring the stars, dear!"

"Celeste, don't disappear on me like that again," he shouted from below. He was stomping up the several flights of stairs. "I thought ..."

Where did you think I'd gone? You've made it impossible to escape. Were you concerned I'd jumped off the side of the boat, hastening my death? She had contemplated it, but she wasn't one to give up without a fight—she wasn't one to give up at all.

He stopped at the top of the stairs, searching for her in the dark. She waved him over.

"There you are," he said. "I don't want to wake up without you beside me again." He sat down next to her, angrily grabbed her cheeks, and shoved his tongue in her mouth. She tasted the scotch on his breath.

"Omar, darling, I'm so sorry I worried you. I was just up here enjoying the lovely evening because I couldn't sleep." She sat back out of his grip and looked into his eyes, searching for any signs of humanity in the man she used to love. His eyes were vacant.

"Can we talk about what happened earlier? I want to make you happy, like I said, and ...," she swallowed, then continued, "... and I'm sorry that I upset you. I ... I want us to get off to the right start."

"I don't want to hurt you, but you forced me to. I can't lose you, I *won't* lose you like I did last time. When you disobey me, you will pay for it. I'll do whatever it takes to keep you here until you prove to me that you want to stay on your own."

"You already have me here, darling. I can't tell you how much I've missed you. But I was afraid earlier, when ... you know. And my face is bruised, Omar. What will the staff think?"

Omar stood up, retrieving a pack of cigarettes from his shorts pocket. He withdrew one and lit it, then walked over to the railing. After a few frantic puffs, he walked back over to her, his eyes ominous in the moonlight.

"I don't give a fuck what the staff thinks, Celeste. And I want to believe you, I do, but we both know you're lying. You see, I've been watching you for some time. I saw the way you looked at that asshole when you were together. The way you salivated when you fucked him, how your pussy, which is for me, was wet just looking at him. Do you really think I'm so blind to see that you don't look at me like that?" He took another drag, then continued. "But you will, my dear, you will. You just need a little discipline, that's all."

He didn't rape me and he didn't hit me, you fucking asshole. But Omar had a point. It was apparent to everyone who saw her with Theodore that she had been smitten, though she had not expected Omar to be so observant. Fred had warned her in Paris, but still she had failed to grasp the extent of his obsession. A chill ran up her spine as she imagined all the intimate things he had witnessed from bugging her apartments and hotel rooms all these years.

"I wasn't thrilled when you were fucking every twenty-something in Manhattan, not to mention your transgressions abroad. And there were *always* transgressions. But I tolerated it because I thought you still loved me. I knew that when we were together again, when it was time, you'd be all mine." His mouth twisted into a scowl. "Then *he* entered the picture, and you looked at him the way I'd always dreamed you'd look at me. I couldn't lose you to him, so I did what I had to do."

As if he were a rabid dog to put down. The emotions Celeste had been suppressing for some time threatened to take over, and her eyes brimmed with tears. *Not. Now.* She had to act quickly. She stuffed her bandaged hand into her pocket and removed the safety on her Glock, which she had sneaked into one of her boots on the plane. Hoping to take advantage of Omar's intoxication, she squirmed past him, intending to run to the other side of the deck, where she could get a clear shot at him. But Omar seemed to have anticipated her move. He tripped her.

Crack. Her wrist took the force of her fall. If her pain level was any indication, it was broken in several places. She yelped, and her blood turned to ice as the Glock flew from her pocket and crashed onto the deck. Omar's eyes widened in rage. *Stand up, Celeste.* Anticipating her next move, he sprinted over to her and delivered several kicks to her rib cage. She bore her weight with her broken wrist as she fell back onto the deck.

Blood sputtered out of her mouth with each blow. "Omar, please! Let's talk about this," she pleaded in a raspy voice. "I was wrong to ... to fight with you, but you have to understand—I was afraid of you, afraid of our love. I couldn't fathom that I deserved to be so happy, so I ... I disobeyed you to screw it up. Please forgive me—I'll be better now."

His expression revealed that he was unconvinced by her charade. "You disrespectful cunt! You fucking disgusting whore! When will you learn?"

Too injured to stand, she began crawling. Omar easily made it to the gun before she did. He stood over her once more, his rage palpable. He kicked her again and again, and while she wept, he snarled, "How dare you threaten me! You are mine, and until you accept that, there will be consequences. There will be consequences, you cunt!"

He'll kill me before anyone could ever find me here. I'm so sorry, everyone. I'm so sorry I couldn't save you; I can't even save myself.

He raised the hand holding the Glock, and she squeezed her eyes shut, bracing herself for a blow from the butt of the gun. Suddenly, words from a Doors song popped into her head: "This is the end, beautiful friend ... The end." She had always wondered if people knew the moment before they died that death was imminent. Now she knew. Omar was going to kill her, either with his next kick or with a gunshot to the head. Blood rushed out of her mouth now, her broken wrist caused her hand to dangle from her arm like a puppet's, and the pressure and pain in her midsection were almost unbearable. *The end.*

But it never came. Instead, she heard scrambling and a loud noise. Celeste slowly opened her eyes. As she took in what was happening, her jaw dropped open.

Omar stumbled backward as a bullet ripped through his chest, blood splattering on the chrome railing behind him. He steadied himself against the railing and pulled the trigger on her gun, sending a bullet to the other end of the deck. She looked back to see a man dive out of the way, the bullet narrowly missing him. The man stood back up and delivered two more bullets, this time hitting Omar in the shoulder and again in the chest.

Celeste watched what happened next as though it were in slow motion. Omar's body went flying over the railing from the force of the final shot.

She tried to push herself up, but she was too weak. She coughed up more blood.

"Who's ... who's there?" she whispered in panic.

SHE HEARD THE MAN'S FOOTSTEPS AS HE RUSHED TO HER SIDE. SHE struggled to see his face.

Then Celeste's eyes widened, and she drew in a sharp inhale, which caused her to wince from the shooting pain in her rib cage.

This can't be real. I'm hallucinating. Or maybe I've crossed over.

"How did … I don't … How is this …?" she muttered deliriously as the sticky blood pooled beneath her. "Is … is it really you?"

"Celeste. My beautiful Celeste. I'm so sorry. I should've been here sooner." Theodore bent down, his face close to hers. His lips brushed her cheek. Then he gingerly took her in his arms. "Yes, it's really me."

"But … Theodore, I … I don't understand. I thought you were dead."

She willed her eyes to focus and lifted her hand, battered wrist and all, to touch his face. His skin was warm and damp to the touch. It was really him. It was her Theodore.

Tears streamed down his face as he rocked her slowly. "Oh my God, I fucked up, baby. You were never supposed to get hurt," he told her.

She felt sleepy, her eyelids heavy, but she wanted to focus on what Theodore was saying. He seemed to spring into action. He was shouting now. "Alex? Alex! … too much blood … she's shivering … when will the chopper get here? … a hospital now … right fucking now!"

She squinted to see that his white shirt was stained. "Theodore … you're … you're bleeding. He … shot … you." Talking was becoming more difficult with each labored breath.

"It was just a nip."

Another man walked up. Blond. Familiar. She struggled to place him. It was Alexsandr. *This can't be real. Why would Theodore be with Alexsandr?*

"Everything's all cleaned up down below, boss," he said to Theodore. "The spooks will take it from here. Here's a blanket to wrap her in."

Theodore's tone softened, and he whispered to Celeste, "We need to leave now, darling. We've got to get you to a hospital." The alarm on his face reflected the extent of her injuries.

To Alexsandr, he said, "She's in shock …" His voice broke. "She's lost too much blood, Alex … We have to get her out of here. Now!"

"The chopper will be here any minute, boss," Alexsandr said.

The two men carefully wrapped Celeste in the blanket, and

together, they moved at a snail's pace up the stairs to the helipad. Once the helicopter arrived, the pilot stepped out to greet them.

Theodore and Alexsandr lifted Celeste into the chopper. She was in and out of consciousness, unable to make sense of what Theodore and the pilot were saying. Her heart raced, and she could not seem to fill her lungs. Theodore held her, his warmth comforting her shivering body. He still wept and repeated, "Hold on, baby. Hold on." She smiled and attempted an "I love you."

Theodore kissed her forehead. "No, no, baby, no talking. Save your strength. There'll be plenty of time to talk later."

He's alive! She drifted out of consciousness with a goofy grin on her bloodied face, the song lyrics playing over and over.

The end, beautiful friend, the end.

EPILOGUE

The evening of glamour Celeste had dreamed of all those weeks in the Nice hospital had finally arrived. She was in her dressing room, adding the final touches to her look. Ty had curled her hair into sleek Hollywood waves, and Patrick's skill was on display with her flawless makeup application. She walked over to the mirrored platform, where she could scrutinize herself from all angles. The emerald Dior gown accentuated her golden locks and artificial tan. There was something else, though, something new in her look. She had a radiance that came from within, the healthy glow of being madly in love. Her relationship with Theodore was stronger than ever, and he'd formally moved in when they had returned to New York. To her surprise, cohabiting with Theodore suited her, and she had never been happier.

Her calm persona that evening had come at a price, though. The trauma she'd endured from Omar's abuse led to seven surgeries and an induced coma. And those were just to stabilize her enough to travel from France back home, where she underwent more extensive medical treatment. Those months of recovery were some of Celeste's darkest days. She had spent many nights in confusion, unable to comprehend why Theodore would have left her and staged his own death. She had dragged him along to her therapy sessions with Anne Marie, shouted at him and cried, questioned how she could ever trust him again. He stuck to his story, consistent with what Alex had revealed to her in Cairo: they'd been trying to take down Omar for nearly a decade, and he'd felt that Omar's behavior was more dangerous and erratic while he, Theodore, was in the picture.

"So you faked your own death? In what fucking alternate universe was that the solution? And why didn't you bring me in on what was going on? How the fuck did my falling to pieces in grief and risking the lives of everyone I love make anything better? I fucking hate you, and I wish you hadn't come back, because then I could've lived without knowing of your unforgivable betrayal!" she had screamed one night, throwing her engagement ring at him and locking herself in their bedroom, forcing him to sleep on the sofa. Theodore had realized she was right, he said in one of their therapy sessions, when Omar had kidnapped Celeste. He thought he was protecting her, he said, but in the end, he realized he had endangered her more by going into hiding and leaving her to pick up the pieces with her grief-driven erratic and dangerous actions.

It had been a long road, but they had put the work in to move to a better place. Once Celeste's rage and pain had subsided, Theodore had formally proposed at a dinner with her and their friends. "How did you know I had left the ring in my Paris safe, and when did you have the time to get it without me knowing?" she had asked.

He smiled mysteriously and asked, "So? Don't keep us in suspense! Is that a yes?"

Everyone laughed, and she kissed him before saying, "Yes, yes, yes, but if you leave me again, I'll kill you myself!"

There were still loose ends, of course. Theodore had shot Omar, but all their intel pointed to the same conclusion—Omar was still very much alive and out there somewhere, biding his time until he resurfaced. Celeste wouldn't let herself live in fear, though, and she found solace in the fact that her entire network including the FBI, CIA, and Saudi government, had the same goal—finding Omar and bringing him to justice.

Tonight is not for dwelling on the past; tonight is about inspiration and a new chapter for me and for D&C. She put on her Cartier diamond studs while she rehearsed her lines for the speech she would deliver later in the evening at the black-tie gala unveiling D&C Philanthropies, their foundation devoted to infrastructure and innovation in developing countries. When she had become well enough to return to work, she and Savin had evaluated where they were, their profits years ahead of their previous projections, thanks to the money they made from taking down Omar's holding company. They decided to pay it forward. That evening, they would name Lorraine as the president of D&C Philanthropies. Her commitment to doing good was unrivaled in their industry, so she was the natural choice. Celeste smiled as she imagined the look of surprise on Lorraine's face when they made the announcement.

"Knock, knock," came Theodore's baritone from the other side of the door. "May I come in and see my beautiful fiancée?"

Celeste took one last glance at her reflection and said, "Yes, of course, come in!"

Theodore walked in, and the expression on his face revealed his thoughts. "You look ... well, there are no words to describe how magnificent you are. I'm the luckiest man alive." He lightly kissed her cheek the way she had taught him, so he didn't disturb her makeup.

"Let me grab my shoes and I'm ready to go!" Celeste said and turned to retrieve her silver Aquazzura stiletto sandals. When she turned back to Theodore, he was holding a large jewelry box. "What's this?" she asked excitedly.

"Well, you'll have to open it to find out, darling," he said with a smile. He handed her the box.

Celeste opened it and her jaw dropped. "Theodore, this is, well, I never thought I'd hear myself say this, but this is too much." A necklace with an enormous emerald gem encrusted with more diamonds than she could count rested on the navy-blue velvet. "I've never seen such a beautiful piece of jewelry," she said. "Help me put it on?" she asked.

Theodore carefully removed the necklace and fastened it around her neck. He whistled and said, "I knew it was made for you, but even I had no idea how perfect it would look."

Celeste hugged him. "Thank you, Theodore. I love it."

"I aim to please," he said with a mischievous smile.

The two walked arm-in-arm to the foyer and donned their coats at the very moment Celeste's phone vibrated with a text notification. She pulled the phone out of her clutch. There were three texts: one text from Monty saying he had arrived, one from Savin saying he couldn't wait for her to meet his new girlfriend tonight, and one from a blocked number.

"We need to talk. Soon. I'll be in touch," the unknown person's text taunted her. A puzzled look came over her face.

"Something wrong?" Theodore asked.

Determined not to let anything ruin their evening, Celeste said nonchalantly, "Monty's arrived, though he's probably been here for hours for fear of being late, and Savin's excited for us to meet—oh, hell, I can't even remember her name."

Not tonight. I'll deal with it tomorrow.

TO BE CONTINUED

ACKNOWLEDGMENTS

Writing my first novel has been a magical journey in introspection, self-discovery, and resilience. It's also challenged me in ways that nothing has before. The desire to tell the story overpowered my misgivings, and I put my heart and soul into it. Now it is out in the world, in the hands of readers. So thank you, thank you, thank you to everyone who has read my book and taken a chance on a fledgling writer. I am indebted to you.

So many people deserve my gratitude for making this book possible.

Claudia Carravetta, you take the cake for your unwavering belief in my abilities. You were my cheerleader, beta reader, critic, and confidante, and this book is stronger because of you.

Traci Medford-Rosow, you have been an invaluable teacher and mentor on this ride, and I'm forever grateful for your time, encouragement, and confidence in me when I would forget why I embarked on a writing career in the first place. (And thanks to Kyra for introducing me to your mom!)

Kelly Campbell, you've always been available to listen, provide ideas for the book, and give honest feedback. You've brought so many new parts of the world to me through philanthropy and travel, which has enriched my life and writing in ways still unfolding.

Swami ji, thank you for making me feel supported and reminding me that my meditation practice is an antidote to nearly everything.

Roxanne, your reminders to be gentle with myself and celebrate this process (I wrote a book! An entire book! That's great!) have helped me more along the way than I can put into words.

I'm grateful for everyone who read early drafts (and many rewrites, in some cases) and provided so much encouragement, including, but not limited to, Jennivere Kenlon, Lisa Riolo, Alex Borchard, Mikki Trowbridge, and Lane Penry.

I'd like to express my gratitude to John Marchant, for introducing me to your supersmart friends who helped me with some background research (and asked not to be mentioned); to Julian Malasi, for rallying support, which makes me feel important and special; and to Chris Pernie and Gary Meltz for helping me keep a sense of humor in these unprecedented times.

Kira Zalan, you helped me move this story forward in two crucial ways: by editing one of the most difficult scenes in the book and by introducing me to Mathina Calliope.

Mathina, my writing coach and editor, I would never have crossed the finish line without you. Joyce Bond, copyeditor extraordinaire, you reminded me of all the nuances of grammar and subtleties of word choices that I seem to have forgotten. You've both helped me learn so much about the craft, and my writing has matured exponentially under your guidance.

Courtney Roberts, you've been my partner in crime as we strive to become the women we want to be and one of my favorite people to discuss the world with over a bottle (or two) of bubbles.

Wasey and Kanwal Kheiri, Mike Carter, Sarah Yekinni, Amanda Koziura Quick, Amy Miller, and Liz Lawson, you always provide me with a laugh or lend an ear when I need it, and I'm grateful for our years of friendship.

Credit goes to my NYC roomies for tolerating life with a writer. Danielle Izzo Zaccardo, you were there when this all began, and your encouragement kept me going through difficult times when all I wanted to do was give up. Denise Bissell, you've listened to me discuss this book for what feels like a decade, and your enthusiasm for my passion project has never fizzled. Alena Amano, watching creepy shows with you on FaceTime provided me with much-needed breaks from writing.

Chris Brescia, I still hear your voice telling me to "write faster, write faster" over cocktails in the West Village when we were neighbs. You'll never know how focused it kept me.

The following people kindly shared expertise on topics in the book: Kern Briggs, who recognized that I needed to learn what it's like to use a handgun and took me to a Virginia shooting range (my first and hopefully last trip!); Cordelia Kim and Nikki Stefanelli, who provided much-needed insights into the mysterious world of finance and made some invaluable late-stage catches; Tendai Gomo, who schooled me on cybersecurity; and Dr. V. Patel, who responded to my incessant medical questions, such as whether a bullet wound is clean around the edges, and also helped me understand what a medical exam is like for a woman who has been assaulted.

Kelsey Olson and Kristin Neely, you provide me and Sassy with so much love, and Manali Patel, you've been a great auntie to Sassy when I've been consumed by my writing.

Abby Hanemann, you listened to me talk through plot points and collaboration ideas for nearly a month during our East African adventures.

To those not mentioned here, either by your request or by my omission, the countless friends, former lovers, and those who've made only a brief appearance in my life—thank you. What you've taught me about love, loss, friendship, and finance could fill volumes, and without your lessons, I could never have developed the empathy to properly tell other people's stories.

Finally, this novel never would have happened without my family. You've all grown accustomed to my grandiose ideas (I'm going to become a lawyer! I'm going to become a yoga teacher! I'm going to become a writer!), and yet you automatically assume that I will succeed. Your faith in my abilities is what has gotten me this far in life.

Grandma Ellie, I'd never know true romance but for your LaVyrle Spencer and Danielle Steele collection. I'm grateful you let me borrow your romance novels when I was way too young and didn't tattle to my parents!

Jessie/Saster, though our paths are very different, we will always be each other's first best friend, and I know you're my number-one fan. Korey and Jordan, you've always been amazing cheerleaders for me!

Sassy, my oft-neglected doodle, I do not love my laptop more than I love you, though it may seem that way. We're going to take many, many long walks to make up for lost time.

Mom and Daddy, you've been incredible parents. Thank you for supporting my love of reading and my insatiable thirst for books, books, and more books. You two are the ultimate storytellers. Your elaborate tales have fed my imagination since childhood and allowed me to grow up and tell stories of my own.

ABOUT THE AUTHOR

Rachael Eckles grew up in the Midwest. After graduating from law school, she followed her heart and moved to the east coast. *Trading Secrets* is her first novel. She currently lives in Manhattan with her puppy, where she is working on her next novel.

rachaeleckles.com

 twitter.com/rachaeleckles
 instagram.com/rachaeleckles

Made in the USA
Middletown, DE
08 May 2020